Second Time Round

Second Time Round

Clifford Hanley

HOUGHTON MIFFLIN COMPANY BOSTON
The Riverside Press Cambridge
1964

This book is for F. E. and H. W.,
and as always, for Anna

Second Time Round

One

THE telephone wakened him from a sleep so sound that he reached out a hand and groped to switch it off, thinking it must be his alarm clock. As the noise forced him into consciousness, he dragged the instrument off the cradle and cleared his throat before saying, "Fletcher!" in a growl.

"Tom?"

"Uhuh."

"Tom Fletcher?"

"Yes!"

"Hugh here. Hugh Winton, Tom. Sorry to waken you up."

"Whaddyou want?"

"You don't sound like the cheerful old Tom Fletcher, Tom," Winton said nervously.

"Listen, Hugh. Oh God, seven in the morning. I'm at home, in bed. I don't get paid for being cheery on the telephone in my own bed. What the hell's up with you?"

"Honestly, I tried to get you last night, but you must have been out till God's own time. I got a buzz."

His irritation was dwindling as he came fully awake. There was no sense in being irritated with Hugh, it only made him sulky without curbing his nervous enthusiasm. Tom opened both eyes and blinked, and then said, "It's the Gaylor Group."

"How did you know?" Hugh hooted. "Have you heard something? I mean, how does it affect . . . us?" He had almost said "me." Hugh would not be too much interested in how anything affected anybody else, Tom realized sadly.

"Don't let it ruin your breakfast, Hugh," he said wearily. "You'll be all right. I haven't heard anything. But you'll be all right."

"Are you sure? I don't know." Hugh waited to be reassured, flattered, comforted.

"Stop working yourself into a decline, Hugh. I haven't got the strength to give you pep talks at this time in the morning. You're all right."

There was a short silence.

"How about you?" Tom smiled to himself. Now that the main point was settled, young Hugh was prepared to be interested in the rest of mankind.

"Well, how about me?" he repeated. "For God's sake stop worrying, they're not the Martians. I've got money in the bank."

"I wish I had," Hugh said fervently, and added, "Yes, you're all right, you've got nothing to worry about anyway, have you, Tom?"

"No, nothing." Did he have anything to worry about? he wondered. He had a quick twinge of apprehension, but he took the twinge for granted. What was the worst that could happen to him? The worst had already happened.

"Look, Hugh," he said, "it's too early in the morning to have conferences. If you like, I'll pick you up on my way this morning and we can talk before we get to the office."

"Good! Good! Right, Tom, I'll be waiting. Eh, um, would you like to come now and Hetty could give you breakfast? No, it's too early, I suppose. You can if you like, you know that."

"Just have your breakfast, and I'll pick you up later, Hugh. Now go away."

"Right. Um, cheers."

"Right."

Tom hung up. In spite of all the training, Hugh still found it almost impossible to finish a telephone conversation. He would say goodbye three times and go on waiting for the other man to hang up.

Seven o'clock. Seven-five, by this time. Another merry laughing day of crisis and panic. Tom examined his own momentary twinge again. No, he was all right, and "what's more," he said aloud, "I don't give a damn anyway. Sorry to disappoint you, but I don't give a damn. The only thing I give a damn about is that I talk to myself, right out loud. I must be going loony, or senile. Senile, would you say?"

He looked at the very empty space round him on the big double bed, and decided he could afford the luxury of feeling sentimental, or morbid. He looked, but the morbid feeling failed to come. He felt nothing, except the profound lack of somebody to talk to. If Georgie hadn't died, he could have talked to her about young Hugh, and about the Gaylor Group.

All other conversations, he realized, were little more than a substitute for conversations with Georgie. He could talk to young Hugh about business, he could talk to old Charles English about the old days, he could talk to a dozen different people about different things, but with Georgie, he could have discussed all the dozen things and in addition, talked about the people he discussed them with.

"So now I talk to myself," he murmured, and lit a cigarette as he sat up in bed. "I do not, however, talk to my dead wife, or to her ghost. I talk to myself. Nothing morbid, merely eccentric." He blew a smoke ring. "Georgie is dead. Georgie's dead. Georgie is dead." He listened to himself, and waited for a rush of emotion, but nothing came. It must be, he decided, one of his unemotional days.

It was hard to know whether to be grateful or disappointed. He put on his glasses, picked up *Barchester Towers* from the bedside table, and settled to the luxury of reading in bed before breakfast. It was one of the trivial pleasures that could be enjoyed when there was nobody else to consider. When he looked at the clock again it was seven-thirty, and he slammed the book shut with a snarl. He had allowed the second crisis of the day to catch him from behind.

At seven-thirty, or within two or three minutes of seven-thirty, Mrs. Crow would materialize through the bedroom door with his tray. He could either defeat her by getting up at seven-twenty and being ready, fully dressed and invulnerable, when she arrived. Or he could linger in bed till she arrived, and play stupid, with the blankets pulled right up round his neck; but he didn't like playing stupid, in his pajamas, especially as he realized he was wearing only his pajama top and the other half was flung conspicuously over the foot of the bed. That kind of sight gave Mrs. Crow ideas, and his mornings were dedicated to preventing Mrs. Crow from getting ideas. She had never actually got to the point of a direct attack yet, but he sensed it coming.

Seven-thirty was a moment for firm decision and careful calculation of risk. He sank back on the pillow, and then threw back the bedclothes and shot out of bed and grabbed his underpants in one movement. No panic fumbling. Calm, unhurried haste. Trousers. Zip fastener. Socks. Slippers. One slipper had been kicked under the bed. He swore as he dropped on hands and knees to find it.

Somewhere in the house a toilet flushed and he heard young Tommy singing; rather shrill. The tune was "Onward Christian Soldiers," but Tommy was making up the words as he went along, as usual.

> Like a mighty army
> Looting as we go . . .

The distant sound of a door being knocked, and the muffled voice of Mrs. Crow, complaining, chiding.

> Ump tum tum tum tum-tum
> Sorry Mrs. Crow . . .

That would petrify Mrs. Crow. He found the slipper, wrenched off the pajama top, pulled his undershirt over his head, and within seconds was at the washbasin with water gushing and his face covered in lather. The lather was definitely good for morale, like hiding behind a mask or a false beard. He discovered he was humming "Onward Christian Soldiers." In the mirror, he saw the door opening furtively, saw Mrs. Crow making her silent appearance and drifting to the bed, where she laid down the tray. He kept the water gushing and kept on humming.

"Oh, you're up, Mr. Fletcher!" Her voice was full of gentle reproach. He couldn't be deceiving himself — he had seen other women on the hunt, and now she was drifting up at his back, hot matronly breath singeing his bare shoulders at one yard's range.

"Right enough, I think that's not right, Mr. Fletcher. It's not right, is it? Blasphemy is not nice in a boy that age. I know the young people nowadays don't care about anything the way we did, but I always say there's a right and a wrong, and that's not right."

"Wuh?" Tom twisted his face and went on shaving. It was fatal, he felt, either to agree or disagree.

"It's well seen he's getting neglected, the poor wee lamb," she sighed. "It's not the same, not having a mother. A boy's best friend is his mother. A boy needs a mother."

She ran out of wise sayings about mothers, and stared at Tom's bare shoulders again. He wiped his face briskly and walked away at a tangent to pick up a clean shirt. Without appearing to move her feet, she drifted in pursuit. He opened the shirt and rammed both arms into it in a practiced gesture.

"Oh. Thanks for the tray," he said. "How is Mr. Crow?" She stared at the open front of the shirt, and her fingers were itching to get at the buttons, to help. The question about Mr. Crow was always good for a few seconds' grace, all the same. My God, he thought, it's a hell of a life when a middle-aged old sinner has to fight for his honor before breakfast. I'll have to start sleeping in a chastity belt.

"Mr. Crow, yes . . ." she said, and went into her Martyrdom of Saint Thingummyjig pose, contriving to bow her head and shake it and stare at his chest at the same time. "Yes, I've got my cross to bear too, Mr. Fletcher, not that I would ever complain, God has been good to me, but what I always say, we have to find our pleasures where we find them and put up with them, it's the will of God, he never changes much."

"Good." She was drifting towards him, and he suddenly remembered something at the bedside and moved briskly in that direction, turning his back. It was a defensive war of movement. If she once got within reach of his shirt buttons, he felt, and he let her help him, something would snap in her mind; or if he tried to fend her off, they would end up wrestling. And giggling, he imagined. He shuddered, and tied his necktie with frightful speed. Then he picked up the cup of tea from the tray, and a piece of buttered toast, and held them in front of him. End of main bout.

"You must take good care of Mr. Crow," he mumbled, through a mouthful of toast.

"Ah, there's not much anybody can do for him, it's just the way of it," she sighed. "That's a lovely tie, Mr. Fletcher." But he fancied he detected an edge of defeat in her voice. You can't rape a man who is brandishing a cup of hot tea and a slice of buttered toast and is almost fully dressed.

"I must have a word with Tommy," he said decisively, and strode from the bedroom. He could hear her halfheartedly complaining that he hadn't finished his lovely toast as he went, but she wouldn't follow him. She was dangerous, but predictable. Tommy was in the kitchen, making toast.

"You making more toast?" Tom asked him.

"No," he said, in the gentle tone you use to an idiot.

"Put something on your feet," said Tom. Young Tommy looked at him calmly and said, "They're hot."

"Put slippers on."

"They're too hot," he said.

Tom took a grip of himself. His son could bring his irritation to the boil in two seconds without trying. But he *did* seem to try; or at least, he worked with the skill of long practice.

"How much toast have you eaten?" Tom asked, reflecting at the same time that it couldn't matter a damn how much toast his son had eaten.

"None."

"None?"

"She doesn't make toast for me. Just for you."

"Oh." That shut Tom up. He poured a cup of tea from the pot on the stove. It was thick and dark and bitter.

"This is hellish," he said. "I'll make fresh tea."

"I had milk," said Tommy. He was buttering a slice of toast, slowly, in the intensely irritating way he had of doing things — spreading the butter right out to the edges and into the corners. Tom forced himself not to look at the process, and turned away to fill the kettle and put it on the cooker: for the sake of occupying himself. Unless he somehow diverted his irritation against his son, he knew, irritation would develop into the other thing, the sense of blank wonderment. He would begin to ask himself what it was all for, why he was drinking tea and standing in a kitchen with a strange fourteen-year-old boy. That kind of wondering did no good whatever.

"She's been counting the bedrooms again," said Tommy.

"What for?"

"She wants to come and live here, you know," said Tommy. "She fancies you."

"Mrs. Crow? She's a married woman."

Tommy swallowed his toast and looked patiently at his father.

"That kind of thing doesn't inhibit a woman like Mrs. Crow," he said. "She's a predator."

Tom felt a rush of gratitude to his irritating son, simply for amusing him. It was astonishing how the boy could display all the exasperating faults of a grubby, sullen child and then suddenly reveal himself as an adult.

"Her husband's a cripple," Tom said.

"He has a limp, that's all," Tommy said.

"He's a cripple!" Tom was already doubting the truth of this while he said it.

"He has a limp," Tommy admitted. "He gets round all right. He works for Conn the bookie."

"Joe Conn?"

"Yeah."

"Say yes, don't say yeah."

"Yes."

"That's better."

"Ye-es."

"All right," said Tom, "I'm a nark. I just don't want you to develop bad speech habits."

"For Joe Conn, the bookie. He drinks."

"Everybody drinks."

"I don't."

"Don't be so damned pedantic," Tom exploded. "You're only fourteen."

"I don't see the point in drinking."

"You don't see the point in a hell of a lot of things, so just wait till you know some . . . till you're . . . the kettle's boiling."

Tommy got up with maddening slowness and lifted the kettle from the cooker.

"I'm not talking about anybody else drinking," he said. "Just about myself. I don't see the point in it for myself."

"All right, all right."

There was a short, hard silence.

"What do you mean, she's counting the rooms?" Tom asked.

"It's a big house." Tommy gave a fair impersonation of Mrs. Crow's servile, ingratiating drone. "It's a black burning shame to see it lying half empty."

"Has she got any particular room picked out for her and Mr. Crow?" Tom asked in genuine curiosity.

"No, not one room. The downstairs room for Mr. Crow and Phil's old room for Mrs. Crow. And if anybody goes sleepwalking, it's nobody's business."

"Do you know what you're talking about?" Tom asked, with only mild irritation this time. "I hope you don't know what you're talking about." Tommy flushed deep red.

"I'm not an infant," he said.

"My God."

"Do you want fresh tea?"

"Eh? No, don't bother." Tom felt the familiar mixture of guilt and exasperation and yes, surely, affection. It haunted him that so much of his reaction to his son felt like simple dislike. But not all the time, surely. It must be a phase that would pass.

"It's time I was away," he said. "There's a panic at the office." Not that Tommy would be interested.

"Oh? What kind?"

"The company's being taken over."

"Oh."

"Just 'oh'?"

"I don't know what else to say," said Tommy. "Is it bad?"

"Ah, it doesn't matter. Well . . . you'd better get ready for school."

"Plenty of time."

"Do you need any money?"

"No."

"I'd better leave some in case."

"I don't *need* any money."

"All right. All right. I'll see you tonight."

"Oh. Right."

What did that "oh" mean? A reproach because the old man hadn't come home till after midnight last night? Or did it simply mean "oh"? Dammit, life was too short for that kind of problem. Tom went to finish dressing, found the car in the drive where he had left it the night before, got in and drove away. As soon as the engine started, the affairs of the house were behind him and he was thinking ahead, towards the office. He chose to turn downhill so that he could spend as much time as possible on the shore road, and opened his window to catch any salt air that might blow in. When he stopped for petrol, he was already Businessman Fletcher. He noticed this with amusement. Salesman Fletcher. Sales Director Fletcher. Now *there* was a small but interesting fact of life. In his entire business life, he could never remember

one occasion on which he had been mastered by personal
irritation. He had been hard enough often enough, he had
sometimes been angry and shown it, but only when open
anger was clearly profitable. Business might be a nonsensical
way to live but it was easy on the nerves and it was no effort
to be agreeable all the time.

In thirty minutes, he would pick up Hugh and pat him on
the shoulder and comfort him. That would be no effort
either. If it was true that the Gaylor Group were taking over
the company, Hugh should have nothing to worry about.
Nobody threw good salesmen aside. In fact, Hugh might have
much better prospects in a big organization than he could expect in the comfortable little office of English Brothers.

Tom ticked off the probabilities. It was almost certainly
true that Gaylor's were taking over. The rumor had been
heard before, often, and always denied. But those rumors and
denials usually meant action in the long run. If it was true
this time, Gaylor's would probably leave English Brothers
alone for a time, to see how it ticked. No change of name,
no menacing reorganization.

Possibly old Charles English would go, but then, old Charles
would have gone soon in any case. Now he could bow out
with hard cash, and doubtless would be damned grateful to
do it.

Then there was Charles Junior, young Mr. Charles. Tom's
nose wrinkled. Would the Gaylor efficiency boys want to
keep young Mr. Charles? It was impossible to be sure. There
must be some people who could like young Mr. Charles, and
it was possible that young Charles' job was safeguarded as
part of the deal. All right, there were three possibilities. One,
young Charles would remain as managing director of English
Brothers, as colonial governor for the Gaylor Group, and become a Gaylor man. Two, young Charles would sell out

along with his father, and vanish from the scene. Three, young Charles would be kept on as managing director until the efficiency boys had time to study the terrain, and would then be quietly removed. Whichever way it went, young Charles had no financial worries.

He dismissed the thought of young Mr. Charles and turned to his own position. It looked like the same treble chance. Gaylor's would keep him on as sales director; or they would ask him promptly to disappear, or transfer him to sweeping floors; or they would keep him on while they sharpened the axe.

At another time, in other conditions, the prospect might have been stimulating. He sensed a faint echo of the old war trumpets and knew that he would have enjoyed the crisis, the blood and treachery, win, lose or draw. But that was when Georgie was alive. As he turned the car into the filling station, he wondered if it was all a matter of sexual energy. It was somehow difficult to *care*.

Charlie Crum himself came out to work the pump, looking fat and sleepy. He hadn't shaved, and the short bristle on his big brown face was like light frost on a turnip. Getting old, that was odd. Fat men didn't get old, they were born middle-aged and remained middle-aged forever.

"You're early enough off the mark," Charlie said. "By God, you must be keen on the money. Eight?"

"Money?" Tom nodded. "Don't you talk about money, you only have to sit on your backside and it rolls in."

"I wish you meant it. Bloody slavery. It's no wonder I'm skinny. No kiddin', Tom, I lost three ounces last week."

"It must be frightening."

"No kiddin'. Hey" Charlie started to shake with amusement. "I'll have to start wearin' the junior size bell tent!"

"Mention my name, you'll get it wholesale."

"Ah, that's it, all the dodges," said Charlie heavily. "Ten per cent here, ninety per cent there, drivin' the fancy Jag, you blokes don't know you're livin'. See me? I'm lucky if I lose less than a tenner a week."

"Why don't you pack it in?" Tom asked him, and the two men chanted the answer together —

"Impossible, it's my livelihood!" Charlie beamed enormously as he hung up the hose, and then leaned into the car window.

"Hey, Tom, hear about this bloke, he says to this other bloke, Hey, do you talk to your wife during intercourse? And this other bloke says, Only if there's a telephone handy. Only if there's a telephone handy! Get it?"

"Charlie, I told you it the day before yesterday." Tom spoke in a hurt tone. That wasn't the response he would have given a client, of course, but everybody called for individual handling. Charlie sagged at the knees and guffawed.

"Ah, Tom, I'll never learn, I'll never learn."

"You're a fat old fraud," Tom said. "You didn't forget, you were trying to con me so that I would laugh and you could tell me I was a hypocrite."

"I should be a hypocrite! The Jag, the forty-guinea suit! Why did I have to inherit a petrol pump? No kiddin', Tom, I wish I had been brought up in the big business racket like you."

"We can't all be lucky, Charlie."

Charlie stepped back and waved as Tom slid the Jaguar out into the road, still smiling. This, Tom reflected, was his game; this meaningless ritual of rubbing along with other people. Garage men, millionaires, typists, barmen, customers. This was the one thing he could do. He wasn't deceiving himself, he was good at it, and he could be complacent about that even if it was a trivial talent.

Suddenly he laughed aloud; and from habit, flicked his eyes to the side to make sure that nobody had heard him as the car swished towards open country with the window open.

"Brought up in the big business racket! Oh Charlie, that is very, very, very funny!"

He reached out one arm, encased in the sleeve of a forty-guinea suit. The movement exposed a gold automatic Omega on a self-adjusting gold band. He pressed a button on the Motorola radio and filled the 3.4 Jaguar with soothing music.

"Very, very funny," he said.

Two

HE WAS seventeen years old, average to bright, and times were hard. Times had always been hard, and Maltdyke was just about the most suitable place in Britain to spend hard times in, because it didn't have any variety that might make people discontented with the hardness of their own lot. A hundred years before, it must have been a quiet little hamlet in the middle of douce farm country. The farm country was still there, but Maltdyke was an ironworks and a sprawl of drab little houses and struggling shops and patches of waste ground.

Looking over the hood of the Jaguar, in time present, Tom found, as he often did, that he was experiencing time present with more vivid clarity because he could still experience time past. Here and now, there was the real leather upholstery, the opulent six-cylinder murmur, the knowledge of power and comfort; and here and now was Maltdyke in the thirties, the period that would never be anything more than a boring old slice of history to young Tommy, even to young Hugh Winton. It wasn't only the look of Maltdyke that was with him, but the human flavor of that place and that time.

In childhood, the flavor of the place had simply been the flavor of childhood. Environment means nothing to a child — any environment is the entire world, everlasting and inevitable. It was only in his teens, with the experience of school in

Paisley, that he began to see Maltdyke as an individual village, a place different from other places. That surely put Maltdyke in its place. Paisley was drab enough, and diminished as a town by lying too near the city of Glasgow. What Paisley was to the city, Maltdyke was to Paisley. Its flavor was partly meanness, the dreary meanness of old small cheap houses and muddy back courts, the meanness of the dark muddy brook running through it, of gas street lamps and rain.

Could it have been as grim as that? Surely not. The old gas lamps were as good as any other gas lamps. The sun must have shone, the sun did shine, the patches of waste ground and the muddy brook were paradise enough, a derelect shed was a secret cave and a submarine and a stockade beseiged by Sioux. But that was childhood, and the meanness slowly revealed itself as childhood vanished.

But it wasn't only meanness. There was another flavor so strong that he could feel it in his nostrils now: surrender. Times might be hard, food might be scarce, life might be bloody, but it was all there was. There was no way of changing it and no way out. Things were as they were. The spirit of the village was dumb acceptance. Off the main street, near the southern end, led another street, Burnett Street. It led nowhere except to the wrought-iron gates of G. R. Burnett and Co., the name, also in wrought iron, spanning the gates in an arch and touched up with brass paint once a year. That was the Works. There was nothing else. Maltdyke was a nursery for breeding Works employees on the spot.

And the Fletchers were all right. They were In. When hard times got harder, other men in Maltdyke walked the streets, but they never got so hard that Joe Fletcher was paid off. Joe Fletcher drove the Major's car, and the Major's car had to be driven in good times or bad. The Major would never let Joe down.

Young Tom Fletcher was almost part of a tribal group, with hereditary rights. When other boys were leaving school to begin a career of unemployment, young Tom was quietly whisked into the office at the Works, and he could think himself lucky.

"You might try to look grateful. You're better off than plenty in this place." His mother. Thin, tallish, anxious but inflexible. She wheeled him round to inspect the back view of his new blue serge suit.

"Look at your shoes!" She sniffed. "It's well seen a good soldier never looks behind."

His father, carefully not interfering, sat on the edge of the armchair, happy and inarticulate, a permanently tidy small man in black jacket and breeches, and leather leggings that gleamed like metal.

"Well, you're the polishing expert," Tom explained to his mother.

"You'll get expert if you put your back in it," she warned him. "Don't think you can get me for a skivvy. I polish your father's boots, you can look for a wife to polish yours, if she's stupid enough." His father smiled, embarrassed, complacent.

"He'll never get one like his mother," he dared to say.

"No, there's not many as soft these days. Don't fidget, Tom." Man and boy suffered the tyranny without complaining until Tom grew bored.

"You would think I was being presented to the King. It's only a job."

"*Only* a job!"

He was sorry he had spoken. There was more in his mother's fussing than ordinary excitement. She was proud, and frightened too. Life was secure as long as the Major smiled on Joe Fletcher. It could improve when Joe Fletcher's son came under the Major's benevolent glow and showed that he too was respectful and hard-working and grateful for his good fortune. But if young Tom Fletcher blotted his copybook, the sunshine would be switched off, and it might stop shining on Joe Fletcher too. All good luck was dangerous.

"Now you listen to me, young man!" His mother started to give him the facts of life, but her pride and her fear were too much, her voice quavered and she had to set herself to furiously brushing his jacket before she could regain control.

"Listen to me," she said, very quietly, and Tom and his father froze into respect. "If it wasn't for your father and the way he's always been a good worker to the Major, and the war, and everything, you might be queuing up unemployed instead of going to work in a good suit with a clean collar and all your orders. Just think yourself damned lucky and don't forget who got you there.

"And if anybody orders you about and it goes against the grain, you can bite the bullet and keep a civil tongue in your head and thank your lucky stars you're in work."

"What if I don't like the job?" Tom asked after a silence. He could see his father wince, but he knew his mother. She needed opposition, she needed the lunacy of men to sharpen her energies on.

"Listen to him! Not like the job! Lord Muck doesn't like the job, so he'll take a long holiday on the Continong and try something else! Aye, it's lucky for you you're smiling or you'd get my hand across your face, Tom Fletcher! You don't *expect* to like your work. You *do* it, do you hear me? Man is put on earth to sorrow and travail and know when he's well off. And you remember this, Tom Fletcher, your father's respected at the Works and he's never had a day's idleness and you'd better be a credit to him. Because they'll be watching you, don't think they'll not be watching you. They know you're Joe Fletcher's son and there's plenty would like to see you come a cropper."

"All right, all right, Mother, I'll be careful."

"Never mind being careful, do your best and speak the truth and shame the Devil. And you'll get on."

The passion was spent, and it was safe for his father to say, "Ah, don't worry, Tom'll get on."

Tom tried to smile at him. But as always, his mother wasn't finished.

"He'd better start learning to bend his stiff neck, God knows I could never bend him. And if you don't bend, you'll break, my lad. There are stiffer necks than yours."

"All *right!* I'll be good."

He was good. Everything was new and different inside the Works from anything he had previously known, and he was taken for a quiet boy. He recognized in himself a feeling that might have been fear and he kept it quiet inside himself until it diminished and he recognized it as insecurity and ignorance. The first sight of the drawing office appalled him. It was a dingy long room with grimy windows along one side, and eight men at drawing machines endlessly working in silence. It jarred his nerves to find the atmosphere of a school examination room with grown men accepting the discipline.

Ironworkers weren't like that. He had seen them every day of his life, pouring down Burnett Street in dungarees and cloth caps and talking, shouting, horny-handed and uninhibited. Without consciously thinking of it, he had pictured the inside of the Works as a noisy place, full of adult jokes and shouts and men who didn't care a damn. But the noise and the jokes belonged in the foundry. The drawing office was a superior place, a civilized silent misery.

Nevertheless, he kept quiet, he listened respectfully to everybody who spoke to him, he took his place and prepared to endure a life of unspeaking boredom until he could find a way of mastering it.

He was quiet in the presence of Mr. Moules. Having decided at first glance that he didn't like Mr. Moules, he stood respectfully and privately undertook to wait until he knew better. Mr. Moules might be a very nice man. He had a paunch and a pale slightly womanish face and wore half-moon glasses and a gray alpaca jacket in the office. Every morning he arrived in a shiny blue suit, maticulously stripped off the jacket and hung it on a hook, and put on the alpaca jacket that hung overnight on the hook.

"So you're Fletcher," he said, and pursed his lips, and Tom became convinced that he would never like him. It wasn't only the pursing of the lips, but the use of his surname. Feeling nervous and youthful, he would have been embarrassed if Moules had called him "Mr. Fletcher," but if not Mister, then plain Tom. The surname seemed a deliberate attempt to patronize him, to remind him that he was no more than a chauffeur's son. Tom nodded solemnly and said, "Yes, sir."

This brought a small pursed smile to Moules' face as he nodded, and Tom disliked him more and more.

"At least your father's taught you decent manners," said Moules. Tom smiled boyishly and promised himself that one day he would kick Mr. Moules downstairs.

"You don't need to call me sir, Fletcher, you can keep that for the directors, if you ever meet them — and if they speak to you first."

"Yes sir. Yes, Mr. Moules."

"So this is your first day, Fletcher. Well, you play fair with us and we'll play fair with you. It's a great chance you've been given and there's plenty would like to be in your shoes." His mother's speech in different words. Everybody kept telling you to be grateful. They might be right. He tried to look grateful and waited respectfully.

"I know your father. A very good worker. I hope you'll do as well as him."

"Yes, Mr. Moules."

"But don't think your father can help you. We've got no favorites in here, so don't think it. It's up to yourself."

"Yes, Mr. Moules." He could see that Mr. Moules would have liked to go on and on. Mr. Moules was enjoying the conversation. He was visibly groping for more words, but none came. Tom stood, respectfully, waiting.

"Well, we can't hang about talking all day. Go along to Mr. Green there and he'll get you started on something." Mr. Moules at once began to read a sheaf of papers on his desk and Tom went along to Mr. Green there. His heart lifted slightly when the other silent men in the office nodded to him as he passed, in friendship or sympathy, perhaps.

Eight drawing machines, eight men. Eight hours a day. Sixty-four man-hours a day. He had fallen into a lifelong habit of making simple arithmetical calculations. Eight electric lamps, 100-watt bulbs; 32 kilowatt-hours in a forty-hour week. At .75 of a penny per unit, two shillings a week. Forty-hour week, two weeks' holiday. Two thousand hours a year. Through one of the grimy long windows, he could see a man in the yard wheeling a bogey of metal into the open foundry door.

"The prisoner's view." He turned in embarrassment to Mr. Green. Instead of the neat alpaca jacket, Mr. Green had changed into an old brown tweed jacket, frayed at the cuffs and torn at the elbows. He was a thin man with a brown leathery face.

"The prisoner's view," he repeated. "That little tent of blue that prisoners call the sky."

"Oh. Yes. I've never seen the inside of the Works before."

"It'll get better when you get used to it. This is where you'll work. What's your name?"

"Fletcher. Tom Fletcher, Mr. Green."

"Tut tut, I'll never be a boss. They call me Dan Green. Dan. As long as you don't call me Danny Boy you're all right."

"Do I call you Dan?"

"It's the only name I've got."

"Oh, I didn't mean that. I mean, I'm only the boy, it sounds a bit cheeky."

Dan Green was taken aback. He stared at Tom and then smiled and put one hand on Tom's shoulder.

"That's a disease that's curable, son. You'll not be the boy all your life. Call me Dan, and I'll regard you as a man." He laughed and patted Tom's shoulder. Tom, still holding to his silence, smiled and felt an extraordinary wave of happiness. Thirty years later he could still remember it. What was it, after all? The most casual gesture of kindliness that any man might offer to any boy.

"Thank you, Dan." The words sounded too formal and precocious, but they passed, and he turned to the drawing board.

After all, there was nothing in it to frighten anybody. It was more important to avoid mistakes than to work fast. Living his days quietly and expressing no opinions, he learned to control impatience and work slowly and ask questions. An hour extra on the drawing board was only an hour of a boy's time. Fivepence, to G. R. Burnett and Company. Plus .75 of a penny for electric light. A mistake could multiply itself into a hundred hours of ten men's time in the foundry or the machine shop. Equivalent, four years' wages for a boy in a drawing office.

"Do you work your brain like a cash register all day long?" Dan Green asked him one day. Tom flushed. His policy of silence was crumbling away. He had just averaged the output of component drawings per man in the office and quoted the yearly production. Showing off, he had mentioned his calculation to Dan.

"It's a childish trick, I suppose."

"It's easier thinking about women. You never get a tidy answer, but there's more entertainment in it."

"Do you think about women?" Tom was astonished. Dan was old, older than Tom's father, and quiet and not given to obscenity.

"All the time!" Dan laughed and Tom laughed with him, not knowing whether he had spoken the truth or an adult joke or a mixture of the two.

Slowly, the eight faceless men in the office evolved into separate human beings. Peter Harkness, the menacing one with the long neck, who turned into Peter Harkness the sad one . . . Robby Sanderson, the one with broad shoulders and the faint air of a Rugby player, who never played any game but would start a fight in an empty house. Yes, Robby was the one who owned Things, or knew people who owned Things. He ran a car, a Morris Eight two-seater, and spent his life and time proving the superiority of the Morris until he traded it in for a Ford. From that moment, Ford was God. Robby was the office bore, the office buffoon, the office butt, who would rise to any bait. His presence was a private comfort to Tom, who thought that he himself might have become the butt if Robby hadn't monopolized the position before him.

Darky Gillan. That was an odd thing, in retrospect — there were half a dozen men in Maltdyke with the nickname of Darky. Darky was the youngest, next to Tom, and in time he accepted Tom enough to spend leisure evenings with him. His hair was thick and black as char and he had to shave twice a day.

In time present, Tom tried to savor the excitement of those leisure evenings, but it escaped him. Evenings in Paisley, sometimes in Glasgow. Walking behind girls on summer evenings, Darky brash and confident, Tom baffled and unsatisfied. Dancing, battling to talk persuasively to girls who giggled or glared. In retrospect it seemed a time of total joylessness, but it couldn't have been, it hadn't been. There had always been the distant excitement of possibility. He had been carried on a kind of nervous exhilaration, in the hope that he would suddenly break through into the excitement, as Darky evidently did. But nothing of the kind happened. Hope persisted, and hope was deferred. In time present, something clicked. Disease, disease! Tom laughed to himself, because he knew he had deliberately buried the memory. He had spent his teens with the dread certainty that he would catch syphilis if he stepped out of line even once. The barrier he couldn't break through was one he had built for himself.

And that one was unbreakable, until the business with Agnes Orr.

Agnes Orr.

There was a memory that couldn't be buried. But a shutter came down in front of it. In time, it wouldn't matter at all.

In the meantime, there was the drawing office and the eight lamps and the careful lines and calculations. And Mr. Moules. And the other one — Robert Moules. Several weeks had passed before Tom realized that the blond, youthful draftsman who worked at the far end of the office, near Mr. Moules' desk, was Mr. Moules' veritable flesh and blood, his own son. No favoritism here, he thought, and watched incessantly for the signs of it. Perhaps because of his own stubbornness, he had never come to change his mind about Mr. Moules. He did not like Mr. Moules, who still called him "Fletcher" while he called everybody else "Mister" and his own son by his Christian name.

No matter how hard Tom tried to be fair, he couldn't alter his first impression that Mr. Moules intended him to remember that his father was only a motor driver. From time to time, Tom was certain he heard Mr. Moules mutter the magic word "batman" as he turned away from Tom's drawing board, but it was impossible to be sure. Everybody in Maltdyke knew that Joe Fletcher had been Major Burnett's batman during the Great War. There were rumors, which Tom had fostered as a child, that Joe Fletcher had saved the Major's life at Passchendale, or Ypres, or Mesopotamia; or that the Major had saved Joe Fletcher's life, the story was good in either version. It was all nonsense, and the truth was much more rational, that Joe Fletcher had been a superefficient batman. Good batmen, Tom now suspected, were better employees than heroes might be.

His deepening dislike of Mr. Moules had nothing to do with any shame of his own at his father's humble war career. It would never have occured to him to be ashamed of his father if his father had been a corporal's cook, he was Tom's father. What angered him quietly was the knowledge that Mr. Moules *did* choose to regard a batman as an inferior, and a batman's son with condescension.

But at home, none of this was ever revealed. Sometimes he would see his father in the yard, polishing the Major's car; sometimes driving past him through the gate. He took it for granted that while he might nod to his father or speak to him while the car was being washed, he would do no more than tilt his head minutely while Joe was at the wheel, on duty, in the presence of the Major. Protocol was established without any discussion. At home, when his father exchanged small gossip about the Works, he would offer his own in exchange, without ever giving an opinion about anybody. Take everything quietly, keep a civil tongue.

"Well, you're not disgracing your father, I will say that." When his mother spoke, Tom smiled. It was difficult for her to offer outright praise to anybody, and a backhanded compliment verged on sentimentality. She probed constantly to discover how he was behaving himself in the office — not whether he was enjoying himself, merely whether he was behaving himself. But she had a desperate curiosity about life in the office. It was impossible for her to visualize what people actually did in an office, in clean clothes, to justify being paid.

Sometimes he would describe closely the shape of the place and the silence, and the process of engineering drawing. She remembered everything. She would take pride in it all once she was sure that it wasn't going to disappear in some disaster. Her bitterest regret was that Tom's young sister Florrie couldn't be embraced in the everlasting arms of the Works. There was a limit to the number of typists the Works could accommodate. Florrie had had to find a job in a solicitor's office in Paisley, and hated it.

The one thing in the Works that she disliked and feared was Darky Gillan. A Bolshie, she described him. She knew the kind, she remembered the General Strike. It wasn't safe to lower yourself to be friendly with that stamp of people, Socialists were all tarred with the same stick — What's yours is mine, what's mine's my own.

"He isn't a Bolshie, Mother."

"Don't you tell me he's not a Socialist. I know his kind!"

"What's wrong with that?"

"Don't you contradict me!"

"I'm not contradicting you, I'm only asking you."

"Joe, you tell him what's what! I'm not going to stand here and be given cheek by a boy out of school!"

His father, who kept a civil tongue in his head and was slow to wrath, glared at him for creating an impossible situation, and said soothingly, "He's just feeling his feet, Alice, he'll learn, it's only natural to be curious."

"By God, he'd better learn in a hurry or he won't stay in this house!"

It was all wrong, Tom felt, that his mother should have grown up as a domestic servant and married an officer's batman before she had time to experience anything else. Her energy was terrifying. She might have been a suffragette or an empire builder on her energy and nothing more. But the energy was ringed round with the knowledge of poverty and peril until it was all concentrated on keeping things as they were, on safeguarding her shaky nest against anything that seemed strange and therefore threatening. New, unsettling ideas provoked her to blind instinctive defensive anger.

Darky was hardly a Bolshevist, except that where Tom quietly and secretly disliked Mr. Moules, Darky detested him and invented obscene descriptions for him. In moments of exultation he gloated over Mr. Moules' fate when the Red Dawn broke.

"Wait till the barricades are up, boy," he told Tom. "The barricades! The day of the revolting workers, boy! see the barricades — right there, bang across Burnett Street. Six drawing machines and Robby Sanderson's tinny wee Ford. See me? Worker's leader. See Mouldy Moules? Sniveling capitalist lackey. See the Red Dawn? Bang, ratatatat! Brrt! Comrade Moules, swinging from the lamppost. Revolution over."

"Make up your mind," Tom complained. "Are you shooting him or hanging him?"

"Who the hell cares? No! Shoot him *slightly*. Brrt, ratatat — one or two in the guts, a smashed kneecap. *Then*, boy, à la lantern! Long jump, short rope, zip!"

Dan Green seemed to Tom to be more of a genuine Bolshie. When Tom produced one of his absent-minded calculations about the yearly output of the drawing office, old Dan looked at him shrewdly and said, "And how much is that worth? In the market?"

"Nothing, unless you're needing a big pile of engineering drawings."

Dan didn't pursue the point. He shifted his glasses on his nose and said, "Well, it must be worth a lot more than it costs to run this office. It gripes me to be selling something to the Works for less than it's worth."

"But if the Works weren't here, you wouldn't have a job."

"And if we weren't here, the Works wouldn't have a drawing."

"Mmm," Tom said doubtfully. "But I thought you liked it here. You must have been here a long time."

"I have." There was a dull note in Dan's voice that depressed Tom unbearably.

At eleven o'clock every morning, there was a ten-minute break in the office. It was unofficial, in the sense that Mr. Moules didn't recognize it although he never actually prevented it. It was initiated each morning by Dan, who left his drawing board quietly and sat down. Once he had done that, everybody else very casually sat down too. And every morning, Dan opened a drawer, took out an apple, and calmly peeled it with a pocket knife which he put back in the drawer.

Dan's apple began to fascinate Tom. The ritual varied so little that it could have been a film, projected at eleven o'clock every morning forever. No, not quite forever. Automatically, Tom was calculating the total of apples, the total weight, the total length of apple peel, represented by Dan's working life up to that moment, and his estimated working life to the age of sixty-five. Twelve thousand apples. Average four to the pound. Three thousand pounds of apples. Perhaps a ton and a quarter to a ton and a half. Tom visualized them in a pyramid, and found himself scribbling calculations to find the size of the base. One, plus four, plus nine, plus sixteen, plus twenty-five, plus thirty-six, plus forty-nine . . . there must be a formula for calculating a squared arithmetical progression; S equals $2n$ cubed plus $3n$ squared plus n, all divided by 6. A pyramid, 33 apples square and 33 apples high, would add up to 12,529 apples.

That would be Dan Green's monument to a lifetime of conscientious labor in the Works. A four-foot pyramid of apples.

And his own? To his stupefaction, he realized that he had already chewed his way through 750 slices of bread-and-something. More than two years. The strange thing was that each day still seemed endlessly long, but a hundred days could slip away unnoticed.

He became quiet again, but nobody noticed except his mother, who noticed everything. She asked questions, and Tom answered them without lying and without revealing the truth.

One fine summer morning he found Darky Gillan staring at him and grimacing constantly. He looked blank, but he guessed the reason. Darky patted his pocket. Tom looked blank. When Dan Green slowly left his drawing board and sat down to open the drawer and peel his morning apple, Darky hurried across to Tom and muttered, "Here, boy, have you got some tart in the family way?"

"No."

"That's your story, boy, but you're in trouble. This looks like a lawyer's letter." He pulled the letter from his pocket. "What's your game, young Fletcher? Using me as an accommodation address?"

"You know what mothers are," said Tom, and very quickly and firmly took the letter and tucked it in an inside pocket.

"Well? What's the big secret?"

"I'll tell you later."

"I know what you're up to, young Fletcher."

"Well, keep your mouth shut."

"You can trust me, boy, mum's the word. My God!"

He was careful to do everything correctly, or as correctly as he could without being able to ask advice from anybody. His only worry was his father, and he had spent hours in working out a formula that would protect his father. On the morning of the day he acted, he was glad to find that he felt quite calm. Perhaps, he thought, he had practiced quietness for so long that he had become quiet inside too. Standing at the drawing board, he crushed the temptation to glance round it in the direction of Mr. Moules' desk. The letter was there, Mr. Moules would read it in his own good time, and in the meantime he, Tom, would go on working.

But no glance was needed. He could hear the clatter of Mr. Moules' feet along the short path between the drawing boards. In the far corner of his eye, Dan Green's unfocussed head turned in curiosity.

"What's the meaning of this, Fletcher?" Mr. Moules was trembling.

"It's a letter, Mr. Moules."

"Don't give me any of your damned lip, I can see it's a letter!" Mr. Moules waited. Tom said nothing. There was a definite quiet shuffling all over the office. Everybody was getting into position to see the show.

"Well, Fletcher?"

Now, to his surprise, Tom found nervous anger seizing him. He tried to relax.

"What is it you want, Mr. Moules?"

"I want an explanation of this!"

"There is no explanation."

Mr. Moules felt about him for words.

"Come to my desk, Fletcher." He spun round and stamped to his desk, and Tom followed, being careful not to put his hands in his pockets. Mr. Moules sat down and read the letter again, or stared at it. He acquired some calm.

"Do you know what this is, Fletcher?"

"Yes, I wrote it."

"Now don't give me any of your damned lip, Fletcher." Mr. Moules had adopted a deliberate tone of dangerous quiet. "This is a letter of resignation."

"Yes."

"How dare you! Insolent young hooligan."

That was the point of highest danger. Tom tightened his lips to keep words back.

"I suppose you think you're going to better yourself."

Tom said nothing.

"That's the rock you'll perish on, Fletcher. You got a chance here through your family . . . connections. I could have found hundreds better than you. You'll never get another chance like it."

It was hard to believe that anybody could get so apoplectic over the mere act of resigning, but Tom's instinct had been right. He had known that Moules would regard it as subversion, defiance, revolution. Tom looked respectful. Moules might stretch the talk to five minutes. At 200 words a minute, a thousand words. With silences, less than four hundred. Five minutes, the 288th part of one day, a minute fraction of a week. For the half-millionth part of a lifetime, Tom could look respectful.

"And where, may I ask, do you think you're going to work now?"

Tom considered this, and didn't answer.

"Has the cat got your tongue?"

"I'm not at liberty to say, Mr. Moules."

"By Christopher, we'll see about that! And I'll tell you one thing, Fletcher. You'll never get back here. Don't try. You'll never get back here."

Silence.

"Don't stand about here wasting my time, get back to your work, Fletcher." Mr. Moules buried himself in what papers he could find. Tom walked back to the drawing board without responding to any of the questioning faces on the way. At ten o'clock, Mr. Moules jumped to his feet and hurried out. At once, Darky Gillan was at Tom's side, punching him in the ribs.

"I knew it, I knew it, young Fletcher. I can always tell when a rat is going to desert the stinking ship. Where's your new job?"

"Oh, here, there, anywhere. I shall be traveling a good deal, old boy."

"Listen, boy, I nearly died when old Mouldy said 'Cat got your tongue, Fletcher?' and you said 'I'm not at liberty to say.' Boy, that was priceless."

"Careful, careful, careful," came the muttered voice of Dan Green. "The walls have ears."

"Jesus," said Darky, "Mouldy Junior, I forgot him." He sidled back to his drawing board with one arm covering his face.

"What do you mean, you've left the Works?" His mother was convinced that she was going insane.

"It's no use arguing, Mother, I've left the Works. I'm working my notice."

"You've got the sack!"

"No, I've left. I'm going to try another job."

"Where will you get another job?" She actually swung

her open hand to strike him in her passion, but he dodged. There was no point in allowing himself to be slapped, it would only make her more hysterical.

Tears were not for her. Accepting that disaster was complete, she sat down in the chair at one side of the kitchen fireplace and stared into the fire, saying nothing, until Joe would come home. Tom sat at the table and opened a book. He knew it would infuriate her to see him reading, she would consider this frivolity when he too should join in the vigil and sit doing absolutely nothing. But now, in his own home, he was too tired to behave like iron. He was nineteen years old.

His sister Florrie came home first, neat, pretty, and bad-tempered. She bit back the first word that came to her as she saw Mrs. Fletcher sitting like stone, and looked at Tom.

"I've chucked my job," he said, and dismissed any further talk by returning to his book. It was a small cheap edition called *What Is Man?* Dan Green had lent it to him. Florrie's face changed to horror, to excitement, to bewilderment, to a dozen other things, and then she burst into dramatic tears. Without a word, Tom took her by the elbow and pushed her out of the room and slammed the door behind her. A few minutes later his father came home. Alice Fletcher looked up at him and slowly prepared to speak.

"I know," Joe said, "He's chucked it." Joe shook his head. The world was beyond him.

"Well, speak to him!" Alice shouted. "Knock sense into him!"

Joe looked at his son, who stood up. Joe remembered his peak cap, still in his hand, and laid it on the table. His wife almost spat at him.

"What will the Major say?" She wheeled on Tom with all the energy stored up during her silence. "What about your

father? You don't care about your father! What's to become
of him when the Major finds out?"

"The Major knows already, Alice," said Joe. "It's all
right."

"All *right?* Is it all right?" she added unbelievingly. When
Joe nodded, she sat down and rested her head in her hands.
Joe shook his head again.

"I don't know what's got into you, Tom," he said. "You
had a great chance there."

"Is the Major all right?" Tom asked him.

"He nearly bit Frank Moules' nose off and spat it in his
face," said Joe. "By God, I enjoyed that. And he says you're
very good-mannered."

Tom's mother looked up from the fireside. Fresh astonishment was nearly too much for her.

"I'm giving the coachwork a bit wipe," said Joe. "Ten A.M.
it would be. Out of the blue, that Frank Moules comes at me
and starts giving me dog's abuse about . . . about Tom. Im-
pudent hooligan, cheeky pup. I thought he had committed a
murder. And what am I going to do about it? he says. I tell
him Tom's big enough to take his own troubles —" Alice
snorted. "— when out comes the Major. 'Major Burnett,'
says Moules, and then as nice as you like, the Major says, 'Do
you have some business with Mr. Fletcher?' *Mister* Fletcher!
That's what he said. Moules! He was a picture." Joe stared
into the fire and enjoyed the picture.

"What else?" Alice very nearly leapt on him to shake him.

"Aw, nothing else. Moules says something about a cheeky
letter from Tom, so the Major asks to see it and stands there
reading it. Then he says 'Very proper,' something like that,
and tells Moules to tell Tom we're sorry to lose him, and to
get back to his work. Quiet, you know, the Major's always
very quiet. Very cutting. So off Moules skitters like a

skinned rabbit. The Major knew all about it already, he had a letter as well."

"Did you write to the Major?" Alice turned her total fury on Tom. Joe, blushing, intervened.

"A very good-mannered letter, he said. A credit to you, Joe, he says. He calls me Joe when there's nobody about, you know. He says . . . well, there was something about me in the letter, and it's good to find a son with . . . respect for his father, something like that. And he hopes Tom will be bettering himself, something like that. He was very nice. Said it was all very good-mannered."

"You'll not lose your job?"

"Not at all, he was very nice. Oh, you should have heard him telling off that Frank Moules. I never liked that Frank Moules."

"I hate him," Tom said.

"You! You hate him! So you're out of a job! I hope you don't expect your father to keep you."

"If he's got something better, Alice," Joe pleaded.

"I'd like to know what *that* is."

"A sales job." Tom was deliberately obscure.

"A sales job? When everybody's on the dole and there isn't a penny for anybody to buy anything with? What'll you get out of that?"

"A change." Tom glared back at her. "A change. And money."

"You were getting good money at the Works."

"I calculated how much money I would make . . ." Tom abandoned that thought. "I want a change anyway, it's not my kind of work. And I'll make money!" He had been quiet too long, it began to burst out. "As much money as the Major. A car, a big house. I want to be independent."

"Haw!" His mother's good humor restored itself. "The

boy's been dreaming. Do you stand there and equal yourself with the Major? You're not fit to lick his boots."

"If I have money, I'm equal to anybody," Tom said doggedly.

"You were making good money at the Works, the same as your father! Do you think you're a better man than your father?"

Tom had a flash of revelation, that that was what disgusted Alice as much as her fear of change: that he, Tom, might strike out on his own and do bigger things; things that would diminish her husband and his life of honest, willing drudgery.

"No," he said. "I don't. But I'll be richer."

This time he didn't dodge. Her hand rang across his face. He shrugged his shoulders.

"What kind of sales job is it, Tom?" his tortured father asked, trying to seem calm. There was no escape from it now.

"I'm selling vacuum cleaners."

His father's face fell, shocked. His mother, with her red hand still waving, burst into a shout of helpless laughter. "Vacuum cleaners!" She collapsed in the fireside chair and laughed, and laughed.

The suburban houses were thickening along the dual carriageway. Four hundred yards ahead, the road narrowed and there was a speed limit sign. Tom eased off the accelerator and slowed quickly from eighty down to sixty, fifty, as he swung over the bridge and into Glasgow.

"That's it, Charlie," he said aloud. "That is how I was brought up in the big business rackets."

Half a mile towards the center of the city, he turned off. Hugh Winton was actually on his doorstep, and when he sighted the car he trotted down to the garden gate, waving his morning newspaper.

"I'm glad you're early, Tom," he said. "I know you said it's all right, but I'm dead worried. I wish I was like you, Tom. You never worry about anything, I don't know how you do it."

Three

WHEN they got to the office, Hugh leapt out of the car and was up the six outside steps in two strides, but paused outside the door, rubbing his hands, till Tom locked the car and checked all four doors before walking up to join him, not too slowly, not too quickly.

"Take it easy," he said.

"Yes, you're right." Now Hugh was prepared to linger outside the door and take deep breaths and look at the view; but when Tom moved on to the door, Hugh jerked round to keep at his heels. He grabbed Tom's arm.

"Tom, before we go in — I'm sorry I sounded so nervous, but this has never happened to me before. No, I know it's never happened to you either, but you're used to this kind of thing. But I want you to know that I'm right behind you."

"You're practically walking up my back, Hugh," Tom laughed easily.

"No, but I mean, you know, in case anything happens, you can depend on me, whatever you say goes as far as I'm concerned. If they get funny with you, well, I'm out as well."

"Don't be silly, don't be silly, Hugh."

"I mean it, Tom. You can depend on me."

"Don't jump the gun, Hugh. And don't say anything silly.

You've got your own wife to worry about. She comes first. But you've got nothing to worry about."

"I hope so." Hugh's voice had sunk to a cautious mutter.

There was a detectable atmosphere in the office. Three of the girls were whispering over a fourth girl's desk, and they leapt apart when Hugh and Tom walked in. Old Meg Macrae was reading mail.

"Any news, Meg?" Hugh blurted out.

"No, but there's plenty of work to be done. *Ladies!*"

The girls broke apart.

"I'll see my mail," said Hugh, and scuttled out of the room. Meg glanced at Tom and raised her eyes to heaven. When he walked through to his own office, she followed him with a bundle of letters. She closed the door behind her.

"It's like the day before a lynching," she said. "The Colton's order's scrubbed. Rowe and Rankin are all right. Smith and Smith are still waiting for that fourth machine. Old Mike Allardyce was on the phone."

"For Hugh?"

"No, for you. He wonders why you never go and see him. He must have heard the rumors. I think he just wants a blether."

Tom put on his glasses and sat down. Meg settled comfortably on the chair opposite him.

"I might go and see the old drunkard for lunch," he said. "Not surprised about the Colton thing, it was only a shot in the dark. Any good rumors?"

"Where have you been? It's in the *Financial Times*."

Tom raised his eyebrows.

"That's a cheaper method than sending interoffice memos," he said.

"You mean they didn't tell you?"

"Not a blind word."

"It's a funny way to treat a director."

"Could they mean it as a wee hint, maybe?"

"Don't be daft, Tom, the only thing Gaylor's bought over here is you, the rest is trimmings."

"Meg! You never told me! Will you marry me?"

"Not on your bloody life. Mr. Charles is still in London. Young Mr. Charles says he may be in later today, I *don't* think. He's keeping away till it's all over. You're not worried, Tom, are you? About yourself?"

"I have no idea, Meg. I never come to a conclusion on insufficient data. How about *yourself*?"

"Ach, the chop. That Gaylor mob believes in putting people to sleep painlessly at fifty. I've been dead for five years already."

"Don't be too pessimistic, Meg."

"Don't you worry about me, Tom Fletcher, I can look after myself. I'm not all that fond of working, anyway."

For the first time, Tom felt that he might enjoy having a fight with English Brothers and the Gaylor Group, if it came to a fight. He got up, savoring a quiet pleasant anger, and walked to the window.

"We need you, Meg. I'll make that quite clear to whoever matters."

"I know that, you didn't need to say it. Worry about yourself, and don't get distracted with me."

She was tall and big-boned, a heavy ugly face under white hair. When he had first known her the hair had been black, but she had been just as ugly. She always wore dark neat suits with a brutal kind of elegance.

"At the worst, what would you do?" he asked her.

"Damn all. I've saved my money."

"Oh, you would get a pension if it came to the worst, Meg."

"Maybe aye and maybe hooch aye. There's nothing in writing."

"We'll see."

"Aye. I know you will, Tom. I see young Master Hugh's got the shits."

"You're a foul-mouthed bitch, Miss Macrae, I don't know who you take it from. He's entitled to have the shits, he's young and he's frightened."

"I was never scared of anything in my life," she said, and glared at him. "Including *that*." She was daring him to be funny.

"Your disgusting sex life is of no concern to the directors of English Brothers, Miss Macrae, so don't start seducing me at this hour in the morning. Hugh'll be all right."

"But you'll give him a helping hand." She wrinkled the bits of her face that weren't already wrinkled.

"Nobody will give anybody a helping hand, Meg. When the bomb goes off we're all on our own."

"Aye." She was skeptical. "Just remember that. How are you keeping? You were on the batter last night, weren't you? Your face is like gray wax."

"Keep your nose out of my face, do me a favor, you're not married to me, Meg," he said impatiently, and she said, "Tom, Tom."

"Sorry, Meg. All right, leave the stuff and we'll get on. Business as usual."

"Stick by the ship."

"Keep the flag flying."

"Shit."

She went back to the general office.

Leaving aside the large crisis, it looked like a routine day. On an impulse, he telephoned old Mike Allardyce and arranged to call on him at noon. Allardyce was delighted. At ten o'clock his son-in-law telephoned. As he waited for the call to be put through to his desk, he prayed that there wasn't another crisis developing in that department.

"Hello, Dad?"

"What can I do for you, Alan?" It was easy to be pleasant to Alan Spurrier because he never asked for anything.

"Nothing at all."

"Good."

"Are you busy?"

"Not particularly."

"I thought we might have a drink at five o'clock. Joan's got the hens coming in for tea and I'm out in the cold."

One of the snags, and it wasn't always a small snag, about not having a wife was that everybody else who did have a wife tended to seek you out to share the occasional bachelor freedom. To married men, it was only one rare night of liberty. To Tom, it could mean a seven-day week of bachelor nights. Still, Alan wasn't the wild boozer type.

"All right. Can you pick me up here?"

"Yes, that would be fine."

"There's nothing wrong, is there, Alan?"

"No. I thought I would like to see you again, that's all."

"Good."

He called in one of the girls and dictated letters. It was the dark-haired one, Sally. There was no doubt about it, he must be getting old. He was sure that even three or four years ago he would have looked at her with some degree of speculation. He wouldn't have expected anything of her, he wouldn't even have teased her, but something would surely have registered.

She had no more effect on him than a paper doll. Maybe it was that inflated football hair style. She seemed a quiet enough kid, but she always dressed to kill, skirt rather tight, a fair show of knee, stiletto heels and eye shadow. There was probably some young fellow who saw all the mystery of womanhood in her, and the young fellow was undoubtedly right; but Tom looked at her vaguely through his glasses and measured her callously and saw nothing. It must be the football hair style. You could never get your hands into a pile of starched hair like that, you couldn't ruffle it or even stroke it without cracking the lacquer. If suddenly she was sitting there stark naked, she would be nothing more than a girl with a football hair style; not an excitement or a torment or an invitation, simply a girl, a female human creature, a person of some kind, a nothing. Anatomically different from a boy, but not in any disturbing sense, merely as a fact of nature. She was a good shorthand typist.

Trying to be honest with himself, he recalled that he had never really been interested in very young women, not, at least, since he was a very young man. They could be agreeable to look at, but the closer you got, the less interesting they were. Unless they were smooth and had soft hair, maybe?

Unless they seemed older than their years, maybe. It was ironic that he had been troubled all his life by the way women could trouble him, and that now he was troubled because they didn't trouble him. When that kind of trouble died away, was there anything left?

Yes, there was lunch with Mike Allardyce and a drink at five with young Alan, and five more letters to get rid of. He finished, and told her there were no more, and she minced to the door in the tight skirt, with the football hair jogging.

"I hope everything's going to be all right, Mr. Fletcher," she said solemnly. Tom looked up in surprise.

"With the take-over bid and everything," she said. Coming from that dance-hall face, her voice was unexpectedly level and intelligent.

"I'm sure it will, Sally."

"I like working here, it's the best place I've been in."

"That's a very nice compliment, Sally. Thank you."

"Not at all." She stammered and smiled and went out.

Good heavens, had she been ogling him? No, she was just a pleasant child who wanted to be nice. This was the best place she had been in. He had a short laugh. It was a far cry from Maltdyke and the thirties, when a job was a job and you hoped to settle in by your toenails and cling for the rest of your life. Nowadays he sometimes got kids of seventeen who had bounced in and out of twelve jobs already. They didn't give a damn. He half envied them. They got along because it had never occurred to them that they wouldn't get along. There were no bogeymen in their lives.

At the bottom of the papers Meg had left on his desk was a folded page torn from a magazine. *Life* Magazine. A small sheet of memo paper was clipped to one corner, bearing no message except a question mark. He picked it up curiously and scanned both sides, which contained a piece of an article on the Europort in Rotterdam. He lifted his telephone and pressed a button.

"Yes, Mr. Fletcher?" Meg always called him Mr. Fletcher in the hearing of the girls.

"This magazine cutting."

"I'll come in." She hung up and appeared a second later at the door.

"The advertisement, ninny," she said, leaning over the desk and stabbing with her finger. It was a glossy announcement of something called the Kutsu Computer. He glanced up at Meg. They both shrugged shoulders and he started to read.

"No price given," he muttered.

"You can always ask."

"Mm. It's a bit beyond our line, Meg, isn't it?"

"I suppose it is. But *that's* the kind of thing I've always said to *you*. I've always been the conservative one. You're the wee wizard who jumps out in different directions."

The photograph in the advertisement showed two slender

hands holding a specimen of the Kutsu Computer in mid-air. The thing couldn't have been any bigger or heavier than a junior adding machine, but it claimed to do everything short of flying to the moon.

"This is a hell of a time to start giving me new ideas," he complained. "Anyway, they must have agents all over the shop already."

"Aren't you even going to ask?"

"Oh, all right, Meg, send Sally in and I'll give her a letter."

She shook her head firmly.

"Never mind Sally. I'll take the letter."

He looked at her sharply, detecting undertones, but she sat down and poised pencil over pad and turned a blank, willing expression on him. He knew she was thinking ahead and thinking of a number of things. There was a whiff of conspiracy. He grinned slowly, but she refused to respond.

"All right," he said. "To the Overseas Sales Director, Kutsu Manufacturing Corporation, Kobe, Japan . . ."

At eleven o'clock, Hugh Winton sidled in with two cups of coffee.

"I thought you would be out pushing up your figures, Hugh."

"I know. I thought you would be out too. I got bogged down in the paper work."

"Weren't you seeing Mathieson's this morning?"

"How do you remember that? I always have to look in my diary. I didn't even know you knew I was seeing Mathieson's."

"You told me the day before yesterday."

"Oh. Yes, that's right. Well, the buyer's hung up in some conference, I'm phoning him later. I thought you would be out, you see, Tom, so I thought there ought to be somebody in the office in case anything came in, or anybody . . ."

Tom hid his exasperation.

"Hugh, if any of the Gaylor hatchet men suddenly come in, the best place you can be is outside, selling like a bastard and showing how keen you are."

"I know, Tom! I *would* have, if I had known you were staying in. All the stuff I have on my plate can be done by telephone, it's one of those days."

Tom took the coffee. It was too hot to drink.

"Well, I'm going out to lunch at East Kilbride."

"Right." Hugh looked thoughtful, and added, "Maybe I should go out there myself. I half promised to call on old Thingummyjig, Allardyce."

"Forget about Allardyce, I'll look in on him while I'm there."

"Good. I'll hold the fort. Eh, tell Allardyce I was asking for him. He's a nice old boy. A terrible blether, though, isn't he? Every time I'm out there I begin to think of the number of other people I could be seeing during the time he takes to gossip."

"Yes, he is a bit of a blether," Tom agreed, but couldn't resist adding, "but there's more profit in blethering with a certain sale than in calling on ten chancers."

"I suppose you're right. I'll get used to it. I'm too impatient, that's my trouble, Tom. I always want to get away and get on with the job."

Hugh sat down in the chair opposite and put his feet up on Tom's desk and stared at the wall and chewed his lip.

"Colton's haven't taken the bait," Tom remarked.

"Colton's? Colton's. Don't tell me. I remember. The biscuit people. I didn't think they would, I warned Cam Jones. I never even got past the commissionaire when I tried them. It's like a Gestapo security office, that place."

"Well, Cam did his best."

"I'll bet he did," Hugh agreed. "Cam really works at it, I'll

say that for him. He sticks at it. But Colton's was hopeless
anyway."

Tom knew what Hugh was thinking: that Cam Jones did
his best, but that he was probably too old for the game. For
a moment he tried to put himself in Hugh's place at — what
age was it? Twenty-eight? — and look at Cam Jones. It was
always the same. He found himself remembering Mr. Moules,
and himself at nineteen. Yes, it was true; under his respectful
quietness he had looked at old Moules and known that time
was on his own side. He hadn't even had to express the
thought to himself, it was a physical certitude rather than a
mental process. He was young and the sap was rising and all
the ductless glands were gathering force and he was the in-
heritor of the earth; and old Moules, no matter how big a
noise he might be in Burnett's drawing office, was simply
wearing away, an old man with all his chances behind him and
nothing to wait for except being pushed aside. The only difference was that at nineteen he had been the lowest form of
life and old Moules had been a mean-minded swine; at twenty-
eight, Hugh was making good money and paying off a mort-
gage and drinking on an expense account, and Cam Jones was
the farthest thing from a swine that the human race could
produce. And Cam was a good salesman. Not brilliant, but
good and dead reliable, with thirty or forty years of hard selling and hard boozing behind him.

When he went out to the car to drive to East Kilbride, he
noticed that the trees opposite the office were unusually brilliant with green. It was a better place for an office than a
good central address. Before the war it would have seemed
too far out, but life in the center of the city was becoming
impossible. Here there were still green trees, and even a few
decent pubs handy, and the biggest bonus of all, a private service road for parking. The office was part of a long terrace of

what had once been elegant town residences. A few of the houses were still residences, but most of them were divided into flats. It was a tall narrow house with three floors and a basement, and in spite of the postwar expansion of the business there was still some unused space in it. He realized that although he could turn his back on it without suffering too much, he didn't want to leave it. As he was eying it up and down and approving of it, Meg Macrae came to the door.

"Congratulating yourself, Tom?"

"Why shouldn't I?"

"Yes, you're a very clever man. Tom, are you going to East Kilbride now?"

"Yes." He moved down to the car, and she followed him.

"Tom, enjoy yourself with old Mike, but be careful of the booze, eh, son?"

"Tut tut tut."

"I know, Tom, but I wouldn't like you to have any accidents or get the jail just at this particular time."

"You're perfectly right, Meg. I'll be good."

She leaned a hand on the car as he climbed in.

"Frankly," she said, "if I was in your position I would get stewed to the gills every day."

"Ah, this'll all blow over, Meg."

"I don't mean the office. My God, that's trivial."

"Ah."

"I shouldn't have mentioned it, but I've never mentioned it before, and I can't bottle things up inside me like you, you know. I've been bursting to say something."

"Ah. It gets better, Meg, everything gets better in time."

"I hope so, Tom Fletcher. I would like to see you looking like yourself again."

"Like myself? What's that?"

"Do you not see the difference these past months, Tom?

The first thing I noticed about you when you came to English Brothers all these years ago? Even in your bowler hat you've always looked like a dog in heat."

"My God!"

"Maybe it's all in my own dirty mind. Oh, don't worry, it was a well-behaved dog. But I'd like to see you looking randy and rotten again."

"Meg Macrae, you are disgusting."

"I know. Give my love to old Mike."

He was halfway to East Kilbride when the desolation struck him, and he cursed Meg murderously. But it would probably have happened even without Meg's reminding him. The fact was that he had nothing else to stretch his mind. The morning had started with a panic, and now the panic was dissolved or deferred indefinitely, the afternoon looked like routine if he managed to get back to the office at all, and there was nothing on his mind except meeting Mike Allardyce for no particular reason. It was at times like this that the hell was liable to engulf him. He realized that he was doing seventy without having noticed it, and he became afraid to drive, because he knew he was capable of going over the edge on a perverse impulse. There was no sense in that. If he killed himself or maimed himself, he might kill somebody else at the same time, and if not, he would leave young Tommy defenseless; And Hugh and Meg Macrae and Cam Jones. He looked in the driving mirror and took his right foot off the pedal, and coasted till he found a turn-off where he could pull in and do nothing. Even so, the near-side wheel bounced on the verge. His eyes were swimming with tears.

This was the worst yet; or maybe it was the best. He sat staring at the fields and waited for the tears to flow. Who was it who had established the inane law that men didn't weep? For months he had periodically felt like weeping, but the tear ducts were absolutely ruined by training. It's probably dammed-up tears that seep back into the system and give executives ulcers, he thought idly.

Now that the first jolt had passed, the tears ceased to flow. What seized him now, as always, was the horror hell of logic. It was logic that made life insupportable. He was a man, healthy, comfortably rich, he had done nearly all the things he had hoped to do. He was the same man now as he had been a year ago. There was one difference only, and that was merely that there was one less woman in the world, one single woman whom he might never have met except for an accident; or he might have met her and passed by. Logically, he was little diminished, everything was almost the same. But there was nothing there.

And the logic of all life was a black torture. You grew up, helpless and ignorant but looking forward to the time when life would begin, and then it never actually began. You married, you reared children, you grew old and you died, and the only thing you were really looking forward to was dying because it was the only positive thing there was. So what was the sense in the long journey? It was all a confidence trick, a waste of effort.

The darkness that flooded into him contained a jumble of a thousand memories and bafflements. His mother, frenziedly bringing him up and building her nest to keep danger out, and suffering agonies merely because he had left his job. What was her life for? Waste, waste, waste; her energy twisted into an endless fight against nothing. In thirty years nobody in the world would even remember that she had existed, nobody would understand how anything could have been important enough to rouse her anger. It was all gone, meaningless, a tangle of nonsense. Old Moules — he remembered how he had promised himself to drive down Main Street, Maltdyke,

in a car bigger and shinier than the Major's, and stare unsee-
ingly at Mr. Moules one day to convince the old man of his
absurdity, to torture him with a demonstration of how his life
had been a mistake. For what? Moules was dead, absurd,
petty, sixty or seventy years of mediocrity. But if Moules was
dead, where did that leave Tom Fletcher? with his life de-
voted to scoring off Moules one day. He could never impress
Moules now even if he wanted to; and in any case, that savage
ambition had melted away long before he owned a car that
would impress anybody.

Carabine . . . Lexie Carabine, that was his name — the man
who had swindled him. Where was Lexie now? Dead, alive,
swindling somebody else? What did it matter? How could
Lexie have found the *drive* to cheat him out of a few pounds,
another few pounds? Was Lexie living a life of any meaning
at all, that he should actually lash himself into a sweat to cheat
for a few pounds? Did he feel it had all been worth it?

What was it *for?* It was for nothing. Technically, he called
himself a Christian, more or less. Christ came to earth, Christ
died. Life everlasting. Everlasting? What for? What was the
sense in going on with it forever? Eternal bliss was impossible
to envisage, except as a drugged state for idiots. Maybe eternal bliss was more like an injection of a stimulant, so that nothing external would be changed, but the Blessed would imagine
everything was great fun and love every second of it. He
didn't want it.

But on top of all that was the simple, routine horror of
knowing that Georgie was dead, gone, a person extinguished.
It couldn't be as terrible as that. The world was full of wid-
ows and widowers, all somehow living and apparently living
entirely. He knew dozens. A widow or a widower was a
routine occurrence, like a man with brown hair or blue eyes.
He could remember meeting them, and registering the fact

without curiosity. It was a natural state. Or did they all have this black hell when the wind was in the wrong quarter? Did they all have it, and go on working and say nothing, as he did? There was nobody to say it to.

But Georgie was dead, and the horror was more terrible because Georgie now wasn't only Georgie alive, laughing, loving, swearing, but Georgie alive mixed up with Georgie a mindless thing on a bed, growing pale and yellow and changing into another thing; Georgie dead, a corpse with the rot, the decay beginning at once, a shape of corrupting stuff.

He had forced himself to look the facts of life in the face when it happened, and that meant facing the facts of death. He would never blink an ugly fact in order to comfort himself. A beautiful woman, dead, wasn't an ethereal sadness, but a piece of material, protein and fat, that somebody had to take physically and dispose of, bury or burn. Burn, burn. He could never have lived with the thought of that thing lying in the ground, corrupting like meat. Even now, he sometimes took a fresh revulsion from meat, a physical spasm. For three months after the funeral, he hadn't been able to eat anything except fruit and vegetables. And whisky.

"You take yourself too seriously. You'll never sell anything with a face like that."

He jumped. No, he hadn't said it. He snorted. No, it hadn't been the spirit of his loved one either, calling to him across the Gulf. His own memory had popped the recording up on the machine, in high fidelity. He tried to hear it again, but it wouldn't quite return, with the solemn tone and the bubbling laughter beneath it and the blue blue eyes mocking him and caressing him.

It was ten minutes past noon when he reached the office block of Fortress Foods in East Kilbride. Mike Allardyce, he reflected, wouldn't be worrying about ten minutes here or there; but in fact, Mike was waiting at the door to push him back towards the car.

"Man," he said, "you've got a terrible habit of giving a man a thirst and then leaving him to die of drouth."

"You mean you've got no bottle in your fancy damned office? I expect it free when I come this distance."

"You'll get the first one free, the same as any other honest man. Come on, put a spurt in it. Man," he said, "it's good to see a full-grown man. That young lad of yours is a fine chap, but he's a terrible blether and he knows nothing whatever about whisky."

"He'll learn," said Tom.

"Ach, to hell with that, I haven't time to wait while he gets his education, I'm thirsty *now*. Be honest, now, Tom, does your pulse no' quicken at the thought of a nice round glass with the golden glow in it?"

"It does that, Mike," said Tom, and it was the truth.

Four

WHEN Mike Allardyce went for a drink, he took an old-fashioned Scotch view that it should be a real drink, neat doubles every time. In the crowded cocktail bar, Tom played his foxy trick of carrying the glasses to the bar for the second round and bringing back his own filled with neat ginger ale. It was touch and go, he realized. With very little encouragement he would join the older man drink for drink and suggest a few extra rounds and to hell with the afternoon. It wasn't until the third round that Allardyce squinted contemptuously at his glass and said, "It's a sad day for honest Scotsmen, Tom. I never thought you would turn into a secret teetotaler."

Without a moment's hesitation, Tom said, "It's the new salesman trick. Get the customer drunk and then bring out the order forms while you're still sober."

"Ach!" The old man snorted. "It's the car business, it's ruined social life. Never mind, I knew all the time you were at the ginger ale, I don't blame you. You'll no' even remember the days when a commercial traveler went about in trains like a gentleman. A man could drink a good bucket and be poured into his compartment and no harm done. The world's away to hell."

"What's the use of fighting it, Mike? You're making money out of it."

"I'm making money for the bloody government," Mike said sourly.

"You voted for them, you silly old man."

"And by God, it's the last time! Conservatives? They're worse than the damned Socialists, they've got the same damned disease."

"Soak the rich?"

"What do you mean, the rich? All they're doin' is cripplin' the real workers — the men who keep this country goin'. I've sweated for every penny . . . By God, Tom, you've done it again, I should be old enough to know better. If there's one thing I can't stand it's a man that gets me started and then sits back and laughs at me. Come on and I'll buy you your dinner and keep my mouth shut." The old man gripped him hard by the elbow as they walked into the dining room.

Over the cheese, he brought up the subject of the take-over by the Gaylor Group. He had an ingrained suspicion of big London companies and their sly ways, and he pressed relentlessly about Tom's own position, but although Tom discussed the company at length, he was careful to be noncommittal.

"Dammit, Tom, you're talking generalities. I want to know what kind of swine they are, you've been at it for ten minutes and you haven't said a damned thing I couldn't read in the *Financial Times*."

"I don't know what kind of swine they are, Mike, I'll wait till I see how they jump."

"Aye, all right, but keep your powder dry. There's no sentiment in these bastards."

"Or in me. Or in you."

"Ach, I've got no time for sentiment, I'm too busy keeping a crowd of fat civil servants in jobs counting the money they steal from me."

They went back to the factory to look at the equipment

English Brothers had supplied for the Counting House. As soon as they went into the place, Tom realized that it was wrong.

"Do you mean you've sent the wrong machines? By God, I'll sue you," said Allardyce.

"You can sue till you burst, you stubborn old pig," said Tom, "the machines are all right. You've got them in stupid places. Where's the room plan we did for you?"

"Ach, it's somewhere or other, I've got no time for fancy plans," Allardyce grumbled, but he was already digging it out of a drawer. The Fortress Foods order was a big one, a completely new installation of accounting and filing equipment for a factory of over three hundred employees. It was all there, but its positioning only vaguely resembled the floor plan Tom had worked out with Hugh Winton.

"This is a dog's breakfast," he said. "You're losing an hour a day with people just walking from place to place."

"Who the hell cares?"

"If you've got ten people here losing an hour a day every day you can work it out for yourself. You're throwing money away. Get me a laborer, or one of your keen works managers, and get out of my way." Tom was already throwing his jacket across a desk and pushing a filing cabinet along one wall to a new position. Soon he was joined by a silent man in overalls, and they worked for an hour while Mike Allardyce sat on a desk and critically observed them.

"I've sweated every drop of whisky out watching you," he complained when they were finished. "Come into my office, Tom, I might have a drop still in a bottle somewhere." Feeling his weary muscles, Tom followed him into his office and they sat silently over a drink.

"Your young fellow should have done that in the first place," Mike remarked accusingly.

"He gave you the room plan. What do you want him to do, hold your hand?"

"Goddammit, when I pay that amount of money I expect to be pampered. Nobody ever pampers me nowadays."

"Tell me, Mike," said Tom, "how long did it take you to get used to being a widower?"

"I would never have brought that up, Tom, it'll do you no good to think about it, just keep goin'. When you've got no wife to fight with you've got plenty of other bastards that'll do you down if you turn your back on them."

"Does it matter?"

"Oh, go to hell if you like." Mike was surprisingly shouting. "You've still got a day's work left in you, it's more than I've got. Get out of here and let me get on!" But he stood up and came to the main door with Tom.

"You kids are always feeling sorry for yourselves," he grumped. "Never mind, it was good to see you working up a sweat. You're about the only salesman I ever met that carried a screwdriver and an inch tape, you know that?"

"That's all a part of the confidence trick, Mike. People respect a man with a screwdriver."

"You mind the day you fixed yon old cash register? I've always had the idea you swindled me on that."

"I did, I did," said Tom. "I made two pounds on that deal."

The old man stared closely at him and decided to believe him. "You were a damned fool, Tom. I would have given you it for nothing if you had held off a bit."

"So I'm a damned fool."

"I think you're a cunning damned fool," Mike said slowly. "Away you go, and for God's sake leave your fancy car at home the next time you come." He turned abruptly and walked back into the building.

Tom patted his breast pocket as he walked to the car park.

Fountain pen, pencil, screwdriver and steel measuring tape. They were all there. Nowadays they would be called a gimmick. He had adopted them as his trademark before the word gimmick had been heard of. Like so many other things, the screwdriver and the tape had been the result of cold calculation . . . no, not entirely cold; by that time he had decided that calculation couldn't be confined to mathematics. It could function in more intangible fields, as an instrument in human relationships.

The screwdriver was standard equipment for anybody who was selling Ajax vacuum cleaners, even for anybody who was merely trying to sell Ajax vacuum cleaners. You could always run into snags if the plug on the demonstration cleaner turned out to be the wrong size for the customer's power point. It was one of the trifling details the Ajax Company blandly ignored. Some of the salesmen bought themselves an adapter plug, or a handful of adapter plugs, but for the sake of saving a few pennies, Tom had started out with a sixpenny screwdriver and worked out a routine that would allow him to change the plug while he was talking.

At once he discovered that the sight of the screwdriver had a bonus effect of its own. The sales talk would drone on half heard, but the housewife's eyes were always drawn to the screwdriver and the brisk efficiency of Tom's hands as he screwed and unscrewed. He spent evenings on his own doing nothing but rehearse with the screwdriver and two old electric plugs, so that the operation had the slickness of a conjuring trick. There was something about a screwdriver, it instantly created an impression of technical expertise and stamped him as a skilled mechanic, which was a more reliable thing than a salesman.

When he joined Mindley's Cash Registers, the screwdriver went with him — a new screwdriver, with a clip for the pocket and three blades that stowed inside the handle. In a way, it was a juvenile trick, probably a form of symbolism. He would pull it out of his pocket as if in mistake for a pen, and hold it between his index fingers while he talked, in the hope of hypnotizing the customer. Then he added the roll-up steel rule, which he found in Woolworth's. If a screwdriver made a man look skillful, a rule made him look farsighted. They were his parlor tricks and his lucky charms.

And Mike Allardyce was one of his lucky charms too, because he bought Tom's first Mindley Register.

Times had certainly changed, he thought. If he had started today, he would probably have been sent away for a high-pressure course in some Americanized sales school to learn to chant the ABC of depth motivation and Togetherness, and then stepped straight into a company car to call on people who had already been battered into submission with advertising. In the thirties, he had finally managed to buy a thirdhand Morris Eight two-seater, but the tires were a nightmare and the motor always sounded quietly ill, and the Mindley Register was too massive and heavy to drag around as a sample.

"Make up your mind to it," the branch manager told him, "you haven't got a hope in hell of selling one of these babies. Is that understood?"

"Why did you hire me?" Tom asked.

"To sell Mindley Registers. But we didn't hire you — you're on your own. That's the first thing you've got to get into your head. That's what a straight commission deal means. You can spend the whole week in a pub if you like, we don't care. You're not on our payroll."

"I've got that."

"Good, good. I've made my point." The sales manager was a bulky restless man with patches of broken veins on cheeks and nose. His name was Cameron Jones.

"And you think — you have the colossal audacity to think — that you can sell one of these to some grocer with a drawerful of bills and bad debts and not a tosser in the bank?"

"Can *anybody* sell them?"

"Oh, oh yes, laddie. *I* can sell them, but I'm bloody *good*. And I've been at the game for a long time, I've got *contacts*. You? What have you done?"

"I've sold vacuum cleaners."

"How many?"

"I made a living."

"You're a quiet kid, aren't you? You don't talk much."

"Not all the time."

"A bit cheeky, as well. You don't give a damn for me."

"I don't know yet," said Tom.

Jones smoothed his black mustache and cracked the knuckles of his right hand.

"Would you like to come out for a drink?" he asked.

"No."

"You don't drink."

"I wish you would tell me what to do, Mr. Jones," Tom said. "Thanks very much, about the drink, I mean, but I can't afford to drink now. I've got to get to work."

Jones stood up and stamped about the office.

"I wish I was in your shoes. I'm not boasting, but I'm the one good salesman we've got here, so I'm sitting at this desk all day listening to the tales of woe about how nobody ever buys a Mindley. Christ, I sold six last week on the telephone. That was three quarters of the total sales for the week. Three quarters! I sold six on the telephone and five other men sold two among them. You can't run a business that way."

"If you can sell them, somebody must be willing to buy them," said Tom.

"That's the spirit, laddie, that's the spirit. I hope you don't get sickened, believe me. You see, it's like this — a cash register isn't like a vacuum cleaner. Who buys a vacuum cleaner? A housewife. What does she know about business? Nothing, she's a sucker. Wave a few sheets of paper and say half a dollar a week and she thinks you're giving her a free present."

"It's not as easy as that," Tom insisted, but Jones went straight on.

"Now. Now then. Take a grocer or a butcher. What does he know about business, money, profit and loss? A damned sight more than you. Money's his business. See the difference?"

"All right," Tom said with some impatience. "If money's his business, he'll buy something that's going to save him money. If he's got three assistants, he can lose more in petty pilfering in a year than a Mindley would cost him."

Jones looked at him with new interest.

"You've been doing your homework all right. But try and tell that to a butcher. Just a minute, son, I'm not trying to sicken you. I only want you to know how hard it is before you get disappointed."

"All right," said Tom. "If he understands money, the way you say he does, he'll understand that. If he doesn't understand that, well, he isn't much of a businessman, so you should be able to wave a sheet of paper and say half a dollar a week and he's just as much of a sucker as a housewife."

Jones was gazing at the window during this speech, and slowly beginning to smile. Now he laughed.

"Christ, you've got it calculated, haven't you? Is this the way you talk to prospects? It would frighten me out of my life."

"I haven't got much experience, Mr. Jones," said Tom. "I only tell people what seems best at the time, as long as it's true."

"Never mind experience, you'll get plenty of that, I hope. In Bellshill."

"Bellshill."

They looked at each other and then Jones raised his hands in a French gesture.

"I know, they're still living in caves out there, but you've got to start at the bottom."

"Okay."

Jones looked at him and smoothed his mustache again.

"I'm sorry, laddie, I'm really sorry. But you have to go in at the deep end. Don't let it get you down. And don't spend more than a week at it. If it's useless, it's useless. Come back and I'll try to find you something a bit easier."

Bellshill, when he arrived there, reminded him gloomily of Maltdyke. He had emigrated to the big city only to find himself back where he started. He stopped the little car in the main street and wondered briefly if salesmanship was the right kind of life. Then he remembered the drawing office and Mr. Moules, and he got out of the car and started working.

It was the most depressing day of his life since Maltdyke. Even selling vacuum cleaners, he realized, had been a pleasant cozy business compared with this. There were always plenty of housewives who had no intention of buying anything, but who were happy enough to have somebody agreeable calling at the door. There was always the occasional welcome, the cup of tea, and after a cup of tea there was always a possibility of a sale.

But in a shop, there was no welcome. The whole village had that air of dumb resignation that marked Maltdyke when Burnett and Company were on short time; the tight belts and sallow faces. The village lived on coal and steel, and nobody was buying coal and steel that week.

If there were customers in a shop, he hovered and hung back until he felt that he was wearing an illuminated signboard marked Commercial Traveler. The customers avoided looking at him, and the shopkeeper would throw him an occasional glance without a trace of friendship in it. If there were no customers, the shop would have the chill atmosphere of a dying business and the words sounded remote in his mouth, the literature in his hand seemed to wither as he held it.

The busiest place he deferred till the last. It was a grocery with two windows and the legend M. Allardyce above, and he had passed it and repassed it several times. Since it was so busy, M. Allardyce might be in need of a good cash register; but M. Allardyce would hardly hold up his business to be told that.

By the middle of the afternoon, Tom realized that he was putting it off because he had lost his conviction. A trail of blank disappointments had convinced him deep down that nobody would ever buy a Mindley Register. He could hear his mother laughing, and Mr. Moules warning him that he would never get another job with G. R. Burnett even if he crawled back on his hands and knees. He stopped glancing at M. Allardyce, Family Grocer, and set off to walk smartly to the far end of the village and back again, to breathe fresh air and slough off the gloom.

When he came back, he walked straight into the shop. It was still busy; with a man, presumably M. Allardyce, and three girls serving. Tom settled himself to wait without showing any impatience, but the man went to the rear of the shop and beckoned to him.

"Good afternoon," said Tom.

"A traveler?"

"Yes."

"What is it?"

"The Mindley Cash Register."

"Never in a million years."

"It could save you money."

"Sales talk."

"I'll prove it."

"I've got no time."

"I'll come back when you have time."

"Seven o'clock?"

"Right."

"All right, but you're wasting your time."

Without another word, M. Allardyce went back to the counter and started serving. Tom walked out of the shop and realized that he had nearly four hours to wait until seven. Plenty of time to drive back to Glasgow and return, or try another place in the district — Uddingston wasn't far away. But driving back to Glasgow and returning would use up petrol, and for what? He couldn't do any business in the city. And the thought of moving to Uddingston and spending another two or three hours being rejected was too sad to bear.

He left the car where it was and started walking along the pleasantest road he could find. He walked for two hours and then turned and walked back. To his horror, the front door was closed on M. ALLARDYCE, FAMILY GROCER, and he cursed at the callous duplicity of a man who would waste his afternoon and then desert him. But there seemed to be a light burning somewhere in the shop, and he knocked loudly on the door.

Allardyce opened it and said "Humph" in surprise, but stood back to let Tom into the shop. One of the girls was still there, measuring sugar into paper bags and stacking them behind the counter. Allardyce himself had evidently been cutting chunks out of a vast cube of margarine and wrapping them in quarter-pound pieces. He immediately picked up two wooden knives and resumed the job, ignoring Tom.

One of those hard men who browbeat people by silence. Tom sat on a barrel and watched him beating the margarine into cubes without saying anything. One thing was positive, he wasn't going to stammer and yammer while Allardyce battered away and ignored him.

"You think I need a cash register," Allardyce said finally. He had been thinking. Probably it hadn't been a nerve-war of silence. This was simply a man who worked hard and was busy and didn't talk much in any case.

"I might be wrong," said Tom. "I don't know as much about your business as you do."

"Is that a fact?" His tone was too direct to be sarcastic.

"This is one shop that keeps busy," Tom remarked.

"Scraping for pennies, every damned penny."

"There's no need to swear," the girl said. Not quite a girl, maybe thirty-five or forty. Mrs. Allardyce, obviously.

"Ach, he's a traveler, no' a customer," said Allardyce. "He'll be telling us dirty jokes in a minute."

"And you'll be telling them back."

Allardyce smiled at Tom, the rueful smile from a man to a man commenting on the nature of women.

"If you don't believe it's a scrape for every penny," he said, "you can have a shot at this." He held out the wooden butter knives. Tom shook his head decisively.

"All right," said Allardyce, "sell me a cash register."

"All right, I will. You work hard for a living. Do you ever lose any pennies? I don't mean pilfering, I mean simple mistakes. How much time do you lose making change? Adding up?"

"Dammit, I've got a cash register already."

Tom went over to inspect it, an ornate mass of figured brass casing.

"Antiquated," he said.

"It works," said Allardyce.

"No it doesn't," his wife objected.

"No, goddammit, it doesn't work — show me a machine and I'll show you a damned nuisance. But new or old, what's the difference? It'll no' save me any money."

"Can I try it?"

"I'll sell you it," said Allardyce. "There you are, I'll sell *you* a cash register."

Tom pressed one of the keys cautiously. A shilling rang up. He went along the line and discovered six keys that refused to drop. Allardyce went on measuring out margarine and eyed him cynically. Tom lifted the front of the machine and could see nothing that enlightened him. Allardyce gave a short snort of amusement.

Tom felt his face hardening, and despised himself for not having spent any time studying the inside of a cash register. He had already decided that on the following day he wouldn't make any calls. He would sit in the repair shop and see a Mindley Register in pieces, and identify every single piece. He took the screwdriver out of his pocket; and out of the corner of his eye, fancied that Allardyce had raised his brows. In a few minutes, while Mrs. Allardyce went on mechanically weighing sugar and Allardyce continued to pound pieces of margarine, he had stripped the entire casing off the ancient machine.

It meant nothing to him. The engineering principle was rudimentary, but it was like the first typewriter he had tried to repair — every maker had his own style of fitting the pieces together, and it could take hours to find out which little lever did what. He walked back round to the far side of the counter and crouched to peer into the guts of the thing, praying for a heavenly guidance.

He got it. There was a piece of something — possibly

cheese, but it was hard to tell — wedged among the levers underneath. He hooked some of it out with the screwdriver.

"Could I have a skewer?" he asked Mrs. Allardyce. She pulled a long metal skewer out of a ham and handed it to him. Pursing his lips to avoid smiling, he dislodged the rest of the stuff.

"You wouldn't have such a thing as a pipe cleaner?" he asked Allardyce, who had drifted along the counter to watch him.

"A penny a packet," he said, and slapped a bundle of pipe cleaners on the counter. Without a word, Tom slapped a penny beside them, and picked one up and worked it carefully back and forth to wipe the last traces of foreign matter away.

"Michael Allardyce!" the woman shouted. Allardyce laughed.

"Aye, aye, it's all right, pipe cleaners are free. I suppose this'll cost me a quid."

Tom was already fitting the casing back into place and twirling the screwdriver.

"No charge, it's part of the Mindley service," he muttered.

"All right," said Allardyce. "Now I've got a cash register, and it works, so that's one sale you'll no' make here."

"You're wrong," Tom said. "You've got the only business here that's getting anywhere. You're only holding yourself up if you work with this old . . . scrap heap."

Allardyce was peeling off his white apron and hanging it on a hook.

"I'll buy you a drink, and that's us square," he said. "I don't expect you've got enough money in your pockets to buy me one back."

"I haven't. At least, I have, but it's not for drinking."

"Now Michael Allardyce," the woman protested. "Don't

you start making this young man drunk and sending him home stupid." She too was hanging up her coverall.

"Wouldn't Mrs. Allardyce join us?" Tom asked. "No, I'm sorry, I've got no right to ask that if I'm not buying a drink."

"That's something that would never cross his mind," she said. "It takes a stranger to teach you how to treat your wife, Michael Allardyce."

"Ach, away and shut up." He pushed her affectionately. "Nark nark nark. The only place I get peace is in the pub."

"You can just bring the young man back for his tea, since he's a gentleman."

"Good," said Allardyce, "he'll be handy for carrying me upstairs."

Sitting in the pub across the street, Tom was grateful that he had been invited for a meal afterwards. Whether from gratitude or from habit, Allardyce stood up big whiskies, once, twice and thrice.

"Have you given up?" he said after the first sip.

"No," Tom answered, "I'm just looking for your weak point before I attack again."

"Not a damned one will you find if you look for a hundred years. You saw that shop. All right, I admit it, it makes money, but it's me that makes it make money, me and Jean. With *work*. None of your fancy machinery. Work. That's what makes money. I can sell cheaper because I sell more. I can sell more because I work harder. Everything in that shop is the cheapest I can buy because there isn't a bugger in this district with two pennies to rub together. It's bulk stuff, no expensive packets. I sell it in packets with my own sweat."

"You could sell twice as fast if the cash register was doing your addition sums — and keeping the books at the same time," said Tom. "The Mindley will give you a record every day of every penny. It could take the place of one assistant. Or at least half an assistant."

"You're trying hard, and I don't blame you, but you're havering. We get two busy days a week. The machine would lie in there seven days a week, *depreciating*."

"Its depreciation is less than a girl's wages."

Allardyce didn't answer.

"All right," said Tom. "Answer it. You're the man that has every answer. Answer that."

"It's an exaggeration. Isn't it?"

"Slightly."

"If you hadn't admitted that, you would have gone home without your tea. I'll think about it."

An hour later, in the flat above the grocery shop, Tom sat wolfing gammon and chips and trying not to look feral. A terrible hunger for food was on him, combined with the certainty that he must pack food into his stomach or he would never sober up as long as he lived. Mrs. Allardyce was constantly pouring fresh cups of tea for him, and offering him white and brown bread, and he kept smiling weakly at her and promising himself that one day when he was sober, he would explain how guilty he felt at abusing her hospitality by arriving in her home helpless drunk.

After the fourth cup of tea, and uncounted pieces of bread and butter, he rose sharply from the table, and found Mike Allardyce's hand under his arm. Muttering something that never quite turned itself into words, he found himself propelled through the flat at horrid speed until he found himself stooped over a lavatory bowl. He was rackingly sick. Between spasms, he mouthed slurred apologies to nobody. He saw Allardyce's face scowling at him, and a glass of water being forced into his mouth. Later still, he was sitting in an armchair, burning his tongue with coffee and gazing at Mrs. Allardyce and knowing that he looked pale and idiotic.

"This is the wrong kind of start for a selling career," he said, very carefully but badly.

"Oh, shut up, you're not the first man that ever had too much to drink," she said. "Don't start preaching about it, it'll not be the last time."

"It will, it will. Never again."

"Oh, Michael Allardyce, you've got a lot to answer for," she was saying. "He's probably never had a drink in his life before you did this."

"He's a grown man, he's a grown man, it's his own funeral."

"Your husband is right, Mrs. Allardyce . . . I ave . . . I *have* had a drink before in my life, I'm zuzz . . . zzz . . . snoss a same thing . . . ssssoo much tso drink asssssa one time . . ."

"He'll have to sleep here tonight," he heard her say. She had gone out of focus and then vanished. Some time later he found himself lying on a bed, but the light was shining, and he opened his eyes and reached out to grasp something. It was Allardyce's arm.

"Just a minute," he said. "I'll forget this if I don't say it now."

"Leave him to sleep," Mrs. Allardyce said, but her husband broke in, "Maybe it's worth hearing. What is it, son?"

Tom raised himself slowly and discovered to his joy that he merely felt ill, not stupid.

"It's this system of packing everything in pounds and half pounds and quarter pounds."

"He's delirious," said Mrs. Allardyce, and Mr. Allardyce said "Shut up and let him rave, dammit."

"It's ssstupid," said Tom. "People have got no money, right? Right. Right. Right. So they've got no money. Right. So they count the pennies. So! So! Just a minute, this is brilliant! I can transform your business!"

"They're all the same," he heard Allardyce say. "One drink and they're God."

"No! No! Listen, honest! People count the pennies. So! Weigh it out in pennies! Simple. Not pounds, not quarter pounds. Pennies. A minute, a minute." He closed one eye and focused on a naked electric lamp in the middle of the ceiling. "This is not drunk talk, this is business. Sugar costs twopence halfpenny a pound. Two and a half pennies. So you weigh it in a bag, two fifths of a pound. One penny. Everything in the shop's an even penny. Or two pennies. Or six pennies. Like Woolworth's. Penny bags. Twopenny bags. Threepenny bags. Sixpenny bags. All honest weight."

"He's raving," Mrs. Allardyce said, and her husband said, "So am I."

"If somebody hasn't got enough for a half pound of sugar, they can buy a penny's worth of sugar. See? Anybody can find a penny. To hell with half pounds and quarter pounds."

"Michael Allardyce," he heard the woman say, "I want my bed, and I want you in it. Put the light out and leave him."

Tom whirled down into a stupor.

At breakfast next morning, at seven o'clock, he tried to explain, to apologize, to make everything clear to Mrs. Allardyce, but she patted his shoulder and told him to stop thinking he was different from anybody else.

Five minutes later, Michael Allardyce came into the kitchen, ruddy-faced, clear-eyed, shaven to a shine.

"Right," he said. He sat down and started at once to eat bacon and eggs. "Right. I trust you. Is your cash register worth buying?"

"Yes."

"I've bought it. But I expect a decent price for the old one."

"Oh."

"What'll you give me?"

"It's worth nothing."

"It is to me."

"Fifty bob."

"Done."

"Jean, you can go and see your mother on Sunday. I'll stay in the shop and weigh up penny bags."

"Any excuse not to visit my mother!"

"Any excuse. If I don't sell penny bags, you can take your cash register back, you."

"Will I hell."

"We'll see."

"Do you want to buy it on easy payments?"

"My money makes less in the bank than it costs me to pay your interest. You can have a check for the lot when you deliver it."

"You'll get it this morning."

"Good. Do you want any eggs?"

"Christ." Tom ran from the kitchen.

When he met Cameron Jones in the office at half past nine, Jones was dumfounded to hear of a positive, outright cash sale.

"I don't know if we can deliver one today," he said thoughtfully.

"The sale is off," said Tom.

"All right, all right." Jones laughed. "I wish I had been with you. Selling a Mindley in Bellshill is the big-game hunt. You must feel good."

"One thing," Tom said, keeping his head still and avoiding sudden movements. "One thing — how much do we allow on the old cash register?"

"Not a cent. Oh, for God's sake, this is business. What can anybody do with an old cash register? Throw it in the river! We can't use it. We're *selling* cash registers." He saw the stricken expression on Tom's face, and his own face softened. "I'm sorry, but it's not my decision. We don't take trade-ins. If you're depending on that for the sale, it's off."

Tom stared at him, feeling dull and remote and unconnected with his body. It wasn't an unpleasant feeling. He calculated. His commission on one machine would be nearly seven pounds. Minus fifty shillings, it would be four pounds ten shillings. It was still a deal.

He arranged to pick up a machine from the store, and walked slowly out of Jones' office, pale and far away, but still calculating.

Half an hour later, he had found a shop in the working class district of Maryhill, at the tenth try, and he was in business. He had a secondhand cash register to sell and he had sold it.

"Five pounds is too much," said the shopkeeper. "I haven't seen it yet."

"Four pounds ten shillings. Guaranteed. I'll service it for three months, free, but it doesn't need any servicing." He handed over his card, with the imposing name of Mindley Cash Registers.

"Too much."

"Two pounds when you get it, and the rest next week."

"All right — if it works."

Nine pounds, in one week. Now he could hear his mother laughing, and laugh in return. Anybody could be rich. He would have a bigger car than the Major's. He would drive through Maltdyke and not see anybody.

He settled in behind the wheel of the Jaguar. It was true. He opened the side window and breathed deeply. There was just time to get back to Glasgow to meet his son-in-law, and discover if the office of English Brothers was crawling with Martians with hatchets. He almost felt in the mood for dealing with Martians.

Five

THERE were no Martians at the office of English Brothers; only the girls and Meg Macrae.

"Mr. Winton went out to make some calls," she said, not quite sniffing. He grinned to himself. There was nothing that Hugh would ever do that could sell him to Meg. Maybe it was a matter of the hostility between generations. Hugh sold hard and sometimes brought in spectacular figures, but Meg had made up her mind that he was a young irresponsible who had life too easy, and her mind had closed permanently on that judgment.

"Young Mr. Charles will be in tomorrow," she added, and this time she actually did sniff. "He had a very busy day. He was speaking from guess where?"

"Bermuda?"

"Aye, well, you're not far out. Turnberry. Busy day!"

"Now then, Meg, now then. It's a good day for the golf, and for all you know, Turnberry was crawling with potential clients."

"No doubt. You have to defend your fellow directors. You're all in the club."

"Well, I've been away enjoying myself at East Kilbride, haven't I? Boozing with the best people while you slave over a hot typist."

"Aye, I suppose so." She examined his face. "You don't look too bad, you must have been taking it easy."

"What do you mean, I don't look too bad?" he complained, and went to the mirror above his fireplace. "I look fine. Young. Classical features. Intelligent. Clean-living."

"Oh, I've got no time to be bothered with you when you start that. I've seen better-looking tadpoles." She did her contemptuous sweep-out-of-the-room routine and slammed the door. A few minutes later there was a knock on the door and Cam Jones came in. Tom found himself seeing Cam with fresh eyes. A very toned-down Cam Jones from the hard-swearing, hard-drinking days at Mindley's. He had somehow smoothed out, rather than aged. Quiet gray suit, rolled umbrella, Homburg. His bulk was quieter and gentler, but he still looked what he was, a formidable operator. His hair, Tom realized, was dead white — it must have turned imperceptibly white in the last few years, but it was so thin and fine and smoothly brushed that it merged into his scalp unnoticed.

"This is a fine pickle you're in, Tom," he started, and sat elegantly on the desk. He still had the talent for the unexpected opening. Another man would have been talking about his own situation.

"I haven't noticed any pickle," Tom protested. "Life goes on."

"Still, it's tougher at the top. You've got more to lose," said Cam. "On the other hand, they're nobody's mugs. They'll probably offer you a bigger job."

"We'll see."

"People always exaggerate these panics," Cam said. "Panic is the natural state of industry. I read that somewhere. Hell, we never had anything else but panics back at Mindley's. I hope you're not losing any sleep over the Gaylor thing."

"No. Frankly, I'm not, Cam."

"That's all I wanted to know."

It wasn't all he wanted to know. Cam would never let anybody imagine that he was worried, but he would probably be pleased to have some word of comfort and assurance all the same. There was no point in offering him any assurance. It wouldn't be honest. Tom said nothing, and after a moment Cam shrugged his shoulders. They understood each other.

"I'm sorry the Colton thing fell through," said Tom.

"It hasn't fallen through."

"We got a letter this morning."

"Oh, that. You don't expect to nab an order from people like Colton at the first try. The buyer says no. So I got myself introduced to the managing director at lunchtime. No sales talk, nothing sordid, by gad sir, we're gentlemen, we never think of business, but by gad, sir, we like to meet a fellow with a good fund of stories."

"No fooling, Cam — have you got to the managing director?"

"Best of friends, dear boy."

"Christ, does he really talk like that? By gad, sir?"

"No, he's all right, a bit overeducated, but good sound stuff, my boy, honest British grit. He may turn out to be a dead loss but I've got the foot in the door."

"You never give up, Cam."

"It's all for the good of the jolly old company, Tom. You know? Ah, the bloody truth is, I feel pigheaded about Colton's, I'm damned if I'll give up."

Yes, Tom knew. At sixty, it mattered to Cam that he should make a sale where young Hugh Winton had never got past the front door. He had always been in competition with the whole world and the habit stuck, only now the competition was narrowed down and failure was more to be feared. And he knew too what Cam meant by "the good of the jolly old company."

"You'll beat them, Cam," he said. The older man relaxed his shoulders suddenly and sighed.

"I'm not worried, Tom," he said, convincing himself. "I can always get a couple of small agencies if these Gaylor bastards don't like my face. I don't have expensive tastes any more."

"Let's jump that when we come to it," said Tom.

"What the hell, I've had a good innings here, Tom."

"A year?"

"Five years, Tom, five years."

"Is it? Yeah. Well, we're not done yet, Cam."

"Sure, sure, that's the fighting spirit, laddie. The big smile, confidence, belief in the product. It's lousy and it's overpriced, but sell it." He picked up his rolled umbella and waltzed to the door. "And the best of British luck, Tom," he said before he vanished.

The telephone rang.

"Fletcher."

"Oh. I wanted Hugh Winton. Hello, Tom, Enterkin here — Filograph."

"Uhuh?" He tried to place the man.

"Nothing important. Hugh was looking for me today. You could let him know I called."

"Right."

"How is . . . everything going up there?"

He couldn't place the man at all. Enterkin. The name was familiar, but he certainly didn't know it well enough to gossip about company business.

"Fine, everything's fine here. How is Filograph surviving?"

"Ah, the usual, we're getting our share."

"Good. Well . . . I'll let Hugh know."

". . . right. Bye."

Filograph. That was slightly puzzling. Filograph were in competition with English Brothers, more or less. They certainly weren't potential clients. He hoped Hugh hadn't started to scramble round for another job — it wasn't a question of loyalty, he would advise Hugh to be loyal to nobody but himself and his family. But people could always smell panic, and you could damn yourself fast by merely having it known that you were worried and looking for a job. And the story could get back to your own boss faster than you realized.

Still, what *could* you do if you wanted another job? You had to make some move, you couldn't wait till somebody came along and begged you. All the same, it was frightening how your best friends didn't want to know you once they heard you were looking around. People who would have actually made you an offer a month earlier suddenly wondered if you were worth having, when you seemed to *need* a job. It was one of the frailties of human nature that had always infuriated him. Nobody seemed willing to exercise independent judgment. They all wanted a man when they knew everybody else wanted him. It was a hell of a way to live.

He stared at the door through which Cam Jones had disappeared. Why had that come into his mind? This was one of those damned days for remembering things. Definitely a symptom of advancing age, he decided.

Five years? It scarcely seemed more than a year. He tried to remember his feelings on that day when Cam was announced. Yes, he had been as bad as all the others. He hadn't seen Cam except occasionally for ten years or more, and his first reaction at the name was honest pleasure, and then . . . yes, positively, he remembered, the instant conviction that Cam was probably on the beach, in need of help, a job, money.

Old old friends didn't turn up out of the blue unless they wanted something.

He could see Cam coming through the door — not nervous, not servile; a bit older, but the same tough hard Cameron Jones who could sell six cash registers on the telephone. The joyful greetings, the happy reminiscences, and then, more and more strongly, the shared tension because Tom knew that Cam would soon have to get down to business, and Cam knew he knew. Tom looked at Cam, and for the first time noticed that the buckle of his coat belt was frayed. Everything else was fine, no frayed cuffs, good shoes, white shirt. The coat buckle was the only small betrayal, and at the sight of it, Tom remembered how well Cam had treated him in the past, and felt like a swine, and decided to help Cam at least through the difficulty of coming to the point.

"You didn't come . . ." he started, and heard his own voice and wondered how the hell anybody could find words that wouldn't sound like the old brush-off. "No. I hope I can do something for you, Cam," he said.

"Right, Tom. For a start, let me have twenty thousand quid for a couple of days." It came with the big Jones smile, the merry joke, never look worried in the presence of a sale.

"Cash or check?" Tom asked, trying to match the smile.

"Good, good! I trained you well," said Cam, and added at once, "No, I didn't mean that, Tom, you trained yourself. You don't owe anything to anybody."

"Aw, come on, Cam, give us it straight."

"The sordid truth?"

"Sure."

"No sugar on the pill?"

"Not a grain."

"Ah! I don't think you can do anything for me, Tom, but I'll give you the sordid truth. I'm flat. Finished."

"You're not with Mindley any more?"

"Mindley? I left them six years ago. Too late. I left it too late. Made a bum move, Tom. Never mind the details. I'm a salesman with nothing to sell. Tough, but that's life, laddie."

The big Jones smile was agony to Tom, but he forced himself to keep looking straight at it because he felt it would be greater agony to Cam if he turned away.

"Would some money help?" He heard himself saying it and hated the sound of it.

Cam waved the idea away. "Thanks for asking, Tom. What's the use? I'm a bad risk. Neither a borrower nor a lender be, laddie."

They both nodded.

"Rugged, isn't it?" said Cam.

"Yup." Tom stood up and put his hands in his pockets and walked across to the window, with the vague idea of getting rid of the desk between them. He was already calculating the possibilities, but they needed slow, careful work. "It's true, Cam," he said, while he thought. "I once lent an old mate a hundred pounds — 'never mind the details' — but he was gibbering when he asked me for it, it was life or death and he fell all over me when he got it, and I haven't seen him since. He avoids me in the street. I suppose he hates me."

"It's true, laddie," said Cam. "I met Joe Hepplewhite in a pub the other day, by the way. See much of him nowadays?"

Tom wheeled on him, grinning, and Cam grinned back.

"I got a sort of feeling," Cam said. "Funny thing, your name came up in conversation, and he said you were a bastard."

"Oh, you're a sly sod, Cam. Never mind Joe Hepplewhite, what can *we* do?"

"Tom, for God's sake let me sell something for you. Anything, anywhere."

"Bellshill?"

"Bellshill!"

"Don't jump to conclusions, Cam. I'll try. I can't make the decision on my own, you'll have to wait."

"Of course, of course, Tom. It's only a passing phase, laddie, it'll pass. I'll . . . I'll give you a ring next week. Good to see you, Tom."

"You are a suspicious-minded pig, Cam. 'Give me a ring next week.' Who do you think you're talking to? Meet me at five o'clock in Kelly's. There may be nothing, but at least I can ask."

"Five o'clock. Kelly's." There was only a momentary trace of withdrawal on Cam's face.

"Surely I could advance you a quid, Cam — you know, as a token?" He had a vision of Cam hovering near Kelly's, afraid to go in until Tom's arrival because he didn't have the price of a single drink. Cam shook his head.

"When I'm rich, you can lend me money. Five o'clock, Kelly's."

It wasn't going to be easy to sell Cam Jones to English Brothers. He knew it, and he was anxious for Cam not to be there when he brought the subject up. No matter how good Cam was, young Mr. Charles would take one look at him and tell him to his face that he was too old. That wasn't going to happen to Cam. Tom went upstairs, knocked, and walked into young Charles' office.

"Yes, Fletcher?" Tom could take that. It was the old Moules trick, the offensive use of the surname, but in Charles' case, it was complicated by his determination to ape the Okay London Chaps he admired so much; or by his upbringing in a Scottish private school where the principal subject was imitation English manners. And it wasn't the Moules situation. Charles might be the managing director, but Tom wasn't the newest drawing-office apprentice and he wasn't a silent boy bent on keeping a civil tongue in his head. He was the sales director and he was the man who got results while Charles was striking poses, and he was ready, if the time ever came, to take Charles on and wipe the floor with him. So he grunted, and sat on Charles' desk because he knew it would irritate Charles, that Charles might utter a well-bred reproof, and that Tom could then look puzzled and innocent and make Charles squirm.

"Yes, Fletcher?"

"I'm thinking of putting a new man on the road."

"Good heavens, Fletcher, you don't seem to understand the weight of our overheads. A new man? The salary budget is ridiculously overspent. No. No no. We couldn't hear of that." He made to perform the Moules trick of reading the nearest paper to his hand, but Tom settled more comfortably and said,

"A salesman isn't a charge, he's a paying investment. If I want a man on the road it's because we'll make a profit out of him." He saw Charles' thin lips twitching, and decided not to make an issue of this. There was no point in trying for a cheap victory at the expense of Cam Jones. "In any case," he went on, "it doesn't go into the staff budget. Commission and no salary."

"That's all very well . . ." Charles tried to find a new objection. "Do we know this man you have in mind?"

"I know him."

"We should want to see him, naturally. I think this ought to be left till next week, when the chairman can vet this chap, whoever he is."

"To hell with that," said Tom. "If we wait till next week we'll lose him. This man doesn't need us, we need him."

"I shall certainly want to see the fellow. We can't rush into . . . putting people out . . . representing the company, when they may be any Tom, Dick or Harry. In any case, the sales staff is quite big enough already." Tom was already calculating an inspiration into existence.

"You can't see him unless you're prepared to go to Edinburgh. He's there, and he's working six days a week. And we've got nobody there, the place is wide open. I only heard about him today, and I telephoned him. He's prepared to take our stuff on to see if there's anything in it for him. If there is, he'll concentrate on it."

"The damned impertinence! Who does this damned upstart think he is?" Young Mr. Charles was about to throw a young slim apoplectic fit.

"He thinks he's Cameron Jones," Tom said brutally, "and he knows he's a salesman, and I'm grabbing him quick."

"We'll see what the chairman says about that!"

"We'll see what the chairman says about selling a few thousand quids' worth of stuff. If we don't get results, we'll scrub the man, naturally. I think you're absolutely right about that. We can't waste our time on him if he doesn't produce the goods. I'm glad you brought the point up."

It was really too easy to fox young Mr. Charles. Tom couldn't remember tangling with anybody who could swallow a switch as blatant as that. But maybe it wasn't only stupidity, it was temperament too. Young Mr. Charles had an effortless genius for starting a squabble, but he hated a fight on equal terms, and any means of saving his face was probably welcome, however absurd.

Or was it nothing but stupidity?

"I brought up the point," Charles said, "because we need sales, not jumped-up salesmen with reputations. I've never heard of the fellow."

"He'll do his best for you, or as far as I'm concerned, he's out on his ear," said Tom. He was already on his way to the door. "These salesmen have to be kept up to the mark, there's no doubt about it," he said as he went out. What a bloody fatuous thing to say! It meant nothing. But young Charles had nodded enthusiastically as if he himself had scored a point.

Tom went through his files and dug out a copy of all the brochures he could find, and stuffed them in a pasteboard file. He made a point of being at Kelly's on the stroke of five, and kept his head down so as not to notice Cam Jones staring into a shop window on the other side of the street. Exactly thirty seconds elapsed before Cam joined him at the bar.

"Lemonade," he said.

"I can afford to buy you a real drink," said Tom.

"Chucked it eight months ago. It doesn't go with unemployment, Tom. And where's the percentage in starting again?"

"Eight months!"

"It passes very quickly, laddie."

"You took your own sweet time about coming to see me," Tom complained. But there was nothing more to be said.

"Well," he went on quickly, "we don't hire you, you're not on the payroll. You're on your own. You can spend the whole week in a pub, if you like, drinking lemonade, we don't care."

"Commission job?"

Tom nodded. Cam let a great gust of air escape him, and clapped his hands and rubbed them together. He cracked the knuckles of his right hand.

"Do you not remember these words, Cam? That's what you told me on my first day at Mindley's."

"Ah, great days, Tom. I'll never forget this. Where? Bellshill?"

"Edinburgh."

"Right," Cam said slowly. Edinburgh meant petrol or more probably train fares — he couldn't possibly be running a car in his present position.

"You'll draw ten," said Tom. "No, twenty in advance. Now, this minute. Repayable to the company." He started to write a check.

"Through you." Cam wasn't deceived.

"Here's my card. Get some made for yourself. Now just a minute, Cam, this is going to sound funny. Don't show your face in the office, don't speak to anybody in the office except me. You live in Edinburgh, you never come to Glasgow. Not for a month or six weeks, anyway."

"They don't like me," said Cam in disgust.

"They don't even know you. Don't sulk."

"I'm not sulking Tom, I'm too damned grateful."

"The first time anybody else in the office sees you, Cam, they won't be seeing your ugly face, they'll be seeing you through a haze of sales figures. You'll look beautiful, then."

"And young?"

"Do you want me to flatter you?"

"No, Tom laddie. You've played it bloody clever. You'll get your sales figures. God," he said. "What a callous bunch of bastards we are. You know this, when I was bashing the old cash registers, I *resented* old men. They were in the bloody way. Clear out and give me room to work, Granddad, that was me. No harm to the old sods, but it was a man's game, they ought to go and get themselves put away when they lost their hair. Talk about the day of bloody retribution?"

"No," said Tom, "don't talk about the day of bloody retribution, talk about the day of bloody annual balances."

"Okay, Tom, buy me another lemonade now you're the boss. I'll leave this for a couple of days. I mean, I'm not rushing to Edinburgh tomorrow before I've done my homework. Okay?"

"You can leave it for a month, Cam, you're on your own."

"Check. Look, this will disappoint you, Tom, because I know you love my company, but I think I'll be off home. I'm a busy man, no time to gossip with old pals."

"Sure." Tom had been wondering how they would get through the next ten minutes. He mopped his brow and had another whisky.

He had never felt more confident of anything in his life than of Cam Jones. Not a word was heard from him until four days later, and that was a small mundane order for a cheap cabinet at six pounds. In the next six days there were four more orders, all small and petty. You could almost plot Cam's movements and his mental processes from the orders alone. A slow, inexorable chipping away at the stony foundations of Edinburgh. In the third week, Tom received a rather coarse comic postcard with an Edinburgh postmark and the unsigned message, "Love to all at Bellshill."

It didn't seem like five years ago; and the five years were as inexorable as Cam himself, chipping away at the foundations. It had been hard enough to find words to say to Cam when he arrived with a frayed coat buckle that day. Maybe it would be easy to speak the next time, when he was telling Cam that the innings was over. Somehow he couldn't picture Cam being fitted in among the keen young men of the Gaylor Group.

"Ah, hell hell hell," he said aloud, just as the door opened and his son-in-law walked in.

Six

THEY had a couple of beers in Kelly's. Tom was slightly restless, half hoping that Alan would be planning to leave him and spend the evening somewhere else, but it was pleasant to sit in Kelly's or anywhere else. Alan was relaxing as company because he talked about other things than business, and Tom realized he had been starved of nonbusiness conversation lately.

"I hope you've taken to Trollope," Alan said. "I always thought it was a rather repugnant sector of social life, but it's a very insidious pleasure if one once gets past that prejudice."

"It's not repugnant," Tom protested. "Odd, that's all. It's got nothing to do with religion or parsons once you get down to it. They're like businessmen, or politicians."

"Or schoolteachers." Alan's somewhat haggard young face lit up. "Trollope's a perfectly *modern* writer, that's what one finds it so hard to convince the kids. All those parsons are modern film characters wearing black frock coats." He was getting carried away. "The tragic thing is that these kids actually love stories of the same period. After all, the Western is contemporaneous with *Barchester Towers*. Nobody ever stops to consider that. No, I'm utterly serious. Doc Holliday and Doctor Thorne were in practice at exactly the same time. Why should schoolchildren think Doc Holliday is modern and Doctor Thorne is a square?"

"You'll never get anywhere with that line, Alan. Doctor Thorne didn't carry a six-shooter. Kids don't like modern stories. They're primitives."

"Yes, I admit the West is a primitive society." Alan was speaking quickly. "But what I've got to teach them is that the human relationship situation doesn't alter from society to society. A six-shooter is merely an externalization of the same element of conflict which you can find in *Framley Parsonage*. I'm convinced we merely confuse ourselves when we divide time into historical periods. We are oversimplifying, or dividing human affairs into categories merely to avoid the trouble of examining them in real terms. That's one of the real faults of the curriculum method of education, it merely divides subjects which in fact are not separate, in order to provide tidier administration."

"Thank God I never tried to sell you anything, Alan. I would never have got a word in. Calm yourself, I'm not the enemy."

Alan shook his head and grinned at himself.

"I have to get things off my chest now and then, I'm sorry. But it's true!"

Kelly's was filling with the five o'clock business trickle. It had remained old-fashioned, with a plain dark wood bar and dark linoleum floor and dim old-fashioned lamps, but it still held its trade, teachers and university people and businessmen and oddities. In another half hour it would be definitely dangerous to be standing there, because two or three or six old acquaintances would have appeared and the rounds would start snowballing.

"I don't want to hold you back," said Alan, who was always hypersensitive to other people's boredom.

"It's young Tommy. I shouldn't be leaving him on his own too late."

Alan's face fell in disappointment as he nodded agreement, and on an impulse, Tom invited him to Helensburgh for a meal.

"You can eat with us and I'll drive you back to town later," he suggested.

"No thanks, I wouldn't want you to drive me back. I can get a train."

"Suit yourself, Alan."

"It's rather silly, but apart from the inconvenience to you, if you drove me home Joan would . . . *might* . . . it's rather difficult to explain, but would probably feel that I shouldn't have gone to Helensburgh when she wasn't there. She's very attached to her old dad," he ended with an embarrassed laugh.

"That doesn't mean I can't see you alone if I feel like it," Tom said impatiently. "She doesn't have to feel possessive."

"I shouldn't say possessive," Alan pleaded, but he didn't sound happy. "It's natural affection, I suppose. Daughters are always possessive towards their fathers, aren't they?"

"Ah, to hell with that," said Tom, steering him out of the dimness of the pub into the sunlight. "Her mother was never possessive about *her* father."

"No." Alan laughed. Georgie's father was the bogeyman tribal legend. "I miss your wife very much. I suppose it's rather eccentric to love one's mother-in-law."

"It's a free country."

"I do miss her," Alan repeated. It was more soothing than sympathy.

When they got to the car, the younger man stood back respectfully while Tom unlocked it. He stood back and absent-mindedly rubbed the paintwork with the back of his hand. It was like a furtive gesture of lust. When he saw that Tom had noticed, he flushed with guilt.

"Would you like to drive?" Tom asked him.

"I couldn't!"

"You could."

"You wouldn't mind?"

"Not much." Tom handed him the keys, and Alan gritted his teeth and tried not to purr as he fitted himself into the driving seat and stroked the steering wheel. Tom sat beside him and refrained from saying anything as the younger man checked all the controls and rubbed his palms on his trousers.

It was a cheap enough gesture of generosity. Alan was totally absorbed in driving, and Tom recognized the feeling of pure sensuality in the way he handled the car. It was the same as his own, but young and sharp . . . virginal, almost, an engulfing passion rather than mere satisfaction. That was a feeling that could never return. And hell, it was just as well. Sensations as keen as that were painful as well as joyful, you had to be young to tolerate them physically. Life might be duller when experienced through the hard thick shell of middle age, but it was easier to bear, it must be easier to bear.

He was making a discovery, in fact. The inexpensive gesture of generosity was even smaller than it had seemed, because after all, there was no nervous strain in sitting in the passenger seat. When he was younger, when he first started to drive, a ride as front-seat passenger left him limp with tension, left his right leg knotted with the effort of jamming on an imaginary brake pedal. It was so long since he had done it that he had taken it for granted that he still felt the same way, but the old tension had dissolved somewhere during the years. He could sit and relax and let Alan get on with it.

There must be other things, he thought, other laws of nature that aren't laws of nature any longer. A man dislikes brandy when he's thirty and spends the rest of his life convinced that he doesn't like brandy. But if he tried it again at forty or fifty he would probably find that his taste buds had

developed, or atrophied, to the point where brandy is delicious. Or he acquires a hunger for money at twenty because
he's poor, and at fifty imagines that he still wants money. But
it's nothing more that a habit of mind, a hardening of the
mental arteries. In fact, any man's mind at fifty must be a
congestion of tastes and habits that should have been retested
long ago and thrown out.

Idly he tried to catalogue his own habits, but it was impossible to pin them down. He must be too accustomed to them
to notice them at all.

Black coffee. Why did he always ask for black coffee? It
was because he had learned unconsciously, when he finally
had enough money to eat in good restaurants, that experienced gourmets *always* asked for black coffee after dinner. No, there was something else — somebody . . . Morris
Isaacs, it must have been . . . whatever had become of big
Morris? Morris had told him that Jews never took meat and
milk at the same meal, something to do with religious cleanliness or primitive hygiene or something. The fact had stuck
in his mind and actually inhibited him from having coffee
with milk.

"But that's silly," he said. "I'm not Jewish."

"Pardon?"

"Sorry, Alan, I think I was half asleep."

"I presume that's a compliment to my driving."

"Your driving is fine, you can drive her any time you like."
It was true, he had been half asleep. Old man's catnapping?
No, surely not, he had been able to drop off to sleep at odd
moments all his life.

"I was thinking," he said. "I don't like black coffee and
I don't like bread. Every day I drink black coffee and every
day I eat bread, and I hate them. I don't hate them, but I
don't like them. Black coffee's too bitter."

"That's curious, I don't like carrots, but I eat them every time I get them."

"It's slavery."

"It's hunger," said Alan, and Tom laughed.

"Hunger is the worst slavery," he said. "When are they going to raise teachers' pay so that you can buy a Jag?"

"A Mini-minor would do."

"Surely you could afford a Mini-minor," said Tom, and then added, "No, strike that remark from the record. Everybody always knows what everybody else can afford."

"Yup." Alan was concentrating on his driving. He was really such an earnest and inoffensive young man, such a non-irritant son-in-law, that Tom had an impulse to offer to help him buy a Mini-minor, but immediately rejected the impulse. He suspected those lavish impulses in himself, in case they were attempts to slough off the guilt he sometimes claimed to feel at making his own money so easily. In any case, Alan would refuse the offer and be embarrassed. The one time he had seen his son-in-law's face closing sullenly towards him was when Tom and Georgie had given Joan the cash to deposit on a new house after she married Alan.

It was quite a pleasant little house they bought, and it was a hell of a lot better than living in flats and being hounded by landlords, but for all Tom knew, it might be a source of arguments and quarrels between Alan and Joan. Alan seemed to have a pure, cultivated love of all the expensive things of life, cars, houses, boats, clothes, without actually needing to own them. He could worship them and dream about them without being really unhappy. Joan, on the other hand, was completely practical. If she liked something, she couldn't be happy liking it unless it was her own.

Yes, Joan had a simple, ordinary greed. Probably too much greed. It amused him that he could now contemplate his own daughter, and like her, and admit that she was spoiled and greedy. She kept her figure and she dressed it, and enjoyed her house and bought things for it. Ideal modern girl. Tom decided, uncomfortably, that it must be easier for a father to smile at such characteristics than for a husband to live with them. He glanced at Alan, still crouching slightly forward and loving the feel of the car, and wondered if that delighted sensuality was a substitute. Maybe the kid wasn't getting his oats. That was probably a filthy way for a father to think about his daughter, but it worried him.

He smiled to himself. One advantage of growing older was that he had learned to conserve his energies, at least. Ten years ago, if he had been worried or curious about a daughter or a son-in-law, he would have nosed into the trouble, asked questions, got everybody embarrassed, probably quarreled with Georgie over it, offered help and had the help refused. The effect would have been no change whatever in the situation, except for the worse. Now, he could scent the trouble, think it over, and keep his mouth shut, and achieve the same result with no action at all. He was dozing off again.

If Tommy was surprised to see him home early, he didn't show it, but he did show pleasure at the arrival of Alan.

"You can do my homework for me," he said.

"That wouldn't do you any good," said Tom, but Tommy made his answer direct to Alan.

"It would, it would do me a lot of good. I would have my homework done. That's a lot of good to somebody in my position."

"I am a salaried employee of an education department," Alan said. "I spent five years in becoming an expert so that I could command a high salary. If you think I'm going to waste all that by working for nothing, you've got another think coming. I am worth ten shillings an hour."

"Teachers can *always* wriggle out of everything," Tommy complained, quite happily. "You can never win an argument with a teacher."

"That's because teachers have power, and grubby school kids have none," Alan said. "We don't have to win the argument because we're bigger than you."

"I'm three inchest taller than Graveney. *Mister* Graveney," Tommy added with a grimace of disgust. "But he's the worst. Is Joan with you?"

"No." Alan glanced guiltily at Tom. "She's entertaining friends."

"I don't mind," said Tommy. "Women are a bit of a bore, generally speaking. They lack the capacity for logic, I suppose that's the reason."

"They have intuition," said Alan. Tommy was already walking into the lounge, and Alan followed him. Tom started for the kitchen to find what food Mrs. Crow had left. As he went, he could hear Tommy's voice piping on.

"I don't underestimate intuition, if in fact its existence can be proved, but how can you sustain an intelligent discussion on the basis of intuition? That's what women don't . . ." The door closed on his voice. It was fantastic how that kid blossomed out into a political orator when other people were about. Hard to believe he was the same brat who sat in the kitchen with bare feet, unwashed bare feet, and moved like a dumb ox and spoke in unwilling dribbles. Tom opened the refrigerator and stared into it without seeing anything.

"He doesn't think I'm intelligent enough to understand long sentences," he muttered. "I'm just the bloody old man with no education, grubbing for pennies." The food didn't look very interesting, and he felt deeply tired. He went to the lounge and suggested that they should go out and eat in a hotel.

"Oh, *no!*" Tommy made his disgusted face, and Tom felt

a surge of anger at his ingratitude. All right, he thought, he doesn't want to eat in a hotel, but he should be old enough to say no without making it an insult. Eating in a hotel is so bad, Christ . . . Tom discovered he was almost on the verge of muttering aloud. When I was his age I had never seen the inside of a hotel, far less eaten in one.

"I'm not extraordinarily hungry," Alan said.

And after all, what was he lashing himself into a frenzy for? So the kid didn't want to eat in a hotel. Well, why should Tommy be dazzled at the idea of eating in a hotel? He had eaten in plenty without being given any choice, it was no thrill to him. He was only a child, the "oh *no*" business was one of the clichés of his generation, they all said it, just like that, all the time.

Watch this sullen bottled anger, Fletcher, he thought, it leads to embolisms and ulcers.

"I'll make something light," he said.

"I'll give you a hand." Alan stood up, and naturally, young Tommy stood up, and they all ended in the big kitchen. Alan was laying the table, Tom was beating eggs, and young Tommy, he noticed, was sitting on the windowsill, complacently inactive and talking without a break. As he beat the eggs, Tom thought this out slowly and decided that resentment of a fourteen-year-old boy was in itself childish. If he didn't like Tommy's laziness, he could order the boy to do something, without nagging, or keep his mouth shut and ignore it and forget all about it.

"Has it ever occurred to you," said Alan, interrupting Tommy in the middle of an analysis of the Chinese population explosion, "that your limbs may atrophy and fall off if you leave them inactive while other people are working?"

That was it. Alan could say it without offense, without creating any situations. It was baffling.

"I do, I exercise my limbs incessantly," Tommy insisted.

"But one must be careful not to indulge in physical movement without purpose. I have a theory that each human being has a certain store of energy when he's born, and that when he has expended the sum total, he dies automatically. That's reasonable, isn't it?"

"You can't want any eggs in that case," Tom said, hoping that his tone sounded light and inoffensive. "Because eating adds hundreds of units to your store of energy and louses up your theory."

"I might live forever, if I kept on adding to the store without subtracting anything from it in the form of work done." Thank God, he sounded earnest and pompous and not sullen.

"You might blow up like a balloon and burst," said Alan.

" 'Tis a consummation devoutly to be wished," Tommy declaimed, and then coughed several times, embarrassed at having chosen the wrong tone. When they sat down to scrambled eggs, Alan found a silent interval and asked Tom how he was managing with domestic help.

"We have a predator yclept Mrs. Crow," Tommy cut in at once. The presence of Alan had stimulated him, and he was fidgeting to get talking again. "She has religious scruples and dark designs."

"Crows are not predators," Alan admonished him. "Is she all right, Tom?"

"I insist!" Tommy said. "This Crow is a predator. Dad doesn't believe it, but she is."

"She's a pretty vigorous woman," Tom admitted. "I think she has a motherly regard for my son."

"I think she's trying to get her hooks in my father," Tommy countered, and turned to speak directly to Tom. "You haven't seen her going about *measuring* the house, red in tooth and claw. Nature in the raw is seldom mild," he added complacently.

They sat over their empty plates and talked till it grew dim enough to need the lights on. Then Tommy asked if he should open cans of beer for his father and Alan.

"This is special," Tom said to Alan. "He doesn't approve of alcohol."

"My attitude is exclusively subjective," Tommy explained, to Alan. "I find the habit incomprehensible, but I tolerate it in other people. People of my age are intensely tolerant. It's the distinguishing characteristic of my generation."

"Oh, *no!*" Tom and Alan spoke in spontaneous synchrony.

With one section of his mind, Tom was analyzing the situation. It was the first time he had had anything resembling a conversation with his son in months. The first time, he now realized, that he had had a conversation, sober, with anybody in his own home for almost a year. The thought was eerie and unbearably sad, even while he enjoyed the slumped, relaxed atmosphere that had been generated over the kitchen table. It was Alan's doing, of course, the third party, the court of appeal. Alan himself had said very little, but most of the talk had been directed at him or through him. A third party was what the house had been lacking for so long. That was what Georgie's death had removed; her presence had mattered not only because she lived with him, but because she made it possible for his son to live with him too.

When it grew late, he was reluctant to let Alan go, invited him to stay for the night and travel up to Glasgow next morning.

"Joan would slaughter me. And you."

"She would, at that," Tommy said judicially. "Women have a lethal quality, I've observed it incessantly." Without thinking, Tom aimed a mock backhand at him, and Tommy cowered away, but laughing. He was half drunk with his own talk. They drove Alan to the station and drove back in silence.

"Will you clear up the kitchen?" Tom asked.

"No." Tommy added quickly, "I mean, I don't think we should, on principle. Mrs. Crow is getting her money dam — getting her money very easy. She never does much when you're not here, you know."

"It's got nothing to do with Mrs. Crow," Tom said shortly. "It's scruffy to leave dirty dishes lying on a table all night."

"All right, I don't mind." The boy went off to the kitchen. Tom decided to have a shower, and forced himself to rinse in stinging cold water.

"To prove something," he spluttered. "Something bloody silly." When he came out, Tommy was on his way to bed.

"Goodnight, son," he muttered, shy.

"Goodnight, Dad."

"Um. Hm, we must see more of Alan. He's a very nice fellow."

"Yes!" The boy curbed his eagerness. "He's not bad, for a schoolteacher. Hm. Goodnight."

Tom felt healthy and relaxed, but decided not to risk bed yet. He took *Barchester Towers* down to the lounge and poured himself a moderate whisky and settled to read. He had gone off Trollope's clerical English, he found. It was unfair to Trollope to read five of his books at a stretch. He laid it down and browsed around discontentedly and finally settled on a paperback Chandler. It was so long since he had read it that it would probably work again as new. After the first three pages he sighed in satisfaction and settled down to reading it whole.

It was half past midnight when he looked idly at the clock, and in the same instant a hideous shriek set his wrists prickling and jerked him rigid. Imagination. It sounded again, and he was racing upstairs. The third scream was sounding as he opened Tommy's door and switched on the light. Tommy stared at him from the pillow and screamed again, long and shrill. The effect was horrific. The boy's arms were stretched out in front of him, and when Tom sat and held one of the hands, it was stiff and shuddering. His own sheer blind startled panic had gone.

"It's all right, Tommy, it's all right now."

The boy kept on staring, not at him but through him, focusing on something else, and shrieked again.

"Mum! *Mum!*"

"Wake up, Tommy, you're all right." Tom gripped Tommy's arms firmly and half lifted him.

"The reeds, the reeds!" the boy babbled. "Turn them down! Turn . . . them . . . *down!*" His body was bent like a bow and he kept on staring into the distance. Tom's nerves twitched. He threw back the blankets and forced Tommy upright, made him stand on the floor. Tommy stood there shuddering, and great tears flowed down his face. His arms dropped to his sides and he shivered.

"What is it?" he asked vaguely.

"You had a bad dream."

Tommy looked puzzled, and climbed back into bed. Tom found a handkerchief and started to dry the boy's cheeks. Tommy lay and gaped at him, disoriented, for a few seconds, and then grabbed the handkerchief and put it to his eyes.

"What was it?" Tom asked him.

"I don't know."

"Can you not remember what frightened you?"

"No. It's all right." He turned his face away.

"Dammit, you don't need to be ashamed. Everybody gets nightmares sometimes."

"It's all *right*."

"Can I bring you anything?"

Tommy turned on his back and looked up.

"No, it's all right. Honestly."

"I'll leave my door open so that I can hear you."

Tommy gave a shaky smile.

"Mrs. Crow'll get you if you leave your door open."

"I'll hide. Goodnight, son."

"Goodnight."

Tom paused at the door after he had switched off the light, and saw a little white point of light where Tommy's still open eyes were staring at the ceiling. There was a quiet snort from the darkness.

"Anything wrong?" he asked.

"No." A nervous giggle. "I was foolishly speculating on what would happen if we both had a nightmare at the same time. Who would come to who?"

"Don't think it couldn't happen," said Tom.

There was nothing more to say. Or there was plenty to say, but none of it would come. He took the Chandler and a less moderate whisky to bed, left his bedroom door open, read with only half his attention, and fell asleep with the light still on and the book in his hand.

Seven

THERE was an unexpected spell of mild sunshine in March, and he started spending time in the garden; not from any enthusiasm but more because the garden was there and had to be tended. When he looked at the sheer size of it and remembered how it had been a prize and a delight, he wondered if the time had come to abandon it, to abandon Helensburgh altogether and move into a small flat in the city. All the big decisions of married life were based on an assumption that everything would be permanent — a big house was needed for a rowdy family, a big garden was a perennial holiday — but in no time, children grew up and went away, a big house was an empty booming cavern and a big garden was only a stretch of brute soil that had to be fought and outwitted. His first-born Philip was in Canada and quite possibly would never return even for a visit, Joan was settled immovably in her bungalow, and Tommy was impervious to gracious living in a big house and completely indifferent to the garden.

Nevertheless, Tom took spade and fork and doggedly fought the garden. The physical activity must be good for him, he considered, and in fact, it did produce a dreamy state that wasn't unpleasant. Almost half an acre, 2200 square yards, 1300 square yards in lawn, say 200 square yards in shrubs and trees, leaving 700 square yards in odd beds and patches of nothing very much. Thirty-six turns of the spade to a square yard. The total sounded frightening, but reduced to seconds for a single movement, it was a feasible operation with visible results. Georgie had always laughed hilariously at the mechanical way he had approached gardening. She was a dasher, she burst in murderous energy where her eye took her and as soon as the momentum had petered out, she threw down tools and shouted in triumph or cursed foully at the earth and went off to do something else.

While he was actually working with the spade, he could remember this with less pain because his energy was concentrated on the job. He took to leaving the office as early as possible in the afternoons, and digging and rearranging till the light went. Coming home early meant that he was there most of the time Tommy was home, it kept him sober and it helped him to sleep. Tommy would stay indoors, doing whatever he did, or sometimes come to the kitchen door and watch. Once or twice he asked if he could help, but he was clearly so uninterested that Tom waved the offer away. Gardening wasn't a kids' thing. Tom didn't want the work done, he wanted to do it.

At times he could believe that his incessant irritation with Tommy was diminishing. Impatient anger still welled up in him, but he felt he was releasing it less often.

Perhaps Mrs. Crow had something to do with the improvement in the family atmosphere, since she provided a diversion for his irritation. Now that he was available for more of the time, she took to lingering later on her work in the house so that she could rush out to the garden with cups of tea and snatches of conservation. She had a peculiarly reverent way of watching him work, a beady-eyed adoration that made his skin crawl.

"Gardening is God's work, Mr. Fletcher," she would say

piously, and then add, "I like to see a man that can use his muscles, your shoulders move lovely for your age."

"How is Mr. Crow?" he would say, in the hope of diverting her, but this trick had lost most of its power with repetition.

"Just the same, tut tut," she would sigh, and go right ahead with her worship, and in the garden there was no convenient escape. He couldn't keep throwing the spade down and stamping off to look at the rosebushes. She simply followed him, and her stupidity wore him down. Tommy's diagnosis was that she had been vaccinated with a gramophone needle. She never really expected answers to questions. A submissive silence was enough.

"Hard work is good for a man, I think. The Bible says that man was born to work so it must be true. There's a lot in the Bible, isn't there? There's a lot of truth in it. Some people say you can't believe all you read, but if you can't believe that, what can you believe? It might be bad for you if you got too much of it, right enough. Some people die from working too hard. I always think you shouldn't work too hard, everything in moderation. That's my experience anyway, everything in moderation and you can look anybody in the face, it's a known fact."

"Uhuh."

"But they're not sensible, people wouldn't be sensible that would do a thing like that, work themselves to death."

"We have to work to eat," Tom said wildly. If you joined in a conversation with Mrs. Crow, you found yourself adopting her mental level in spite of yourself.

"That's very true, that's what I always say. We have to work to eat. That's why the farmers work so hard. They've got to eat, you see, to make the things grow. Or where would we be?" she added with a merry laugh.

"Dead?"

"Well, you can't live without food, I always say that." Tom could see her thinking: *It's nice talking to Mr. Fletcher, it's such interesting talk. He's got nice shoulders for his age, it's not right he hasn't got a woman in the house. That's what it says in the Bible, and God created he woman. He's always worrying about Mr. Crow, but Joe and me aren't like that, Joe knows when he's well off.*

"I think I'll make you a nice sandwich, Mr. Fletcher."

"All right."

"Men must work and women must weep," she laughed. "And a man can't do a man's work without eating. Not a *man's* work." Her tongue rolled the word deliciously and she minced into the house, high heels ridiculous on soggy grass. She was around forty-five and spreading fast, but she doggedly wore stiletto heels, at least he had never seen her feet in anything else, and she always wore bright thick make-up and a bright scarf round her head. Her calves were enormously plump above the foolish shoes, and her buttocks ballooned out under a tight cinched waist. The middle part of her body, he fancied, was encased in high-tensile steel . . . mentally he designed the heavy-duty corset that she must be wearing, metal sections swaged for torsional strength, hinged at one side and closed at the other with turnbuckles in place of the feeble old-fashioned lacing system. Perhaps Mr. Crow's first duty every morning was to take a square key and twist away at the turnbuckles till her face turned black, and then slacken back two turns. Above this hypothetical cincture, her bosom burst outwards. Bosom was the word, rather than breasts, because it was singular, one enormous frightening shelf of tissue. She had a habit of placing her hands delicately beneath it in thoughtful moments, in a quiet, proud gesture.

On that occasion, she returned to the kitchen door after a

few seconds in the house and called in a tortured accent that was intended to be formal, "Mr. Fletcher! There's a lady inquiring for you by telephone. What shall I inform her?"

"I'm coming." He dropped the spade thankfully.

"I don't think that's very good manners, disturbing you with matters of business in your own home," she sympathized as he went into the house. Short of biting her, he couldn't answer that. He lifted the telephone in the lounge and she remained, hovering.

"Tom! It's Alice. Alice Wardell."

"Oh. Hello, Alice."

"Where have you been hiding yourself?"

"Nowhere, Alice. Busy."

"Yes, I know, Tom. Tom! I'm in Helensburgh. I didn't think I would catch you at home as early as this, but what the hell, always have a bash, I thought. Come and buy me a drink before I go back, skinflint."

The jaunty bantering tone was perhaps forced. Maybe not.

"Sure. Where are you, Alice?"

"I'll meet you at the Royal. Are you decent?"

"Not more than usual."

"Oh, *good*. Can you be there in twenty minutes?"

"Yes, Alice. It's a pleasure. Thanks for phoning."

"It's no effort to telephone . . ." There was a little dig in that remark. And there was a violent clanking from the kitchen. Mrs. Crow had heard enough, and was away smashing the saucepans.

"I'll see you in twenty minutes," he said. "Bye, Alice."

"Don't be late." She hung up. He found Tommy in his bedroom and said that he was going out to have a drink with a client.

"I don't blame you," Tommy said. "If you protract your absence to half an hour, the Crow will have flown."

"Maybe I'll bring this . . . this woman back for a bite to eat . . ." He was ill at ease. "I don't want to, but she's a client."

"I know what women are." Tommy's face had gone guarded. Still carrying his book, he went downstairs, and Tom went to his bedroom to change. While he was there, there was a muffled sound of Mrs. Crow giving voice in complaint, and then he heard Tommy coming upstairs, singing something to the tune of "Le Pont d'Avignon."

> Le corbeau
> Has to go
> Le corbeau has got to go-o.

Yes, undoubtedly the Crow would have to go. If she had been an employee at the office, he would have disposed of her painlessly without a tremor. It was different in his home. He couldn't find a formula. He began to wonder if he was the kind of man who used up all his power of decision in business and had none left over for his private life — something like young Tommy's theory of the limited store of energy that everybody was born with.

As soon as he saw Alice in the lounge of the Royal Hotel his natural suspicion started operating.

"This a stroke of luck," she explained. "Imagine, I've known for years you lived in Helensburgh, but I've never seen you here against your natural background, Tom. I had to deliver some papers to one of the big brass and it suddenly hit me on the way to the station. Helensburgh. Tom Fletcher. Bingo."

No doubt she wouldn't have delivered papers to the big brass dressed in an old boiler suit. It was unjust to be suspicious of her fur coat, the little hat made of feathers, the simple black dress and the strand of pearls. Was he so desirable that he had to be suspicious of any woman who turned up apparently by accident? A man could get delusions of grandeur in middle age. And yes, he decided he *was* so desirable. Alice, in spite of the neat shape and the elegant style, was also middle-aged, by some reckoning. What happened to girls like Alice, who liked men and could like a particular individual man, and who were *there*, unmarried as a permanent condition? Nice, agreeable, good-looking girls with pleasant faces and figures and sex. The entire marrying business was an unbusinesslike mess, the selection process was too wasteful.

Very attractive legs, really very attractive legs. Not long, but smooth and interesting. That was something about the career girls — people might say that marriage fulfilled a woman, made her bloom, but those lasses who were married to their jobs remained fresh; they didn't use themselves up in the muddle of cooking and housekeeping and childbirth. She was wearing a white slip with a frilly hem under the black dress and there were just a few pleats of hem showing where the skirt tightened on her crossed knees. Very white. Fastidious. She must be only a few years younger than his own forty-seven . . . about the same age as his mother had been when he left G. R. Burnett's drawing office. Now *there* was a bizarre thought.

"You are a terribly damned independent male," she complained, over a whisky. No gin, no vodka, no chic feminine tipples.

"Am I?"

"My dear Tom, when people have troubles, that's what friends are for. Remember me?"

"Other people's troubles aren't very interesting, Alice."

"They are to me. I've got a broad back."

"Yes. I remember."

"I'm glad." She stared into his eyes.

"And a little smile played mockingly round her lips," Tom said.

"Loose lips, loose hips."

But he had no wish to exchange private phrases of old memories. She was trying too hard, too quickly. He sympathized with her, but it wouldn't do. Quickly, almost too quickly, she sensed his own mood, and she turned and looked out of the lounge window at the sea.

"It's a very nice place to hide . . . to hide from your friends, I mean, you dog." Her smile was bright and unsentimental.

"That's a funny coincidence," he said. "I was wondering only the other day if I should give up the house here and get a flat in Glasgow."

"Oh, no! It would be a shame. You couldn't get a handier place and you'll never get a view like this in Glasgow. Not, that, it's, any, of, my, business, Tom. I'm not trying to worm my way into your life."

Tom smiled and shrugged. Any answer to that would be precarious.

"Tell me about yourself," he said.

"Well. Old Mr. Mathieson had a stroke. You knew that. He's more or less recovered. He's a bit dotty, the old soul. They're talking about moving to new offices. Again, I'll believe it when I see the furniture going out. Bill Forsyth . . ."

A catalogue of small events, office, gossip, itemized in the manner of an efficient secretary. Fluent, sharp, good brain, she enjoyed talking. He listened amiably. It would be a shame, in a way, to leave Helensburgh. Even without the car, the train service to Glasgow was good, and if he didn't look out at the salty view of the Firth very often, he was always pleased to be aware that he *could*. That had been the big glorious step, abandoning the city and becoming out-of-towners;

comfortable successful people who could live as they chose,
where they chose. Back to the village life and the sea air and
the hills. He couldn't have found a village less like Maltdyke.
No ironworks, no pale despairing faces. The grass was green
and the hills were purple and you could find cherry blossom
blazing right outside in the street; not behind walls, but right
out in the street. ("Christ, it *stinks* of money!" Georgie had
shouted. "We're up to the ears in it!")

"And tell me about *your*self. Or is it a military secret?"
Alice was asking. Her glass was empty, and he ordered fresh
drinks. He hadn't really had a drink for three days. He asked
for doubles. She raised her eyebrows but didn't protest. He
felt reckless, but it was the recklessness that wanted a drink,
it wasn't directed towards Alice. If she got any wrong ideas,
he would simply remove them. Nevertheless, it was he who
invited her back to the house, and she who held back.

"Okay, you can come or not, Alice," he said. "I would buy
you dinner here, but I've got the kid at home and I have to
get back. It'll only be a cold salad."

"Right." She demonstrated the process of coming to a firm
decision. "It is good to see you again, Tom, and I'm not in
a hurry to go anywhere else. But I'm *not* trying to worm —"

"Okay, okay, stop wriggling, then." He laughed and fitted
her fur coat round her.

They ate in the dining room, and again Tommy behaved
well in the presence of a third party, except that this time he
laid the table and declined Alice's help. It was not a hilarious
meal, all the same. Not unpleasant, but not hilarious. Tommy
was quiet and polite, and Alice talked too much.

"And how do you like school, Tommy?"

"All right."

"That's not very informative, is it? I don't know why men
are always so secretive. Do you like your teachers?"

"Not bad."

"Oh, it's a marvelous age to be — you probably don't agree, but believe me, it's marvelous. Do you play tennis?"

"A bit."

"I like strong silent men."

Soon after the meal, Tommy announced that he was taking his homework to bed because he was tired.

"Don't let me chase you away, Tommy," Alice pleaded. "I'm not staying very long in any case."

"No, it's all right. I'm fairly tired . . . Well, I'll say goodnight. Goodnight, Miss Wardell."

"*Very* formal." She flashed him a rueful smile, and after he had gone, she threw herself back on the sofa and whistled.

"God, did I louse that up!"

"What do you mean?" Tom asked politely.

"Oh, don't try to let me down lightly, Tom, for God's sake. 'How do you like your school, Tommy?' and 'How do you like your teachers, Tommy?' How is it that I can natter like a silly old spinster, and know it, and damn well go on doing it? I'm surprised he didn't throw up at me." She stubbed out her cigarette and glared at it.

"He doesn't talk much to anybody," Tom said. "Don't get yourself in a paddy about it."

"Oh hell, I feel like a fool. Let's face it, I'm no use with kids — I haven't the faintest damn clue what to say to them. You know what he thinks, of course. I'm a designing female chasing his helpless dad." She defied contradiction.

"Have a drink, have a drink, Alice, and let it evaporate. This isn't like you." They sat in an uncomfortable silence.

"Maybe I *am* a designing female. If you turned round and asked me to marry you I would do it like a shot and Mathieson and Company could go to hell tomorrow. It's all right, don't dive for cover, Tom. I know you're not likely to ask me and you're not going to be seduced into it."

"Have a drink."

"I've got to hand it to you, Tom, you can change a subject slicker than anybody I know. Don't get me blind drunk, that's all I ask."

"You mean, 'ply you with liquor'?"

"Since when did you have to ply me with liquor?"

She drank and said, "That's better. And this is straight gen, Tom. I don't want to marry you, really. I don't want to marry anybody. I would do it for a lark, and to get a rest, but I don't feel strongly enough about you, personally, to make an honest wife. I would, however, not object to seeing a bit more of you than I've seen for the past year. We used to have fun."

"That's true."

"Tom, I haven't contracted leprosy, honestly. It's not rational, that you enjoy taking a woman out when you're married and then drop her when you're *not*."

"No, it probably isn't. It's bad manners, too."

"I'm beginning to think I know what it is. The little bit of sin is a load of laughs when you've got a wife because it's something extra on the side, but when it comes to the pinch, the little bit on the side doesn't measure up as a substitute. That's true, isn't it?"

"Don't hound yourself, Alice."

"I sound more like I'm hounding you. It's true, though, I think it's true."

"That is not the situation, Alice." He would definitely have to lie. What she said was true, but as soon as you said it, it distorted the truth because it was only a small part of the whole truth. And no woman could be allowed to think of herself as a little bit on the side, because that wasn't entirely true either. And even if it had been true, it was wrong. "When you're married, you never know what's going to hit you. I've been knocked out. It's got nothing to do with bits on the side or anything else — that's a horrible phrase, incidentally — I've had certain habits for twenty years or more and one day bang, they're gone. I'm a different man. And not much good to anybody."

"Oh, the Gaylor Group." She had switched abruptly into the tidy-minded businesswoman. "Why should I be giving you my worries? I'm sure you don't have to worry about Gaylor's."

"Maybe not." He accepted the change of subject with relief.

"They ought to be damn glad they got you with the package."

"I hope you're right."

"You *must* have changed. It's not like you not to be sure of yourself." She set out to restore his shattered business morale, and he let her go on about it. There was no doubt about it, Alice was loyal, and she talked sense when it came to business. Anybody can talk sense when it's only business, he reflected.

"Well, now I've got the Gaylor Group sorted out, *and* Mathieson and Company, *and* English Brothers, *and* you, I'd better be on my merry way." She stood up.

"I'll drive you to the station, at least," he said, but she contrived to move the wrong way so that they bumped together, and she laughed.

"You can't wait to get rid of me. Tom, stop being frightened."

"Of you? That'll be the day."

She patted his cheek, then put her arms round his neck, and he kissed her.

"That's better," she said. "Just good friends." She kissed him again. He could see himself standing there in the lounge, holding her and kissing her. A suitable occupation for, say Tommy, at fourteen, but surely a macabre charade at forty-seven. What was it the Duke of Whatsisname had said about it? The something is something, the expense is damnable and the position is ridiculous. When you got to the stage of trying to place quotations while in a clinch, that was old age.

"I do like you, Tommy."

"I like you, Alice."

The time to stop was now, but it was true, he did like her, and he admired her, and there he was, sitting on the sofa with her. He patted her back in a vague brotherly way as she closed in on him. That was the great difficulty, he knew: Alice wasn't the cool mental type who advanced in steady gradations. Some people were like machines, which gently gathered momentum, and others were like those chemical fire extinguishers, one thump and the whole thing boiled. But she was a girl with immense self-respect and self-control, and she was still speaking with iron calm.

"I *like* you, Tom. Don't let that worry you." He patted her vaguely again. Pleasant. Women were still beautiful things. She giggled, determined to be gay, treat it lightly, brother, it's just good clean fun.

"On a couch, at my age! Nice Tom." But her hands were eating him of their own volition; and his own hands were going through motions from long practice. Beethoven fingering melodies long after he could hear nothing. Soon she grew frantic, and then incredulous and pleading.

"It's no use," he muttered into her neck.

"Hell damn damn, it *is*." But she was beginning to believe him. "Tom, do something, do *something*."

"No." He wanted to get up, but he squeezed her firmly and she shuddered against him.

"Now I know what they mean by the polite rebuff," she said.

"It's not a rebuff, it's no use, it's got nothing to do with you, Alice."

"Don't say No, do something."

"No. You wouldn't like it, and you would hate me. It's no use, Alice." He let her go and stood up. "It's not the kind of thing a man says unless it's true." She lit a cigarette and dragged on it.

"You mean it's no use at *all?*"

"No." He was looking at himself again, and calculating: it was better if she could feel sorry for him, rather than think he felt sorry for her. Sneering at himself, he sat down and rubbed his brow, weary, old helpless man. At once she rose and put her hand on his shoulder.

"I'm sorry, Tom, that must have been awful."

"It's all right."

"My God, what is it *like?*"

He stood up and pressed a finger on her nose.

"Don't be a nosy little girl."

"Yes, teacher."

She sat with one hand on his shoulder as he drove her to the station, and when he left her at the train, she squeezed his arm, and said, "It would still be nice to hear from you some time. You do still eat."

"If I get somebody nice to spoon-feed me."

"I'm your girl."

"I'll make it soon, Alice. Thanks."

"You'll get your health and strength back." She squeezed again and got aboard the train. He drove back to the house wondering if he should feel mortified and wondering why he didn't. Tommy was in the lounge looking for a book to read.

"She didn't stay very long," he said.

"Busy businesswoman. Did you like her?" he asked in honest curiosity.

"Quite nice-*looking*. I suppose she's all right."

"Other people's female friends are always a puzzle."

"I wouldn't presume to have an opinion," said Tommy, and blushed dark red.

Eight

MR. FINNIMORE was tall and slender, and he wore a dark lightweight suit of some mixture that gave off a dull sheen when it moved. The trousers were very narrow and had no cuffs, and ended above suede half-boots. His shirt had an unusually narrow collar and a tie pin was fastened across under a very thin dark red tie with a small knot. He toured the office saying almost nothing, and hardly seeming even to look at anything, though his eyes flitted from side to side occasionally. Tom thought he performed like a high-class spy in a television series. When he was introduced to Meg Macrae he only nodded. He was waiting, Tom suspected, for Meg to offer him a hand to shake, so that he could fail to see it, but he wasn't getting any change out of Meg. She nodded back, barely avoided sniffing, and her nod was even briefer than Mr. Finnimore's.

Young Mr. Charles was in London, meeting the new masters of the Gaylor Group. Young Mr. Finnimore was in Glasgow, surveying the colonies on behalf of the masters of the Gaylor Group. It looked like an imperceptible exchange. Old Mr. Charles was on hand to exude his diffident, old-school welcome to the visitor, and after the cursory tour of inspection, Tom was invited to make a third for lunch.

"When the weather is mild enough," he said to Finnimore, "Thomas and I — Mr. Fletcher and I — have the habit of strolling as far as the Botanical Gardens before we take a taxi. If that suits."

"Anything you say," said Mr. Finnimore. He measured his pace to match old Charles', and said very little while they walked, but examined the old terraces with that sideways flicking of the eyes, as if he didn't want to be caught in the act of deliberately looking at anything.

"Not unlike Chelsea," he remarked, and old Mr. Charles turned eagerly.

"Yes, I've often thought that. The great convenience, of Glasgow, I've often thought, is that one can find such a pleasant ambience so near the center. The city is only a few minutes in that direction —" he gestured with a thin dry hand, "— and Loch Lomond is less than half an hour in that."

"Not much recent development," Finnimore muttered.

"No, thank Heavens," said old Mr. Charles. "It would be a great pity to see all this swept away. We have a splendid Mackintosh terrace only a little way away. Are you interested in architecture, Mr. Finnimore?"

"Not much." He followed the direction of Charles' hand, westward along the broad rise and fall of Great Western Road, and viewing it through Finnimore's eyes, Tom could see it ruled off in small squares with price labels.

In the taxi on the way to Carrera's, Finnimore kept his eyes flitting from side to side and Charles, who appeared to have used up his conversation, sat back and looked dry and benevolent. Tom, on the fold-down seat facing them, kept his eyes on the side window. He had said nothing since they left the office, and it amused him to go on saying nothing. While Finnimore gave all his attention, respectfully, to old Charles, his mind was palpably on himself, on Tom. Old Charles was only an old man, soon to disappear, and to be treated nicely in the meantime; but Tom was a situation, a problem that had to be surveyed. Tom found himself smiling, and was aware that Finnimore had noticed the smile — smiling was almost as dangerous as talking aloud, but he smiled regardless, and Finnimore could deduce what he liked from it.

Tom was idly calculating the probabilities, and in their simplest form, they were that Finnimore had been sent to Glasgow to make him an offer — good, bad, or indifferent, but in any case, an offer that had been decided before Finnimore's visit, in which case Finnimore was merely an errand boy; or Finnimore was instructed to examine him and report back, in which case he was a person with power. Certainly he was acting up to the role of the man with power, silent and confident and all-seeing, but after a lifetime of selling, Tom had no interest in the approach. The reality — the quality of the goods, the price, the profit margin, the balance sheet — these were the only things that mattered, and he would consider them when they were revealed. If Finnimore had been given the job of examining him, he could react by trying to create a good impression, or by deliberately declining to make a good impression (which amounted to the same thing) or he could refuse the rules of the game and amuse himself by sizing up Finnimore instead. He had already decided to do that before he had even seen Finnimore.

At Carrera's, old Charles agreed to have a dry sherry before lunch.

"At my age," he smiled gently — a bit of a faker, old Charles; it was true he was thin and austere and diffident naturally, but he acted it up just a little — "At my age, most indulgences have to be cautiously limited."

"Whisky," Tom said shortly.

"What brand?" Finnimore asked him, and the question seemed important.

"I trust the cellar."

"Oh? Whisky for me. Teacher's."

Alfonso's face showed a momentary doubt.

"Try Glenfiddich," Tom suggested.

"Don't they stock Teacher's? Oh, all right." Alfonso swooped away. When he returned after an interval with the drinks, Finnimore tasted his neat, and judicially said, "Not bad."

Alfonso, beaming, had already started saying, "For your guest, Mr. Fletcher, I brought some Teacher's from Donnelly's across the street. No trouble, sir." He swooped away again. There was a brief silence.

"The joke's on me," Finnimore said. He looked at Tom and Tom looked back. It was one of the moments when two men can become enemies permanently. "I should know better," Finnimore added, "than to pose as a connoisseur of Scotch among Scotsmen." So he wasn't quite such a twit as he might have been.

"I'm a Scotsman, and I would hate to be blindfolded and asked to name six brands," Tom said, willing to get him off the hook.

"It's all part of the with-it fashion," Finnimore said. "Everybody in London asks for Teacher's. These things go in fashions, of course."

"Ask for Famous Grouse and start a new cycle." Tom smiled openly.

"One-upmanship! What was that name?" Finnimore took out his pocket diary and wrote it down. There was some kind of person inside the shiny suit. There always was. But Tom kept judgment suspended and waited for more data. They talked over lunch in generalities, about industrial prospects in Glasgow and economic growth.

"We know all about the situation in these provincial towns," Finnimore said, and Tom prickled irrationally. "You have to push them like hell to get them off their backsides." He had had two more whiskies and they were on their second bottle of claret. "No offense, but everything's a damn sight slower than it is in town. It's a matter of record. I haven't seen a single new office building since I arrived here."

"You haven't been looking," Tom said. "I can show you twenty within three hundred yards of here."

"Big blocks?"

"Is twenty floors big enough?"

Finnimore digested this, but he wasn't beaten. "'Built with local capital?"

"No, by London speculators."

"Well, there you are, old man."

"So what?" That sounded childish — it sounded like young Tommy, in fact, and he added, "I mean, what has that got to do with our particular business?"

"I'm not *criticizing*, old man, don't misunderstand me, it's a matter of *attitude*. You either accept the dead-and-alive local situation or you go out and beat the hell out of it, old man." Alfonso, on his swooping route past the table, glanced at them, and Tom caught his eye. Alfonso, for an Italian, was a chauvinistic Glaswegian, and he would sometimes do impersonations of the lunchtime conversations of visiting London executives, consisting mainly of "just a second, old man, come come, old man, Balls, old man, Who are you calling Old Man, old man."

Old Mr. Charles pulled out his watch and looked at it in surprise, the gold pocket watch another of the props of his inoffensive elder statesman role.

"I really must be going, now — no, don't get up, Thomas. I know Mr. Finnimore has much more to discuss with you, so I shall leave you in this amiable atmosphere and take myself away. Shall I be seeing you again later, Mr. Finnimore?"

Finnimore stood half erect and held out his hand.

"I'd better not promise, Mr. English — bags of paper work back at my hotel before I catch my plane."

"Well, then! It's been a great pleasure, Mr. Finnimore. Safe journey. I leave you in Thomas' capable hands."

Tom ordered a whisky with his coffee, and after a moment's hesitation, Finnimore said, "Same for me, why not? I usually have Courvoisier, but when in Rome, do as the Romans do."

"What if the Romans are jumping off cliffs that week?"

"Um? Ha! Ha ha! Is that new?"

"I don't know, I only just thought of it."

"Just a tick." Finnimore took out his little book and scribbled. "No, honestly, Tom — your name's Tom, isn't it? My friends call me Jack." They shook hands. "No, honestly, Tom, I can tell you in confidence, the Top Man isn't too worried about English Brothers. Small firm, a bit comfortable, you know what I mean, a bit of dust in the corners here and there, but good figures, you're doing a good job."

"Seriously, you're doing a grand job."

"Yes, that kind of thing. Not to worry, old man, there isn't going to be a blood bath, nothing like that, old man, N.G. doesn't believe in working that way."

"How is Nick Gaylor?"

A small shadow flitted across Finnimore's face at the use of the first name.

"Fine, he's a great operator. Ever meet him, Tom?"

"I was drunk with him for two nights in Paris once."

Finnimore stared at him. "Christ, nobody told me that," he said resentfully.

"We're not close friends."

"No, but still, old man. Still, I don't suppose that has anything to do with it, it's strictly business with N.G. You know that he won't even have any of his family working in the company?"

"Neither do I."

"No, but I mean, Tom. Anyway, cut cackle, get to horses, we want you as managing director of English Brothers."

"What happens to young Charles?"

"Well, for Chrissakes, old man!" A trace of American was beginning to show in his accent, plus a trace of some other hidden intonation that Tom couldn't quite identify. "I dump the directorship in your lap and all you can ask is what happens to young Charles. He's going into the London office, I can tell you in confidence."

"What's in it for me?"

"You can't get a Scotsman excited, can you? Canny Scotsmen. Good question, I agree. Well, salary-wise it isn't too exciting. Same figure as you're on now as Sales Director, but naturally, subject to review, old man."

"Upward or downward review?"

"You Scotsmen! Well, figure it out for yourself, Tom; that depends, obviously. In strict confidence, Tom, the point never came up. But I never heard of anybody being reviewed downward."

"Only upward or outward."

"That's defeatism, Tom, negative thinking. Take it from me, if you play it N.G.'s way, the only direction is up. We'll want changes, naturally — streamlining. But no hurry, not to worry. N.G. always knows what he's doing."

"I accept."

"Well, for Chrissakes, Tom, I would *hope* so."

"What would you have said if I had refused?"

Finnimore grew deep and solemn.

"Tom, old man, this is in strictest confidence, but now that the joke's over, let's face it, you can't buck the organization. We all get fits of independence, naturally, but let's stick to the facts, none of us are indispensable. You only stay in the game as long as you play by the rules."

"Like Nick Gaylor?"

"Well, I mean, he wrote the book, didn't he? He can make his own rules, old man. That's okay with me, the big boys make the rules, the small boys play the game and collect the salary check for being good boys." Finnimore was now at the stage of alcohol when he could feel that the ice was broken, the stern silent executive act could be dropped among friends, it was time to be all buddies together in the comfortable club of the junior executive suite. He couldn't be more than thirty-five, with a lifetime spent in one big organization or other — probably not more than two, all told — keeping his nose clean and watching the man above and picking up the tricks and the attitudes, and now happy and secretly surprised to have arrived somewhere with a salary and an expense account. An inoffensive man without an idea in his head, arrogant and confident and absolutely terrified that the world would change overnight and leave him stranded in a desert with nobody to take orders from.

He had drunk too much at lunch; not any more than Tom often drank himself, but too much to drink in the company of a stranger, a possible enemy. That level of drinking was fine among friends who didn't give a damn what you might say out of exuberance. In the present situation, Tom saw dispassionately and soberly, Finnimore had sacrificed his position of authority by drinking to the point of becoming confidential. He would never be able to perform the strong, enigmatic, silent role to Tom again, he would always be a younger man who did his best but was eager to drop the play-acting and work for sympathy.

"I'll admit in strictest confidence I was rather chary about this interview — no offense, Tom, old man, but what I mean, wild Scotsmen, you might have been completely different. God, some people can be shockers."

Tom smiled happily. Finnimore was really a rather likable boy.

"I should have worn a kilt and carried a two-handed sword."

"Too true, old boy! Strike a blow for freedom and whassisname, well for Chrissakes, how was I to know you *wouldn't?* But it only took one glance to size you up as one of the Chaps, definitely one of the Chaps. Funny thing, that, how you can tell straight off that a chap is one of the Chaps. Incidentally, old Charles is a funny old trout, isn't he? He's like something in the movies, I swear it."

"H. M. Pulham Esquire?"

"Something like that." If he had been a little more sober, Finnimore would have pulled out his diary and noted the name. "But let's not dissipate our mighty intellects on discussing old Charlie-boy, I can take it you're happy to accept the great gifts of the great N.G. and we're all palsy-walsy. Strictly in confidence, I'm very glad about all this, Tom, I hope we'll be seeing more of each other."

"Yes, that would be nice."

"You have a very dry sense of humor, did you know that, Tom? I suppose that's a Scotch thing, of course, but it's very, very effective. You don't say much, but every now and then you come out with something that shows you're bang on the ball. I admire that, I honestly do. I don't miss much, you know — I could see you having a wee quiet Scotch smile to yourself all the time. I like that. Do people usually have a second whisky with their coffee?"

"Why not?"

"That's what I say, why not? N.G. is not a stingy man."

"Do you like working for The Organization?" The capital letter was a small all-buddies-together note that Finnimore noticed and appreciated.

"Well, I mean, look what I've got! Ah, for Chrissakes, I've worked for it, they're not paying me for looking pretty, you know what I mean? But let's face it, grammar school education — that's in strictest confidence, ha ha. No, honestly, there's a helluva lot of university types in the Group, good thing I've no doubt. But look at me, very ordinary grammar school education but it hasn't held me back. I've only just bought a new house at the, oh, trifling figure of nine and a half thousand. It's not peanuts, is it, old boy?"

"It sure ain't."

"So I should buck the organization? I should be so schizophrenic. Ah hell, let's face it, we all have our gripes, it's not a bed of roses, but what the hell, you get what you pay for."

"Less ten per cent."

"Uh? Yeah, you're with it, Tom, old boy. Incidentally, Tom, I hope you're happy about this deal — remembering that it's subject to review, finance-wise."

"We'll see how it works out."

"Eftsoons and gadzooks, old boy, you Scotsmen really believe in playing it cool. Don't misunderstand me, old boy, I respect you for it. It's an honest answer, Tom, and let me tell you, that's damn rare nowadays. It's good to get away from the damn rat race occasionally."

"Can I take you back to your hotel?"

"Not for a moment, old man, I wouldn't dream of it. I've kept you late long enough with wining and wassailing and quaffing the flowing bowl, I'll toddle back and have myself a small snooze. That's one of N.G.'s tricks, know that? He has an absolute bloody bed in his office suite for catnaps. He's a very original character, N.G."

"Like Churchill."

"Check, old boy. Know something, I bet he dreamed up this English Brothers deal in his sleep. He's like that. Sleeps like a baby and suddenly he wakens up and zowie, all hell breaks loose. Well I mean, for God's sake, who else would have even *noticed* English Brothers? Talk about ripe plums withering on the bough? N.G. has a better nose for real estate than Charlie Clore, believe me, Tom."

At the words "real estate" Tom smiled into his coffee and knew himself for a fool. Finnimore was still talking.

"But seriously, don't forget to give old Jack a buzz when you're in town, will you? Sincerely, Tom, I enjoy listening to you."

"Roger."

When Tom arrived back at the office, he went straight up to old Charles' room. Charles was sitting gazing calmly at the window, an elderly gentleman passing the day in an elderly gentlemen's club.

"Please come in, Thomas," he said. "You've caught me preparing for a life of leisure. Finnimore seems a pleasant young man."

"He's all right."

"Ah, reluctant to make a hasty judgment, as always, Thomas. Very wise, very wise. At any rate, you concluded your business with him satisfactorily?"

"You knew about it, of course."

"I was told informally, yes. I suppose I should regret passing from the scene, but to tell you the truth, Thomas, the life of leisure will suit me admirably." He smiled a sheepish little smile. "I don't possess the tycoon temperament, that's the truth. All that apparently concentrated itself in my late brother."

"Not quite all of it," Tom said politely.

"It's a great pity you never knew John. He had many points in common with you, Thomas, I assure you. It's a question of endocrinology, of course. I wonder if John would have sold to the Gaylor Group. Perhaps not."

"No."

"Still, Thomas, John would have been, let me see, three years older than I am. And one can't go on forever. I'm sure you will have no regrets in any event."

"I have my regrets now," Tom said brusquely. "I've been so busy thinking about other things that I missed the best chance in my life to make a fortune."

"Really, Thomas? I don't understand."

"I could have bought the company myself."

"You're not serious, are you, Thomas? If so, you must be a great deal wealthier than I ever imagined."

Suddenly Tom was filled with impatient dislike of the gentle, foolish old man. It must be true that the long-dead brother John had cornered all the business aggressiveness of the family, and carved out a business that could absorb and support the more pallid relatives like Charles and son. Tom had no doubt of any kind that without his own arrival in the company, it would have diminished year by year to vanishing point.

"I wouldn't need money to buy over a company, any more than Nick Gaylor uses his own money. The Prudential Insurance Company or the Midland Bank can fork out all the money anybody needs."

"But not to any Tom, Dick or Harry." The old man was nettled. Yes, always the kindly old gentleman, always thoughtful of young Thomas with his aggressive business energy, but Charles was still the boss and Tom was still an employee, however favored with empty titles, and it was an act of insolence to talk of taking over the company. Tom, Dick or Harry! Tom stared coolly at old Charles and realized how much he himself must have aged to spend so many years in the company simply growing with it, instead of jumping to something bigger.

"What do you imagine Gaylor intends to do with the factory?" he asked, quite pleasantly. "And the London show-room?"

"I don't think you need to fret about things like that, Thomas." Old Charles' complacency had returned. "They hardly affect your own situation. In fact," he added, "I don't expect any changes in either place. Oh, the factory may well be modernized. It's the kind of thing one can do more easily with large capital . . . integration into the group operations . . . one imagines they will wish to avoid duplication. However," he was complacent again, more and more complacent, "I should be prepared to say that for its size, the factory is by no means inefficient. My son has always been very conscientious in his management down there."

"No doubt." The little factory, which hadn't expanded output ten per cent in ten years, kept going thanks to a hard-working underpaid foreman and survived despite the periodic meddling of young Charles. "And what about the London showroom?"

"Ah, I may say Gaylor is very happy about the London showroom."

"He already has a showroom in their London office."

"No doubt he can make use of two."

Tom stared at Charles in disbelief. "You can't be as innocent as that. Do you imagine for a second that Gaylor is going to leave that property standing as a showroom and a couple of offices?"

"It's in an excellent position," Charles said defensively, and in that moment, Tom knew that the old man wasn't innocent. He knew, but he didn't want to know. He didn't want to be bothered. He wanted out and he didn't care if he was mildly swindled as long as everything was easy and comfortable.

"In six months," Tom said, "the place will be a few broken

bricks and the builders will be in for the redevelopment. My God, these few broken bricks are worth more than Gaylor paid for the whole shooting match. I could walk into any bank tomorrow and raise a hundred thousand on the bare site."

"I don't wish to hear any more in this vein, Thomas." The old boy grew stern. "You seem to have developed some foolish sense of grievance because Nicholas Gaylor is a powerful successful businessman and you are . . . well, what you are, very fortunate and successful in your more modest way. This is hardly the attitude that will serve you in your new position, which you owe entirely, I may add, to Nicholas Gaylor. And since you are clearly so preoccupied with the London property, I can tell you that I have Gaylor's personal assurance that it will continue in its present form."

Tom declined to accept the gesture of dismissal.

"Personal assurance? What the hell will that count for when you're sunbathing at Nice and Nick Gaylor is in there with the bulldozers?"

"That will be quite enough, Thomas. I find your attitude completely incomprehensible. Good heavens, man, you have so much to be grateful for."

"You're right, of course." There was nothing at all to be gained by flogging the old fool for his folly. It was done, and he himself was more of a fool than Charles, because he had the wit to have done something and Charles hadn't. He left the room flogging himself. All the calculation and all the drive that had taken him out of Burnett's drawing office had deserted him in the one situation that could have meant something really big.

Meg Macrae looked up as he passed her desk and said, "Nothing is as bad as your face looks."

"It's my natural nastiness, Meg, when I relax it shows, that's all."

Maybe she was right. What would he have got if he had seen the situation earlier and moved in ahead of Gaylor? Charles and Son would never have sold to him, of course; that would have smacked too much of encouraging the lower classes to get above themselves. But the whole deal could have been done through a nominee, a fast little company set up for the occasion. Raising the finance would have been child's play, and the appalling fact was that the London showroom, bought long before the war, *would* fetch more in the present property market than Gaylor's had paid for the entire company.

And so what? He could have tucked perhaps £100,000 in his pocket. Maybe quarter of a million for all he knew, if he joined a developer instead of simply selling the site. And he would have complete personal control of English Brothers as well, a nice prize for a week's work.

But what could you do with £100,000? The deal itself would have been a satisfaction, of some kind, but how much more money could you enjoy? It was many years since he had decided that he didn't want more and more and more money. As a drawing-office apprentice, he had wanted, needed, craved more money because he had so little that it was a humiliation; but once you had made enough to buy pride, it meant very little to have more. The theory of marginal utility. The first thousand was worth everything, and every further thousand made less and less difference, until you could reach the stage where an extra ten millions couldn't affect a single moment of your life.

No, it wasn't the idea of making a tax-free £100,000, it was the bitter knowledge that his situation in life could still be bought and sold over his head. The indignant patronizing attitude of Charles had no power to anger him — Charles was a pathetic fool who would have starved to death without somebody like himself to take care of the business, and if

Charles refused to admit this, he was merely more of a fool.

No, it was the echo effect. Old Charles' angry contempt was the same absurdity as Tom's mother's bewilderment and old Moules' outrage all those years ago when an upstart boy called Tom Fletcher had dared to claim human equality with "the Major" or with anybody on earth.

At nineteen, he had taken their derision, an ignorant boy with nothing but greed and energy in his favor, and he had done what he started out to do, he had carved out his little triumph. But you didn't win and then stay on top. At forty-seven, a tough old jungle creature with a man's strength and all the tricks of the game, he was back where he had started. The Major had fallen back into the past, now there was Nick Gaylor. And still, people like old Charles and young Hugh, and the highly trained frightened Finnimore, accepted the aristocratic principle: Gaylor was Big, they were Small, a law of God ordained for the stability of society. It was no use being angry with them, they were the hen-people whose only worry was to be sure of the pecking order so that they could find their place in it. If they had met Nick Gaylor when he had two hundred pounds in a savings bank and a broken-down old Bedford truck, they would have howled at *him* for classing himself in the same species as Lord Nuffield.

"What I need is a woman," he said to his desk calendar, and he meant it in the most rudimentary sense. Ideally, he wanted an entire woman, a Georgie, who would understand everything and laugh and be a comfort as well as being a physical relief; but short of that, a mere woman, a crude bash. "No," he added, "it's worse than that. What I need is to *need* a woman." Because he had given himself the prescription from mental habit, from the knowledge of his previous self. His mental responses still operated, but strangely, they operated more readily in a vacuum, in private fantasy, than they did in the living presence of any individual woman. And even then they remained mental, the glands didn't leap to conform. It couldn't be simply age, look at Charlie Chaplin.

Meg Macrae walked unannounced into his room.

"What you need is a woman," she said.

"What a curious coincidence," he said. "You are a woman."

"You're getting above yourself, Tom Fletcher. Did you get the push?"

"No, I'm the managing director, tra la, tra la."

"True or false?"

"True."

"What's to become of young Mr. Charles?"

"Fa Chrissakes, you Scotsmen — I give you the big news of Bull Run and all you can say is What's to become of young Mr. Charles!"

"It's because Charlie is our darling, the adorable little stoat. Have you a bottle in the office?"

"Yes."

"Why don't you and I get boozed, Tom? Just this once."

"Why indeed?"

"I like this room, as pubs go. You meet a good class of people here."

Nine

HE SAW his father-in-law hunched outside a cinema in Sau-chiehall Street, looking at the stills of a double feature: *Dealers in Love*, and *The Natural Flesh*. Shaw was peering with his face close up to the display frame and his leathery face twisted in disgust.

"You might as well go in," Tom said. "Nobody's watching you." The old man turned round on him and made a humphing sound of recognition.

"They need their backsides tanned," he snarled. "The bitches."

"Away inside and have a good look," Tom told him. "Get it out of your system."

"I would sooner have a dose of arsenic!" Shaw spat. "Filthy bitches."

"Some people sell fish," Tom said equably. "Some people sell their backsides."

"A good dose of the cat, that's what they need on their backsides." The old man's eyes had returned, screwed up, to the stills in the display frame.

"Some of them let you do that," Tom remarked. "You can take down their pants and flog them for a few quid."

"Where's that?" Old Shaw was provoked to outrage and disgust and wild curiosity. Tom laughed in his face.

"I'll get some addresses for you if you like, you dirty old swine."

"Dirty? Dirty? I'm disgusted. By Christ, if I was twenty years younger I'd knock that sneer off your face."

"You were twenty years younger twenty years ago, you silly old pig. You should have taken your chance when you had it."

Old Shaw's jaw worked from side to side. It was too easy to touch him on the raw, it was too easy to manipulate him. Twenty years ago, there would have been satisfaction and delight in doing it, twenty years ago when he had still been an object of apprehension, an ogre to be feared. Now, it didn't matter; it was no more than an absent-minded game, but there was still a small satisfaction in prodding the old man to fury. Shaw spat into the street.

"If I had laid a finger on you I would have killed you," he snarled.

"I would have died laughing." Tom walked away.

"Just a minute, just a minute! Old Shaw pattered after him. "Don't you walk away from me! I haven't finished speaking to you."

"Right, finish and get on your way." Tom looked at his wristwatch. It was brutal, but he couldn't find a trace of compassion in him for the old man. Shaw took a hold of himself and produced a sneer from long practice.

"You thought you were helluva smart twenty years ago," he said, "but you've got your punishment, you got your punishment. I hope you're satisfied, you cheeky young get."

Careful, careful. Tom smiled blandly and pushed his anger away.

"Yes, it served me right," he said. "You must have been a happy man when you knew your daughter was dead. Up to the crematorium, whoosh! Burn her, she deserves it."

Old Shaw jerked and twitched, and tears suddenly poured down his sallow cheeks. He looked as if he might collapse there on the pavement. Tom put a hand under his elbow as the old man pulled off his glasses and wiped his eyes with his hand, and Shaw shook his supporting hand away.

"You're a hard . . . a hard bastard," he wept. "You don't know what's like . . . don't care, nobody . . . nobody knows what I done for her. Georgie. My jewel. She was my jewel."

"Dry your eyes for God's sake," Tom said callously, wishing that he had never run into the old man. Nothing had changed in Shaw, the gloating sex righteousness, the vicious morality, the slobbering sentimentality. Nobody but Georgie had ever been able to cope with him, because nobody but Georgie could find him amusing and be amused without anger or fear.

"What did you have to burn her for?" the old man cried out in anguish. "She hasn't even got a grave. I could have went and seen her grave," he muttered to himself. "My jewel. They burned me when they burned her."

Tom was now cringing in horror from Shaw's performance and, he reflected, he had brought it on himself.

"She wanted to be cremated," he said, trying to sound sympathetic and calming. "She always insisted on it."

"Aye." Shaw blew out a solemn sigh. "She had a mind of her own. She would never bend, even if she broke." And with a sudden total change of mood, he added, "She was a good girl, Georgie, you know that, and you and me are the ones that miss her."

"Yes." It was nonsensical, to be standing in the main street, with people walking past and staring, and to be suffering the histrionics of a silly selfish old man. "You're not surely in all that much of a hurry," Shaw said, wheedling. "It's not very often you have to put up with the old man. I've got a right to know about my own grandchildren."

There was no doubt about it, the old pig was invincible, simply because he had no taste and no sense of good manners or consideration. He would snarl and spit and curse because he wanted to, and within seconds he would cajole and smarm because he wanted something, and expect to be pampered and accepted. He would bear a grudge for a hundred years, but he was so totally self-centered that he would simply never understand how anybody could bear a grudge against him. Georgie had been right, the only approach to him was amusement without involvement.

"Do you feel like a drink?" Tom asked him grudgingly, to get him off the street and out of the public eye. Shaw's face immediately assumed the mock-cunning, the mock-stinginess that wasn't more than ten per cent mock.

"If you're offering to pay for it!" He probably had two or three hundred pounds in his pockets, grubby, in single notes, rolled in a wad and counted to the last pound. He smirked to himself as Tom led the way into the nearest pub, and sneered at the thick carpets and the plastic surfaces. "I'll have a glass and a pint," he said quickly, before Tom could ask. Tom bought himself a small whisky, and gave the old man his double and his pint of beer. Shaw drank it in Glasgow proletarian style, throwing the neat whisky back over his throat and holding his breath to withstand the shock, then carefully dripping the last few spots of whisky from the glass into the top of the beer.

It was a greedy way of drinking, the shortest route to drunkenness. There would be some element of man-pride in it with old Shaw too, whisky and beer together made a man's drink for a man who could hold his liquor. A man had to be a man, strong and hard and no bloody womanish fiddle-faddle or weakness. He lifted the pint of beer and poured half of it after the whisky in one go, and when he put the pint pot back on the table, his eyes were watering and Tom reckoned that he was halfway drunk already, with an old man's feeble resistance to drink and a young man's arrogant drinking habits.

"Oh, fancy that!" he said coyly. "My whisky glass is empty already." Tom waved to the barmaid, and Shaw's face wrinkled in contempt for his meanness when he held his fingers to indicate a small whisky. The small whisky vanished instantly. It was like a greed of a child at a party, a child who is convinced that everybody else is out to hog the supplies and that the only way to survive is to grab everything visible and eat fast.

"Don't think I'm buying you one back." Shaw was already slurring the consonants. "I'm an old-age pensioner, you know that. I haveny got money to throw about in fancy pubs."

"Keep your money."

"You're tellin' me! How is my wee Joanie? She's the best of the bunch, you know that? These two boys of yours? I wouldn't give them house room. Cheeky young gets, the pair of them. Joan's worth tsss, ten of them. Ten."

"Joan's all right."

"She threw herself away on that bloody schoolteacher, you know that? Threw herself away. Oh, I know, you think I'm going to say, 'Just like her mother.' Well, that'ssss all water under the bridge. I was never against you, you know that," he added amazingly. "I never had anything against you, I only wanted Georgie to be careful, I only wanted her to be sure she was doin' the right *thing*. I never interfered. Now! You've got to admit that. I never interfered."

There was no possible answer to this. Tom grunted and got himself another whisky, and Shaw watched him petulantly. The old man's eyes moistened again, with liquor and the easy emotion it brought. He stared dimly at his son-in-law and was heartened to see Tom waving for another whisky for him. It was only right that Fletcher should be spending his money, after all he had taken from him, from Philip Shaw. He wasn't a bad son-in-law, maybe, others might have been worse. But Fletcher could have been a better son-in-law if he hadn't been such a selfish young get in his time. And sneaky, there had always been something underhand about him in those days; nice as ninepence to your face, and planning the usual filth behind your back.

Now, at seventy-five, old Phil Shaw was probably the richest fishmonger around Glasgow. His ten shops in the city and around it worked away every day of the week to keep him rich, and he deserved it. He had made them all or bought them all and there wasn't a man in the fish trade more respected (he knew) and even liked, except by a few people who didn't matter a damn. He had been an honest man all his life, and a generous man, and plenty of people had tried to cheat him or do him down, but he was still what he was and he would outlive the lot of them because he was hard and he took care of himself and he hadn't a lazy bone in his body.

"I gave Georgie everything she ever wanted," he said thickly. "I never grudged her anything."

"You grudged her the air she breathed, you old dotard," Fletcher said. That was only Fletcher's manner, he had to be insulting because he thought it was clever to insult an old man who couldn't knock him down. Phil Shaw nodded wisely to himself. He knew, he knew. He could remember

Tom Fletcher when he was a tuppence-halfpenny salesman trying to get rid of cash registers, and butter wouldn't melt in his mouth, he touched his cap and said yes sir no sir three bags full sir. And all the time he was up to his tricks on the sly, making up to Georgie, like a dirty-minded young mongrel in heat, plotting away to lead her astray, seduce her, probably putting his hand inside . . . no conscience, no honesty, it was all water under the bridge. He stared at Tom and felt like weeping for the waste, the time that was gone.

"She was a jewel, you know that? A jewel." Fletcher only nodded and looked at his watch. No time to waste on the old man now, the old man didn't have anything to steal.

A jewel, oh yes, Georgie had been a jewel. She was *still* a jewel. Shining like diamonds, the sunshine of her smile, I love the sunshine of your smile I love the laughter in your eyes, my world forever, the sunshine of your smile.

"I'm leaving my money to Joanie," he said suddenly. "She's the best of a bad lot. She's like her mother."

"I'll make her give it away," Tom said. The idea frightened him, and the old man was quite capable of doing it, from spite. Joan would love to inherit a fortune, but what would it do to Alan, her husband? He would think of that when and if it happened.

Yes, the sunshine of her smile. Georgie had been the best of the bunch, he had given her everything, a good school, piano lessons, he had paid nearly fifty pounds for a piano, and fifty pounds was a lot of money when money was real money. She could talk French, and sing. It was a treat to see her in the big shop, banging up the cash slips with a smile for everybody.

Bridie, her mother, never wanted him to put Georgie to work in the shop. A silly woman, Bridie, cowed and whining and aggravating, God rest her soul but she had been no wife for a real man. She didn't see why Georgie should work at all, but he knew that hard work was good for anybody, and Georgie wouldn't come to any harm in the shop. There would be no smarmy bosses giving her dictation and looking at her legs and keeping her late in the office, as long as she was there in the shop where he could protect her. And Georgie herself had never complained, she liked it. She enjoyed everything, she never complained, she laughed and sang and joked with the customers. She was worth her weight in gold.

Georgie could always make him feel better, even if it often seemed cheeky and disrespectful when she laughed at him. It was only her manner, she didn't mean any disrespect. She loved her father the way a daughter should. She would waltz past him when he came into the shop and pretend she was tickling his ribs, although he had never been ticklish, and he would slap her bottom as she passed, and she would wag her finger and say, "Naughty father!" and life was glorious, people could see that here was a beautiful girl who preferred her father to anybody else.

He was a hard man, but it was his job to be hard. Children needed a strong hand, and if you were soft in business you were finished. He could boast that he had never cheated anybody, and anybody he did cheat, a bit, had been asking for it. Anyway, he wasn't too hard. Treat Phil Shaw right, and Phil Shaw would treat you right, he often said, and nobody had ever contradicted him yet. He didn't approve of Georgie's joining a tennis club, but he gave his permission gracefully enough because he realized her heart was set on it.

("*You're damn well not joining it and that's my last word.*"

"*I've joined it, and that's MY last word.*"

"*Jumping about half-naked to show off your bare legs in front of . . . in front of everybody!*"

"*That's the idea, Dad. You never make a sale if you don't display the goods.*"

"*I'll come and drag you home by the hair, I'm warning you, my girl!*"

"*Marvelous, Dad! Make it at eight o'clock when there's a good crowd to cheer.*"

"*Get up to your room, girl. You're going to be locked in.*"

"*Yes, oh great father, but later, when I come home. I'm playing in the mixed doubles first.*"

And she was away, laughing.)

He had given in to her because he was a reasonable man and he would never stand in the way of healthy exercise. She enjoyed life so much that it was a joy to see her happy.

When she said — she, Georgie, said — that the big shop needed a new cash register, he had given her one without a moment's hesitation. Well, a bit of hesitation, but that was business, a matter of putting your money in the right place. And he had been perfectly open and generous with the kid who was round trying to sell the cash registers. Yes, Tom Fletcher wasn't worth a handful of coppers then, and it had been an act of Christian charity to give him an order that would save him from losing his job.

("*Take your cash registers to hell out of here, I can make more money counting on my fingers than you'll ever see in your life.*"

"*You can lose money counting on your fingers.*"

"*Don't tell me my business, you cheeky pup, or I'll fling you out of the bloody shop. Get out.*"

"*You could save yourself money if you moved your old cash register, without buying a new one.*"

"*And what do you get out of it?*"

"*Nothing.*"

"*Just a minute, you'll go when I tell you. Let me see that paper.*"

"It's only a plan of the shop with the counters moved so that the customers move faster and the cashier works faster."

"It's a piece of damned impertinence. Who gave you permission to hang about my shop and make drawings?"

"Okay, Mr. Shaw, it's torn up, forget it."

"Cheeky young devil, I haven't seen it right yet. Come back here!")

Yes, he had been generous with Fletcher when Fletcher was a po-faced kid who knew nothing, couldn't have sold a cabbage to a rabbit. And all the time, if he had realized it, Fletcher had been getting round his innocent Georgie and pulling the wool over her eyes.

Tom, seriously concerned in case the old man became drunk and helpless and had to be carried home, gestured carefully to the waiter to bring only a half pint of beer and no whisky. Shaw was sagging in his chair, focusing with difficulty, and his mouth was slack. It was the routine strangeness of life that this ineffectually venomous old man had once loomed in his life as the great terror.

Selling seven cash registers to Philip Shaw was just tough enough to be interesting. It was a cunning and skillful Tom Fletcher who had taken on the job, cunning after three hard years with Mindley's Cash Registers. Old Shaw was tougher and nastier than most, in that he made more of a *point* of being nasty, made it a matter of pride. But he was greedy, and greed was there to be calculated and manipulated.

Young Tom Fletcher — not so young, either, almost twenty-five — was still given to silence. The habit of keeping a still tongue in his head had lingered. And he still wasn't as big a man as the Major. But in the company of Cam Jones and others, he had truly broken away from Maltdyke. His silence was not a means of avoiding trouble, but an instrument that could be employed or laid down as he chose. He had learned to speak as fast as a circus barker when he needed to, and this he had learned as another man might learn to play triples on the trumpet. Fast-talking salesmen wearied him because so often their fast talk was a string of words saying nothing. But fast talk could have its place and therefore had to be mastered.

He doggedly memorized passages from novels and practiced them in the privacy of his lodgings, before the mirror, till he could machine-gun them at more than two hundred words a minute. When he was driving in the country — the old Austin Seven was long forgotten, he had an almost new Ford Ten — he would choose a commodity from a billboard and rehearse a spiel for it. Patent medicines, perfume, Conservative policy, rubber boots, ball bearings, anything.

He had worried, sometimes, when people told him he was too solemn for a salesman. He practiced smiling in the mirror. It looked all right, but he analyzed his face coldly and decided that it was the kind of face that would look dishonest and be dishonest if it smiled all the time. A smile was also a mere instrument, and it worked better if it was held in reserve and used occasionally. He was a calculating young man and a hard one, and he never started to speak without knowing how he was going to finish, or without being prepared for any question whatever. He could calculate, while he talked to a client, how much he might earn, gross, from the sale, and how much of his expense in petrol, in cigarettes, in drink, in telephone calls and time, had to be deducted from that commission alone, including the percentage of expense from failures that had to be spread over the year and set against the successes.

In a period when skilled engineers were lucky to earn £4 a week, he had banked £200 in a year. He had bought his father a set of golf clubs which were his father's delight, and his mother a fur coat which she adored and never wore because such ostentation in Maltdyke might seem like a blasphemy against the natural superiority of other people like the Major.

When he visited Philip Shaw's big shop, he already knew what most people knew about Shaw, he knew the reputed turnover of the seven shops and he knew what most people knew about Shaw's temperament, which was no secret in the fish trade. He could take on Shaw, with the calm certitude that he wouldn't die if he didn't make a sale. Shaw was an exercise that would stretch his muscles. He knew what to expect.

What he didn't expect was the luminous beauty of the girl behind the cash register in the big shop.

"You'll have to go over there for fish," she said. "We only sell money at this end."

"I'll buy some."

"A pound for twenty shillings, sir." A banal joke sounded delicious on her lips because it wasn't intended as a joke, it was nothing more than an expression of happiness. Her hair was dark and cut short and swung loose and she had great brown eyes. Nose coming to a point, long thin lips — she wasn't beautiful, surely. But she was, she lit up from inside. He wanted to make her smile, to see the thin lips swinging out to make two little mounds high up on her cheeks. She must have had freckles as a child. There were still three or four. He could have eaten them. He felt extraordinarily light and strong and filled with sunshine.

"I'm not buying money today," he said lamely. "I'm selling cash registers."

"You're not!"

"I am."

"Not to *us!*"

"I fully intend to try." Why couldn't he think of anything merry and light? But perhaps it was even more delightful to see her face grave and gloomy, see her shaking her head and her short hair tossing.

"You take yourself too seriously. You'll never sell anything with a face like that."

He hated his face, he would have torn it off and put on another. She laughed, and he felt himself smiling, and he pushed the smile to make it bigger, to hell with it even if it was a dishonest smile, a big salesman's smile, he had to smile. He could have wept or shouted. She looks as if she's quite small, he thought, pity, I like long legs, her legs will be little brown legs, it doesn't matter, it's the customary sex business, why do I have to hunger for every good-looking bird I ever meet? There'll be another one tomorrow, or five or six, I want them all, I could jump across the counter and ravish her but you can't do that, get on with the business, the world is full of eatable women, this is merely another one and you can't have them all so why let them bother you at all? And he went on trying to switch on the hundred-candle-power smile and feeling drunk.

"Mr. Shaw isn't expected till the afternoon," she said, quite formally but it was no use, the bubbles still danced in her voice no matter what she said. Watch it, boy, watch it, this one could be dangerous. Tom had already made his calculations concerning women. At thirty, he would marry a girl of twenty-two, thus balancing out the differential rates at which men and women aged, and ensuring that he was well fixed for money before he had to make large capital outlays on furniture and housing. A man also needed a variety of experience for his wife's benefit, and that experience could only be acquired legitimately as long as he stayed unmarried. And gazing at this girl in a fish shop in Bridgeton, he knew with all the certainty of Archimedes' Principle that he either had to leave her entirely alone or have her permanently. She was that kind.

"I'll come back in the afternoon," he said, turning away. "Any particular time in the afternoon?"

"Oh, very early. We're closing for lunch now, he'll be back soon after that."

"I'll look in."

"Stay and have something to eat," she said. "You're awful thin, you know that? *Awful* thin. You look as if you hadn't sold anything for years and years and years. I think you're too sad to sell anything. People would look at you and know it was no good."

"Do you stare at everybody like that?"

"No," she said, "I was waiting to see if you'd say it should be 'awful*ly* thin,' so that I could win a bet with myself."

"You've lost your bet."

"I could lend you a sandwich," she said. "I wouldn't, if you were fat, but I think you need it. I eat mine here in the shop."

It would hardly do him any good in business if Shaw came back to the shop early and found him sitting there eating sandwiches. He shook his head.

"I'll get something to eat and take a walk on Glasgow Green," he said.

"We'll take my sandwiches on Glasgow Green. Would you like that?"

"I would love it."

"Come on, then."

They sat on a bench on Glasgow Green in the sunshine. It was too dry, and in the dry weather it was too dusty, and the river was dark and dirty, but the grass was green and the girl had a lot of sandwiches.

"People don't do this enough," she said. "I mean to say,

look at all this grass and water and everything, but nobody comes out to have a picnic. People are hidebound."

"What's your name?"

"Georgie."

"Georgie what?"

"Just Georgie."

"You're very nice."

"You're only saying that because I'm feeding you. I'm only feeding you because you looked so sad and hungry; mind you, I have no romantic interest in you."

"I thought perhaps you were a fast worker," said Tom, warily.

"I do anything I like, that's all." She munched bread and tomatoes. "Girls are afraid to speak to men in case they seem forward, when all the time all they want to do is *talk*. I don't give a damn. If I want to talk to somebody, I talk."

The mild swearword sounded bizarre and enchanting, coming from her. He wondered how it would sound if she uttered a string of obscenities. Delicious, probably. But all the same, she was young and certainly spoiled.

"You do anything you feel like." He tried to sound old and mature and indulgent, because she bothered him.

"Anything I feel like," she nodded vigorously as she tore a sandwich in two. "I'm selfish. Selfish people make life easier for everybody because everybody knows what they want. I mean," she munched away half of the sandwich, "if somebody asks me whether I would like tea or coffee and I say it doesn't matter because I don't want to ask for the one they don't want to make, nobody gets anywhere, but if I say coffee, because I do want coffee, they can make the coffee and if they wanted to make tea in the first place, well, they should have made the tea, they shouldn't have asked me, I would have been quite happy with tea if I hadn't been asked. That's what I mean by selfish."

"You're quite a talker, Georgie."

"Yes, I know. I like talking."

"So I see." He searched for light bubbling words. Nothing came.

"I hope you don't imagine I'm trying to impress you or get off with you," she said. "I would talk to anybody."

"No, I don't think you're trying to get off with me."

"You do."

"I don't."

"You do."

"I don't."

"You do."

"I don't."

She had started smiling and the smile had broken into laughter, and now he was laughing without operating the big salesman smile.

So he sold the cash register to the tough, invincible Philip Shaw, and he sold six more, and Shaw took his little bits of paper with sketch plans scribbled on them and used his ideas and worked them so enthusiastically that he was able to cut the staff of each shop by one; which, Tom felt, was typical of the Glasgow business disease. When a Glasgow businessman found he could save money, he saved it, instead of going right ahead spending and making the business bigger. But there was nothing he could do to manipulate Shaw on *that* point.

And he visited the main shop again. And again. He was too honest with himself to deny that Georgie was the reason for repeated visits, but he still had enough dishonesty to persuade himself that his interest was carnal and casual. It wasn't until his third visit that she told him that she was Georgie Shaw, not another employee of Philip, but the favorite daughter.

"My God," he said.

"That's put you off, hasn't it?" She laughed delightedly.

"Put me off what?"

"Put you off the prowl."

"I don't care."

"Have you got intentions towards me?"

"What kind of intentions?"

"That's the next question. The first thing we establish is whether you have any at all. Then we can get to the details."

"I have some, but I haven't decided what kind they are."

"No, neither have I. I mean, I haven't decided what mine are, but I've got intentions too. What are we going to do about it?"

"I haven't done my homework on that question."

"Can you play tennis?"

"A bit."

"Meet me at seven o'clock tonight and we'll play some. If you like."

"I don't know."

"Don't, then. Stop looking solemn! Oh, why do you have to look so solemn?"

"I will meet you at seven o'clock."

"All right."

He would play tennis and then retreat. He couldn't quite bring himself to not seeing her at all, but once was enough. He had made his sale to Shaw and got his commission and he didn't need to get entangled in anything else. He went home to his lodgings and looked at this thought and knew it was a deceit. He hadn't made his commission. Shaw had kept him going till the sale was about to be closed, and then demanded eight pounds each for his old cash registers. Cunning old Shaw.

But there was no point in blaming Shaw for being a shrewd operator; he had always known that, and he would have walked out on the sale, laughing, if it hadn't been that he wanted to keep contact with Shaw. And why did he want to keep the contact open? There was no dodging it, it was Georgie. If and when he sold the old machines, he might be a few pounds poorer all over. Or a few shillings richer, at best.

He should have known that the tennis club Georgie took him to would be a blaze of white flannels and white shirts. His gray trousers made him feel like an intruding pauper. Embarrassment was something he had long ago crushed down, but this wasn't business, this was something else, and he looked at the dashing young blades about the courts and knew they were inspecting him from inside the armor of their whites. They would be ready to hate him a priori because Georgie had brought him, and unless they were all imbeciles they would all want Georgie. And his gray flannels were a convenient focus for their resentment. He decided not to play, to finish the whole thing, to go away and forget Georgie.

"There's no rule about wearing whites," she said to him, shaking her head close to his face as if she wanted to shake him and laugh at the same time.

"Nevertheless."

"Men!" She strode into the pavilion and came out wearing a black skirt and went straight onto the court. That was Georgie. She did not give one damn and when she wanted to do something, she did it.

And neither did he, of course. He didn't give a damn for her formidable father, business was war and he knew how to fight it. But Philip Shaw as a tough prospect for cash registers was nothing like Philip Shaw as a father, he discovered. He was startled and loath when Georgie proposed to take him home for supper.

"What's wrong?" she asked. "Do you think we're the Borgias?"

"No. It's just too sudden."

"Do you think I'm getting you into something against your will?" She squeezed his arm and laughed.

"Yes."

"You can talk your way out of it."

What the hell, she probably acted like this with everybody. If she wanted to talk to somebody, she talked, and if she wanted to take somebody home, she took somebody home. Maybe she had taken dozens of bewildered young men home. It was hard to tell from the sidelong sullen glares of the tennis-club mashers whether they were sullen because he had made spectacular progress or because they had all been home with Georgie once and never again. In any case, he went, and in any case it was a disaster. Georgie's frightened mother turned ashen at the sight of him, and Georgie's jut-jawed father flew into a demonic rage and ordered him out and threatened to report him to Mindley's Cash Registers.

"Mindley's aren't interested in my private life," Tom said levelly. In Shaw's home, he had no weapons and felt utterly vulnerable. The best he could do was look calm and keep his voice down.

"We'll bloody well see about that! Snake!" Shaw spluttered and frothed, trying to find a name that would really hit the jackpot. "Rat, you're a rat, I know your kind. Rat!"

Tom shrugged his shoulders and left, but Georgie followed him, in spite of Shaw's high-pitched stuttering.

"Is he like that with everybody?" Tom asked her, and she looked thoughtful.

"No, he usually takes more time to warm up. He hasn't swindled you, has he?"

"No, no. Yes, he has, but it was my own fault."

"That explains everything! He's a scream when he gets going, isn't he?"

"Oh, yes, I'm hysterical."

"Has he got you frightened?"

"No."

"I knew I was right about you."

Old Shaw had gone to the toilet, and when he came back, he ordered two whiskies with the most hammy show of reluctance and resentment. He seemed to have found his second wind, and there was something fresh on his mind.

"You've been bought up." He said it with joyful malice. "That'll have shaken you up."

"It doesn't make any difference to me."

"I always knew you would never get any higher than a ten-a-penny clerk. Nobody buys up Philip Shaw, you know that? I'm the boss, there's nobody over my head."

"Bully for you."

His casualness angered the old man, as he had known it would.

"Don't try and pass it off, oh, you don't care, you're the high-and-mighty. They can sack you like that!" He snapped his fingers inefficiently. "If you had had anything in you, I could have set you up for yourself, you know that? If you hadn't been so rotten and underhand you would have done all right."

"You could still do it," Tom said, laughing. "If you put up about forty thousand I could swing it."

Shaw jumped to it like a stung horse. "Ha ha! Ha ha! I knew it. Not one penny. Not one penny, you know that? I would sooner give it away — I would sooner give it to Joanie, as long as I was sure you would never smell it."

Tom got up.

"You can stuff it up your nose, in small change," he laughed. "I've got an appointment. Buy yourself another drink." He threw some loose change on the table and walked out before old Shaw could find the words to blast him to ashes. Altogether, it had been a pleasantly stimulating meeting, and one consolation about growing old was that the ancient monsters shrank to their correct pathetic size. His formidable father-in-law was a threadbare joke with no power to wound any more.

But two days later, while he was reading through the very long, very obscure contract that he was expected to sign with the Gaylor Group, his son-in-law telephoned in a state of bewildered panic to tell him that old Shaw was in the process of making a deed of gift of £10,000 to Joan.

"Without strings?" Tom asked automatically.

"I don't know," Alan answered, in deep misery. "But Joan is delirious. She wants me to give up teaching."

"And you don't want to give up teaching."

"What else would I do? The old bastard, I don't want his money, he's doing it to insult me."

"No, not you, Alan. Me."

"How does that work?"

"Keep the heid, Alan, don't do anything, don't say anything. It may never happen."

"I suppose I sound mad, not to want ten thousand pounds."

"No, I think you're perfectly sane, Alan. But it may never happen. Let's keep our guns clean, bright and slightly oiled, and do nothing for a while."

"And then shoot Granddad?"

"Hold your fire till you get the signal."

Meg Macrae walked in without knocking, and looked nosily at the contract.

"Have you put your ear close to it to see if it's ticking?" she asked him.

"I'm enjoying it, Meg," he said. "Everywhere I look, we've got troubles. That's what we need to keep us young."

"Could you spare a few for Cam Jones? He's had a letter from the great panjandrum as well, and he looks about a hundred and ten."

"Out?"

"Out."

"Shall we dance?"

She answered with surprising obscenity.

Ten

It sometimes seemed to Tom that what life required to make it work properly was a new life form, a divisible human being; one self-contained part-man for business, one for living at home, one for boozing with acquaintances, one for listening to music, one for brooding and a few others for odd areas of existence. Everything was a full-time job, and none of the jobs seemed to belong to the same man.

It had been simple enough when he started to sell vacuum cleaners. How on earth had he managed to fill each day then? There was nothing to do except get the hang of the trade and make a lot of money in order to prove that he had been right to leave Maltdyke. Then, bit by bit, life acquired other things, and there was never going to be an end to any of them. There never came a Friday when you could add up the figures and shut the sales book and stop everything until next week. No matter how zealously you kept up to date, a fresh mixup was growing at your back or under your feet. The whole thing was a guddle, and everybody was always aiming hopefully at the magic time when it was smoothed out, The Day When the Guddling Stopped. There was no such day, the guddle would last forever.

There was nothing he could do about Cam Jones, nothing at least that suggested itself easily. The old war horse was being heaved out to pasture, and was taking it calmly, saying nothing. Tom tried to picture himself at Cam's age, suddenly shut off from the only life he knew, and felt it must be similar to death, but there was nothing he could do about it, he couldn't die anybody else's death. Young Hugh Winton was hurling himself into work like a demon, so thankful to be still in a job that he was turning endless cartwheels to show that he was worth his place. And at the same time Alice Wardell was appearing oftener and oftener, moving in for the kill. Marriage might not be on her mind, but something was, and it had to be something *resembling* marriage. And at the same time young Tommy was turning difficult and irritating again, and at the same time Tom was growing more aggrieved at the feeling of growing old. He would have to cut down on food and start playing golf again; but there was never any way of squeezing in a game of golf, and to be frank, he despised the game except as a coldly calculated exercise, a dull but useful therapy for lung and muscle. And at the same time there was the perfectly ludicrous affair of his daughter Joan and her husband Alan and old Shaw's eccentric threat to give Joan ten thousand pounds as a malicious joke. And at the same time his mother was probably dying and he would be embroiled with the glutinous sentiment of his sister Florrie, who could make a big juicy drama out of anything but needed a funeral for her wide-screen epic act. And at the same time there was a hell of a lot of other things and what was the point in cringing? It was the guddle, the guddle was destined by God and the guddle would go on forever.

Hugh Winton came into his room with coffee, wearing a new dark suit with very narrow trousers and no cuffs; and a very narrow tie with a tie pin fastened across beneath the knot.

"Too bad about old Cam," he said, and that was all he wanted to say. He had to say something, to make the gesture of sympathy and show he wasn't a callous swine, but he didn't want anybody to go on and on about it, so Tom said "Um" and stirred his coffee and looked at the new suit and said, "Get you."

Hugh shot his cuffs and executed a mannequin turn with cup and saucer in his hand.

"Favorite!" he agreed. "Favorite" was his favorite word that week. "Well, you have to put on the big-time front if you're in the big-time business, haven't you, Tom?"

"Favorite. You look like number one hatchet man for Standard Oil."

"Not bad." Hugh twisted his neck to examine the back of his trousers and admire them. A little absurd, but clever and well organized. Tom recognized in him the same quality of calculation that he knew in himself. Clothes might be trivial, but they were also an instrument, like a smile or a silence, and if they could impress some people, it was right to use them to impress. In a few months Hugh would have picked up the speech patterns and some of the accent of people like Jack Fillimore, he would be dressed exactly like them and he would be recognizably one of them, the In boys. If he had learned nothing else from Tom, he had learned that details could make a profit.

"I think it's a good style," Hugh said defensively. "You see, it's all right for you, Tom, you're a big man, you've made your mark, you don't need to put up a front any more. Me, I'm still trying to get noticed."

"Well, *I* noticed you, Hugh. The minute you came through the door, I noticed you right away."

Hugh would survive, as he himself would survive. There was no question of kicking anybody in the face. A big crisis was like a shipwreck, and you could love everybody on board, but if there were three swimmers and a two-seater lifeboat, you grabbed a seat and *then* had time to love everybody.

"I'd feel better if I was more like you, Tom," Hugh said enviously. "I've had the jumps for the past month, but you just carry on, everything's a big laugh, you've got it under control."

"Away and don't sicken us, for God's sake," Tom pleaded. "You could fight a lion in that getup. If you got the sack now you could get a job as an ambassador, or a front man for a high-class brothel."

"Yup, it's not bad." Hugh admired himself in the dim reflection of the glass door. "These London guys know their stuff. I think you're laughing at me."

"Perish the thought." Tom sat back and laughed helplessly. There are always consolations. If you've developed the habit of laughing, you find something to laugh at. Life is composed of small moments, and some of them are always funny. No doubt when God sent down the forty-day flood, some of the evil and the damned choked over a joke before they had time to drown.

By the time he got to Maltdyke in response to Florrie's hysterical summons, his mother was hardly conscious. He had seen her two days before, when she was merely tired and dispirited. It was hard to tell whether she had progressed to a different, a graver condition, or had simply become a little more tired. But Florrie had no doubt, Florrie could hear the beating of dark pinions overhead and she was braced for the big moment.

"She doesn't look too bad," Tom said after studying the old woman and trying in vain to get a response from her.

"It's a coma," Florrie said brokenly.

"What does the doctor say?"

"Sh!"

"What did he say?" Tom repeated in a whisper. Florrie shook her head in a pregnant gesture which he always thought of as the doom-waggle, and he snorted in irritation.

"What does that mean?"

"Sh!"

"Why the hell are we talking in whispers, if she's in a coma?" he demanded, and she clenched her teeth to hold back her outrage and anger, and dragged him out of the bedroom.

"Do you not realize our mother is dying?" she asked, in the narrow hallway, still keeping her voice to a passionate whisper.

"Is it positive?"

She nodded.

"Then why are we talking in whispers?"

"How can you be so hard, Tom Fletcher? She always said you were hard."

"She said damn all of the kind, so for God's sake stop wallowing in it."

Florrie immediately burst into tears — her favorite indulgence, he thought. He patted her shoulder and led her into the kitchen, and she clung to him and wept. There was nothing to do but suffer it. Over her head he met the eye of her husband, and the two men exchanged helpless glances.

"Make a cup of tea, Andrew, I'm too upset," Florrie sobbed, and sank into Father's old armchair. Andrew dutifully filled the kettle. *Andrew*. Thus time changed everything. Good old Darky Gillan, the Bolshie sex maniac, married to Florrie and podgy and middle-aged and addressed as Andrew. In all the years at G. R. Burnett and Company, Tom had never known Darky's real name till he popped up as Florrie's fiancé. The coal-black hair that had given him his nickname was dull gray now, and there was a sad solid look about him; he looked like one of those men who have always been ponderous and middle-aged. It was as well that there had been no children — men like Darky, who womanized obsessively in youth, often aged into moralistic heavy fathers, like reformed drunks who campaigned against drink.

The wild colonial boy who had dreamed of the red dawn and the barricades. He was still with G. R. Burnett and Company, chief buyer or something, a gold watch every twenty-five years and a radio phonograph and a pension when he retired. And he was a Labor member on the County Council. None of your wild-eyed revolutionaries, a careful, reliable middle-of-the-road Labor man respected by the voters and approved of by the management as a living symbol of their tolerance and progressiveness. Changed days too when a wild rebel — even a rebel in name only — could earn promotion in that staunch old Tory company. Good Lord, Darky probably had sherry in the boardroom with the Major himself.

And Tom's mother, who lay in the little bedroom presumably dying, had lived to see the dangerous subversive Darky marry her own daughter and evolve into a sound man and a credit to the village. This was the man she had warned Tom against because he was dangerous, corrupting company.

"It's only a matter of days," Florrie crooned to herself. He felt very much like upending her chair, to see if she could maintain the Eleanora Duse act sprawling on her rump. Every time she spoke, you could tell that she had been turning the words over in her mind several times to choose the proper epic syntax, and even the proper tone, choosing meticulously from a range between sobbing passion and bleak despair. The silly bitch lived in front of an imaginary movie camera.

"When is the doctor coming back?" Tom asked. She buried her head in her hands and did a bit of swaying, and Andrew, very quiet and solemn, said, "Not till tonight. There's very little he can do." Damn him, Darky had picked up the infection from Florrie, or else he had developed a parsonical intonation from too many sessions at the County Council.

"Where's wee Tommy?" Florrie asked wildly, and when Tom ignored this, she burst out, "He should be here! It's the last chance he'll have to see his gran."

"A fat lot of good that would do his gran, or him," said Tom.

"He's entitled," she sobbed. "He shouldn't be kept away."

"Florrie," Tom said gently. "I know you're upset, but if you want to have a big emotional orgy, you can leave Tommy out of it, and that's the last word I want to hear about him. You can slobber over somebody else."

"You're not even giving him a chance to say goodbye to his gran!" The sobs were momentarily forgotten in her frustration.

"Do you think a fourteen-year-old kid wants to say goodbye to an old woman in a coma? Now I'm warning you, Florrie, that's enough."

"You haven't got an ounce of feeling for anybody!"

"Now, now," said Andrew Gillan. "You can understand Tom's point of view. There's something to be said on both sides." The judgment of Solomon.

"Joanie's coming anyway," Florrie said in triumph. "I didn't think you would telephone her, so I did."

Tom looked at her in distaste, and he didn't trouble to disguise it.

"Don't tell me you forgot Phil," he said. And he wouldn't have believed it, but Florrie raised hands, head and eyes in guilt and shock.

"I forgot all about Phil! You'll have to send him a cable, Tom, it's only right that he should have the chance to come if he can."

"I'll call him on the telephone," Tom offered.

"But the *money!* It would cost *pounds.*" The horror of her reaction was mixed with a reluctant approval. Already she was savoring the romantic quality of this extravagance, a wild expenditure to match a historic crisis. Already, she would be contemplating the incident in retrospect, rehearsing the breathless or the casual way she would tell it later, a telephone call all the way from Maltdyke to Canada. And wouldn't *that* give a shine to the dignity of bereavement. Heartbroken Grandson Flies 4000 Miles to Deathbed. And already, in her imagination, Florrie would have the taxi racing to Maltdyke from Prestwick Airport, and a mob of invisible photographers ready by the door as she appeared dramatically in black. Too late, sobbed grief-stricken, attractive Mrs. Andrew Gillan, popular wife of County Councilor Andrew Gillan, J.P., chief buyer of the world-famous engineering company of G. R. Burnett and Company, as her nephew leapt from the cab after a tragic transatlantic dash. At a press conference later, attractive Mrs. Gillan broke down in the luxurious lounge of her home at 35 Garry Crescent, Maltdyke and said . . .

"There's no telephone here!" she cried. "You would have to go to our place."

And why not? She might as well have her extra shot of drama, and the money was nothing. Three pounds, not more than six. It was strange how most people would unthinkingly spend three or four pounds on drink or on some gadget they didn't want, but quailed at the idea of spending less on an international telephone call because there was nothing to show for it. Much impressed, after Tom had undertaken to pay for the call, Andrew agreed to take him to the luxurious Gillan residence to make the call.

It was nice to see Florrie's heart wrenched between the

lust to get in on it and sob direct to Toronto and the glorious call of deathbed vigil. Luckily, duty won. It would have been a macabre experience for Phil in Canada to get a burst of Florrie's Grand Guignol squirted into his ear without warning. Tom and Andrew left Florrie on the doorstep, wringing her hands and waving a brave farewell and showing her better profile for that movie camera.

Maltdyke hadn't changed, except for the number of strange faces. The main street was as mean as ever, merely older and more decayed. Most of the new people presumably lived in the scatter of Council houses that had grown round the old village. He looked at the place as he walked, and found it unpleasing, and wondered what he was doing back in it; undoubtedly a callous reaction. He had never regarded himself as callous, but he found no emotion of any kind in him. He could contemplate the probable death of his mother with total detachment, and while this seemed abnormally callous, even to himself, he could think of no reason to pretend any other feeling.

The telephone call cost a little over six pounds and he enjoyed it for its own sake. Andrew crept out of the lounge while he was speaking, crept out with the thunderous tact of a rhinoceros and, Tom imagined, went to pour himself a sly drink. Phil, of course, wasn't at home in any case.

"Hello, Mrs. Fletcher?" Tom said. "This is your father-in-law."

"Talk about a fabulous surprise! Mr. Fletcher! Dad? I hope there's nothing wrong."

No, nothing wrong. How could anything be wrong for this girl, this Margie, who had never even met Tom's mother or seen Maltdyke? He explained the situation to her and was grateful to find that she sounded sympathetic, unhysterical and intelligent; and that her baby was expected in five weeks.

It sounded as if Phil had been lucky in his marriage. What pleased Tom most was that Margie was grateful for the call but quite positive that Phil would not be making any dramatic dashes across the Atlantic to any deathbeds.

"There's no question of that, Margie. I made this call to please his aunt, but he's got more to do in Canada than he has here."

"I absolutely concur. I like the sound of you, Mr. Fletcher."

"I like the sound of you, Mrs. Fletcher."

"Why don't you come and see us some time? Phil has a new job, in advertising."

"Advertising! You're joking. Phil's an engineer."

"That fact had occurred to me too, but I guess he's what you might call an advertising-type engineer now."

"Oh God. No, never mind."

"You mad?"

Tom laughed. "No, never mind. I was just going to repeat history, but I won't. Give him my love and skip the advice."

"That I will."

Tom's suspicions about Andrew were proved accurate when Andrew drifted back into the lounge, after hovering outside to wait for the goodbyes, with two drinks.

"How do you like that?" Tom said. "Phil's chucked engineering and gone into advertising."

"That's a waste of good training, Tom. I wouldn't advise that. There's a great future in engineering." Then he caught Tom's eye, and the old wild Darky showed briefly through and they laughed and tossed off their drinks. It was only then that Tom remembered that Tommy would be home and unaware that anything was happening. He called Helensburgh and had a casual but worrying conversation with the boy, because Tommy rose to the occasion and insisted that he would be fine on his own all night if necessary, but there was a gray sound to his voice that bothered Tom, and on an impulse, he telephoned Meg Macrae at home and told her what was going on.

"Don't start fretting yourself, Tom," she said. "I'll take a train to Helensburgh and stay the night, and there's nothing to bring you into the office in the morning either. Now stop trying to give me instructions, I was sucking eggs when you were still in one. Get off the phone and leave me in peace." Ironically, Tom felt moisture in his eyes for the first time since he had arrived in Maltdyke.

And still there was nothing to be done and nothing to do. He cursed himself for not bringing a book, and on the way back to his mother's house he stopped and bought half a dozen paperbacks. And a bottle of whisky. Andrew Gillan was ponderously understanding, Florrie was shocked. There was a continual mouselike tapping at the door and a continous stream of neighbors to ask for news. Some of them Florrie kept on the doorstep, some of them she brought into the kitchen. The selection was according to a formula that doubtless made sense to her. She enjoyed it, Tom found it wearying to the point of frenzy. Some of them, he realized, were as anxious to have a look at him as they were to inquire about his mother. He was the One that had Run Away, the one that had made all the money.

Adopting Maltdyke habits, he hid the whisky; rejecting Maltdyke manners, he settled into his father's old chair with a book in his hand and feigned sleep every time anybody was ushered into the kitchen. His callousness towards the good, nosy neighbors outraged Florrie, but since her outrage didn't influence him, she adopted the tale that her poor brother had been up all night and was exhausted. Soon she grew to like this story, and with each successive visitor it developed extra circumstances, frantic drives through the night from England, transatlantic phone calls to numerous relatives, nervous prostration, the lot. Tom lay back in the chair and assumed a look of unconscious nervous prostration and worked out exercises in trigonometry to divert him from the danger of giggling.

Late in the evening the doctor arrived, made a short examination, and took Tom aside to explain that it was merely a matter of hours before his mother died. The doctor was a fat little man with a brusque bedside manner, and Tom guessed that he was glad to give the information to him in a business-like style rather than have a harrowing conversation with Florrie. Florrie, resentful but respectful, waited till the doctor had gone and then demanded the exact words he had used, so that she could memorize them and inspect them properly.

Later still, Joan and Alan arrived. Joan was ready to be deeply moved — that was interesting, his daughter Joan was quite like his sister Florrie. They both liked a good wallow. But Joan didn't go for it in quite the baldheaded manner of her aunt. She wept easily, but remained lucid. Florrie would cheerfully have slept all night on a three-legged stool if that seemed the proper procedure for grief-stricken kin, but Joan preferred a comfortable bed, and blandly proposed that she should be put at Florrie's house for the night. Alan demonstrated his capacity for easy self-effacement. He and Joan had not exchanged a word since their arrival. Their mutual silence could have been no more than the effect of an imminent death, but Tom reckoned that they had not exchanged a word for some time before. Once or twice he caught Alan looking helplessly at him, as if he would have liked to talk about other things than illness and death, but there was no time or opportunity for Alan's problems.

It was a little dismaying, all the same, to see how firmly Joan was set on spending the night at Florrie's, and how equally firm she was that Alan should go home to Glasgow.

It all sounded logical enough, and considerate, but she was surely too positive about it, and Alan was very quiet and expressionless in the way he agreed, and left to catch a train home.

In the end, around midnight, after yet another pot of tea — Tom swore that he would never drink tea again in his life — Florrie could find no good reason for staying any longer, because Tom flatly decided to spend the night with the old woman and Joan had to be taken away and given hospitality. Andrew Gillan remained with Tom, pointlessly, for a little while after they had gone, and Tom at once poured two resounding glasses of whisky and relaxed for the first time. Andrew was looking solemn and reverential, and Tom had no patience with him.

The sight of this tubby man, inside whom was imprisoned dauntless Darky Gillan, had jolted his memory, and he was impelled to talk of anything rather than his mother.

"Whatever became of young Moules, Darky?" he asked suddenly.

"Robert Moules? He's in Birmingham or somewhere. He got married to the grocer's daughter."

"Agnes Orr."

"Aye, that's right, Agnes Orr. Quite a nice-looking bit. Agnes Orr. Ah, it's a long time, isn't it, Tom?"

"No."

"Remember the way you used to torment old Moules? Ah, it's sad, mind you, Tom, when it comes to this. Who would ever have thought?"

His prosiness was maddening.

"Who would ever have thought what?" Tom asked.

"Ah, sitting here like this tonight, in these circumstances."

"By Christ, Darky, you do talk like a county councilor."

"Now, now, Tom. The circumstances are very melancholy."

"Oh, for God's sake shut up, Darky. Everybody's mother dies. Don't make a meal of it. Did you know Agnes Orr, Darky?"

Gillan's face poised on a memory and he nodded slowly, a bizarre mixture of the young devil and the middle-aged pudding.

"Aye, aye, I remember Agnes. I'm not as old as that, you know, Tom. I had an eye for them in those days."

"What are you talking about, 'an eye for them'? You were a roaring sex maniac. I know what eye you mean."

Gillan started to laugh aloud and then checked himself suddenly, in the house of sorrow. Moved to guilt, Tom got up and went to the bedroom, where he found his mother still sleeping and breathing steadily. When he got back, he waved a hand at the eager, inquiring, reverent face of Gillan, and refilled the whisky glasses.

"Ah well," Darky capitulated. "It's not very often, and the circumstances are out of the ordinary run." His prose style must have been a joy and a delight in the County Council chamber.

"Tell me this, Darky," said Tom, and settled well back in his father's chair. "Did you ever do anything really foul? Have you ever done anything that makes you curl up when you think about it?"

"Oh, we've all had our moments, Tom," Darky said soothingly. "None of us are perfect."

"Agnes Orr," said Tom, and repeated the name in wonderment. "Agnes Orr was the first girl I ever shagged."

The turn of conversation was bothering Darky.

"Now, now, Tom, as I said, none of us are perfect. That's all water under the bridge. Everybody sows their wild oats. What's past is past. Ha! There's not many cupboards without one skeleton or two tucked away!"

He looked slightly sad and fearful as Tom sloshed two

more big shots into the glasses. It amused Tom to pose as slightly drunk, because a drunk man must be humored, and by humoring him, Poor Darky, pillar of society, head buyer and county councilor, would have to take half of the bottle of whisky. That would be good for Florrie, Tom thought, and also thought, amiably, was ever man such a monster as I? He went to the bedroom to check on his mother, but was back before Darky could do anything clever, like pouring his whisky down the drain.

"No, no, Darky," he said, and hoisted his glass and forced Darky to drink deep in unison. "I know all about that water under the bridge, we've all had a swim in it; but this is ink, Darky. Nobody else has ever heard about it, and you're going to hear about it, because I'm drunk and half crazed with grief, of course, and because you have to humor me, haven't you? Of course you have. Drink up."

Darky was now perfectly willing to drink up. In fact, he took off his shoes and undid his tie and collar, and refilled his own glass.

"I don't know how well you remember Agnes Orr," Tom said, and he was going to get this off his chest because the sight of Maltdyke had reminded him of the weight of it. "I don't know, if we had lived in a bigger place she would have been nothing, but down here, in this pit bottom, she was something extra. She was too thin, I have to admit it, she was too thin, but she was *extra*. Always loaded with dough too, I suppose that must have made a difference. She *had* things. Clothes. She had a beautiful bottom, though, I can assure you of that because I watched it night and day for weeks. Small, but beautiful."

"Night and day? You never watched it night and day, Tom." Darky was growing quite happy and sympathetic; the years were blurring.

"Night and day. I watched it in my sleep. *And* I did all right with Skinny Agnes. I'll tell you the truth, Darky, she wasn't much at all, she was solid bone from ear to ear, but I never noticed that at the time. I knew she was a dizzy dame, but my God, Darky, every dame I ever met then was a dizzy dame. I thought it was a law of nature.

"Anyway, just a minute, don't interrupt, we're not in the council chamber, Darky, I did a very strong line with Agnes. I joined the tennis club, high-class stuff, backhand swing, leaping over the nets, sport it, partner. It was after I started on the old Ajax cleaners, but I was still living at home. She went for me too. This, I would remind you, Darky, was a large social achievement. Old man Orr was a big wheel in this here one-hoss town, I'll have you know. That guy sold a lot of margarine."

Darky stirred pleasurably and said, "She was okay, Agnes. Don't think you're the only one that noticed her bum, Fletcher. Ay ay. Here, don't say anything about this to Florrie, will you?"

"Forget it, forget it, Darky. This is taking too long with your interruptions and your slavering at the mouth. What I want to tell you is that I had started to make dough myself, and it was noticeable. Old man Orr sold a lot of margarine, I sold a lot of Ajax cleaners. I was *in*, boy, I had a future. Then there was Comrade Moules. Robert Moules. Poor old Robert, I hated him, the poor bastard. He was doing a line with Agnes before I turned up, and he was in as well, because he was a young chap with prospects. Funny, now I look back I realize old man Orr had everybody sorted out, and Agnes played the same rules as him.

"Anyway, the funny thing is that Agnes always tried to be adult, you know? Sophisticated. You know this, I think we read a lousy collection of books in those days. Everybody wanted to be adult and sophisticated. Agnes had to be terribly terribly honest with everybody, that was the sophisticated thing to do. So one day — listen to this, Darky — one day she explains that she can't make up her mind between Robert and me. I suppose she gave Robert the same story. Oh, it was hellish sophisticated. Actually, she was a hot little bitch on the quiet, but she had always kept that dark until this day when she announced the Great Plan.

"She had been reading some mush about sexual compatibility, and she had decided that she would spend a weekend with me, and a weekend with Robert, so that she could come to an intelligent decision. Now how, in God's name, do you like that, Darky?"

Darky waggled a thumbs-up sign.

"Get in there, Fletcher!" he said.

"Ah, you don't get it, Darky, you were always an insensitive ram. I was nearly crazy about this dame, man. I wanted her for keeps! And you know, the minute she said that — you should have seen her, it was a great performance. Sincere. She wanted to do the best for everybody. The minute she said it, I didn't want her any more. I *wanted* her, but rotten, you know? I just wanted to let her have it and then scram."

"Sure thing, Tom."

"Can you imagine what that dame was doing to one of us? Imagine being the guy that *won*. Imagine going through this rigmarole and then marrying the dame."

"Have another whisky, Tom."

"If I'd had it before I would never have done this. I would have caught a boat to South America and been sick. But it's a hell of a thing when you've never had it, you're so damned greedy to get it that first time. I took her to a hotel down at Largs and I had it, and I knew that was going to be enough for me. I told her it was no good. What good did it do me? I could have left her alone and let Robert have the lot. I just had to be rotten and spoil it for him. That is the filthiest thing I've ever done."

They sat and stared at the fire, and then Tom went to the bedroom to check. When he came back, Darky was running water from the tap into his glass, on top of a decent-sized tot.

"It's all water under the bridge, Tom," he said. "Let the past bury the past. We've all committed our little peccadilloes, my friend. One moment, sir, before you ask your question. What makes you so sure she ever told Robert anything about this?"

"It was a flaming contest, Darky, you haven't been listening. We were both in it. Robert and me. That poor sod, I used to hate him. I've never got him off my conscience, do you know that? I'm beginning to talk like Florrie, it must be the whisky."

"Now now," said Darky, "recapitulate, my friend. You never discussed this with Robby-boy, you haven't got a jot or tittle of evidence that he knew anything about it. Just a minute, now, listen, Tom. If she told him about you, why wouldn't she tell him about me? And Arthur McConnell? And that fellow, whatsisname? Tosh. Tosh Mackintosh. Eh?"

"You're kidding, Darky." Tom glared at him, and Darky shook his fleshy county councilor's head, his solid gray head, and grinned to himself.

"I lived in Maltdyke as well, you know. You're not the only pebble on the beach, Fletcher. Oh, you're a dark horse, all right. I never had an inkling you had been there. You're a dark horse. Hey, do you remember a lassie called Maggie Low? She lived up the back road. Kind of sallow skin, you're bound to remember her, her old man only had one arm."

"No."

"You *must*. Everybody knew Maggie Low." Darky was shaking his head again, and grinning, and Wandering Down Memory Lane. Tom forced his thoughts into focus and started to laugh. When Darky shushed him, he obediently fell silent, but kept on laughing, holding his stomach muscles in pain. Darky watched him in owlish concern.

"Away you go, Darky," he finally managed to say. "You're no' a bad chap even if you're a county councilor."

"I've never lost my faith," Darky agreed complacently.

"You stick to that, Darky-boy, and here, I'll tell Florrie you felt ill and I gave you a wee medicinal drink, if she asks any questions."

Darky lingered at the outside door and laid his hand on Tom's shoulder.

"No offense, Tom. No offense, Tom?"

"Sure, Darky."

"Ach, I've said a lot of things about you when you turned capitalist, but there's worse than you, Tom, you're all right. And I'll tell you something, Tom. I thought the world of your mother. A fine type of working-class woman."

"Aye, right, Darky." Even spoken and heard through drink, Darky's words had intonations that needled him, and he didn't want any quarrel. "Goodnight, Darky."

"Night, Tom."

The county councilor walked, not too shakily, up the main street of Maltdyke.

Tom looked into the bedroom, and then switched on another light in the kitchen and put on his glasses and picked up a book. But he was still thinking about Agnes Orr. It was a great puzzle. He felt, or rather he felt he should be feeling, a great load lifted off his conscience. But when he studied it, he discovered that the weight had never been as heavy as he had habitually believed. Had it mattered at all? Maybe he had nursed the terrible load on his conscience as a matter of pride, as well as guilt.

That was the puzzle about the whole insane sex thing. Pride and guilt were the same thing, if you turned either of them over. Did you *take* something from a girl like Agnes Orr — or from any girl — or did you give something? Or both? Or what proportion of each? He recalled how he had decided, at twenty-three, that sex was a simple physical need, like the need to go to the toilet. That was a nice escapist theory, if you liked. You didn't need another person when you went to the toilet, or when you ate or drank. And two people could get into a bed and each could be doing something entirely different from what the other believed he or she was doing. Both were doing the same thing, but each was still separate, getting or giving or both.

In fact, the same two people could get into a bed a hundred times and each be getting or giving something different each time, and there was no way in which the other could tell.

He poured himself a glass of water and drank it in one swallow, and then another. Then he walked into the bedroom, and in the light of the low-power bedlight he looked at his sleeping mother. He knew himself to be callous but his mind insisted on speculating consciously, and not pushing speculation out of conscious sight.

It was no novelty to look at a dying face. The bones showed (or it seemed to the watcher that the bones showed) and it was possible to see the face with flesh dissolved away, a bare skull. And that was a human person, the mother who had borne him and loved him. He had no doubt that she had loved him, even when she hated him. She had loved him in the best way she knew, and loved his father too, and the two things must have been a hellish struggle to match at times.

Her skin was pale and yellow, but peaceful. If she was dying, it was easier than some deaths he had seen. The breathing was steady enough, the blood was flowing. What was inside that skull? Was it still a human person, or a machine, with the humanity gone and the components still ticking over from habit, without personal power? Was his mother still in there? The quiet face diminished, as if it were moving away, by some trick of his eyes and imagination. It receded into the distance without growing smaller. This was where calculation ended and there was nothing left but puzzlement.

Georgie had taken longer to die than his mother would. The car had struck the truck and she had lain for months before the machine, her own machine, stopped operating. But she, Georgie, hadn't been there, surely; without speech or sight or voice, an assembly of bones and organs couldn't be Georgie. Had she died at the beginning? Was the object in the bed for all those months nothing more than an assembly? Or had Georgie herself been hidden away inside it all the time, screaming to get out? No, that was too dreadful to believe. Hidden away inside it, in a dream, living a life as real as his own.

Or reliving life a thousand times.

And at least Georgie had a life to relive. Life had been full and joyous for Georgie. It must have been, since she made it full and joyous for other people, without effort or strain. He wondered what kind of life his mother could relive, in the dream of coma. A hard, angry struggle against unknown forces, against the prison bars which she thought were the world, but which she had made for herself. A life wasted in a struggle against nothing.

But this was arrogance, to dismiss his mother's life. She had been herself, and she had lived it, and nobody else could know how it had tasted to her. She wasn't a complaining woman, and Tom decided, in a woolly way, that people who don't actually complain are probably succeeding.

But at least by now he had flogged himself into some kind of emotion, perhaps as an act of self-indulgence because he *wanted* emotion. He was filled with a vast sadness for the entire sad human kind.

"And when anybody feels that," he told his unconscious mother, "he's been at the whisky."

He was too weary to read, so he arranged three chairs in the kitchen for comfort, and lay comfortably enough with the two doors open between him and the bedroom. But his sleep was mottled and jerky, with half-dreams, and periodic jolts into wakefulness when he found himself straining for the sound of breathing, and hurrying into the bedroom when he could hear none.

At seven o'clock he made himself tea, wrinkling his face at it, and went to the bedroom again. He was almost terrified when his mother's eyes opened, and her limbs moved. She was trying to get out of bed. He laid a hand on her shoulder and tried to calm her, but she looked straight at him, with glazed eyes, and mumbled, and he understood. He carried her to the toilet, marveling at how small and light she was, and lifted her nightdress and held her upright on the seat. She mumbled something that he strained in agony to understand, but couldn't. There was a tiny tapping on the door as he carried her back, and he ignored it until he had laid her straight and covered her over.

"As the mother to the child, so the child to the mother," he said, quietly, and it was possible that she was smiling.

Florrie and Joan were at the door, fresh and hushed and eager.

"No change," he said.

"Not a sign of consciousness?" Florrie asked tearfully.

"No, nothing."

Eleven

IT WAS Joan's idea that he should preside over a family conference, or perhaps referee a punch-up, on the question of Grandfather's Gift. He didn't want to know about it. He felt that the funeral had given him his ration for the year of family reunions, but there was no easy way out of it. Joan was his daughter, after all, and Alan was his son-in-law, and he was responsible for them. It was a father's natural duty.

That's what it said in the book, anyway. It was damned funny that he and Georgie had never thought of holding crisis conferences, or calling in the U.N. to mediate when they got mixed up about money or about anything. It was probably funny, in fact, that he couldn't recall any time when he and Georgie had quarreled about money at all. They had worried about it when they were broke, and enjoyed it when they were flush, but neither of them had ever considered which money was whose. Money was a means of negotiating with the outside world, not with each other. And that was true even though Georgie, unlike Joan, had been a sharp and energetic businesswoman. She had helped him to *make* money, but it was all a game. People might sneer at moneymaking, but it was a lot of fun, and money ought to be fun or it wasn't worth anything.

He disposed of Tommy by bringing him to Glasgow with

a school friend and giving them enough money to see *Ben Hur*, and taxi fare to Joan's afterwards. He didn't think a sordid financial discussion would be good for the boy, and the boy agreed willingly that it would also be a living death. Tom had telephoned Alan at school earlier in the day, and had rejected the idea that they should meet first, because that would look to Joan like a conspiracy against her. Joan was very quick at sensing conspiracy. Instead, he killed time in a pub with Cam Jones until he could drive out to the South Side just a little late for a meal in Joan's tidy shining bungalow. It was a rather silent, slow session with Cam. For the first time in years, he found himself having to think of things to say.

"What did people do before they discovered alcohol, Cam?" he asked suddenly.

"Chewed betel nuts."

"I'm thinking about my parents. I don't suppose my mother had more than a dozen drinks in her life, and the old man would get drunk once a year, at New Year, but he never saw it any other time. But he never seemed to miss it. Why do we have to be at the booze all the time?"

"I don't," Cam said. "Except at New Year. I don't miss it, honestly."

"No," Tom said, and was on the point of adding automatically, *but that's because you're an old broken-down swine*, when he realized that that was too near the truth. Cam lifted his lemonade and sipped it and smacked his lips and smiled, as if he knew what Tom had nearly said and why it hadn't been said.

"I don't know," Tom said, "You're all right, Jones, with your creeping-Jesus principles, but the middle classes are drinking themselves to death, if we're the middle classes. It must be boredom."

"It's funny you should mention that, young Fletcher," Cam said. "I've been hearing that you're on the bottle."

"That's what I said."

"I mean I heard that you're half canned all the time."

"Fair enough," Tom said, but Cam wasn't speaking casually.

"You're an insensitive young hoor," he said. "The story's going around that you're drinking yourself into a stupor. Now just hang on, Fletcher, and don't start punching an old man like me or I'll punch you back. That is what I've heard, Tom. For God's sake we know it's baloney, but it can be dangerous."

"Who the hell told you?" Tom was coldly enraged.

"Uh-uh. Whoever told me is of no importance."

"Come on, Cam, don't tell me half the story and then clam up. Who was it?"

Old Cam shook his head in finality.

"No names. Aw, be your bloody age, Tom, what difference does that make? Anybody who would tell me a thing like that would be repeating a hearsay and he would be somebody who doesn't know you, so what good will his name do you?"

"I could bloody well find out who told *him*."

Cam looked at him in disbelief.

"You're losing your grip, Tom."

Tom thought about this. Finally he laughed.

"Yeah, you're right. You can never find out how that kind of story starts. But God, Cam, it must start somewhere. Ach, I don't know. Look at Big Morris — you remember Big Morris? He had a hell of a name for chasing women, and the poor sod was practically a virgin, but there was nothing he could do about it. He used to say he had picked my reputation by mistake. It never did him any harm, though."

"I know, it means nothing. Nevertheless. I've told you."

"So what do you expect me to do about it?"

"Damn all, Tom," Cam said impatiently. "Just be careful. You don't think I told you for fun."

Tom laughed. "No, you told me as a father."

"What's so bloody funny about that, you cheeky little get? I practically raised you from a yokel."

"And turned me into a dissipated aristocrat."

"Jesus, you're modest. Once a yokel —"

"— always a yokel. I'll never be a distinguished old bastard like you."

"You haven't got the breeding, Fletcher. By gad, birth still means something." He did his imaginary monocle act.

So what? If somebody in a pub had repeated some vague story that he, Tom Fletcher, was hitting the bottle, that was no more than somebody in any pub was saying about somebody at any hour of any day. In a way, it was true, as he had said. It bothered him to reflect that people of his father's generation could live for weeks on end without ever drinking, while he in his generation seemed never to be far away from a bar.

It wasn't that his father's generation had been pure and restrained; there had been plenty of drinking in the old days and plenty of genuine drunks. But he felt sure that it was people like miners and bricklayers and engineers who had really drunk hard, and then only at weekends, after their work was finished. Nowadays it was the comfortable merchants, the buyers and sellers, the businessmen and executives, who were packing away the hard stuff, and they were doing it in working time. But *everybody* was on the booze. It seemed a terrible waste of time and money.

On the other hand, there was the positive fact that he *liked* drinking. He didn't, he felt sure, do it to escape reality or make him witty. There had been a period of danger just after Georgie's death, but that was past. He simply like the taste of good whisky, and the relaxation, and the atmosphere of pub conversation. Still, it added up to a lot of whisky in a year. Seventy or eighty bottles. More. Perhaps as much money as his father had earned as a chauffeur.

And to conclude, he said to himself in the car as he drove towards Joan's, and to conclude, there is no profit in it, and I'll go on doing it anyway and to hell, so why am I giving myself a sermon? You are stony ground, Fletcher, and the seed of truth will not grow on you. You are *pickled* stony ground. Your mother always said you would come to a bad end, so get on with it and shut up.

He arrived at Joan's in time for cold ham and salad, and careful conversation that avoided the big problem throughout the meal. Everything looked fine. It wasn't the kind of house he would have chosen to live in, but Joan had chosen it and loved it, and presumably Alan was happy about it. It was like nearly every house that people were building nowadays, small and square and tidy and somehow *thin*, without space or grace. Joan fitted into it as into a frame, it was her nest, or her hive, and she was the queen. Everything was new, everything was shiny, and it could have been a show house built and furnished by a speculative builder as sales promotion. It had a lounge-dining room running from front to rear, with a picture window at each end to let the heat out in winter, and there were two other rooms, one the bedroom and the other fitted up as a sewing room that could be converted into a nursery.

This had always troubled him, though he had never mentioned it either to Alan or to Joan. The idea of a sewing room must have come from an article in *Good Housekeeping*, one of those smooth pieces all about how a wife should have some small corner of the house that was entirely her own; and this was absolutely peachy except that Joan hardly ever sewed. Alan, on the other hand, obviously brought work home from school all the time, but it was piled neatly on a small table at the far end of the lounge, next to the television, and no doubt he would work at it there in competition with Perry Mason. Maybe Alan preferred it that way himself. Or maybe all young husbands nowadays had to fit into a woman's world and scratch along as best they could. A man's home is his wife's castle.

"Now Dad," Joan said, and she spoke with that determined commonsense that always sounded overtight and too near the edge of tears. "I want you to explain to Alan that having money doesn't do people any harm." Since Alan sat glumly silent, and Tom tapped his lips and pondered, she felt she had to go on, and she burst out, "Well, it doesn't! You would think anybody would be *glad* to get a bit extra. I simply don't know what all the fuss is about!"

The tears (of vexation or guilt?) were very near now, and Tom had to say something.

"There's something in that." He slumped in his chair and tried to emanate a soothing influence. "This isn't the worst thing that ever happened to a young couple."

Joan relaxed slightly and sat down, and turned to Alan and said, "That's exactly what I've been saying. It's *fantastic* not to want a bit more money. We *need* it."

"*I* don't." Alan was saying his piece, but he took pains to sound apologetic and placatory. This was going to be hopeless, and Tom could have slapped his daughter, not for wanting the money, but for bringing him into the business at all. She wasn't interested in having a judicial opinion, she had already made up her mind and she merely needed Tom's influence to increase the pressure on Alan. There was going to be no calm courtroom procedure with the case for the plaintiff and the case for the defendant and the careful impartial judge analyzing the evidence. it was going to be more of a People's Trial in Omsk, with the judge and jury and prosecutor assembled to steamroller the insect in the dock, Alan.

"It won't make any difference to us, Alan," she said impatiently, and it was clear that she had said this many many times before.

"If it isn't going to make any difference, we can do without it." And *that* had been said many many times before too. It sounded weary and hopeless from repetition.

"But think of what we can *do* with it! Dad, for heaven's sake try to get some sense into him. I'm *baffled*. I think I must be going *mad*. I never heard anything like this in my life. And anyway, if Granddad gives me the money, I can't *refuse* it. It's a *legal* thing. It isn't as if Granddad comes to the door with the money in his hand and I refuse to let him *in*. It's all done in the lawyer's office and there you are, I've got ten thousand pounds whether I like it or not. There's nothing we can do about it. We may as well . . . make the best of it."

"If rape seems inevitable, lie back and enjoy it," said Alan sourly.

"Oh!" Words failed her, and she prepared to burst into flames. It was time to say something.

"There there there." He sounded to himself like a starched nursemaid with a mountainous bosom. "Money is very nice, Joan, but I think what Alan means is that he wants to provide for his own wife. He may be wrong —" (right or wrong, he's had it) "— but it's, um, natural enough."

"Oh, I know all about that." Joan had no patience with this kind of silliness.

"I do provide," Alan said quietly to a spot on the carpet.

"It's the same thing," Joan said, ignoring him, "it's the same thing as if I wanted to take a *job*. He wouldn't object if I went out to work."

"I would!" Alan was puzzled. "But you've never wanted to have a job, anyway."

"No, I know — but I *might* have wanted; but I didn't, because I knew you wouldn't want me to."

Tom's head whirled with the logic of this, but Alan didn't react at all. He looked like a man being sucked under a quicksand, knowing he would drown but determined to breathe as long as he could. If he could have taken Joan and shaken her till she rattled, he might have got somewhere, Tom thought, and felt a great impatience with the soft and gentle people of the earth who let themselves be enslaved because it didn't seem fair to fight back hard. But it didn't do any good to be impatient with Alan, he was what he was and wouldn't change. He transferred his impatience to Joan.

"What good is the money anyway?" he demanded. "The old pig's doing this to cause trouble, he doesn't like Alan. And he doesn't like me either. He thinks he can get at me by giving you this ludicrous heap of money."

"It's got nothing to do with you, Dad!" Joan protested. "He's not trying to cause any trouble to anybody. I would do the same thing if I was rich. What's the use of waiting till you're dead before you pass on your money? He's quite right, and I admire him for it."

"Joan, Joan, Joan." Tom left the impossibility of getting past her greed with any explanation. Ten thousand pounds was certainly a high-class piece of brainwashing. "Never mind me, it wouldn't worry me if you had a million. I don't know if you should take the money or not, but you've got to decide whether it's good or bad. Don't get *dazzled* with money, it's only stuff. You've got more than old Phil ever had in his life. You're young and healthy and you're married and you don't need help from anybody and you don't need money from anybody . . ."

"Hear hear," said Alan.

"We need a car! How can we buy a car, on a school-teacher's salary?"

"We don't need a car," Alan protested.

"Oh! Listen to him. Suddenly we don't need a car. He thinks about nothing else but cars. Austin-Healeys, Cooper Specials, station wagons, he dreams about them all the time."

"But I don't *need* one!"

"People buy cars without having ten thousand pounds," Tom suggested, but Joan was away, away beyond argument, and the tears had started, but she let them spring quite happily now.

"I thought you were going to talk sense to Alan! You don't remember what it's like, doing without things. You and Mum had a car long before you were our age. Anybody would think I was a . . . a *criminal* . . . because I want to enjoy life while we're young. It's *my* money."

Tom watched her in detached calculation and counted the seconds till she would fling herself hysterically from the room and throw herself on her bed in order to think up her next move. Four seconds exactly. Alan got up, shuddering, and muttered, "I'd better go to her."

"Don't be a bloody fool."

Glad to be restrained, Alan sat down again. A nice, honest boy, but absolutely clueless when it came to a fight. With ten times the intelligence of Joan, he would always be three moves behind, he would always be on the defensive, he would always understand exactly what was being done to him but would never find the brute resolution to fight it.

"It's true enough," he was now saying miserably. "Teachers never get rich. A girl is entitled to more than I can buy."

"Shut up and don't be a flaming hypocrite, Alan," Tom said harshly. "You don't believe that guff. A girl is entitled to what she gets from her husband. There's a hell of a lot of people worse off than Joan and she knows it."

Now it was Alan who wouldn't be brought to reason. He was broken, there was no doubt about it. Tom felt he could almost dislike him for betraying himself. He had the pride of Lucifer, but he was going to let it be eaten out from underneath because he wasn't strong enough to be one kind of man or another. He either had to be proud and hard, and make Joan accept his pride; or be soft and uncaring, take the money and enjoy it. But he was neither, he was proud and soft. He would let Joan take the money and he would hate it and he would die slowly of shame from this moment on.

"She's right," Alan said, convincing himself. "You did have a car, and all that jazz. You were able to get everything for your wife when you were young."

"I wasn't a schoolteacher," Tom said slowly and savagely. "And I wasn't you, and you're not me and Joan isn't her mother. Christ, you might as well say that Rockefeller got his wife ten yachts when she was young. What has that got to do with any other married couple? I've got no advice to give anybody, Alan, don't expect any. It's your own life you're living. Don't compare it with mine or anybody else's. If we had a car or anything else, that's because we lived that way. Georgie never asked me to live up to her old man's standards. I would have booted her out if she had."

"She was different."

"Ach, away and make a cup of tea. Joan'll want a cup of tea when she gets rid of the sulks. You can go and comfort her if you like. It's your marriage."

Alan went into the kitchen, however, and avoided the bedroom.

It was impossible that two young people should be torturing each other over money. Money was a great joke to young people, surely.

There would be no point in trying to explain to Alan, or to Joan, how he and Georgie had treated money in their wild youth. As he had said, Alan and Joan were different people. He realized again how lucky he had been in finding a girl who could understand money without giving two hoots about it. And yet, Georgie had been as hard as flint about money when it mattered.

There were still two joyful memories of the splendid, buccaneer way she had approached money; and they were both connected with old Shaw, and Shaw had been the loser both times.

When it finally became clear that Georgie was perfectly determined on marrying a conniving penniless salesman, Shaw produced his secret weapon, and it *always* had to be money. He would consent to the marriage (damned generous, since he couldn't stop it) as soon as young Fletcher had 1000 in the bank. It was like everything Shaw did, a caricature of the Victorian heavy dad.

Tom was so simple and earnest that he clenched his teeth and told Georgie that he would make a thousand in a year, if he had to rob a bank. Georgie laughed gaily and kissed him till his misery was mixed with delirium.

"Oh, Solemn Tolemn," she cried. "Do you think I'm going to lie a barren virgin till you get out of Dartmoor? I want Whatsitsname before I'm too old for it to be fun. I want it now, if truth be told."

"What, in the car?" He still felt crushed and resentful, but he joked because she wanted him to.

"No, it's too utterly utterly squalid, dahling," she giggled. "You'll have to smuggle me into your digs, but on second thoughts you'd better not because your landlady would know you were being unfaithful to her."

"My *landlady?*"

Georgie waggled a finger in his face.

"I have watched your landlady watching you, Solemn Tom, and I for one am of the opinion that she has enjoyed your favors."

Tom was aghast, but he smiled secretly and said, "What would you say if I said you were right?"

"Tom, don't take me for a cretin merely on the basis of my besotted passion for your fair white body, I *know*. I *know* she has. As long as she's been good to you and taught you things and *as long as it has stopped.*"

"Georgie, Georgie. For God's sake, of course it's stopped."

"Ha! Ha ha! Trapped by our own words, oh, you sordid seducer. No wonder my honest upright father says you're a whited catapult or something — no, don't say anything." She pressed her mouth to his and chewed his lips. It was delicious. "The hideous story shall never sully our lips again. No, listen, Tom, we're having no long-engagement nonsense, I would end up screaming with desire. If my dear papa wants a thousand pounds, we shall give the poor dear a thousand pounds. You're the sharp salesman, I can't understand how I have to conjure up all the brilliant financial schemes. But I have, and it's so simple you'll kill yourself for not thinking of it first."

Tom was aghast again. The jocular vision of five years in Dartmoor took horrible shape as he tried to dissuade her from her idiot plan, but Georgie laughed; Georgie always laughed. It wasn't as if she was actually going to defraud anybody, she laughed.

Next day she opened an account in the Savings Bank in Tom's name, and came to his digs in the evening with a crisp, new-smelling passbook. He put his head in his hands and moaned, but she kept on laughing. The first and only deposit in the account was ten shillings, and while he exhorted her to think of the police and the High Court and the prison bars, she giggled in delight and meticulously backdated the book by five years. Then she took three pens and three bottles of ink, one diluted with water and one with strong tea, and painstakingly entered a five-year history of deposits to total £1013.

"You can't do it," he wailed. "I don't think they *let* you deposit more than a thousand pounds."

"That, Thomas, is the kind of detail a big businessman like Papa would never have heard of. Oh, please don't whimper, Tom, I have to do this for the sake of my hormones. You're not involved in it at all, and they're such willing little hormones that it's not fair to spurn them. Get me some dust to blow over the yellowing pages before I wrinkle them a bit. I know, I'll rub the covers with my shoe . . ."

It worked, of course, because Georgie worked it. Her power of hypnotism must have been even stronger over old Philip Shaw than it was over himself, because Shaw could never have been taken in, surely, not by any trick in the book. Maybe it was so simple that it couldn't fail.

"Have you thought of anything?" Alan Spurrier asked him. Closed up inside himself, like a sea urchin, he had brought a tray from the kitchen, and now he was looking at it without interest and wondering what good it was going to do anybody.

"No, Alan, I haven't thought of anything. You think I've deserted you. I haven't. Or maybe I have, because I can't help you. I can only advise you to be yourself, and what's that advice worth?"

"Not much. I know nobody can help anybody else very much. Oh, I can tell you I hate money."

"I think it's a great laugh. Incidentally, Georgie took money from your kindly old grandfather."

"Didn't you mind?"

"Mind? Alan, I rolled on the floor. She didn't get it, she *took* it. And he squealed. It wasn't like this business, he wasn't flinging fortunes about, he kept his money hidden under his toenails, and she dragged it out."

"I would feel better if it was that way now."

"No . . . no. Nobody else could deal with old Shaw the way Georgie did."

They had been married a month. What was all this about money? He still had his little Ford, and he was selling in a frenzy to heap things on this female creature who had suddenly become his property, but there was never any money to spare. Not in those days. They had found a big flat in Hillhead, near the university. It was just about as far away from Shaw's house as they could get it, because Georgie had decided to cut her father off with a shilling. And it was marvelous, a collection of big rooms with a door that locked with three locks and left him inside with the endless delight of Georgie. But they lived from week to week because he had spent everything he had on furniture and sheets and pots and pans and all the time they needed more things.

They should have been buried under wedding presents, but for the fact that their wedding had slipped away unnoticed. Maybe Shaw had divined that he had been tricked over the fake bankbook, and maybe he had simply wanted to dream up another obstacle. In any case, he fought a ceaseless delaying action, he developed a heart condition, he pleaded that business was bad.

"I hate to insult your father," Tom said to Georgie one day, "but it strikes me he's jibbing at paying for the big wedding reception he always promised you."

"That's not an insult, Tom, it's a compliment; it shows he hasn't lost his mind, he's still foxy old Papa who promiseth much and performeth little, that's what made him what he is today, Tom."

"To hell with him, then, *I*'ll pay for it. I would enjoy making him ashamed."

"Tom, Tom! It would be the biggest joke of his life! *You* pay for it? He would never stop laughing. We'll give the dear soul a fortnight and then have the job done by a vet or somebody if he doesn't cough up. Quiet wedding. Ah! Ha ha! Then everybody'll think it was a hushed-up affair because Miss Shaw was in the family way! That would take the smile off his sweet old face! That's the plan, Tom."

"But I don't want people to think you're in the family way, Georgie. Hell, no."

"Solemn Tolemn, if you would stop treating me like a fragile flower and *put* me in the family way, we wouldn't have any of this trouble, it would be what you call a *fait accompli*."

"Oh no, Georgie. I don't want a pile of kids round your neck before I've had a chance first."

"Okay okay, but scratch me on the spine again, and this is an ultimatum. Two weeks' grace, and then we get the wedding ceremony done by a quack, one of these traveling preachers that sings about damnation and seduces all the village maidens."

They got it done by a quite ordinary Church of Scotland minister, quietly, in his vestry. They could still have made more of a splash, but Georgie had her mind set on the most frugal of arrangements. It was her big day, she said, the most thrilling day of a young girl's life, and she was damned well going to have it stark because that was the way she wanted it. There was no wedding gown, the bridesmaid was a girl from the office of Mindley Registers and the best man was Cam Jones, half full of whisky but utterly grave and correct. After the ceremony, the bridal party went to Guy's for lunch, which Cam Jones donated and at which the girl from the office got tight and burst into tears. There was no honeymoon. Georgie said a honeymoon meant Paris or nothing, and since Paris was out, everything was out. She and Tom took a taxi to the echoing rooms of their half-furnished flat and stayed in bed from Friday afternoon till Tuesday morning, rising only to make meals together and have baths together.

No, they hadn't gone straight to the flat. On the way, Georgie stopped the taxi at a kiosk and telephoned the glad news to Papa. He didn't believe it, or he refused to believe it, in the hope that that would make it untrue.

"You've finished yourself now, my girl!" he spluttered. "You were going to get the biggest wedding anybody ever seen, but you've eloped, you're for it. You've made your own bed, you can lie on it."

Georgie, half tight herself, was crushing Tom's head against the telephone so that he wouldn't miss anything.

"Yes, Father, I'm on my way to do that now," she laughed. "Nature is wonderful."

A strangled silence followed at the other end.

"You're no daughter of mine," old Shaw shrilled. "Don't show your face in my house again."

"Don't be a donkey, dear Papa, *I* am a housewife, it's *my* house *you* can't show your face in, silly. Bye-bye!"

* * *

"Does this go on forever?" she asked Tom, late on Friday night.

"That's up to you," he said. "If I have to decide, yup, it goes on forever. I calculate that's . . . with the normal expectation of life, say, forty-five thousand shameful ordeals facing you, minus a few thousand for natural interruptions, broken legs, piracy and acts of war."

"We'll have to increase the average rate in normal times to cancel out the natural interruptions in that case. But does it not peter out after a while?"

"It does with some people."

"It had better not. I think if we had a quick bath, and a cheese sandwich and champagne, we could catch up some of the slack in, oh, an hour . . . *half* an hour?"

"The champagne's finished."

"Who wants champagne? People drink too much."

It had petered out, very slightly, after a month, by the day when Philip Shaw gave up waiting for his repentant daughter to collapse on his doorstep and plead for forgiveness. She was afraid to plead for forgiveness, he reckoned, and therefore he decided to show his big heart by taking it to her. Georgie was sitting in the bow window of the lounge, three stories up, when she saw him getting off a bus in University Avenue.

"Lo, the father approaches!" she cried. "A visitor, at last."

"I won't have him in my house!" Tom shouted. "The boot's on the other foot now. This is my palace. No hawkers, no canvassers, no beggars. No buggers either."

"Don't be silly, Tom, we're not going to deprive ourselves of the great reconciliation, it'll be a shriek, honestly. Dignity is the keynote. Hee hee. Calm and aloof and terribly

terribly posh. Oh, the poor old pig, he'll never know what hit him."

"I'll have to get dressed in that case."

"No, no, Tom, we'll feel terribly terribly superior in our pajamas and dressing gowns, make him ill at ease."

"I'm not wearing any pajamas."

"Christ, neither am I. Isn't it convenient to be a woman? Look."

She dropped her dressing gown to the floor, stood for a second stark naked, picked up a dress from a chair and was inside it at once.

"And with a wave of the wand, she turned into the beautiful princess," she said. "Now you have to fiddle about with all those sordid trousers and shirts, and you haven't shaved. Ooh, I love your face when it's bristly, Mister Fletcher. Maybe we should ignore him and go and have a bath instead, we haven't had one since last night. No no," she cried as her lover's hot breath singed her blushing cheek, "We must be strong. We'll have a bath as soon as he's away, it's curious, this has put me bang in the mood again, it must be psychological."

"All right, don't offer him anything to eat and he'll go sooner."

It took Shaw several minutes to locate the flat and climb to it, and by that time Georgie had gone the length of putting on stockings and make-up, and Tom was giving his face a few quick swipes with the razor after dressing. They heard the despairing clunk as the old man dragged on the ancient bell pull, which wasn't connected to anything except rusty wires; and then an angry hammering on the door.

"Ssh." Georgie silenced Tom as he came into the hallway. "Who is it?" she called through the door.

"It's me, who do you think it is?"

"Who is that, please?"

"Open this door and stop your nonsense." Shaw pounded again. With an expression of profound seriousness, Georgie carried a pair of stepladders to the door, climbed to the top and wrestled with the transom till it opened in a cloud of old dust.

"Look who's here!" she cried joyfully. "Tom, it's that nice man Shaw who throws all those big receptions for his daughters, you must have heard him."

"Come down out of there and open this door this minute, girl!"

"Don't shout, the neighbors can hear."

"I'll damned well shout if I like!"

"Okay, so will I. Tom, it's that old man Shaw that was up in court for beating his wife. You know the one, he has a lot of fish shops, you know those shops that stink so much the Health Department is threatening to close them up. *That* Mr. Shaw."

"Let him in for God's sake, Georgie," Tom muttered, but he knew there was no stopping her.

"Open the door, Georgie, I'm your father!" Now the voice was low and strained. Georgie leaned on the transom and made herself comfortable.

"I don't have a father," she said chattily. "I did, but he disowned me, he said I was no daughter of his, so I thought to myself, well what does a girl want with a father, especially a father who disowns her? And I thought, nothing, she's fine by herself, so I disowned him too, especially a father who never even sends his daughters a wedding present, would you believe this? I had a father who weaseled out of paying for my wedding reception. Now who would want a father like that?"

"That's all in the past, Georgie, I don't bear any grudges, let bygones be bygones. For God's sake open this door."

"Ah, but I bear grudges, I'm well known for it, everybody tries to cure me of it, but it's in my character, I bear grudges permanently. After all, I was cheated out of three hundred pounds."

"How? Who cheated you?"

"That's what it would have cost for a real slap-up reception. And after all, a girl's wedding day is the biggest day in a girl's life and these things leave a mark on her soul if nobody coughs up the three hundred pounds for the big reception she's been looking forward to since she was a tiny baby on her father's knee."

"Let me in, Georgie, and stop this nonsense, the neighbors will be listening."

"No, I couldn't entertain a man who would cheat his daughter out of a three-hundred-pound reception."

"Dammit, I would have paid five hundred if you had been decent and straight about it."

"Done. I'll take five hundred."

"You'll take damn all."

"Goodbye."

She climbed down from the ladder.

"This is the last chance you get, Georgie. I'll not be back."

She crossed the hall to the bathroom and turned the cold tap on full. She started to sing. Shaw's footsteps could be heard descending the stairs.

"Well, you got rid of him," Tom said wildly.

"Tom, how can you impugn my family's escutcheon like that? Nobody ever got rid of a Shaw."

In ten minutes there was a reasonable, restrained knocking on the door. Georgie was at the transom in a flash.

"Aw, come on, Georgie, you've had your fun, I can take a joke. Let me in. I am your father."

"I know, I admit it. Still, business is business, that's what you always taught me, Father, and we can't resume our friendly old relationship till the slate is clean. I think you said five hundred."

"You'll get no five hundred out of me!" It was extraordinary how fast old man Shaw could hop from wheedling to fuming. "Anyway," he said, "you said three hundred."

Ah, he was as good as cooked. The salesman in Tom warmed to Georgie's sheer technique.

"Okay," she said. "Three hundred it is."

"Two hundred."

"Done. But no tricks. Put the money through the letter-box."

"Through the letterbox? You don't . . . I haven't got that kind of money on me."

"You have, Father dear, you have."

And he had, Tom knew he had. Nobody had ever seen Shaw without a roll of cash in his pocket. It was his symbol of success and his clincher to every argument and the tool of his trade. He might not have as much as two hundred, but he would have plenty.

"I'll . . . I'll write you a check. Tomorrow. I'll write you a check tomorrow. By here," he added in admiration, "you can drive a bargain all right."

"Yes, I can. And Father dear, you'll put the money, in cash, through the letterbox now, or you will never see me again as long as you live."

"I never heard of a man wi' a daughter like you," Shaw said brokenly.

"That's right, Father, it's spoiling the hang of your suit anyway."

And miraculously, money started falling through the letterbox. Georgie signaled, and Tom picked it up and counted it.

"That's it. Open the door now," said Shaw. Georgie looked down at Tom. Tom shook his head.

"A father, trying to cheat his own daughter. On a *Sunday!*"

The trickle of money started again.

The odd thing was that when Georgie finally let her father in, and Tom gave him what whisky was left in the flat, the old monster was as merry as a lark. It was nearly four hours before they were able to close the door on him again and have their bath.

"I hope you've seen some sense," Joan said, with her lower lip trembling but no noticeable sign of tears after her orgy of weeping in the bedroom.

"I don't want the money," Alan muttered.

"Well, I've thought it over, and there *isn't* anything we can do to stop it, so there's nothing to discuss."

"We can give it away," said Alan.

"Some hopes!"

"Put it in a trust, for our children."

"Ye-es, we might . . ." Joan clearly saw a loophole, a way of solving the present dispute without letting go of the money. "We can think about something like that. For *some* of it," she added, giving her game away. Alan put his head in his hands.

"Yes, the only commonsense thing is to wait and see what *happens*," Joan said brightly. "Heavens, he might change his mind and we'll wonder what all the fuss was about!"

Alan gave her a weary glance. Tom wished he hadn't arranged for young Tommy to meet him at Joan's. It was going to be a long, unfunny evening till he arrived.

Twelve

It was about this time that Tom began to feel that life was reasserting itself. Things didn't appear to get any better, but one day he realized that they were growing stronger, that he was actually interested in what was happening, rather than merely showing an interest. The sensation must have been developing slowly, but he recognized it quite suddenly, and it was like the feeling of a man who has somehow groped his way through the day with a frightful hangover and then, late in the afternoon, has been grateful to discover that he still doesn't feel healthy, but he doesn't feel like dying either.

It happened, in fact, on the day he went to look over the factory. The place had never interested him much before, because he was interested in sales, and he had been content to let young Mr. Charles worry about big industrial nonsense; and in any case, the factory was trivial stuff in the overall business. Once it had been the lot, now it had shrunk to a tiny dog attached to a large tail.

It was a tired little brick building out in Lanarkshire, where the English family had originated, and it had been the family business when old Mr. Charles was a lad. The original English, Charles' father, had manufactured solid wooden furniture in an age when people had actually bought solid wooden furniture. His son, the late John English, had taken over the business when cheap mass production and veneers were already abolishing it, and had reorganized it and concentrated on office furniture, where solidity still counted for something. But John, the only English of his generation with any restless ambitions, had also been more interested in selling than in making things, and from opening up a sales company to sell his own furniture, he had expanded to sell anything faintly connected with office furniture.

The company now sold eight times as much steel furniture, made by other people, as wooden furniture made by itself. Or, to be bang up to date, steel furniture made by its parent company. And for that matter, furniture of any kind was merely an item that had become less and less dominant since Tom had become sales manager. In spite of discouragement from both old Charles and young Charles, he had taken the view that there should be nothing in an office except girls that wouldn't be supplied by English Brothers. Typewriters, paper clips, ashtrays, everything, ought to come from English Brothers. Even if some things had to be bought at retail, English Brothers should supply the last pin. It created an enormous amount of trivial detail work, but that could be calculated and the profit in the end could be calculated, and while furniture might last for a century, pins had to be replaced all the time.

Pins meant nothing in themselves, he had often told young Hugh Winton, but they could be used to create a habit, and what had to be sold was the habit of asking English Brothers for every mortal thing. It was years since he had made a call without a stock of typewriter ribbons and pencils and pins permanently stored in his car, to cure clients of the bad habit of buying anything, however small, on their own initiative and bypassing the company.

Still, the original factory was there, and it turned over a

small profit and was worth its keep. The only question was how it looked, fitted into the streamlined setup of the Gaylor Group. Nick Gaylor too was a great calculator, and he worked on the basis of a firm, buoyant proportion of earnings to capital. It was hard to know whether the English Brothers factory compared as an earner with the big Gaylor steel-pressing plants. Sometimes these big operations had complications of labor and planning that trimmed the margins ludicrously. But one certain thing was that if the little wooden factory didn't match up with the Gaylor profit formula, it would be reorganized from the top in a hurry, or turned into something else, or sold for the land value. It was important not to leave the decision to anybody at the top of the group, but to be in on it first and keep ahead of the game.

He offered to take Hugh Winton with him for a visit of inspection, but surprisingly, young Hugh shied off. He could see the factory any time, he said.

"I know you can see it any time," Tom said, irritated. "I'm asking you if you want to see it now, with me. One day you may be the managing director, boy, and now's the time to get clued up while I'm still here to explain the difference between a rotary plane and a Rotary Club."

Hugh grinned, embarrassed. He had settled determinedly into a new elegance with his imitation-London suits, and even seemed less fleshy than his normal plump self, but he hadn't yet acquired the cold fish-eyed poise of the top chaps, and he could still blush.

"Me? I've got no ambitions, Tom. Managing director? That's out of my league — once a salesman, always a salesman. You know this, I don't think I should look too keen, I've got a theory that in the Gaylor mob they like you to keep your nose clean and not get too many ideas."

Tom stared at him, baffled, this inordinate pusher whose eyes were always on the big money.

"What the hell are you trying to sell me, Hugh?" he asked. "I bet you've got yourself measured for Nick Gaylor's job already, so don't give me that humble rubbish."

Hugh actually blushed, and then laughed.

"Hey, how about that?" he said. "Christ, I could see myself sitting there making these toffee-nosed slobs shiver. But anybody could see I wasn't the type — these people like Gaylor have got something, haven't they?"

"Yes. Money."

"No, but seriously, Tom. Yeah, I know what you mean. But seriously. I mean, I could see you doing your big tycoon act all right, but I'm not a good enough *actor*. Nobody would believe me. You know what I mean, you walk into the office one day and tell one of the top brass, Okay, you're fired. I mean, it *sounds* all right, but what if he just stays there? I mean, what if he says Up you Jack and carries on regardless? I mean, what could you *do?*"

"Drop a note to the cashier to stop his dough, and then let him carry on if he feels like it."

"Oh. Yeah! Well, naturally. Ha! You know, that had me worried, Tom. Hey, I bet that's just what Gaylor would do — tell the cashier first. These big outfits are terrifying."

"They're only Joes. And you don't want to come to the factory."

"Ach, I've got a lot on my plate today, Tom, I see the place every few weeks any way. Are you in a hurry?"

"No."

Hugh clearly was in the mood for conversation. Now that the panic had cleared away and his job was still safe, he felt like philosophising about it.

"What do you think of the Gaylor mob?" he asked, and

Tom wearily saw another long discussion of life and Big Business coming up. He shrugged his shoulders.

"What gets me about them," Hugh went right on, "is they're such *vicious* bastards. Well, look. They buy up companies — they must have bought up twenty or thirty by this time. You never think that every time some poor sod is going to lose his job — maybe five or six poor sods in some places."

"Aw, for God's sake, Hugh, be your age. We've all seen it a dozen times."

"Oh. Um, I suppose you have, when you've been around long enough. But they don't *care*. They come up here and they don't know anybody, but just because we're not in London they think they can do anything they like to us. We're not on their side, so out you go, chum, we don't like the look of your face."

Tom got up and found a sketch pad for his pocket. He couldn't find the patience for a long harangue against the upper classes.

"Don't exaggerate it, Hugh," he said. "You were right when you said they don't care. That's all. They're not vicious. They just don't care. They're not anybody's enemies, they're only operating their business. If they took the time to get to know everybody in every company they buy, they would have no time to run a business. They do what we do — the best they can. If we bought them over we would probably look like hatchet men as well, to them. I've never let anybody stand in *my* way."

"Yeah . . . but you've never bought anybody over. You're not the same type as them, Tom. It's a different kind of world they live in."

"You'd better get used to it, then, because it's the world you live in as well, Hugh. Away out and sell something."

"I might do that." Hugh had a squint at himself and his suit in the glass door before he went out. Tom clapped his hands and rubbed them together and then wondered what he felt so vigorous about all of a sudden. He had been a little brusque with Hugh, and that must be a good sign, after months of effortless patience. You could be patient merely because you didn't care about anything, but today he felt like action, he was already seeing the factory mentally and seeing it as a stranger would see it. It must be ready for changes because it hadn't changed in ten years. He felt happy and enthusiastic.

It certainly hadn't changed from the outside. It still looked shopworn and drab, but there was nothing wrong with that, the customers never saw it. Inside, it had the clean airy smell of fresh-cut wood that always pleased him, and the sharp nose-tickle of cellulose. Fifteen men and five girls. A neat tidy little labor force. There was a lot to be said for a small operation in terms of staff-management communication. There was hardly any turnover of staff, everybody knew everybody else and it was comfortable. On the way in, he noticed a stack of typists' tables in the dispatch room, and made his first calculation. Cheap typists' tables sold steadily, but offices were changing and wood had become a luxury material. It was the first thing anybody would have thought of — Nick Gaylor might have thought of it already, without even seeing the factory.

He found the foreman, George Stiles, checking a pile of blockboard, and waited till the check was finished before he greeted him. A good solid man, Stiles, in a brown factory coat and a cloth cap which he wore all the time. He was a big man, with big hard hands and a big calm face, and although they had never known each other well, Tom had always felt attracted by the calm competence of him. He addressed him as Mister Stiles and shook his hand. Stiles was either thinking of something else, or even more taciturn than Tom had realized. He took Tom's hand and shook it without looking at him or saying anything.

"Everything fine?" Tom asked him, as an automatic greeting.

"Usually is." It was hard to tell whether Stiles was nettled by the question or merely preoccupied. It was of no importance in any case.

"I'll have a look round," Tom said, and Stiles said, "I'm kind of busy."

"Good. I can find my own way."

"Suit yourself."

Tom walked into the factory with his lips pursed. Stiles was an employee, but an employee was the same kind of problem as a prospect. If he was thinking of being bloody-minded, it was automatic procedure to let him get on with being bloody-minded till he got tired of it. You could be unpleasant in return, but that merely wasted time and energy. He wasn't surprised to discover after a few minutes that Stiles had followed him into the factory and was drifting along behind him. This was Stiles' little kingdom, and few men were capable of letting an outsider inspect their kingdom without being there to watch. Or maybe he had misjudged Stiles, and the man was only anxious to be self-effacing.

He stopped at a bench and turned to Stiles.

"What does this machine do?" he asked pleasantly.

"It does its job all right." Stiles blurted out the words in half surprise, as if he had been caught eavesdropping and was trying to recover his poise, and then brushed past Tom and walked on busily. Uhuh. Right. He had something on his mind, and Tom braced himself cheerfully to deal with it. In the meantime, he stayed at the machine and walked all round it. It was perfectly obvious that it was cutting grooves in blockboard, for drawer runners or fixings, but he lingered to talk to the man operating it, and made some meaningless notes on his sketch pad, and as he did, he could see Stiles in the distance, watching him.

He spent an hour in the factory, timing it deliberately by his watch. His first thought had been to spend the hour as a psychological trick, to force Stiles to wait and wonder and fume until he wore down, because he knew that Stiles wouldn't now be able to rejoin him after brushing him off so obviously. But as he went round the machines, Tom realized that time was too precious to waste on psychological warfare alone. The machines interested him despite himself.

He filled pages of the sketch pad and without straining himself, he had already decided in half an hour that the factory was ripe for changes. It didn't take any specialized skill to see them. Every old factory was probably the same, it grew naturally as new machines came in, and the machines were dumped in the handiest available space and people got used to them and got used to their being *there* rather than *there*. Lack of planning was easily compensated by human effort and habit, and in a small family factory it wasn't really fatal. But it mattered, especially when a flying squad of Gaylor efficiency boys with narrow pants and stopwatches might swoop on the place any day.

After an hour, exactly an hour, he put the sketch pad back in his pocket, went to the glass-walled cubicle where Stiles was sitting, and walked in without knocking. Stiles didn't look up. Tom lifted some books off a chair and sat down at the desk opposite the foreman, took out the sketch pad and started to make calculations on the top page on which he had already sketched a series of rectangles. He heard Stiles breathing heavily, and refrained from smiling. He also re-

frained from rubbing his hands, but he knew beyond doubt
that a fight was in the air, and he was ready to enjoy it. He
flipped over the pages of the pad and kept on writing, not
nonsense but every sensible question that came into his mind
on the subject of furniture production. He glanced at his
watch. Ten minutes had passed.

Fifteen minutes passed. He had a strong urge to laugh for
pure pleasure. Whatever Stiles had on his mind, Stiles was a
good hard man who could keep his mouth shut for fifteen
minutes if he wanted. But he wasn't going to be hard enough
because he didn't have the training and he didn't have the
cards. At the sixteenth minute he broke.

"You going to be much longer?"

He probably needed to go to the toilet. Ah, that was very
sad, the way a trivial physical condition could unman a man
in a fight. Tom looked up from the pad, without focusing on
Stiles, and pondered into the middle distance.

"Mm? Mm, it shouldn't take more than three or four
days."

"Eh? What to do?" Stiles was startled.

"To do my job."

"Eh? Here, any jobs here, I can do them. I'm in charge
here."

"That's right."

"Well!"

Tom kept on pondering and brushed him aside like a fly.
"Don't interrupt for a minute."

Stiles stood up, boiling with energy and holding it down,
and after a minute, Tom flipped the pad shut and sat back
and smiled at him.

"What's your problem, Mr. Stiles?"

To give him credit, Stiles wasn't upset by that.

"There's no problems here, *Mister* Fletcher. Everything
here's fine, the way it's always been."

"Yes, it's not bad. Not bad." Tom put enthusiasm into it.

"Oh? Oh. Aye. Well, as long as there's not going to be any interference."

"But . . ." Tom tapped his lower lip and looked thoughtful, ". . . but you don't *own* the factory, Mr. Stiles."

"I never said I did. But there's never been any complaints before."

"There are no complaints."

"You come barging in here and snoop about the place and make drawings and interfere with the work without so much as a by-your-leave. What do you call that?"

"I'll be glad to explain that, Mr. Stiles." Tom smiled winningly and infuriated Stiles.

"I hope you will!"

"Now then, Mr. Stiles, it's very simple. This is the English Brothers factory. It is owned by English Brothers —"

"— by Gaylor and Company, Mr. Fletcher."

" — by English Brothers, and don't interrupt me, Mr. Stiles. You are in charge of the factory. I am the managing director of English Brothers. Any time I visit the factory, or anybody from the office visits the factory — even a message boy — you will ask him politely what he wants and then you'll get busy doing it for him, and if you can't do it, you'll telephone me and explain — respectfully — why you can't do it. Be quiet, Mr. Stiles, I'm speaking. The next time I come here, at nine sharp tomorrow morning, you'll have a cup of tea ready for the boss and you'll be free to show me round the works or show me the books or answer my questions I have to ask. You can hate my guts if you like, but you'll do your job, and your job includes doing what the boss tells you."

"Oh?" Stiles was bothered, but he didn't retreat entirely. "I never had any trouble with young Mr. Charles. He never interfered."

"Good."

Tom left it there. He was fascinated to know how Stiles would go on, and interested in discovering whether Stiles was as stupid as he had sounded, or merely an angry man with something gnawing at him.

"I'm not afraid of you," Stiles said. Not bad.

"Why should you be? You haven't any guilty secrets."

"You're damn right I haven't!"

"That's right."

Tom was determined now to give nothing away, to make no suggestions, but to leave Stiles to talk on. He might be simply a good man who was angry, but there was a strong strain of ordinary stupidity in him too. Odd, how he had always seemed such a calm, likable individual. No doubt he was, and no doubt he was a competent factory overseer, but only stupidity could explain the silly way he had behaved; stupidity and an active dislike which Tom had never suspected.

"And what's the big idea, coming back here tomorrow?"

"To do my job."

"Maybe I could help you better if I knew what you were up to."

The beginning of a retreat? It sounded more like plain curiosity.

"I'm looking over the factory."

"All right," said Stiles, "but there's nothing wrong with this place. You might be the managing director or whatever you call yourself — *for the moment* — but you'd better not start poking in and upsetting the one bit of the business that pays its way. I know my business."

It was hard to see how stupidity could go so far, but people were always surprising. A man could get an idea into his head, a grudge or a principle or a piece of cussedness, and he might throw over his livelihood and his life rather than give it up. Tom decided on the spur of the moment to see if Stiles could be softened up in another way.

"That's true," he said genially. "You've been foreman since John English was manager. In fact, since he died you've practically done a manager's job. You should have the manager's title and a manager's money."

"Aye, maybe." Stiles had gone so far that he couldn't find a quick way of changing his tone, or maybe he was determined not to be bribed out of his principles, whatever they were. "I've never complained about money as long as I'm left alone." But he had glanced involuntarily out of the office window to the yard where Tom's Jaguar was sitting, obnoxiously opulent. That was probably part of it; Stiles seemed like one of those men who could never hoist themselves into the position of owning vulgar cars and therefore hated anybody who did. His attitude to young Mr. Charles would be different — young Mr. Charles was *entitled* to be rich, he had always been the boss. It was the sight of an upstart that griped, a man who had used some unfair advantage to claw himself up. If Stiles was really like that, there would be no cure for him.

Stiles turned back from the window, sullen and guarded.

"But who's got the authority to make me the manager?"

"Me."

"I'll believe that when I see it."

No, there was no cure for Stiles. Tom wondered what the man would do if he suddenly said *You're fired*. He would probably act like the executive in young Hugh's nightmare — say Up you Jack and carry straight on till somebody actually dragged him physically out of the factory. Stopping his wages wouldn't make any difference to him, he would stick to his cubicle and do his job for nothing rather than leave. Tom decided not to try it, even as a joke.

Young Hugh wasn't so silly, odder things had happened in big companies. He remembered a story which Cam Jones had sworn was the unvarnished truth, about a young fellow who worked in a television station writing publicity handouts. When the station manager got tired of his handouts and transferred him to another job, he refused to be moved. For three or four days his replacement found his room locked and had to work on half of a typist's desk, while the rebel barricaded himself in and kept on writing handouts regardless. For the next couple of days, after the office had been forced open, the mutineer scampered around the building clutching his typewriter and refusing to give it up, and all the time writing publicity handouts when he wasn't actually wrestling with the new man for possession of the machine. Tom couldn't remember how the battle had ended, but it was quite possible that the station manager had been worn into the ground and surrendered in the end. Stiles would be like that, clutching his carpenter's pencil to his chest and bawling out orders to the workers while a strong-arm squad carried him out of the factory.

"Do you ever take a drink, Mr. Stiles?" he asked.

"Aye . . . sometimes."

"Come on down the road and we'll have one."

"Na, na, I've got my work to do, I'm not one of your expense-account people that drink when they're supposed to be working."

"You won't get the invitation again," Tom said blandly, and Stiles wrestled with it, palpably tempted.

"Aye, all right, then, just this once, at least I've earned it," he conceded. "It gets dry on your throat in here," he added, to justify himself. He took off his factory coat and put on a jacket in silence, and when Tom opened the door of the car, he lowered himself gingerly into the genuine leather upholstery and furtively smelt it.

"I wouldn't like to drink if I was driving a thing like this," he said piously. Tom didn't answer.

In the quiet, inelegant, noonday pub, Stiles accepted a pint of beer and sipped it with caution.

"Here's a problem you might help me with," said Tom after a decent interval. "There's another factory I'm interested in." (Surely Stiles couldn't fall for this, but Tom felt cheerfully reckless.) "It's the layout of the machines that puzzles me. It's . . . roughly this shape." He sketched a rectangle. " — and the machines are in two straight lines, like this. Here, saw . . . jigsaw . . . machine plane on one of the lines . . . sanding, something like that . . . and there's a door at this end leading straight into the paint shop. Why would they put the machines like that?"

Stiles looked at the rough sketch, and his lips tightened. He hadn't been fooled.

"You get a straight run," he said. "It doesn't always work, mind you — what happens if you want to use one of the machines twice? You have to bring the job back up the line."

"Yes, I thought there was something wrong about it," said Tom.

"Oh, there's nothing wrong wi' it, I'm not saying that. If I was laying out a shop it would be *something* like that. Starting from scratch, like."

"But what if you had a workshop already, with the machines laid out some other way?"

"Ah! That's no' a foreman's job, that's for the man that put the machines in. In my position, you should understand this, my responsi-bi-li-ty is to get the work out wi' the machines I've got."

"Uhuh," said Tom. "Shifting the machines is more of a manager's job."

"Aye, maybe." The lips had tightened again as Stiles saw the trap.

"Right. As the manager, you can make any rearrangements you like."

"What, in our factory? Ah, but just a minute, we've got to produce. Produce. You start moving a machine, that's a machine that's no' producing. That's a fact and a fact is something nobody can shift."

"So you lose a few days. That's a manager's responsibility."

Stiles narrowed his eyes. He still wasn't sold.

"Maybe aye and maybe no. You've just come in wi' a lot of ideas that anybody could have had, anybody that knows the trade, there's nothing new in that. But if anybody's going to hold up production for some idea, it's not gonny be me, Mr. Fletcher. I know what they think at the top, and what they think at the top is, everything here is fine, it's to go on the way it is. And as far as I'm concerned, that's it."

Somebody had been getting at Stiles. Maybe young Mr. Charles, before his departure to higher planes. If it had been young Charles, Stiles was probably misinterpreting a vague assurance as being a firm instruction. Short of sacking him, or demoting him, it was going to take an almighty struggle to get him moving at all, and sacking or demoting would cause more trouble in the factory than it could possibly be worth. It might be better to throw plenty of new, frightening ideas at him all at once, and give him time to digest them one by one.

"There's another thing," he said. "By the time these typists' tables reach the customer, we're hardly making a few quid on each. Yes, I know, they're steady and they're reliable. But offices are changing, and you'll have to take my word for it, because I've been in them all and you haven't. People are paying enormous sums of money for big wooden desks — executive desks. Metal isn't classy any more, but mahogany and teak and afrormosia are. We might double or treble the profit if we got a good design for a big fancy job."

"That's speculation, that's not business."

"Mr. Stiles," Tom said patiently, "You can saw and plane and I've no doubt you can hand-carve better than I, but don't tell me what business is. I know."

"You'll never convince me."

"Och, you're a stupid man." Tom lost patience. "I don't need to convince you, but I'll have the job done."

"We'll see about that. I was warned —" Stiles stopped short. Tom looked at him and nodded without saying anything. Somebody had got at Stiles, there was something odd going on behind his back; maybe something that was merely a mistake or a piece of confusion, maybe something deliberate and planned. With Stiles himself he had lost patience, it was too wearying probing among the man's dogged reflexes, when in the end he might find that Stiles had nothing to reveal. He debated to himself whether he should revisit the factory on the next day, rather than have Stiles think he had been scared off. But that kind of thinking was feeble. There was no useful purpose in visiting the factory next day and Stiles' opinion of him didn't justify wasting time.

"I'll skip my visit tomorrow," he said, rising. "It's time I was getting back to town."

Stiles looked at his empty pint pot with a trace of regret, and said, "This is not one of your drinking days, is it? I would have bought you another one."

"Next time," said Tom, and then wondered lightly what exactly Stiles had meant. He dropped the man at the factory and drove back to the office, and he drove with both windows down and took deep pleasurable breaths. Even if Stiles was his only problem, Stiles was a problem. Life was hard for a middle-aged businessman, and he liked it that way. He booted the Jaguar up to ninety on a straight stretch and handled it like a well-coordinated twenty-year-old. It was a splendid car. He was rich and rugged and he could take on anything, any damned thing at all.

When he got back to the office he sounded out Meg Macrae for her opinion of Stiles, but she had no particular opinion except that Stiles must be all right because he was hardly ever heard of and the factory ran along without creating any fuss.

"Do you think he's sharp?" Tom pressed. "Shrewd politically, I mean?"

"What do you want, Tom — Andrew Carnegie? Here, look at you — you're getting that look again."

"What look?" Tom grinned at her.

"Like a flaming boar in rut. How is Tommy?"

"He's all right. He thinks you're formidable. Boar in rut? Lay off, Meg, I think I'm mellowing into a middle-aged queer."

She made a vomiting noise which he found rather charming, and emptied a bulky envelope on to his desk. A glance told him that it was a pile of literature put out by the Kutsu Manufacturing Corporation, Kobe, Japan.

"Oh, that," he said. "You've got a damn cheek, opening my mail."

"All right, fire me. They're exhibiting at Lausanne next month. You should go."

"Ah, it's only another smart Japanese company, Meg, there's one in every telephone box in Tokyo. Can you see Nick Gaylor letting me screw the expenses for a holiday in Switzerland?"

"Screw Nick Gaylor," she said. Always the puritanical Scots spinster. Tom shuffled the brochures absent-mindedly.

"What was all the furtive carry-on about this, Meg? Secret code letters to Japan and all that nonsense?"

"There's none so blind, Tom Fletcher. You're not out of the wood yet, you could use some wee quiet contacts that Nick Gaylor doesn't need to know about."

"That's what makes women horrible," he said, "they don't know anything about loyalty or principles. You're rotten, Meg Macrae, rotten to the core. But honestly, I don't see much in this Jap stuff, everybody's imitating their designs now, somebody's rechristened a village in Lancashire Tokyo so that they can make like a Japanese trademark. I've got other problems anyway, there's something funny going on at the factory, or in London, or somewhere."

"Oh God, men! That's what's different about women — they know everybody's out to do them, so they're never surprised. You bet your life there's something funny going on. Since when was there not?"

"Thank God Nick Gaylor's a man, that's all I can say. Will you try and get me that Jack Fillimore in London? Maybe I can fish something out of him."

He was connected with Fillimore in under a minute, and faraway Jack sounded crisp, sober and keen; no symptoms of lavish business lunch befogged his diction. When actually on duty at headquarters, the bright young men probably lived out their days in frugal toil and got by on a cheese sandwich and a glass of milk.

Fillimore warmed up at once, however, on hearing Tom's voice.

"Urrrr, it's you, Tom, old boy, the wild Highlanderrrrr, hoots mon! How's every goddam liddle thing wid you?" he added in his New York voice.

"Fine." Tom had developed a revulsion from small talk on the telephone, whose function he considered to be confined to rapid messages followed by silence. "A couple of things, Jack, merely for your information."

"So that everybody knows what everybody is doing, old

boy, first rule of the Organization. I've got my tiny ear pressed to the receiver and a well-sharpened chisel poised above my tablet of stone."

"Nothing very big, Jack. I've been looking at the factory up here, and I'm proposing to rearrange the machines."

"Mmm." Fillimore sounded dubious, and Tom contained his irritation.

"There's no particular cost involved," he went on, angry at having to make any explanation at all. "It'll only take a few days, and it should save plenty. The other thing is that it's time we changed the line from the factory. The same machines could make big executive desks and boot the profit margin sky-high."

"Uhuh. Yup, you're right on the ball, Tom, old man, it sounds fine. Only one thing, old boy, I think — don't want to get out of line, but I think, maybe-maybe-maybe, you should make haste slowly, know what I mean? No, as a matter of fact, it sounds great to me, but there is the point that we already have a line of executive desks from Slocum and Company. You've probably seen some of them."

"Not many in this neighborhood."

"No, Tom, old man, but there will be, when you apply your well-known Highlander's enthusiasm to the problem."

Fillimore was no fool; at least he knew what the Gaylor Group were producing. All the same, Tom pushed a little harder.

"Slocum's do a nice job," he admitted, "but you can't buy the things, they don't make them fast enough. I've tried them before."

"Good point, Tom — I'm not trying to be obstructive, old man, cross my heart, anyway, what the hell? I'm only a lance corporal in this man's army. No, Tom, between you and I, I would play it cool, just for the nonce. It's a political thing, actually, I just deduce from the old bush telegraph that your young Mr. Charles still feels paternal about the factory up there, and our N.G. feels paternal about young Mr. Charles. Nobody's said anything, but they may have something else in mind, who can tell? I'm telling you this off the record, natch, old boy, so that you don't get any wires crossed."

"I see. Thanks for the tip, Jack, it's best to know these things," Tom said, very calmly. "But according to my contract, I could have gone ahead and done all this without saying a word to London."

"Now, Tom, old boy, be reasonable, you don't mean that, I know. Contracts are contracts, but N.G. is, in a manner of speaking, N.G."

"Of course, I was joking," Tom said, his calculation mechanism spinning like a fruit machine. "We'll play it cool. Oh, by the way, Jack, I noticed some interesting electronic stuff advertised by a Jap firm the other day. I was thinking of getting in touch with them."

"Don't, Tom. Very good, you know, it's good to hear people are on that ball, but we have a whole department doing nothing else but combing the overseas stuff, and you know what they say, duplication is the thief of margins."

"Is that what they say?"

"Yes, they say it all the time."

"I could let them have the details, then."

"Well spoken, but I shouldn't bother, old boy, you know how it is, these departments get very touchy, interference-wise. Good of you to mention it, all the same."

"Right," said Tom. "That's all I had on my mind."

"Good, Tom, it's always good to hear from you. Um, Tom? I hope I haven't offended you, you know how these things are, I'm only trying to keep you in the picture."

"Not at all, Jack. We're in business. I hope to see you soon again."

"Check, old boy, and don't make it too long, we pine for a

new face down here. Don't forget, there's always a bed for you at old Fillimore's when you come to town. I mean that, Tom. Have you fixed up your holiday yet? I'll be away during September."

"Yes . . ." Tom reshuffled the literature from the Kutsu Manufacturing Corporation. "Me too. I'm thinking of going to Switzerland."

"Lucky old you. Our kid's too young for long-distance work, so it looks like dear old Cornwall again. I envy you."

"Have a good time."

At least many things were plainer. Tom laughed, and went to look at his face in the little mirror above the fire-place. He couldn't detect any resemblance to a boar in rut, or a young ram, or a mongrel in heat. He looked like himself, a much less interesting object than a boar. Still, maybe Meg's eyes were sharper. He felt like *something*.

No doubt the Gaylor Group were very happy to have him in charge of English Brothers, and he knew without doubt that they were getting their money's worth out of him. But his job was an exposed position that could always be surrounded or undermined or worn away. He knew without rancor that in an organization like that, he wasn't one of the elite, he was a colonial subject; or more properly, a piece of machinery that could become expendable for any of a hundred reasons.

The organization was an impersonal machine that protected itself regardless of any of its members. But it wasn't only an impersonal machine, it was a mob of highly personal people concerned with self-protection, and any of them might find it necessary at some time to stab him in the back. Or he might get a knife in his chest while he was looking over his shoulder. And this situation, he discovered, was just fine. He would rather die of sleeplessness, he decided, than of fatty degeneration.

Meg Macrae had come back in and was leaning against the door waiting to hear the score.

"It's a hard life," he said.

"That's news," she said sourly. "How is that nice young Mr. Fillimore?"

"Oh, very with-it. But we'll just keep our backs to the nearest wall in the meantime. It's a comfort to know that at least I own this office."

"Yes, that was clever, Tom. If they cut your salary you can always put their rent up. Are you going to Lausanne? I wouldn't mind coming with you."

"Don't be filthy. I'm thinking about it."

"I know. I was listening in."

"By God, you're a champ, Miss Macrae. Is that the way you bring up your office girls?"

She walked out, sniffing.

It was a small comfort to know that he owned the office. That could never have happened in the late John English's day. John English would have bought property as he expanded, but old Charles was terrified of any risk at all, and when the old office in the center of the city had grown too small, it was Tom who had bought the big house in the West End and offered the tenancy to the company. He had thought of it as insurance, but it had been as much for a laugh as anything.

That had been in the days when Georgie started him on what she called the landed gentry jag. She had studied property the way some other women study the stock market or antiques, and during three (or was it five?) years she had dragged him into an orgy of buying little bits of land and buildings and selling them. Sometimes it had wearied him, but Georgie was an irresistible force, and luckily she was too smart to make any mistakes.

"It's money in the bank — for *nothing*," she would say.

"A woman has to make some money so that she won't feel financially dependent, you know what Karl Marx says, the sexual subjugation of women is the result of their economic dependence, or the other way round, and they have to submit to their husband's bestial desires because they need the housekeeping money, either that or they need housekeeping money because they're too busy submitting to their husband's bestial desires to have time to earn a living — anyway, whatever he said, if it *was* Karl Marx, this is the best way to develop a hilarious marraige because I don't need any housekeeping money so we can submit to our bestial desires for fun, if only the blasted kids would stop waking up in the middle of the night. That's logic, isn't it?"

"It's something," Tom agreed. "But you're too tired shopping for bits of property to submit to anything these days."

Tears started to Georgie's eyes instantly and she squeezed his arm.

"I know, Tom," she said, "but it's got nothing to do with buying bits of property, it's only a phase or something, oh, I know it's rotten, I don't know why you stay with me, you're not getting anything out of it, but it must be only a phase, it'll be all right, I love you desperately, honestly. Everything'll be all right again."

He groaned when he thought of that. The property-madness had died out like every other craze, and in time everything was all right again. He was sure now that that long period of apartness in his marriage had been a chemical phenomenon, and the property-madness was another symptom rather than a cause. But it had lasted long enough, and it was during that time — he could remember the day precisely, a Tuesday — that he had first spent the night with Alice Wardell. Morally speaking, that had been mean, to Alice more than Georgie. He had used Alice, but it was hard not to, and Alice had not been the only one. It was fantastic how easy it was for a man past his youth to find clean, convenient sex, when boys in their teens mad with hunger couldn't get it at all. And it was all rather ordinary. Necessary, but ordinary.

From the outside, it must have looked like the old sordid story of a long-married man rutting round for extra excitement. Maybe it was nothing more than that, though his passion for Georgie herself had scarcely diminished. Alice and Denise and the others had never been anything better than substitutes, and *that* must have been eccentric, a married man who shut his eyes and thought about his wife while he was lying on his mistress. Ah well ah well, the whole thing was unbearably sad if you concentrated on thinking about it. It was wiser to take it as it came and live it. He could also remember the end of that long time of half-estrangement, the night when Georgie sat up at three in the morning and tinkered with the clock on the automatic tea-making gadget so that the light flashed on and the water started boiling there and then, and how they had drunk tea in the middle of the night and Georgie had said, "Remember the first weekend in University Avenue?"

"Mm."

"We thought it was marvelous."

"Mm. It was."

"It's better now."

"Mm. But if I was ten years younger I could do it again, now."

"You could still do it again, now."

But a few minutes later he had muttered into her ear, "What did I tell you? I'm falling asleep."

"So am I, but stay there and fall asleep, it's lovely. And anyway, I've set the alarm for six o'clock to see if anything develops."

The alarm had rung at six o'clock, and three minutes later

young Tommy had ambled in to ask if breakfast was ready. That was a good time to remember. It had happened, it was still real.

He hadn't made up his mind about going to Switzerland when he arrived home. Tommy had decided, out of character, to do some work in the garden. The abandoned lawn mower, hoe and rake were lying on the lawn ready to gather rust and Tom yelled at his son with the rage of righteousness. At least three times a week for years on end he had delivered careful lectures on how tools must be tidied away, and it was too infuriating to see the deliberate stupidity with which Tommy ignored every word. The boy answered his anger with one of his sullen unwinking silences, and went out to spend almost thirty minutes putting the tools in the shed.

And it was almost impossible to withdraw from one of those rages, Tom knew. The noise of it echoed long afterwards, any subsequent conversation became grunting mono-syllables, and father and son had both to endure a shared meal while avoiding each other's eyes, so that anger and resentment, instead of dying away, fed on the silence. After the meal, Tommy rose without a word and began to clear the table, washed the dishes and then put records on the gramophone. Even they failed to clear away the sullen silence, because they maddened Tom. He had nothing against popular music, in fact he had told Tommy so regularly, but the current songs seemed to have entered a condition of whining monotony, idiot chants sung by sexually precocious children who sounded as if they had IQ trouble and grubby underwear. He forced himself to endure the noise in silence for a while, thought of escaping to the garden to finish mowing the lawn, and decided that that would look too much like piling insult on contempt.

He thought of a book, but couldn't bring himself to enjoy

Trollope, and cursed Raymond Chandler for having been a lazy bum and having written too little. His final choice was a paperback thriller by an Englishwoman he had never heard of, and it was so precious and well bred that he fumed over it until finally it seemed so bad that he began to enjoy it and relax. Only then could he bring himself to mention the possibility of a trip to Switzerland, and he could feel his anger rising again when Tommy shrugged his shoulders and was positively apathetic.

"In any case," Tommy said, "the school holiday's practically finished. They don't like us going away in term time."

"I can fix that with the headmaster."

"What would we do in Switzerland?"

"My God, I don't know what we would do. I would have jumped at the chance when I was your age."

"Uhuh. Well, I suppose it's fixed."

"You could practice your French."

"Oh, great."

"What the hell's wrong with you?" Tom exploded. "You can stay at home if you want to."

"I wouldn't know anybody there, and you wouldn't want me dragging after you all the time."

"Oh hell, you can bring one of your pals with you if you like, I wash my hands of it."

"How much would it cost him?" It was the first time Tommy had shown even a glimmer of interest, and Tom felt guilt and anger too — it was always hard to distinguish how much of his anger with Tommy was anger at himself.

"I'll pay for him," he said. "If he gets permission."

"I'll see." That was the nearest thing Tommy could offer to an enthusiastic acceptance. Tom was practically decided to give up the idea.

On the following morning, however, Mrs. Crow moved into Stage Two. She had been quiet and unaggressive for some weeks, and Tom expected no forays, so when she brought the morning tea (whatever had happened to that automatic tea-making machine? Machines didn't try to rape their owners every time they came to the boil) he roused himself and thanked her and started to drink without a care in the world.

Later he decided that she must have left the room and then lurked on the landing outside, timing his movements with her built-in stopwatch. He finished the tea, got up luxuriously, let his pajama top fall to the floor and stepped out of his trousers; and with splendid timing, Mrs. Crow hurtled into the bedroom, crying wildly, "Are you finished with the tray, Mr. Fletcher?" and eating up his nakedness with her darting blue eyes. Her entrance was so sudden that Tom had an electric jolt of adrenalin and leapt several inches, and with a laugh that was meant to be embarrassed and knowing but sounded horribly rehearsed, Mrs. Crow stopped in her tracks, near enough to have touched him and thrown him on his back.

"That'll teach me to knock on a gentleman's bedroom!" she shrilled, while he gathered himself for escape. "But och! We're past the age to get worried about a thing like that, Mr. Fletcher, it's only nature and what I always say, nature is only natural, isn't it?" Tom had already pondered the wisdom of rushing from the room shouting *Fire*, or *Good heavens, the minister's at the front door*, and this idea brought him dangerously near to giggling, which would have been utterly fatal. Now he was nipping to the far side of the bed and shoving himself into his dressing gown, and Mrs. Crow, complacent in her disappointment, was picking up the tea tray.

"Some people are dirty-minded about things like that," she said piously, "but you and me are people of the world, well I mean, it's nearly like living in the same house, there's no secrets between . . . Anyway, you're not embarrassed, Mr. Fletcher, and no harm done, I always say, and I'll say this, if a man is still a fine figure of a man at your age he's got a lot to be thankful for. Was your tea all right?"

You couldn't be actually angry with the monstrous old bitch, her pleasure was so simple and squalid.

"Tommy and I are going away for two weeks, Mrs. Crow," he said, abolishing the incident. Her face crumpled in disappointment. "We're going to Switzerland," he added.

"Oh, that'll be nice, the mountains and that! Oh, I was always a great one for the traveling, but I never had the chances. That's my tragedy, Mr. Fletcher, I never had the chances."

"Shame." He started shaving.

"Here, you'll have to watch the house while you're away, there's a lot of burglaries about, Mr. Fletcher. I'll keep an eye on it for you."

"No need to trouble yourself, Mrs. Crow, I'll warn the police."

"Them! No, don't you worry, I'll be here to keep it tidy." And she added with horrifying coyness, "That's if you don't mind me being in the house while you're not here, that is."

"No, not at all. Welcome. You'll want to keep it dusted anyway, I suppose," Tom said airily.

"Yes, you leave it to me, Mr. Feltcher, and don't you worry about the money, we can settle all that when you get back. Oh Switzerland! It must be rare, you deserve a break, it'll set you up." Her eyes were eating his spine again. Yes, he was definitely going to Switzerland. There might be a hotel with a *young* nymphomaniac chambermaid. He couldn't handle a nymphomaniac of any age whatever, but it would at least be fun to dodge somebody young and beautiful as a change from dodging Mrs. Crow. He called a travel agency and booked plane seats and a hotel that morning.

Thirteen

THERE were many mundane experiences that had never entirely lost their excitement for Tom. Everything connected with a bank account, for instance — depositing money or withdrawing money, or writing a check. Even after thirty years, these ordinary actions had a dramatic quality that pleased him; a symptom of permanent adolescence, he fancied. He always felt he was writing checks in sight of an audience, and the audience was his own younger self, the self who had chafed against life in Maltdyke and had dreamed of a rich full life full of thrilling moments like the moment of writing a check. Driving a car retained some of the same delight; hearing a waiter address him by name; seeing nine or ten suits of clothes in his wardrobe, and even better, not being sure whether it *was* nine or ten. The pleasure wasn't always conscious, but it was always there. His temperament was a rubbish heap of disguised status symbolism, and the knowledge that this was childish merely increased the pleasure.

Air travel was best of all. It was a pity in a way that everybody no longer traveled abroad in big liners, because that had even more of the expansiveness he had craved as a boy. In those days, the transatlantic liner had been the essence of wealth and success and magic — hooters blowing, people throwing streamers, stewards serving champagne, hysterical farewells, and Tom himself indulgently smiling at them, obnoxiously blasé, exuding the world-weary charm of the man who has done it all too often. The big liners definitely had something you couldn't get in an airplane, but flying was fine too; there were tearful farewells in airport lounges just as on liners, and people were hurtling off to strange wonderful places a million miles from Maltdyke High Street.

Air travel was of course a damned nuisance; getting to and from airports was always a bind, and the insane delays, the endless hours spent waiting for delayed flights, they were all a curse. They must be, because air travelers talked about them incessantly. But when they talked about them, Tom was always struck by the note of hidden pride, the hint that they were entitled to complain about flying because they belonged to the magic group who flew everywhere while other people drove buses and licked stamps and sold soapflakes to housewives. It would be another generation, or at least a half-generation, before people complained about air travel with perfect simplicity because they genuinely took it for granted. Young Tommy's generation, for instance, who had grown up weary of television at an age when he himself had never yet heard a radio.

To be fair, young Tommy was openly excited while they waited for the flight to Geneva; probably because he had a schoolmate with him, to share the excitement and encourage him. The other boy, Albert Enterkin, was a plump kid whom Tom had never seen before. He wore glasses and giggled a lot, and to Tom's surprise, his own son giggled too. Kids were a self-infectious shower. At home, Tommy's laughter was always short and often derisory. In this other kid's company he chattered and sniggered. It was impossible to know exactly what was going on in their minds, and it was useless to try. Were they grateful for the trip? If they were, they wouldn't make a song about it. Gratitude was one of those uncomfortable processes. When he found himself committed to offering a free holiday to one of Tommy's schoolmates, he had wondered briefly how it would feel to the other boy, but there were no standards of comparison. Kids nowadays had plenty, they were used to it. The ideal boy to be offered the trip would have been himself, at the age of fourteen, in Maltdyke, when foreign travel was a strange remote adventure that only happened to other people in books or the movies. *That* would have been something: if some total stranger had arrived one afternoon in Maltdyke and told him that he was going to Switzerland the next day. The excitement would have been too painful to endure. Nowadays it would be taken for granted.

But no, he would have endured the excitement, he would have said thank you quite quietly and kept the thrill locked inside, he would have looked calm and unruffled and shown that he was adult and poised. So this kid Enterkin might well be bursting with gratitude and why was he, Tom, brooding about it anyway? It must be the air-conditioning in the air-port lounge that was making him sleepy and reflective. The flight was called and the boys strained beside him, forcing themselves to walk as slowly as he did; and they chattered without end. They were excited enough, but they didn't chatter about the trip; they seemed to be going through a long private joke about some other kids in their class at school. People looked round at them, listened to the burst of giggling and smiled.

Young Tommy was wearing his school blazer and flannels, he had insisted on it although Tom had bought him a new lightweight suit for the trip, and now Tom realized that the boy had probably wanted to look as much like his friend Enterkin as possible, since Enterkin was dressed identically.

Enterkin was an only child, the son of a widow, and might be short of money for fancy clothes. Seeing the boys together, and remembering how impatiently he had bawled at Tommy for not wearing his new clothes, Tom recognized that his son had shown tact and taste in his decision, but wondered why the hell the boy hadn't mentioned the reason. There would be no way now in which he could let him know that he understood and approved. Being a father was a doomed enterprise.

He wouldn't exert himself on this trip to Lausanne. Meg Macrae regarded it as a big-time secret conspiracy, but Meg still had some curiously romantic views about business. It would be nice to see the Comtoir Suisse and do some very gentle sightseeing, and if the weather was good, a little swimming and a lot of sitting around in the sun. The boys would obviously enjoy themselves on their own and he could spend a couple of weeks doing nothing whatever, no big deals, no business, no women; a fair amount of drink and good food and a lot of peace.

No women. That was going to be an agreeable change. The women business was grossly overrated. If you paid for it, it was unsatisfying, and if you wanted it for nothing, romantically, it was a constant drain on the nerves. He was glad he wasn't young, in his hungry youth when he couldn't relax unless somebody was falling in love with him, which meant that most of the time he couldn't rest at all. Age might be dull, but it didn't wear you out.

On the plane, the boys dived into the flight maps and were off on a long giggle about pilots losing their way and crashing into dung heaps and bailing out without telling the passengers. He ordered himself a whisky and dug out one of the books he had brought, a new abridgment of Gibbons' *Decline and Fall* running to nine hundred pages. The sheer weight of its title made him feel slightly self-conscious, but he had found a new pleasure in the decision that he now had time to read all the books he had missed in youth. He was tired of talking about classics without reading them, and Gibbon should be a good beginning. As he read, he wondered idly what kind of man he would have become if he had been born into a comfortable family with money and leisure. Totally different, because money would have been as normal as air and he would never have had to point his energies to earning it. He might have taken an arts course at the university, read Anglo-Saxon, played the piano — Bach, probably, in that at least he would have been unchanged. Bach was the boy for people who loved mathematics and calculation.

He had speculated on the subject often, without regret or frustration, and he found it cropping up in his mind more often in recent months. In the twilight of our years we look backward. He grinned at himself for thinking such a corny thought. Maybe he could still learn to play the piano — not well, but for private satisfaction.

Or Greek? He had never met a Greek scholar, never felt that Greek was a loss in his life, but if so many intelligent people adored it, it clearly had something, and it too was a piece of equipment, a tool, just as good psychology and quick calculation were tools, that made a man more efficient and more of a man. The stewardess was blond and brown-eyed and French-speaking, the straps of her brassiere showed through her white blouse, and her buttocks moved with sweet charm under the fine cloth of her skirt. He surveyed them with absent-minded, avuncular approval. He was most decidedly on holiday, he realized, because his mind had gone into a soothing coma and he liked everything; the weight of the book on his knees, the taste of the whisky, the whine of the engines and the sight of a live girl; he liked them all without being bothered or overstimulated by any of them. As the girl walked up the aisle of the aircraft he noticed Tommy too was following her with his eyes, and he sighed amiably to himself. The boy was coming to the age, the terrible thrills, the wild discoveries, the panic curiosity. He would be easier to live with, surely, when he emerged into manhood and all its delights, and he was welcome to them. Tom stared, unfocused, at his open book, and saw Tommy nudge Albert and mutter something, without ever taking his eyes from the female sweetness of the stewardess. Albert prattled on, and Tommy nudged him again.

"So what?" he heard Albert's high-pitched voice cutting through the hum. "Women are for the birds."

"No, birds are for the birds," Tommy riposted, and they were off on a giggle again.

The sun shone and the lake sparkled, and it had been a brilliant idea to stop everything and have a holiday. The hotel, booked at short notice during a busy season, wasn't the best in Lausanne, but it was fine, and although it was some distance from the shore, the two bedrooms had balconies overlooking the water. After the first morning, when they all three breakfasted in the dining room, Tom asserted the privilege of having his coffee and rolls alone, on his private balcony, and left the children to manage for themselves, and to his relief, they appeared grateful to be abandoned. He established a daily routine of waking, switching on the radio and taking whatever came out — soothing music or long educational talks in French, of which he caught every sixth word — and persuaded himself this was improving his mind by brainwashing. While it played, he showered slowly, in blessed leisure, and for fun, pretended to do pushups for five minutes, and then usually had another shower.

Then he half dressed and called for breakfast, and sat on the balcony for at least an hour, drinking coffee and working slowly through all the newspapers he could get, in any language, and tried to get the gist of them. On the table beside his coffee he put an English-French dictionary and his current book. He had interrupted the *Decline and Fall* and switched to *The Idiot*, and had no guilt about this uncharacteristic behavior because he was on holiday and Gibbon would still be in his bag when he got back home.

After breakfast he usually joined the boys and strolled through the town. They swam in the pool; they took a trip on a lake steamer, they shopped for cheap souvenirs, they sat in the sun and drank lemonade. The boys alternately slumped happily in the warmth and conducted conversations with most of the sense missed out. They had a rapport, or a secret code, that Tom couldn't recall from his own youth; it was as if everything they had ever seen or known together had been boiled down to one word or phrase, and they could hold discussions by simply connecting a series of the private phrases. It would have irritated him if the atmosphere hadn't relaxed him so much. The Enterkin boy — and in a way, it was a relief to discover this — irritated him slightly more than his own son did. His giggling didn't seem entirely spontaneous, you got the impression that he was in favor of hysteria and kept trying to drum it up when it wasn't there naturally. But what the hell, that was what it was like to be young; you were afraid to let any excitement die out in case it never came back.

The town, and especially the pool, was well supplied with splendid healthy young girls, of whom Tom approved dispassionately but whom the boys appeared not to notice. One morning, sitting on his balcony, Tom overheard them talking on theirs, with reckless clarity. Albert was saying, "Ach, you always want to go to the pool, it's square, swimming all the time."

"You could improve your crawl," Tommy said, not too interested.

"Who wants to crawl? And all those dames would give you the pip. Look at me, big boy —" Albert's voice changed to a whining female impersonation — "look at me in my bikini, you can see my belly button!"

"They can't help having belly buttons," Tommy said. "I don't mind them."

"Ach! They give me the pip."

When Tom found himself alone with his son later in the day, he remarked casually that there were a lot of good-looking lassies in Lausanne. Tommy shrugged.

"You're too young to be interested, I suppose," Tom said.

"No," Tommy said airily, "I'm quite biological, actually. Albert's not very keen on girls."

"No. So I've noticed."

"Actually," Tommy said, "I suspect that he's a potential homosexual. His physique and his environment are very suggestive of the tendency."

"Eh?" Tom was startled. "What the hell goes on in your mind? You're moving out of that room today. You're not sharing a room with anybody like that!"

"Keep the head, keep the head, Dad," Tommy said wearily. "His tendencies are only potential and you've got nothing to worry about. I'm too normal. The alternative theory is that he's frightened of girls because he's got a potbelly and they laugh at him. He's all *right*. Adolescence takes different forms in various people."

Tom gave up.

On the fourth day he took the boys to the Exhibition, and they rapidly succeeded in losing themselves. He consciously became a tourist and walked very slowly round the pavilions gawping and admiring and not giving a hoot. It was only by accident, or perhaps because of the presence of a spectacular Negro girl near the exhibit, that he found himself looking at an array of the products of the Kutsu Manufacturing Corporation of Kobe. He wasn't certain at first whether the girl came with the exhibit or whether she was a tourist like himself, but she was delicious to behold, tall and slender and magnificently black in a slim straight green dress. He found himself naturally standing beside her.

"Wonderful people, the Japanese," he said.

"There is no conceivable way of denying that," she said with a beautiful smile. She was American.

"Are you interested in electronics?" he asked.

"They have their engaging qualities. Or is it 'it'? I never know whether electronics is singular or plural. I'm only a woman."

"I noticed that."

"Well, thank you kindly sir," she said and laughed. She had been joined by a short young man, a Japanese, in a dark silk suit. "This is The Man himself," she said. "Mr. Kutsu. I'm sorry I didn't catch your name — I know, you didn't throw it." She was a delight to the senses.

"Call me Harry," said the Japanese, and held out his hand.

"Fletcher."

Kutsu shook his hand firmly and looked him straight in the eye.

"Fletcher?"

"That's right." And since something else seemed to be called for, he added, "Call me Tom if you like."

"Thomas Fletcher. Of Glasgow, Scotland, England. It's a small world, man." He pronounced Glasgow 'Glass-cow' instead of Glaz-go, and everything else in his intonation was flawless American, not of any particular region but a generalized American accent and without a trace of Japanese.

"Astonishing," Tom said. "You must have one of your computers built into your brain."

"Hey, quit stealing my gags, man," Kutsu said, grinning and pumping his hand. "That's Harry's own line, let me tell you. I use magnetic tape in place of gray cells — Kutsu products last longer than people. How about that?"

"Good line," Tom agreed. "People are finished anyway."

"That is what I keep telling people, man! The human race? Pfui! It's a lousy engineering job, it'll never get off the goddam ground." The only un-American thing about him was a faint excess of Americanism, and perhaps that too was merely an illusion caused by the contrast between his appearance and his speech. "Run along, doll," he said, "and mix our good friend Tom some quaint old folksy Yokohama wood alcohol."

The colored girl smiled and disappeared through a doorway, and when Tom held up a hand in refusal, Kutsu thumped him on the arm and said, "Easy, man, it's only a fiendishly clever Oriental gag — a precise chemical replica of whisky obtained by importing the goddam stuff from Glasgow, Scotland, England."

The colored girl returned bearing a small tray with two glasses, and Kutsu sniffed his with greedy enthusiasm.

"Neat ginger ale?" Tom asked him.

"Goddammit, man, you must have Nip blood in you, I should try to fool a Scotchman yet." Kutsu smiled and drank, and said, "Our beautiful handmaiden is Hildegarde, by the way. Hildegarde, Tom. Tom, Hildegarde. Hildegarde is black but comely, ain't that right, honey?"

"That's what you keep telling me," she agreed amiably. Tom smiled at her over Kutsu's head, but she was looking at

Kutsu and not at him, and he had a twinge of disappointment. The girl was so relaxed and self-contained, and Kutsu was so boyishly exuberant that Tom had half expected to exchange an indulgent smile with her. It pricked his vanity that she should ignore him. She discreetly withdrew, and Kutsu took his arm and swung him round to face the exhibits.

"Now man," he said, "I want to get you drunk enough to act reckless, but sober enough to sign an order blank. I don't aim to give you a hard sell on Kutsu products, Tom, they're merely the greatest; why try to employ the inadequate tool of the language of Shakespeare to describe something beyond words? How about that?"

"Yes, I appreciate the soft sell."

"That's my boy. Dammit, I'm not a salesman, I'm a simple engineer, an electronic hick, man."

"Good. I'm not buying anything."

"So we start even, man!"

On the evidence of his products, Kutsu was no hick of any kind. Tom found him a mass of mysteries. It was difficult to assess his age, but he sounded like thirty-five or even less, so presumably he wasn't the original Kutsu, but a son or a nephew or even a grandson of the boss. A Japanese company would always have plenty of sons to manage its departments. Or was it the Chinese who went in for a lot of sons? The other intriguing thing was the range of Kutsu stuff. Without going into the question, Tom had assumed that the new Japanese precision industries had boomed through close specialization; one company, one product. Kutsu seemed to produce anything that occurred to them, the inevitable pocket radios, intercom sets, laboratory oscilloscopes, radio testing equipment, echo sounders and of course the midget computer. This last was surely, it must be, fairly crude and rudimentary as computers went, but it was a long way ahead of a mere office calculating machine. And the tiny size was a bit of a swindle because for many of its operations it had to be linked to a data-printing machine that was bigger than the computer itself. Even so, it was a tidy piece of work. Even confined to simple payroll work, it could pay for itself in a company of anything over a hundred employees. He itched to get his hands on it and play with it in private, and he had to remind himself that the thing was of no serious interest to him unless some of Gaylor's top boys decided to import it to Britain.

Kutsu was completely unperturbed when Tom repeatedly assured him that he wasn't buying anything. It was only money, he said. It was possible, of course, that the Kutsu Corporation wasn't a manufacturing company at all, but merely a big sales outfit putting its own brand name on stuff from a dozen little companies. That would explain the diversity of the machines. If it was all reliable stuff, at least it was interesting, and he found his own computer filing figures away.

When he was leaving, Kutsu shook his hand again, and said suddenly, "Hey, man, are you alone in this town?"

"I've got two kids, but yes, I'm alone."

"Great, great. Be my guest for the evening, we'll louse up the joint. I get tired of these goddam foreigners, and that's the truth."

It was impossible not to laugh.

"A deal," Kutsu said. "Give me your hotel, I'll call for you. Everything will be arranged of the best, but the best. See you, Tom."

"Check, Harry."

He was still on holiday, and he was determined to remain on holiday, but he found himself back in his hotel room putting through a telephone call to Glasgow and asking for Meg Macrae.

"Get off that telephone, Tom Fletcher," she shouted at him. "Away and chase women, you're wasting money."

"I will in a minute, Meg," he said. "How is everything?"

"I'm not giving you any information, Tom Fletcher, you're on holiday. I admit big-man N.G. is looking for you, but I expect he only wants to sack you, so don't you be fretting about such trivialities. I've told him you're touring and that there's no forwarding address, so go and get drunk or something and stop bothering me."

"I'll see him in London on the way home."

"Don't be a bloody fool, let him come and see you. What's up? You're not in jail again, are you?"

"Not yet, I'm too lazy. Shut up, Meg, for a minute. I want you to find the price of the cheapest radio telephone you can buy. Radio telephone for small yachts."

"Oh God! What kind of business are we getting into? Smuggling?"

"Shut up and just take a note of it, Meg. Also echo sounders, you know, for checking the depth of the sea."

"Get a grip, Tom, you must be getting senile. All that stuff was in the garbage that Japanese company sent you."

"I know. I want the prices of the competition, you silly old bitch."

"Less of your lip, Tom Fletcher, I clipped that to the Japanese garbage last week and you haven't had the wits to look at it. The cheapest echo sounder here is about forty quid. The cheapest radio telephone is about a hundred and ninety. But what are you going to do with an echo sounder? Lark about in the sewers?"

"My God. No, forget it, Meg, I was just nosy. I'll send you a postcard."

"Never mind the postcard, bring me some sexy scent. And don't let me hear another word out of you, I thought I had got rid of you. Is that all?"

"Yes."

"Have a nice time. Goodbye."

The telephone was firmly hung up.

Tom found himself looking forward to an evening with Harry Kutsu. Solitude from adult company had been soothing, now he was ready to be social again. Tommy and Albert wanted to go to a cinema to see *Ben Hur* in a French-dubbed version, so that they could giggle at the translation, and at eight o'clock Kutsu knocked on his bedroom door and zoomed into the room cradling a bottle of Johnnie Walker.

"You're my guest in here," Tom protested, and took a bottle from the table at the bedside. Evidently it was going to be a big wild night. Harry stood grinning up at him and radiating happiness. Tom grinned back and sat down on the bed.

At once Kutsu gave him a shrewd look and said, "Tact, man, that's tact. But you don't hafta sit because you're a yard taller than me, for God's sakes you can't spend the entire evening on your tail just to be *polite*."

"I'm only a few inches taller than you."

"Inch, schminch. Be comfortable like me. Be emotionally integrated, you know what that involves? Emotional integration consists in knowing your potentialities and your limitations and not getting your categories confused, man. Me, I accept my identity. I honestly do not give one frigging goddam what size I am or anybody else is except from the neck up."

"Even women?"

"Women are a totally separate problem, I said don't get your categories confused. Hey, I haven't forgotten that small detail, Tom, when you get quaint old Oriental hospitality you get the works: dine, wine and poon. He is all arrange, señor."

"Really?" Tom laughed helplessly.

"You know this fact, man?" Harry waved his glass at Tom. "You hardly speak a friggin' word, you know that? How come I want to go on the town with a dummy like you? But you have a way of not saying a friggin' word, Tom. I like that. I admire a man that can keep his big blabbermouth shut."

"You haven't given me a friggin' chance to open it."

"Yeah, I know. We make a great team, see what I mean? You're one of those tightlipped Englishmen —"

"Scotsmen."

"— yeah, so Scotsmen, sorry, and I'm the original self-made Westernized Nip. I invented myself, you know that? I invented myself from nothing, man."

"Jolly good show."

"Jolly good show! I like that." Harry waggled his head with pleasure and poured more whisky and lay back in the armchair. He was wearing a dark green suit, almost black, and a white shirt with a dark green bow tie tucked under the collar. He looked very neat and handsome. "Where I come from, my boy," he said solemnly, "we go for the ancestor bit, somewhat. I started life with one great asset. No ancestors. Not one smidgin of blood kin in the entire universe."

"Tough."

"So am I. I'm tough, man. I invented myself, didn't I? So I had the choice, tough or nothing. But what's with the life story? Who cares? Forget it."

"Tell it anyway, the town doesn't waken up for an hour at least."

"I should be so cruel to a stranger? Have another snort." He poured another snort and went on to make with the life-story bit regardless. None of it surprised Tom very much. It rang familiarly and was different from his own, he felt, only in degree of toughness and in the greater distance Kutsu had traveled. Perhaps the extra toughness had made him travel farther. Orphaned just before the war, he had started to fend for himself when he was hardly more than infant, owning nothing, owing nothing, believing nothing except survival. He had actually enjoyed the war because it tended to make people equal — life was suddenly rough for everybody, and as a half-starved urchin he felt better trained for it than most people. His English, as anyone might have surmised, had been acquired from the Americans after the war, and unlike many Japanese with a firmer grip on old traditions, he had embraced the Americans with joy. They were simple, guileless and generous and frantic to be kind. Kutsu set out to get everything these millionaires could offer, starting as an energetic beggar and working up through casual messenger to houseboy, secretary and protégé of the sentimental, kindly wife of an Air Force Colonel.

He boasted that throughout three years he had spent no money at all. Hardship was so ingrained in him that he couldn't bring himself to believe that the plushy new life wouldn't suddenly vanish. He worked at picking up money with total concentration, and kept all of it, and at the same time ate like an emperor, chauffeured his employer and had the use of her car when she didn't need it. He was utterly reliable, utterly indoctrinated, one instant convert to democracy and honesty and the Western way of life. Mrs. Carson had worn him like a diadem. Mrs. Carson paid for his correspondence course in radio, heaped equipment on him and knew that her skill and her sound Iowa instincts had bridged the gulf between East and West. She wept when her husband was transferred home. Harry opened a store at once, and it prospered at once.

He stole ideas from everybody, took out a subscription to *Fortune*, studied the stock exchange, and when the transistor arrived, designed a radio that could be assembled in anybody's living room. It was manufactured by three hundred women working at home.

Suddenly everything was booming. He built and bought and borrowed and still studied the world at large so that he could keep level or a jump ahead with what the world would want next. At thirty-two he was a millionaire.

"So I throw in a few ideas now and then," he admitted modestly. "I travel around now and then. I do what the hell I please. Say, man, are you ever going to break down and buy some high-class Kutsu junk? I don't care, but you could make a lot of dough, man. I never bothered about England till now, I don't need it, and another funny thing, nobody in England ever bothered about me till I got your letter. Is everybody dead there or something? If you don't want to talk business, forget it, Tom, let's live a little."

"I like the stuff," Tom said, "so I'll tell you now that I thought about it when I wrote the letter, but I can't see it now. My own company's changed, and I'm only a small man in a big outfit. Somebody else does the buying."

"Shit, buy it yourself with your pin money and sell it on the side, I don't care. I'll give you credit — for anything up to two hours," he added. Then he looked questioningly at Tom. "Forget it?" he asked. "It's okay with me."

"Forget it. I think."

"Keep on thinking, it's very healthful. Have another snort and we'll blow."

They never quite succeeded in getting to solid food — Harry kept insisting that they could eat later, that it was all arranged. They moved from place to place listening to music and drinking and looking at people. Tom wondered what had become of the beautiful Negro girl. Late in the evening they were at a ringside table in a night club, still drinking, and Harry suddenly said, "Hey man, the stripper's about to appear. Have you anything to read? Any old letters, books, anything?"

"A French dictionary?" Harry sounded merely merry, and Tom felt merely merry.

"The greatest," said Harry. "Let us read together. Aw, go on, it's a gag I've always wanted to pull. They fling on these broads to peel off, and what the heck is the use of that to a healthy American boy? Just *watching?* Anyway, any broad looks alike in a G-string, it's an insult to emotionally integrated manhood. I propose we bow our heads and study the beautiful French language all the time this bag is pulling them down and show the world that we're above all that trash."

The idea appealed strongly, and Tom moved his chair so that they could both pore over the tiny French dictionary. Somebody at an adjacent table shouted cheerfully to them to warn them that flesh was about to be stripped, but Tom turned and smiled politely and returned to the book. The room darkened, there was a roll of drums and the first stripper came on. The band played Ellington's "Caravan."

"They wrote real pop music in those days," Tom said happily. A girl shimmied past the side of his head, a foot away, with one hand running up and down her own spine.

"What's the French for nuts?" Harry asked him. Somebody nearby shushed savagely.

"I think it's *noix*," Tom said, and they bent their heads together over the book. It was too dark, outside the spotlight, to read the small print. Harry struck a match and held it close to the pages. Somebody shouted, "Hey, don't set it on fire!" Harry, with the match burning down to his fingers, had crouched over the table and was holding his stomach with the other hand. In the dim light Tom could see his face twisted and his eyes bulging, and his first thought was that the little man had been stabbed by an ulcer. Then a little spurt of sound came from Harry's tight lips and Tom realized that Kutsu was having hysterics. Tom frowned, and heard himself tittering.

A high, terrifying wail came from Harry, the shriek of indrawn breath, followed by a seizure of laughter. Tears were running down Tom's face.

At half past midnight he was in jail.

He and Harry were sharing a cell. The Japanese sat on one of the bunks on crossed feet, with the grave smile of a yogi.

"I imagine this is a capital charge in Switzerland," Tom said placidly. "This Meg Macrae must have the sicht, the bitch. Second sight. It's an old Highland custom. Thank God they keep clean jails in Switzerland. They're horrible in Spain, I hear."

"How about your kids?" Harry muttered, without moving his lips.

"Oh, you crafty Oriental Buddha," Tom said, and Harry grinned. "You've remembered you can speak English." Harry shook his head violently. "I'm not worried about the kids," Tom said. "They'd go to bed without looking for me." Harry nodded.

A little later the cell door opened and an inspector came in, a heavy milk-fed Swiss who moved slowly and rubbed the back of his neck.

"You are Mr. Fletcher," he accused Tom, who nodded, "and you are Mr. Kutsu." Harry smiled and shook his head and emitted a long sentence in Japanese. The inspector rubbed his face.

"He doesn't speak English?" he asked Tom.

"I've no idea."

"But you are known to each other."

"Only today."

The inspector gave him a long skeptical look. The no-spikka-da-lingo routine must have been old stuff, but since Harry had started it, they had to go on with it. He looked down at Tom, and Tom moved along the bunk and motioned him to sit, but he remained standing, wearily.

"Would you like to explain your version of the incident?" he asked. Harry stared up at him with an expression of eager stupidity.

"No," Tom said. "I would rather have your explanation. Also I would like to telephone my lawyer. In London," he added. He had the happy knowledge that his head was clear, his diction precise, and that at the same time the liquor had relaxed his nerves. It could be a dangerous condition, he also knew, but the danger pleased him. "Also," he said, "I would like to telephone the London *Daily Express*."

"That is not possible." The inspector was impatient. "You were drunk and you started a fight."

"Your English is perfect," Tom said. The inspector didn't respond. "As you can see, we are not drunk. We didn't start a fight, we were attacked."

"You started a fight."

"Is that the charge?"

"The charge is not yet made."

"Whom did we attack?"

"I will ask the questions, Mr. Fletcher."

"You will not."

"I advise you not to be insolent, Mr. Fletcher, you are in prison."

"I advise you," said Tom, "that this is Switzerland, it is not a banana republic in South America. This country is the model democracy and the liberty of man is sacred." He was near the danger line, and he drew back from it. "I am sorry, Inspector, I don't mean to embarrass you, but what I say is true." He forced himself to look earnest, because he could hear himself winding up for a speech to the jury in an American TV series, and it would be fatal to laugh and ruin the atmosphere. "Mr. Kutsu and I were attacked. Obviously, neither of us is drunk. Do you usually lock up the injured parties in Lausanne?"

The inspector sat down heavily and did some more face-rubbing.

"Mr. Fletcher," he said, "it is not my choice that you are here. We do not like to arrest visitors. We like that everything is peaceful and nice. But it will not help to deny the facts."

Tom decided to attack, and to take the risk of standing up.

"There are no facts," he said impatiently. "And there aren't any witnesses either. Don't try to intimidate us, Inspector —" an expression of gross outrage crossed the inspector's face — "because the entire affair is nonsense. We were sitting peacefully at a table when a drunk man attacked us. Where is *he?*"

"You are not helping yourself, Mr. Fletcher. It is a fact that . . . Mr. Kutsu . . . attacked a young woman, a performer in the club."

"Attacked her? She sat in his lap!"

"He bit her, Mr. Fletcher. In . . . in a particular place."

"Did he? I didn't hear her squealing." He tried not to look at Harry, who was still sitting on the bunk, darting his eyes back and forth eagerly to follow the ball. The crafty little opportunist, thought Tom. If he had bitten the stripper, he must have moved with the speed of a cobra.

"He bit her," the inspector said firmly.

"Does it show? Is she going to give evidence?" Tom demanded. "It's more likely she pushed it in his mouth." It was too much. He burst into laughter. Fortunately, Harry remained grave and eager and soundless.

"It is not amusing."

"It might sound amusing in court, all the same."

"I hope that will not be necessary."

"Oh? Oh! In that case, what's the purpose of this discussion, Inspector?"

"We are not to be laughed at, Mr. Fletcher. Also we do not like people who make trouble. If you are thinking of leaving Lausanne, you will be free to go. It will be more pleasant for you in another place."

"I'm sorry, Inspector, it will not be more pleasant. We are not tourists. Mr. Kutsu is president of the largest electronic company in Japan. He is an official guest of the Swiss government. I am the managing director of a British company on a buying mission. We are in Lausanne to support your trade fair, not to be victimized by the police."

The inspector digested this and was weary of all of it.

"Do not imagine, Mr. Fletcher, that Swiss justice can be influenced by a man's position in society."

"Good," said Tom. "I would despise you if you had said anything else."

"Good."

"So what are you going to do about it?"

The inspector had stood up. Now he sat down again, and sighed.

"Keep your friends away from the night clubs, please. We like to be peaceful. We don't like Swiss citizens to be bitten."

"Not in public?"

"And not in a particular place."

"You are very kind, Inspector."

"It is true you were laughing at the performer."

"Yes, it's true. We thought she was funny."

"Some are better than others. There is one who is quite artistic."

"I don't think I'll bother seeing her."

"No. No, there are many other entertainments. Lausanne

has much to offer. Oh. If I might make a request, Mr. Fletcher. Please try to look sad when you pass the sergeant."

"Sad and frightened?"

"Not too much. Yes, a little frightened, that would be acceptable. We understand each other."

Tom held out his hand, and the inspector shrugged before he took it. They left the cell and went to the sergeant's desk. Harry overplayed it wildly, cowering his head into his shoulders and cringing away from the inspector. He was a very dangerous man, Harry.

It was after one o'clock when they reached Harry's hotel suite. A table was set for four, with salad and fruit and champagne. A portable phonograph was playing Brubeck. In one armchair Hildegarde, the Negro girl, was sitting calmly reading a book. She wore heavy horn-rimmed glasses; and a simple shapeless dress of some soft stuff in pale blue. Stretched on the sofa was another colored girl, whose spectacular torso had been sprayed with flame-red silk. The second girl leapt at them as they entered and engulfed Harry.

"Honey lamb, wheah have you *been?*" she cried. "We was like to grow old and die, waitin' and wonderin'."

"This yere is Jennifer," Harry's muffled voice said from the girl's bosom. "That's Tom." He swung the girl off her feet and threw her back on the sofa, zoomed round the room and patted Hildegarde's hand as he passed her. She took off the glasses and smiled at him.

"You'll never believe it, we just been sprung from Alcatraz!" he said. "Zowie! We was framed, I tell ya! Come on, move it, Jennifer and make with the bubbly and listen to the sad story. And man, this man is the most, you shoulda *heard* the bum, Tom, you shoulda been a big time lawyer, this I tell you. Come on, park it here, like it was reconstructing the crime, and I'll sit here, and Jenny, you're the stripper."

Jenny, recklessly overfilling glasses with champagne, squeaked with joy and started to swivel her hips instantly. Hildegarde sat up in her chair with a gentle happy smile and Harry launched into a wild reconstruction of the affair at the night club. Tom was not surprised when Jenny threw herself into the performance as the stripper; in fact, Harry had to order her back several times because she wouldn't wait for her cue. The whole thing was funnier in Harry's version than it had been in fact. In pleasant fatigue, Tom sat beside him and enjoyed it while Hildegarde continued to sit in the arm-chair with a maternal smile, and occasionally applauded. When the story reached the big climax, Jennifer abruptly unzipped the flame-red silk and sat on Harry's knee, and his head darted towards her and back again.

"Ayeeee!" she said. "What in the world was the lady complainin' about? Do it again, honey lamb, quick like that."

"Ah hell," said Harry, "I need some cold food first. Let's eat, and Tom can do the big speech bit in Alcatraz."

Tom, however, didn't have to do the big speech bit, since Harry was still continuing the performance as they sat at the table and ate cold meat and salad and drank champagne. Jennifer gobbled excitedly and bobbed with excitement and urged him on. Hildegarde was the quiet one. She was happy without hysteria, and when she laughed it was low and warm. What was exercising Tom was what was to happen next, when the meal was over. It wasn't too difficult to guess at the relationship among the three, Harry and the two girls. They were secretaries or traveling companions or social assistants, either casually acquired or permanent; and if it seemed eccentric for a Japanese to have two Negro girls, well, everybody in the world looked eccentric to somebody. What interested him was what would be expected of him. In a gently growing lassitude, he decided it couldn't be too important.

"Do it all over, honey," Jennifer pleaded. "I want to get the stripper part *jest* right."

"Ah, nah," Harry said. "It's gettin' late, private performances only after 2 A.M."

"For me, honey?" Jennifer squeaked. Harry's eyes flickered round all three of them and then he shrugged in Yiddish. "Why not?" he said. "Make yourself comfortable, Tom." His eyes lingered momentarily on Hildegarde, and she returned a small smile as Jennifer took his arm and urged him through the door to an adjoining room. A peaceful silence followed.

"He's quite a man," Tom said.

"He is all of that." Hildegarde gave him her warm smile. There was a soothing quality about her . . . ladylike? Yes, he decided, ladylike. She rose gracefully from the table and said, "Shall we go?" Her hand indicated the other door. Tom looked slowly at her.

"It's late," he said. "Maybe I should go home."

"He might be offended if you did."

"You wouldn't be?"

She smiled the slow warm smile.

"No. But he would. You can rest here."

He followed her into the bedroom, and the sight of the bed brought a sigh of pleasure from him. He slipped off his shoes and lay back against the pillows. Hildegarde was standing, unconsciously graceful, at a dressing table, taking off earrings and ring. As he watched sleepily, she undressed without coquettishness, as if she had been alone; or like a woman undressing in the same room as her husband with the casualness of years. Just as casually she turned round when she was finished.

"Lumme," he muttered. "You don't know how beautiful you are, Hildegarde."

She smiled.

"A girl has to be something. Excuse me."

He watched her dreamily till she disappeared through a door, and then heard the hiss of a shower and his eyes closed gratefully. He opened them to find her unbuttoning his collar.

"I can do that," he protested mildly. ·

"Not lying down." She urged him to his feet and went on loosening his shirt.

"You're rather pretty too," she said.

"I'm a tired old man, Hildegarde." Impatient with such nonsense, she pushed him playfully and he fell back laughing onto the bed. She pushed him aside and lay alongside him.

"Which do you prefer?" she asked. "Conversation or amorous dalliance?"

He raised himself on one elbow to enjoy the sight of her. Her skin was dry and smooth and matt to his fingertip.

"Which do *you* prefer?"

"My only aim is to please," she said. The warm smile was almost a barrier defending her thoughts.

"I have a suspicion," he said, "that you wouldn't prefer either."

She looked at him, still smiling, till the smile wavered, and then said, "I'll be most happy to suit your mood, Tom."

"You haven't answered the question," he said. "I suspect you would prefer neither. True or false?"

"You're a very gentle man, Tom," she said after a pause. "All right, I would prefer neither. Why don't we pull the covers over and sleep?"

"If we do that something's bound to happen," he protested.

"If it happens, that's different," she said. They got under the covers. She put one arm round him and cradled her head on his shoulder. Almost at once, she was asleep. He would never sleep, he knew. The unique excitement of this girl was too much; he turned his mind to the fact of her body where it

touched his and as a matter of logic he knew . . . he knew
. . . and then on the other hand, he pitched into a coma.

Hildegarde was sitting on the edge of the bed touching him
gently on the shoulder, and the smell of coffee was in his nostrils. It was daylight.

"Hi," she said.

"Hi."

"I thought you would want to get home before breakfast.
It's six o'clock."

"Do you want rid of me?"

"No, Tom, I enjoy your company, I honestly do."

"Why have you no clothes on?"

"I thought you liked me this way. Why not? It's not cold."

"I'm more dangerous at this time of the day," he said. "At
least, I *think* I'm more dangerous."

"Will I get back into bed?"

He looked at her, and they both laughed.

"Nope," he said. "I'll regret this for the rest of my life, but
if I've stuck out the night I can restrain myself at six in the
morning. Put clothes on, though, not that it makes any difference. You look just as good dressed."

She started to dress, and then came back and sat on the bed.

"You're a very nice man, Tom. You don't talk much."

"A relief from Harry?"

"Ooh, I wasn't thinking about that. I'm just wild about
Harry."

"Are you?"

"Naturally."

"Are you?" he insisted. She lay down on the bed and put
her hands behind her head.

"I surely am. You may now laugh."

"I never laugh at this time in the morning. How long have
you known him?"

"Ah, now we've spoiled it. I thought you were wonderful because men always have to ask *questions*. You didn't, but now I've started you off."

"Don't answer the questions."

"I don't mind," she said. "I've known Harry for years and years. We met him in Japan. Jennifer and I were in the Wacs. Harry liked us, we didn't want to go back home, we stayed."

"And here you are."

"Yup. And don't think it hasn't been fun."

"But you're wild about Harry."

"Women are funny that way, Tom."

"And how do you feel about people like me?"

She gave him the slow smile again, and then said, "No, let's not go into that."

"You clever Hildegarde, you!" he said. "You talk them *all* out of it!"

"Usually. Do you mind?"

"No, I'm glad."

"Men are funny like that."

"What about Jennifer?"

She didn't understand the question.

"I mean, Jennifer and Harry."

"Oh, that. Jennifer's fine with me, she enjoys a good time. Harry takes care of us very well, you know, we're very lucky girls."

"And you don't mind."

"Leave my unconscious mind alone, will you?"

"Lucky old Harry."

"Uhuh."

Tom rose and dressed and she sat on the bed and watched him, a gentle undisturbing presence. Harry and Jennifer were still asleep in the other bedroom.

She came to the door with him, and on an impulse, he said, "Come and have lunch with me."

"Why?"

"I'm on holiday. I like lunching with beautiful women."

"I'll be delighted. But I was going to kiss you goodbye now."

"Do it anyway."

He walked down the corridor shaking his head and laughing quietly. That was the charm of Switzerland. Everything was clean, everything worked, and everything was well regulated and predictable for a restful holiday.

Fourteen

TOMMY and Albert were sitting on their balcony drinking *citron pressé* and impersonating millionaires.

"Do you want a cigar?" Tommy asked.

"Yes, I think I could force myself to have a puff at a Corona-Corona-Corona, my man," said Albert, and giggled.

"I've *got* cigars," Tommy insisted, and pulled a tin of cheroots out of his shirt pocket. He was dressed in a sports shirt and swimming trunks. Albert wore a shirt and flannels. He didn't like to expose his bare legs to sunshine, drafts or view. They lit up and lay back.

"Do you inhale?" Tommy asked. "It makes me dizzy."

"I always inhale," said Albert, who didn't. "They're not very good cigars. Come on, we'll have some cream cakes sent up."

"We'll never be able to eat any food if we have cream cakes."

"I can eat anything. I bet I could eat twelve cream cakes and then lunch as well."

"Ah, don't sicken us," Tommy protested. "These cream cakes here cost about one and a half francs."

"Well, it's all a part of the service, isn't it? Your old man always tells us to order anything we want."

"I know. Yeah. But he doesn't mean twelve cream cakes at a time. That's nearly thirty bob."

"All right," Albert said sulkily. "It would be all right if it was you that wanted them."

"I've got plenty of money," Tommy said. "We could go out and buy cream cakes."

"I don't want any outside. I know, we can go out and buy cream cakes and then you can pay the bill. I get fed up with that — you always want to act the big man."

"You can have some money if you want."

"I don't want *your* money," Albert snapped. "I want to order them on the telephone."

"Okay, okay. Don't order any for me. I don't want to spoil my cigar."

"I bet you're sick before me," said Albert, and padded into the bedroom to telephone for cream cakes. "Not a bad hotel, this," he said when he came back to the balcony. "The service in some hotels is really crummy, but this is okay." The note of spurious sophistication jarred slightly on Tommy because it sounded like himself. He nodded gravely and puffed slowly at the cigar and inhaled and found that he disliked it intensely, but he persevered.

"You'll be as sick as a pig if you eat six cream cakes," he coughed.

"Well!" Albert said defiantly. "You'll be sick with that cigar. We can be sick in the dining room. The Romans used to vomit all over the shop, byugh byugh byugh. They had slaves to clean it up."

"To *eat* it up," Tommy sniggered.

"Hee hee hee! Get down, slave, and eat up that nice boak. No. No. Open your mouth, slave, so's I can boak in it! He he he!"

Tommy leaned over his chair and became a Roman patrician vomiting, and as a refinement stubbed his cigar in the upturned eye of his imaginary slave. Albert started to kick his slave. "For kicks!" he giggled. There was a tentative knock on the bedroom door, and a pale girl in her teens came in with a plate of Swiss pastries. Albert leapt into his chair and lay back and called, "Ici, mademoiselle, vite vite!"

The girl came out to the balcony and put the plate on the little table. Albert counted small change in his hand and picked out a small coin which he handed to the girl. She took it in some embarrassment.

"Parlez-vous anglais, mademoiselle?" Albert asked her, and she shook her head. She would be perhaps fifteen or sixteen, thin and childlike.

"She would be all right for a slave," Albert said.

"Not sufficiently buxom."

The girl looked from one to the other, anxiously uncomprehending.

"I bet she would be all right for a wee feel," said Albert. "How would you like a wee feel, mademoiselle?"

"Comment?"

"Ah, lay off," Tommy said. "Somebody'll hear you. Merci, mademoiselle."

The girl smiled, puzzled, and backed through the french windows.

"You're a right spoilsport," Albert complained. "She would have done it, I bet. These foreign dames are dead certs." He picked up a pastry and bit off half of it. "You're always talking about dames, but when you get one you're scared."

"I thought you hated women."

"Maids are all right, they know you're the boss. We're payin' through the nose for the service, aren't we?"

"You're daft, Albert. If you try and touch the maids you'll get flung out."

"Scared, that's your trouble. In a good hotel you can get away wi' anything."

"Some hopes." Tommy uncomfortably puffed his cigar

and tried to blow a smoke ring against the sunlight. "You better watch the old man doesn't hear you."

"Ach, your old man knows all about it," Albert sputtered through the pastry. "He was out all night, you know."

"How do you know?"

"Oh, I know more than you think."

"*You* know. Huh."

"*I* know. I know my way around."

"Aw, shut up."

Briefly and disloyally, Tommy wished he had come with his father and without Albert. It would have been dull, but between giggles, the quiet stretches of boredom were beginning to stretch longer and longer. If he had been alone, he would have been able to spend all his time drifting about in the swimming pool, and maybe meet a French girl in a bikini, or a German, or something. A couple of girls at the pool had smiled back when he smiled at them, but Albert was always there to sneer at their belly buttons and accuse him of treachery. Albert was perfectly justified, it was true, because they had agreed that they hated women and would stick together. Still, it would have been nice to play truant from this noble principle and just see what happened. He knew this was mean, but he recognized his treacherous urges and wished that Sonny Blackett had come instead of Albert. Sonny didn't have any principles about women.

"Hey," Albert said. "I know something you don't know."

"All right, I'll buy it."

"I'm not selling it! Hee hee hee."

"Okay."

"Your old man's picked up a nigger."

"Negro."

"Nigger. It's a *dame*."

Tommy edged up in his chair so that he could look over the

parapet of the balcony to the far side of the terrace, three floors below. A man was sitting at one of the tables with a black girl, but he wasn't sure for a few seconds whether it was his father.

"It's somebody else," he said.

"It's your old man," Albert said with weary impatience. "You don't recognize your own father."

It *was* his father; but as Albert prattled on, Tommy was staring down at the couple on the terrace and tasting a strange experience. After the instant of seeing the man as merely a man, and not his father, he was now looking at the man as if it still wasn't his father, and seeing him as Albert or a stranger might see him. Not his father but a person, sitting at a table on a terrace, who happened also to be his father; a man with a bony face and a dark suit, talking to a woman and living a life of his own. The hair wasn't quite as gray as Tommy had always seen it, it was gray only at the sides. The thought disturbed Tommy deeply and unreasonably.

"Huh?" he said.

"Dreamy dreamy Daniel," Albert said. Albert disliked it when you sat or stood too long without saying anything.

"Mm?"

"What's up with you?" Albert said. "You look helluva bad-tempered."

"It's my natural face."

"You always say that. Well what do you know? A nigger. Come on, we'll get your old man's binoculars and have a look at them."

"They're locked up."

"I wonder if he's had a go at her, eh? Niggers are dead certs. Byugh. They smell. I bet he was screwing her last night."

"You better belt up."

"What's eating you?" Albert complained. "Can you not take a joke?" There was never any answer to that question.

"He's seen us, he's waving," Tommy said, and waved back.

"You're not going down, are you? I don't want to go and meet any niggers, do you?"

"Okay, stay here and sulk." That was a foul little blow, since Albert had acquired a monopoly of accusing him, Tommy, of sulking, and would be outraged at having his line stolen, but Tommy had momentarily lost patience. He was pulling on a pair of shorts over his swimming trunks, and after brooding on the balcony, Albert followed him downstairs.

His father half rose as they approached the table, and waved them into chairs. Looking at him still afresh, Tommy thought he did it very smoothly. Maybe his old man was one of these suave people when he wasn't being a father.

"This is my son Tommy, and his friend Albert. Miss Hildegarde."

"How do you do . . . ma'am," Tommy said awkwardly, and held out his hand.

"I'm fine, Tommy." She reached out a long arm and shook his hand, and her easiness made him feel pleased and uncomfortable at the same time. Albert said hello and perched on the edge of his chair.

"Will we have lunch together?" Tommy's father said, and Tommy smiled eagerly, wondering how it was that his middle-aged father could meet terrific women like this exotic black beauty. I'm in love with her, he thought. Imagine being in love with a darky.

"No, we had arranged to go out, Mr. Fletcher," Albert was saying.

"That's all right, some other time." Tommy's father was completely pleasant and unconcerned. Tommy hated Albert.

"Yes," he said. "We've got a date at the pool." And he saw Albert's blushing face tightening.

"All right for money?" his father asked, and Tommy nodded and said, "Well, it's been a pleasure meeting you, Miss Hildegarde." He held out his hand again, determined to touch her cool smooth skin again, and he was sure that she took his hand with a secret little caress as she smiled straight into his eyes. Instead of walking down the terrace steps, he vaulted over the low parapet.

"You don't know how childish that looked," Albert muttered. "You would have looked a right Charley if you had tripped."

"So what?"

"I don't want to go to the bloody pool."

"Well you should have kept your bloody mouth shut."

"I don't like eating wi' strangers. They're always looking at you to see if you use the right fork."

"Ah, fork you."

"Fork you. I've a good mind to catch the next plane outa this dump."

"Bloody well do that. I'm going to the pool."

"Yah, cry-baby always has to get his own way!" Albert sneered, and trailed two paces behind Tommy down the hill.

"Nice kid," Hildegarde said.

"He's a damn nuisance," said Tom.

"Not to me. He jumped over that wall for me."

"All the Fletchers are show-offs."

"He'll grow up handsome," said Hildegarde.

"I wouldn't be surprised," Tom said gloomily. She laughed, and he joined her. He was glad that it was his own son and not the other kid who had vaulted the parapet.

They were sitting, talking pleasantly about nothing, when a touring coach pulled up outside the hotel, and watching the tourists pour out, a sight that made him feel settled and superior, Tom became conscious of a small drama in the party. The courier, harassed as always with his handful of lists and timetables, hurried ahead into the hotel and then hurried out again to herd his passengers towards the Number Two dining room. At the tail end came a youngish woman with an old woman leaning heavily on her arm.

"Why do they do it?" Tom wondered aloud, and at the same moment the younger woman called imperiously at the courier.

"Mr. Archer! Come back here at once!"

Gritting his teeth, the courier pattered back and complained, "I've got a thousand things to do, Miss Appleby."

"This has first priority," the young woman snapped, and the courier sighed at the bloody-mindedness of tourists.

"It's only a wee bit coach fatigue," he said. "She'll be all right when she gets a breath of air. I've got all these other clients to take care of."

As he hurried away again, the young woman distinctly said, "Sod!"

She looked despairingly round the terrace, where all the tables were occupied, and Tom hesitated for a second before he stood up. He was determined not to get mixed up with a bus-party squabble, but the old woman looked ready to collapse on the young woman's arm. He took her other arm and they helped her to one of the chairs at his table.

"Your mother?"

"Dithering, incompetent swine," said the younger woman. "Sorry, I didn't mean you. I think she's really ill."

"Your mother?"

"No, only a fellow traveler. How do you feel now, Mrs. Thorpe?"

The old woman muttered something and fanned herself ineffectually with her hand.

"It's cardiac," Tom said. The younger woman turned with sudden interest.

"Are you a doctor?"

"No, but look at her lips."

"I knew we should have got her off at Geneva. The courier is impossible. What can we do for her?"

It was interesting, Tom thought, how people assumed that he would know things. He saw endless complications and involvement, and wished he had been safely at lunch when the party had arrived.

"Get a doctor," he said.

"Yes, of course. Would you?"

Hildegarde patted his arm as he sighed, and he went into the hotel to find the manager in the Number Two dining room talking cheerfully with the courier.

"Could you get a doctor?" Tom interrupted without ceremony. The manager immediately excused himself and whisked Tom towards his office. The courier sighed with vexation.

"Are you ill, Mr. Fletcher?" the manager asked.

"No, it's an old lady from that coach. Heart trouble."

"Strange, the courier didn't say anything."

"The courier is an idiot."

"Amateurs, Mr. Fletcher, amateurs. I have a good friend who is a doctor. Where is the lady now?"

"On the terrace."

"He will come there."

Tom left him and returned to the terrace, to find the young woman from the coach kneeling in front of the old woman while Hildegarde fanned the patient with a menu. The courier was fidgeting beside them.

"I told you there was nothing to worry about," he was saying. "She's feeling better already."

"I've sent for a doctor," Tom said, ignoring him, and the

courier said petulantly, "I was going to do that anyway." He spoke with a strong Scots accent that riled Tom.

"She'll have to stay here," said the young woman.

"In this hotel?" The courier snorted. "Are you kidding? This isn't in our category. Maybe we can find her a pension or something," he added grudgingly.

"She'll stay here," Tom said.

"I'll thank you to mind your own business, whoever you are!"

People at the other tables were now frankly turned round to look and listen, and Tom eyed the courier with cold dislike.

"Come inside for a few minutes," he said, and when the courier stubbornly stared back, he muttered, "Come inside, unless you want to be punched in front of all these people."

The courier backed away, and Tom followed him into the hotel, where he took the man's arm and steered him to the manager's office. The manager was just coming out of the room.

"Can we use your office for a minute, monsieur?" Tom asked.

"Certainly, certainly. Do you want me, Mr. Fletcher?"

"Yes, please." He pushed the courier into the tiny room.

"I'm warning you, now!" the courier said. "You'd better not try anything!"

"A fine damned Scotsman," Tom said. "I've seen more nous in a tuppenny rabbit. You damned fool, man, you've got a serious illness on your hands. You'd better arrange for that old woman to stay here and be taken home when she's fit."

"I'm not authorized to put people in a hotel of this class."

"Get on the telephone and get authorized before I wring your neck."

"It's a storm in a teacup," the man muttered, and put his hand unwillingly on the telephone. The manager touched Tom's arm.

"Mr. Fletcher. I'm sorry, the hotel is full, completely. I'll be glad to arrange something, but we're full, completely full."

The courier's eyes lit with triumph.

"They can have my room," Tom said. And to the manager, "Could you put a cot for me in the boys' room?"

"Ah, certainly, Mr. Fletcher. But this is an inconvenience for you."

"It doesn't matter."

"And who pays?" the courier demanded.

Tom saw the manager smiling quietly.

"You pay," Tom said. "Get on that telephone." He left the room with the manager.

"Ah, life is very difficult," the manager said.

"But you don't mind."

"O-oh. Why do I mind? Can you promise that the old lady will not die? That would be a favor, Mr. Fletcher."

"No."

"No."

"Are you, um, unhappy about it, monsieur?"

"Ah, come, Mr. Fletcher. It's the hotel business. One is accustomed to difficulties."

"Professionals are accustomed to difficulties."

"I should have said that, Mr. Fletcher. He is an amateur, that one."

"He's a shit."

"It is not my place to say so." The manager laughed. "You don't mind giving up your room?"

"I'm a bloody fool. I hate giving it up."

"It's life."

"A nice restful holiday," Tom said. "That's what it said in the brochure."

He lunched with Hildegarde, pleasantly enough. The boys didn't reappear, but on the way back to the Exhibition, he thought he saw Albert moodily walking alone, and wondered if they had quarreled. It was none of his business. The fair was crowded, and after a few words with Harry Kutsu, he went back to his hotel and slept, resentfully, in the temporary bed that had been put in the boys' room. He was wakened by Albert creeping about the bedroom just before dinner, and in a rush of paternalism, he took the two of them to see a French film in the evening, and afterwards to a small club where they drank lemonade and listened to a solitary pianist.

Both boys were subdued, doubtless because he was with them, he thought. They all went to bed together, and he vowed never again to interfere in anybody else's troubles.

Fifteen

DURING the next few days, Tom succeeded in recapturing his original program of a restful, mindless holiday. He saw Harry Kutsu once or twice, and Hildegarde three or four times, but everybody was sobering up and getting down to business. Harry insisted that the offer of a free gift computer was firm and legal, and Tom agreed every time it came up, but it was like a shipboard romance, in a way. They had all used one another up.

After two days, the sick old Englishwoman, Mrs. Thorpe, was driven to Geneva and flown to London. There was some small professional satisfaction in this business. Tom was able to put hard pressure on the tour agency (Evergreen, of all names) to give her V.I.P. treatment, because he suspected that the company was small and slipshod and would have shrugged her off if nobody had defended her rights. His grossest insult to them had been to telephone their London office, transferring the charges and using the name Archer, and then to promise to bring the company to court, have it banned from entry to Switzerland and give the whole story to the *News of the World*. This punitive operation pleased him because he detested a company that didn't fulfill its bargains; and the young woman, Gladys Appleby, although she was calm and competent, didn't have the experience to frighten a big company.

He knew why this little business pleased him. It was his meat. It vindicated the training and the experience of his life to be able to get things done when nobody else quite knew what ought to be done. And with the old woman gone, he was able to move back into his own hotel room and become solitary and selfish again. The young woman, Appleby, was found a small room in the hotel on the same day and elected to abandon the tour altogether and finish her holiday in Lausanne. Tom advised her to send the bill to the tour agency, and washed his hands of her.

Tommy and Albert pricked his conscience now and then. He noticed they hadn't been giggling so often recently, and suspected that they were bored with each other. One night he left his favorite bar early and went back to the hotel, determined to find them before bedtime and organize some more exciting projects — a trip to France, perhaps, or up to the mountains of the Valais. They weren't in their rooms, and he laughed at his good intentions and went downstairs to the bar of the hotel. It had music, a trio in gray tuxedos and a tiny space for dancing, and to his astonishment he found Tommy sitting at a table while Albert was actually on the floor, dancing with the Appleby woman.

"We're going to bed in ten minutes," Tommy said defensively.

"You're not on a curfew," Tom said shortly. "I haven't got a clock on you."

"Oh. I thought you might be annoyed. We're not drinking alcohol or anything."

"I didn't say you were."

"Oh. Right. This is, er, quite a nice woman. English, of course. Miss Appleby. Her name's Gladys."

"Oh."

The music stopped and Albert came back to the table with

Miss Appleby. What, forty? Forty-two? No chicken, anyway. He used the phrase mentally with automatic callousness, and resented the fact that she had tarted herself up in a white flowered print dress with a full skirt and little black bows at the shoulder. She had looked downright dowdy when she got off the coach with the sick old woman. Deliberately dowdy, almost. Her mousy hair had been pulled back and tied with something and her face had been sweaty and dusty. Now she looked all right, for her age.

"It's late," she apologized. Everybody seemed to be apologizing to him. It nettled him.

"There's no school tomorrow," he said, with false-sounding jollity.

"It's late enough for me," she said. "Thanks for the dance, Albert, I'm off to bed."

"I want another dance," Tommy protested. She looked at Tom, and he shrugged irritably. She was one of those quiet dames, the dangerous kind. Maybe. The truth was that she had surprised him and he didn't like being surprised.

There was a slow lazy look about her that nagged him — no, not lazy, but unflurried. She wasn't at all pretty, her nose was buttony and her upper lip was thin and her eyes were gray and none of these things were his favorites. She was passive, that was it. Passive women irritated him.

But young Tommy took her arm eagerly and led her onto the floor, where she was half a head taller than he was, and they disappeared in the crowd, dancing too close together for a boy of that age. All right, the closeness was doubtless Tommy's idea, but passive women of that age were a lousy idea for a boy of fourteen. This was a little friendship he would discourage rapidly.

The woman didn't need any discouragement, however. When she came off the floor with Tommy, she remained standing and said, "I hope I haven't kept the boys up too late. Goodnight."

She was gone before he could answer.

"I suppose we'll have to go to bed too," Tommy said, in neutral tones, neither cajoling nor protesting. Tom recognized the technique. It was designed to lower the temperature and avoid irritating him. It was irrational of him to be angered by the knowledge that his son was averting his anger, and he knew it was irrational, and he nodded without words.

"It wasn't her idea," the boy said defensively. "She was sitting all alone, so I asked her to dance. She's quite nice. Respectable."

"She's a bit old for you." Tom tried to make the words sound genial.

"It was just . . . to dance. Nothing like that. She's old enough to be my mother."

"Oohoo!" Albert hooted. "They're all right at that age! Hee hee."

Tom tried to hide his dislike of the fat boy. It was natural in the teens to try to sound mature and it was natural to sound obscene. Tommy, he noticed, had taken his friend by the arm and was urging him out of his chair and mirroring his own disapproval. He smiled his genial tolerant Dad smile and let them go, and ordered a drink; and inconsistently was annoyed at the Englishwoman for leaving so abruptly. He resented her and he disliked her, but he didn't like sitting alone and drinking. It was necessary that women, or a woman, should be *there*. Even now that they had no functional importance, the habit of the company of women was deeply ingrained. He finished his drink and went to bed.

Next morning he discovered that Tommy and Albert were off on a trip to the mountains with the woman, and he was excessively irritated, perhaps because he had never got round to arranging a trip himself. He saw them go, and promised himself he would scare her off as soon as they came back. Watching them leave together, he felt a foolish twinge of resentment . . . not that he resented not going with them, but because he now couldn't decide to go at all, even on his own. The woman was spoiling his contentment. If he had been simple and childish, he could have insisted on going with them, but since he wasn't, he had to stay behind, and maybe he was simple and childish enough to let this ruin any other idea he might have had. He didn't want to see Harry Kutsu again simply because he felt like somebody's company. It was always wrong and fatal to seek company because of mere loneliness. He despised himself for his foolishness and took a cruise on the lake, and found it impossibly uninteresting. But he was accustomed to days that were impossible and uninteresting. He returned to Dostoyevsky and read it resolutely until it became interesting. Late in the afternoon, he realized that the boys were back, and were just leaving to cool off in the water. He was on the point of following them when he saw the Englishwoman in the lounge, and stopped to speak to her.

"I'm going home tomorrow," she said, before he could speak.

"Pity." He didn't mean it.

"I didn't mean to monopolize the boys. I hope you have a good holiday." She swung away, to end the interview.

"I'm having some fruit juice," he said. "Will you join me?"

"It isn't necessary," she said, and her indifference stung him. He sat down beside her.

"I didn't say there was any need to," he said. "Would you like some fruit juice?"

"All right."

He shouldn't have bothered. He was glad to know she was going, he could have walked away and left her, and now he had put himself in the absurd situation of forcing his company on her.

"I haven't thanked you properly for helping me with old Mrs. Thorpe," she said. "It was very useful."

"Spoiled your holiday."

She didn't quite shrug. She didn't go in much for physical movement, in fact. He wondered if she had been brought up in a convent and trained not to fidget.

"It's been a change," she said indifferently. "I wanted a break before I start . . . back home."

"To work?"

"Mm." She sipped her fruit juice, enclosed in herself, not interested.

"What kind of work?" He could hear himself pushing the meaningless conversation on, his tongue asking the questions everybody asks everybody without direction from the brain.

"You're not really interested in what work I do, Mr. Fletcher," she said. "So why go into it?"

"Why shouldn't I be interested?"

"I irritate you. I didn't mean to, but it doesn't matter. I'm going home tomorrow."

"You don't irritate me," he lied, and she looked calmly at him.

"I don't know," he said. "The human race is not on my side today."

"Tough."

"You nearly smiled," he said. It was the automatic routine again, the old salesman's compulsive drive to break down indifference. He found himself looking forward to the day when it switched off finally and left him in peace. In any case, it wasn't working. She ignored the remark.

"Do you work in London?" he asked.

"You asked that already." She smiled gently, and he laughed.

"Okay," he said. "It doesn't matter. We always ask one another too many questions."

"Yes, I do work in London, or I did." She breathed deeply. "I've left one job and I'm looking for another."

That was it, people always needed something, it always came to that, and he forced his casual interest down; but he couldn't help asking, "What kind of work?"

"Private secretary. You don't need one?" She wasn't asking, she wasn't interested.

"Nope, I have one."

She did her invisible shrug again.

"I know some people in London," he said. "I could ask."

"Why should you?" she asked calmly. "You don't know anything about me. I can find a job for myself. For all you know I may be useless."

"That's true."

"So."

Her utter bland apathy wouldn't let him rest.

"I could offer you a job as a housekeeper," he said, with a laugh that didn't quite convince him.

She stood up.

"I don't think I would really want to join your black and white minstrels."

The cool derision of it stung him so hard that he almost liked it.

"You're twenty years too late for that," he said, and her open palm rang across his face. He looked round the lounge and then laughed.

"Nobody noticed," he said. "I admit I deserved it."

"I enjoyed it," she said. "Goodbye, Mr. Fletcher."

"And," he said, "she swep' out leaving him gasping."

And she did.

"It's time," he said quietly to the empty lounge, "that I started to meet normal people. That's funny, I can't remember the last time I met normal people."

Sixteen

THERE had been a few moments when he actually played with the idea of making a complete break in his life and settling in some foreign town — some town like Lausanne, perhaps, where there would be a reasonable school for Tommy and he might simply retire, convert himself into a leisured exile. The notion was romantic and absurd, of course. Already there was an old restlessness in him, and he decided he was either too energetic by nature to be lazy, or that he had evolved into one of those businessmen in sad American films, who work like beavers to get rich and retire, and then find they have killed their capacity for leisure in the process. He restrained himself from telephoning Meg Macrae to talk shop, but he wanted to know about the office and he was glad he would be home in a few days. Tommy came to his room while he was sitting on the balcony staring at nothing.

"Do you think we could go and see Miss Appleby off?" he asked, in the voice that meant it doesn't matter, anything you say, I was only asking but it isn't important so don't go berserk.

"If you like," said Tom. "You must be short of something to do."

"Well." Tommy shrugged. "We've more or less exhausted the local possibilities of entertainment."

"How are you getting along with Albert?"

"All right."

Tom didn't feel any guilt about the unpleasantness he had had with the Englishwoman, but looking at it objectively, he felt he might offer to make peace by hiring a car to take her to Geneva. Tommy, however, said that she already had a train ticket, and that the train was more fun, and he was relieved, on the whole. She knocked at his door later in the morning, and came in dressed in a thin dark suit, very much a bland efficient impersonal secretary.

"You look very nice," he said.

"I looked in to say goodbye."

"Damn it, I said you looked nice."

"Thank you." She dismissed the courtesy as irrelevant. "I was probably unpleasant yesterday. I'm not a very social person."

"I was unpleasant too." He laughed. "I wasn't trying to make a proposition. You're not the housekeeper type, but I needed a housekeeper. It came out without thinking."

"No, I'm not. I suppose I should thank you for the offer."

"It's not a bad offer. You're not getting any younger. I don't mean to be offensive."

"No, it's a fact."

"You're a self-contained bitch, aren't you?" Tom spoke without rancor, but her complete lack of interest was an automatic challenge.

"I don't know. I've never thought about it."

"I do know people in London," he said. "I work with the Gaylor Group. It can't do any harm in any case," he added truthfully. "Life is always full of coincidences. I'll be spending Monday with Nick Gaylor, and it wouldn't surprise me if I found everybody scrambling to find a good secretary. You can give me your address in case I meet a coincidence."

"Sorry, I don't like giving people my address. Oh, that's silly. All right. But I don't expect you to do anything about it."

She fished in her handbag, found a letter and gave him the envelope. He put it in his pocket without looking at it. He watched her from the balcony as she walked down the street. Tommy and Albert were carrying her two suitcases. From this distance, they all seemed to be chattering merrily. She was probably one of those women who get on better with kids than with people. He found himself looking at his own suitcase, and on an impulse, he began to pack some things in it. The holiday was over.

They left Lausanne on Sunday morning. On the flight home, the boys looked listlessly at the countryside below them. The giggle had gone out of them. At London, he put them on the Glasgow plane and promised to be home in two days.

"If you need anything," he told Tommy, "phone Meg Macrae."

"All right." Tommy didn't want to need anything, he was a man traveling alone and independent. "I'll be all right."

"Maybe you could stay at Albert's," Tom suggested, but although both boys nodded thoughtfully, he could tell they both shied away from the idea.

"I'll phone you tonight," he said, and Tommy insisted, "It's all *right*."

His mind had been working from habit, the habit that dictated spending at least a couple of days in London when the chance came up, to meet old mates and see a show or visit one of the clubs, make an occasion of it. On the following morning he awoke with the happy thought that he was under no compulsion to do any of these things. He could spend that day visiting Gaylor's, purely as a formality, and be home on the evening plane if he was lucky. He telephoned Jack Fillimore and found that he wouldn't be able to see Gaylor himself until three o'clock. Jack was harassed and apologetic at not being able to lunch with him.

"It's the good old rat race, old man," he explained. "We rats really race on Mondays ha ha. Poor show, I wanted to show you the town. You should have *warned* me, old man, I promised to be home early tonight. You wouldn't like to come home for a bite of food?" The invitation was so apprehensive that Tom invented another date and was rewarded with a happy sigh. With the joyful feeling of playing truant, he went to the Tower of London and took the conducted tour. In all his scores of visits to London, he had never sampled any of the guidebook attractions. There had never been any time to spare between meals and drinks. In an access of simple tourist economy, he lunched in a café and gave himself plenty of time to walk along the Embankment and up through Trafalgar Square on the way to Gaylor's, and he indulged the sense of freedom by buying some corn and feeding the pigeons. He was in Jack Fillimore's office at two forty-five.

The building was new, the foyer was coolly overwhelming, there was glass everywhere, but Jack's office was one of a long line of cubbyholes, with two steel desks squeezed into it and a plump uninterested girl at the other desk, and three filing cabinets and a lot of papers piled on top of them and no more grace or opulence than a factory bench.

"Forgive the mess, old man. Tom, you wild Highlander, it's marvelous to see you, marvelous. This is Eunice. Why didn't you call me, you dog? I'm absolutely up to the optics. It's great to see you, Tom, I mean that. Sit down and have a cigarette. I can't think what became of the cigars — the charwomen pinch them, you know." He laughed merrily and

Tom sat down to endure ten minutes with dauntless courage and a stiff upper lip. Fillimore glanced constantly at his seventeen-jewel wrist chronometer and finally stood up and shot his cuffs and dropped his voice to a cathedral hush.

"Time to approach the sanctum, you've never seen the building before, have you? It's a humble little cottage but we manage ha ha."

He led Tom to a lift and took him up four floors, to the level where the corridors were carpeted and the doors were veneered in unicorn hide.

"It's all yours now, old man," he said. "This is it. See you later, perhaps? We won't tie ourselves down to anything. Give me a buzz if you can manage."

Tom entered a secretary's office paneled in dark wood in which a girl with a typewriter and a woman with a desk shared a small parkland of dove-gray carpet.

"Mr. Gaylor won't be long," the woman said, not hostile, not chummy. "He's somewhere in the building. Would you like to sit down?"

Tom looked at his watch, not ostentatiously, not furtively. It was one minute to three. He sat down on a wickedly deceptive couch in black leather which sank under his weight and kept sinking till he was trapped in a nest eight or nine inches deep. He picked up a magazine and read. At three-ten he glanced at his watch again, this time with the merest trace of ostentation. At three-fifteen he looked across at the older woman.

"Could you get a hold of Mr. Gaylor and let him know I'm here?" he asked. Smile.

"Oh dear." Smile. "It isn't possible, I'm afraid. He could be anywhere, any of a dozen places."

He kept on looking at her, smiling, waiting, but she made no move to try any of the dozen places. He resumed the magazine.

At three-thirty the woman looked across at him and pursed her lips. He looked at his watch.

"I'm very sorry," she said. "It's most unusual."

Planting his feet carefully on the carpet, he started to rise. It was tricky, he knew. Without proper balance, you could either fall back or pitch forward on your face.

"Perhaps you'll let Mr. Gaylor know I called," he said. Smile. Walk towards door.

"Oh! I should really wait, Mr. Fletcher." She had spoken too shrilly, and she controlled herself. "He can't be more than a few minutes now." Smile.

"Sorry." Smile. Open door. Pause in doorway. "Thank you." Smile.

Nick Gaylor ruined the whole thing by striding in from the corridor and crossing in front of him.

"Fletcher! Sorry to keep you. How do you do?"

"Hello, Nick. I was just going."

"Don't be daft, you were showing off. Come into the office. How are things in Scotland?"

"I haven't the faintest idea."

That one genuinely turned the woman to stone. It was the wrongest answer in the language. He gave her the big candlepower smile, the vacuum-cleaner-salesman special, as he disappeared into Gaylor's room.

"You shouldn't upset the secretaries, they've got no sense of humor," Gaylor said. "Have a chair. Cigar? No. How do you like it?"

"Is there a choir of two hundred behind the paneling?"

"There should be, at the price. How are things in Scotland?"

"All right."

"Happy?"

"I'm planning to reorganize the factory."

"Forget it, I don't know if we'll keep it."

"Make up your mind, then."

"Eh? Eh?"

"Make up your mind whether you're keeping it or not, Nick," Tom said. "If we're keeping it, I want to reorganize it."

"Take your time, take your time," said Gaylor. "You don't have to start proving anything to me, I know you know your business. Leave it in the meantime, I'll let you know."

"When?"

"When I feel like it. Are you looking for a fight? All that business, walking out of the office because I was a few minutes late. I'm not impressed."

"No, no," Tom said, in suave surprise. "I want to get on with my job."

"That's what we all want. I've got every confidence in you, Tom."

"So have I."

"You're a cool bastard. Do you think there's room for both of us in this company?"

"I don't take up much room."

"You would have this chair if I turned my back," said Gaylor.

"No. I wouldn't. If it comes to that, you would sack me if I turned my back."

"No, you're wrong. I never sack people. If I have to get rid of a man, that means I've made a mistake in picking him, and I don't make mistakes. All right, not often. What are we fighting about?"

"I never said a word."

"Happy about your contract?"

"There's a clause that lets you revise the commission percentage. Unilaterally."

"It's the standard contract, don't worry about it."

"I won't, yet."

"Anything else?"

"Let me know about the factory."

"I'll let you know, it isn't important right now. I *thought* you would notice the revision clause. Don't let it worry you, Tom. I wouldn't like you to think it's the thin edge of the wedge."

"I know you wouldn't like me to think that."

"What the hell's wrong with you?" Gaylor's easy, flip aggressiveness seemed to be giving way to genuine suspicion, and Tom wondered if he himself had played it too hard. But he couldn't have played it in any other way. Gaylor had the confidence and the absent-minded brutality of power, and Tom knew he could never accept power easily when it was somebody else's power over himself. In spite of himself, he had to assert his independence, to claim some kind of equality in his own person, to balance the equality that he didn't have in his position. He wasn't too unlike the Jack Fillimores, in fact, except that Jack would assert his personality over his subordinates, while Tom had to outface his superiors if it was going to mean anything.

"I don't mind a bit of a barney," Gaylor was saying. "I like a man that doesn't crawl, I've never crawled in my life. But I hope you're not a sorehead; if you've got a grudge about anything let's have it and stop fencing."

"No. No. I've got no grudges. Business is business, that's all." He laughed, spontaneously. "You don't expect me to recite the oath of allegiance to the Group, do you?"

"No, I don't." Gaylor wasn't much amused. "I get plenty of that. But I expect an honest bargain."

"You'll get—" The telephone rang as Tom was answering, and he halted at once. Gaylor picked it up and said, "Gaylor." Then he looked surprised and handed it over.

"It's for you," he said. Tom smiled happily. He was doing all the wrong things in the secretary's book, and having a telephone call right there in Gaylor's office must be the ultimate in sin. Gaylor pulled a mimeographed sheaf of foolscap from a drawer and began to read, with pencil in one hand.

"Mr. Fletcher?" said a woman's voice in the telephone. "This is Gladys Appleby."

"Appleby?"

"I left you in Lausanne on Thursday."

"Oh, yes."

"Are you too busy to talk?"

Tom glanced at Gaylor, who was totally engrossed.

"No, not at all," he said. "I haven't had time to make any inquiries. I'm sorry."

"It wasn't that. Are you serious about wanting a housekeeper?"

There was a small pause. It was one thing to make a flippant suggestion . . . but this woman clearly didn't think or hear flippantly. And after all, an offer was an offer. Maybe it was some other woman she had in mind for the job, her old auntie or her mother.

"Yes, quite serious," he said.

"Can I have the job?"

"This is pretty sudden," he said.

"I know. You can say no if you like, I don't want to rush you."

"No, I think it's all right. You could try it anyway."

"I would need —" She paused, and he had the impression that she had been nervous before, but was now the smooth efficient secretary again. "— I would need five pounds a week and all found. Is that too much? I don't know what other people get."

"It's worth eight," he said, thinking quickly.

"Five is enough."

"When do you want to start?"

"I can travel now. I'm free. The sooner the better."

He laughed.

"Where are you?"

"I live in Kentish Town." She recited an address at dictation speed and he pulled an envelope out of his pocket to write it down, and then discovered that it already appeared on the envelope.

"I'll come there," he said. "In . . . about an hour."

"I'll wait for you," she said. "Goodbye."

"Goodbye."

"Okay?" Gaylor asked. His secretary might be shocked, but Gaylor was clearly untroubled by subordinates taking calls in his private office. Tom nodded.

"I have somebody else coming in," Gaylor said. "I'll let you know about the factory in a fortnight."

"Good."

"Keep the figures up."

"Right. Goodbye, Nick."

"I'll see you some time." Gaylor returned to his papers; not as a performance, but as a job. Tom left, and gave the older woman secretary a ravishing smile on his way out. She smiled brightly in return, in case he was a bigger man than she had imagined.

The address in Kentish Town was a dingy yellow-brick terrace, and he had to climb to the attic flat. It was decorated in white and pale colors and clinically bare, and evidently all the little personal ornaments that a woman would have had been tidied away or packed. The Appleby woman had a pot of tea and two cups ready. She was wearing the same dark suit he had seen in Lausanne, or another very like it, and she wasn't at all a bad-looking woman, tall but not too thin; not pretty but very presentable.

"Do you think this will work?" he asked at once.

"I don't see why not," she said. "I've never kept a house for anybody else, but I know how to keep my own. I cook quite well. And I'm efficient and honest."

"If that's all you've got to offer you're unique," he said dryly. "I won't ask you why you want the job, as long as you can do it and take it off my mind."

Obviously, she had prepared her next speech, and he looked at her without expression and didn't interrupt.

"Why not? I've been a secretary for fifteen years, but since you mentioned housekeeping, I've thought about it and I'm not dedicated to being a secretary. Besides, I want a complete change, I want to get away. I left my last job with good references. I'm forty-two. I don't know if I could get another place with the same salary. I was the boss's mistress."

"You don't need to make it sound so crude."

"I would rather make it sound crude. I'm finished with all that. It *was* crude — it seems rather romantic and tragic at first, but years go by and you find it's turned into a habit and there's nothing special about it. There's no future in it."

"So you've chucked it."

"He ended it. His daughter's getting married," she added inconsequentially.

"I see," said Tom. "And that makes him want to turn respectable."

"I can understand it. I don't know if anybody else would."

"I do. He sounds like a louse, but it's none of my business."

"You don't mind?"

"No."

"And the housekeeping job is strictly business? I don't intend to make a habit of . . . of it," she added, laughing a little wildly. Nevertheless, she looked so composed and self-sufficient that he found it difficult to visualize her involved in a passionate intrigue, waiting in her little flat for the illicit lover, opening the door in trembling submission. People were odd. He had no doubt that she was as efficient and as honest as she claimed. Her boss had probably been a little-boy-lost type of parasite.

"I can leave immediately," she said. "I was going to move even if you had changed your mind. I've packed everything I want. I gave the rest away. I didn't want any of it."

There were emotional overtones he didn't want to know about. The whole affair had an abrupt recklessness that ordinarily he would have shunned, but in the taxi ride to Kentish Town he had considered this and concluded that every first meeting of employer and employee was a lottery. He might interview ten women as housekeepers, and because of their shyness or their accidental appearance or their availability, he could very well overlook the treasure among them and land himself with a monster. A total stranger, with the habit of reserve, was just as likely to be ideal as any plump little buddy in an apron, and the Appleby woman appealed to him, as a theory, because he had always believed that it ought to be possible to run a house with the same efficiency that trained women like Meg Macrae ran offices.

There was another thing in Appleby's favor, and that was his recollection that he was going back to Helensburgh to Mrs. Crow. The Crow problem would be solved automatically by the arrival of a new housekeeper. If Appleby proved to be useless, it would be a simple unemotional matter to give her notice, to dismiss her as a businesslike employee, and no doubt she could find another secretarial job in Glasgow or anywhere else.

"You could travel with me this evening," he said.

"Certainly."

He telephoned Cook's and managed to book another seat in the Clansman, and arranged for Appleby's trunk to be collected and sent north by rail. It was all enormously simple. At five o'clock he recalled guiltily that he had never telephoned Tommy, and put through a call from the coin-box telephone downstairs from the Appleby woman's flat. Tommy answered at once.

"Sorry I didn't phone last night," Tom said. "Is everything all right?"

"Yes, I suppose so."

"Well, is it or isn't it?"

"It's okay, no burglaries or fires or anything."

"What's the matter?" Tom asked, his antenna quivering towards trouble.

"Nothing that can't wait. When are you coming home?"

"Tonight."

"That's fine, then."

"What is it? Damn it, what is it?"

"It's not worth talking about on the telephone. I'll see you tonight. Goodbye, Dad."

"Eh?" He held the dead telephone for a second before he hung up, and Miss Appleby looked a question but didn't express it.

"It's nothing, some of Tommy's usual mysterious business, there's something wrong but he isn't talking. Never mind, it's nothing you need to worry about."

"You'll have to tell me what I need to worry about," she said. "I don't know where a housekeeper's responsiblities end."

"Neither do I," he said. "We'll work it out by ear."

She hardly spoke at all during the journey, and he was grateful because he hated talking in airplanes. He distrusted his own optimism, but he couldn't help thinking he had been lucky in finding a woman who knew how to be silent and was probably as efficient as hell. When they landed at Renfrew and he got the Jaguar from the airport garage, she stood

easily by, the trained self-effacing secretary, and seemed a little surprised when he held the door open for her and closed it
after she had got in. They had to queue at the river.

"A ferry!" she said, astonished.

"It's a nuisance."

"I like ferries."

He looked at her, but she was staring out of the window.

"I feel a little like Jane Eyre," she said.

"Jane Eyre? Oh. Don't worry, I haven't got any loony
wives locked in the attic." The words stirred a discomfort
in his mind and he tapped the wheel in impatience while the
ferryboat slid with infinite slowness across the dark river. He
drove very quickly.

He wouldn't have seen Tommy if Miss Appleby hadn't noticed him first. The boy was standing at the corner where he
turned up from the shore road in Helensburgh, and when the
woman cried out, Tom looked again and saw that Tommy
was wearing a light coat and shining a torch into his own
face.

"Maniac!" Tom muttered, and pulled sharply in to the
curb. "What the hell are you playing at?" he demanded.

"I was trying to give myself maximum visibility," Tommy
said. "I'm the welcoming committee. Oh! Hello." He had
just distinguished the woman's face.

"Get in," Tom said wearily. "You should be in bed." And
then added, "I suppose you were fed up being in the house
alone."

"I'm not," Tommy said. "The house is replete with human
beings. That's one of the reasons why I deemed it advisable
to act as welcoming committee. Mrs. Crow is there."

"Oh." Tom was not very interested.

"And Mr. Crow. Mr. Crow sleeps downstairs and Mrs.
Crow sleeps upstairs."

"What!" Tom drew into the curb again, and stopped.

"She claims that you gave her instructions to that effect," Tommy said. Tom noticed that when the boy was embarrassed he talked in a strangled prose, and wished he would lose the habit.

"The woman's insane," he muttered. Miss Appleby had sat silent, offering no questions or comment, and he had to explain. "She's a local woman who's been doing some cleaning and so on."

"She also has illicit designs on the master of the house," Tommy interjected, and Tom impatiently told him to shut up.

"This is insane," he exploded. "The crazy bitch said she would keep an eye on the place while we were away. I never said anything about taking it over."

"It's the latest phase in a long-prepared master strategy," Tommy said. "Infiltration and consolidation. She wouldn't listen to me," he added, and the high-flown prose was dropped and there was a hint of suppressed tearfulness. "She said you had arranged everything with her and that she didn't want any . . . any lip from any kids. 'It's a private arrangement between your father and me so you can like or lump it.' "

"Oh, Tommy!" The Appleby woman had also detected the hint of tears. "You didn't make any arrangement?" she asked Tom levelly.

"Never in a million years, she's stark staring mad."

"She's a predator," Tommy said, recovering his poise.

"I'll get rid of her," Tom said, and the car moved away. And how in God's name will I get rid of her? he thought. He stopped the car in the driveway and went to the front door without helping Miss Appleby out. The hall light was shining and the door swung open as he was reaching for the keyhole. Mrs. Crow was standing in the doorway.

"Welcome home, Mr. Fletcher!" she cried, and his senses reeled. She was wearing her special chrome steel hourglass corset, and the shelf of her bosom soared over the top of it in frightening nakedness, in a black velvet dress with a deep square neckline that barely stopped above the nipples. Three ropes of pearls were strangling her and red glass earrings tinkled above them, and the fragrance of Soir de Paris was dense enough to lean a ladder against it.

"I've got something nice for you, it's nice to have something nice when you've been away on a journey, I knew you would like everything nice when you got back so I've made a nice wee supper, poor man you must be needing it." She had grabbed him merrily by the arm and was dragging him towards the lounge, and there was a hectic note in her cheerful prattle. As his face hit the perfume zone he realized that there was brandy among the Soir de Paris.

"You could have knocked me down when I heard you were planning for to return this evening instead of the morra," she babbled. "But I always say never say die and it's as well I've got my health and strength and a nod's as good as a wink, I says, and if Mr. Fletcher is depending on me I'm the last one to let him down, we all have to do our humble best at least that's the way I've always lived and that's the way I always will so what do you think of *that?*"

The table was set for two with what appeared to be a brick-sized slab of corned beef, tomatoes and a vast dish of dank steaming chips; and candles. The sight unmanned him. He should have thrown a fit of outraged dignity at the door, before she said a word. Now she had dragged him into the house she had almost established his complicity. But she halted and stared beyond him.

"Tommy!" she snapped, and then smiled a thin spurious smile. "That boy!" she cooed. "It's well seen he's been needing a woman's guidance, he will *not* go to his bed, now just you run away to your bed Tommy your father and me are going to have our supper." Then she saw Miss Appleby, and the sight seemed to trigger some crazy defensive reflex.

"Yes?" she asked in a shrill tone. "Yes? What was it? I'm sorry Mr. Fletcher is too late to see anybody this evening. And it's manners to *knock*."

"This is my housekeeper, Miss Appleby," Tom said, and when Mrs. Crow smiled he realized with horror how ambiguous the statement was. "I mean that Miss Appleby is my housekeeper. This is Mrs. Crow."

"How do you do?" Miss Appleby inquired in the most natural manner.

"You'll pardon me for contradicting you, Mr. Fletcher, but I'm not aware of any alteration in our arrangements. You stated to me in black and white, *black and white*, that I was to do the running of your household."

"You're talking nonsense," Tom said feebly.

"Black and white! And I'm not going to stand here and let anybody interfere with my rights without so much as a by-your-leave. That's my last word and I can't say fairer than that. You made an arrangement and to that arrangement you will have to stick, and that boy there was a witness to it, he'll tell you himself because he cannot tell a lie."

Her combination of brandy and stupidity and cupidity left Tom with a panic feeling of unreality.

"Black and white?" Miss Appleby asked him, and he shook his head firmly.

"And you're not called upon to interfere in matters that doesn't concern you in any way, while you're at it," Mrs. Crow assailed her. "*You*'ve shot *your* bolt, so don't think it. Don't think I don't know there are wheels within wheels, *I* never came up the Clyde on a bike!"

Miss Appleby broke into a peal of laughter. Tommy was backed somewhat away from Mrs. Crow, and half sheltering behind the Englishwoman, dying of embarrassment but fascinated as well. Tom made an effort to introduce a rational note.

"Where is Mr. Crow?" he demanded.

"Mr. Crow, God rest his soul, is sleeping on his bed of pain, the soul, for all the sleep he gets in his condition, and he is not going to be disturbed not for you nor nobody else, no offense to you, Mr. Fletcher, but there he is and there he stays."

"Oh, for heaven's sake shut up, woman," Tom said. "You'll have to get out of here, and Mr. Crow too. You could be prosecuted for trespassing. I don't want to hear any more about it."

"Oh! Oh! Oh, that's the way the land lies, is it? Off with the old, on with the new. Is that your gratitude after all I done for you and the comfort I've never grudged you, giving up my beautiful home and humble it may be but don't think it wasn't a sacrifice." She could go on like this all night, obviously. "You can't wait till your poor wife that never complained is cold in her grave but you've got your fancy woman in, well the devil will protect his own and I will not stir a foot from this house."

"I don't want to call the police," said Tom.

"The police? Oh, that will be the rock *you* perish on!" She hitched the corset. "Defamation of Character!" She stabbed the words with a fat forefinger. But Miss Appleby was already at the telephone, and Mrs. Crow's eyes darted towards her in fearful suspicion. The Englishwoman had lifted the telephone, and Tom watched her coil the cord absent-mindedly round one hand, in a rather graceful gesture. She had a good slim hand. The cord was pulled hard down over the cradle so that the line wasn't connected. She stood calmly for a moment and then said, "Operator? Good evening, would you connect me with the police, please? Thank you." She looked vaguely past Mrs. Crow, and Tom left the room and walked into the little bedroom beside the kitchen. It was rancid with the smell of stale smoke, and a man in shirtsleeves was sitting in bed reading the *Daily Express*. There was a crystal decanter on the table beside him, and a full glass beside it. He looked up, owlish and amiable.

"Oh, you got back. I was havin' a bit read in bed here. I'll keep out your way, don't you worry about me."

"Get up and get out," Tom said.

"What? Whass the matter then?"

Tom had no inhibitions or compunction towards this total stranger.

"Get up out of that bed," he said, "and get out of this house. Now."

"Now here, here now surr, fair's fair. You better talk to the wife, she does all the arrangements. I mean, fair's fair."

"You can get out or get thrown out."

"Hey, here! I'm crippled, you know. You better not lay a finger on me."

"Okay, you can wait for the police. They should be here in ten minutes."

He left the bedroom as the man was yelling "Wait a minute, here!" In the dining room, Tommy was trying to shrink into the shadows and become invisible. Miss Appleby was leaning, very calm, against the sideboard and looking coolly at Mrs. Crow, who had fallen silent; but only till Tom returned.

"You're not going to get away with this," she spat. "Your fancy housekeeper has been telling the tale to the police, but I can tell a few tales. Housekeeper! There's no smoke without fire, let me tell you!"

"You should be able to pack in half an hour," Miss Appleby

said. "If you're gone by then there'll be no charges. Would you mind fetching my luggage from the car, Mr. Fletcher?" She looked at him hard, and Tom realized with amusement and humiliation that she wanted him out of the way because he was the weak point in her defenses. With him absent, Mrs. Crow was defeated. He left the room in instant obedience, but stood outside in the garden, looking into the brightly lit dining room, till he saw Mrs. Crow flounce out. Then he got the bags and took them into the house. Thumping scrambling sounds came from the little downstairs bedroom.

"Have I overstepped a housekeeper's authority?" Miss Appleby asked.

"No. No, not at all. Jane Eyre could never have done it." She smiled a small formal smile.

"My other job was with a solicitor," she said. "Difficult people are nothing new to me. Is there another room? I don't think you should be here when she comes downstairs."

"I can't leave you with this on your own," Tom protested.

"I would rather. I work better if I'm left alone."

"Mm." Tom nodded in unwilling agreement and went into the kitchen. She motioned Tommy after him.

"What is she doing here?" Tommy asked.

"She's our new housekeeper. Do you never listen to anything?"

"I didn't think you liked her. She isn't a housekeeper type of individual, is she?"

"I don't have to like her," Tom said impatiently. "Ssh."

The difficulty about an old stone house was its good soundproofing. Through the massive door of the kitchen it was hard to hear anything precise, but the voice of Mrs. Crow was angrily raised, and there was another sound as of Mr. Crow trying to pacify her, and only an occasional low murmur that might have been Miss Appleby. Tom and his son sat with straining ears until a resounding crash signaled that the front door had been slammed, and then they furtively went out into the hall. Miss Appleby was turning from the front door.

"That seems to be that," she said, but instantly the voice of Mrs. Crow rose shrill and passionate from outside.

"I know you're in there, Fletcher! You haven't got the guts to show yourself! You canny hide from your judgment. Everybody knows you killed your wife, tell that to Miss High and Mighty English tart. Tart! You'll get your punishment for what you've done this night!"

Tommy had gone dead white and he trembled. Tom touched his arm and felt the boy shudder.

"I suppose you didn't kill your wife," Miss Appleby asked with what seemed hideous callousness. Tom stared at her wondering whether to hate her.

"A lorry crashed into her car," he said. "I was away at the time."

"Sorry. Excuse me." She went into the dining room and lifted the telephone, and he heard her asking for the police and went to dissuade her.

"She has to be stopped," the Englishwoman said. There was no arguing with her tone and of course, she was right, but he didn't want the police, he shrank from any action that would stimulate more abuse and awkwardness. Why? The woman was using her brains, the police were the only answer.

"What's this address?" she asked him.

"Twenty-four Floors Avenue."

"Police? Ah, good evening." Miss Appleby switched on, very faintly, a touch of class, though her natural manner was already impressive enough. "I'm speaking from Twenty-Four Floors Avenue. Some people are screaming in the street outside. Could you send someone right away? Of course. Thank you. Fletcher. No, my name is Appleby, Gladys Appleby. I am the housekeeper. Thank you so much."

The noise outside had risen again. Tom went into the lounge, which was in darkness, and stood well back in the shadows to look out. Mr. Crow was trying to pull his wife away, and she kept throwing off his arm and taking breaths for fresh shrieks. There were no other lights showing in the street, but darkened windows would be gently opening in this quiet, straitlaced neighborhood. Somewhere else in the night, he thought he heard a car engine.

"You'll never get the good of it, Fletcher! I'll see you hung first!" This dramatic line was spoiled by a violent jerk from Mr. Crow, who pointed far along the street, and in a wild scramble, husband and wife bolted out of the front gate and streaked across the street to a dark lane, the crippled Mr. Crow showing a notable turn of agility and dragging Mrs. Crow as she jounced on her impossible high heels. They were only seconds out of sight when a little van stopped at the gate, blue lamp flashing on the roof, and a tall figure emerged from it.

"You couldny make out what the shouting was about," the policeman said.

"It was difficult to distinguish any words," Miss Appleby said. In some curious way she had monopolized the questioning. "It sounded like a woman, but she may simply have been drunk."

"Aye, you're likely right there, miss," the policeman said, and closed his notebook. "It wouldn't be anybody local, not in this district. Some of these hooligans from Glasgow."

"Oh." Miss Appleby exuded respect for his superior experience.

"Oh aye, it's too handy here for them, you see, miss. We'll keep an eye open for anybody suspicious, you can be assured of that."

"You're very kind."

"It's a pleasure, miss. Well. Goodnight, sir. Let us know if you have any more trouble, but I doubt it."

"Goodnight."

The tall man and his tall shadow strode out to the little van.

"It'll not be like this every night," Tom said vaguely to Miss Appleby. "Not *every* night."

"Could you show me my room, and where you keep the sheets?" she said. She had a disconcerting talent for abandoning a subject and passing on to next business. "After that I'll make some food for you."

"There's food on the table."

"I would rather make something," she insisted. "Do you mind dogs?"

"No. I don't like them much, but I don't mind."

"I would like to buy a dog. I've always wanted a dog. I've always wanted a Labrador."

"Suit yourself," said Tom. Already he was thinking that he might have taken on more than he would want.

"Are you going to stay here?" Tommy asked. Tommy couldn't get it through his head.

"Yes, if you don't mind."

"I like breakfast in bed," he said.

"You can have it," she said, "if you like to come downstairs and carry it up."

"Huh," Tommy said. "Women."

She swung her hand and smacked his rump in derision. That was fine, she and the boy had an easy familiarity; as long as she confined herself to Tommy's rump, and kept her hands off the master of the house.

Seventeen

IT WAS good to be back in the office. There was a palpable atmosphere of suspense in the business, which he couldn't precisely identify, but it brought out his stubbornness and in this sense, he enjoyed it. He was exercised over the fate of Cam Jones, who was just about to depart finally, but it wasn't the case of Cam Jones that gave him the prickling feeling of impending struggle. He had a talk with Cam and tried to think of some way to help, but the older man wasn't as interested as Tom had expected.

"In the old days," Tom said, "I could have left you on your own and let you earn some commission, but that's out with the Gaylor shower. It's a house rule. They're bloody fools."

"I'm easy," Cam said. "My tastes are simple and few and I haven't got the hormones even for that."

"I haven't given up," Tom insisted. "If you want to pick up some sales, I can always put it through the books as a sale to you, at discount, and you get the check at full rate from the sale and pay me. There's always a loophole, even through Nick Gaylor."

"Don't fret yourself into the gutter, Tom," Cam said. "That's the kind of jiggery-pokery that gets people the jail. Tell me one thing, Tom, you're not on the booze, are you?"

"Why don't you belt up about the booze?" Tom asked him. "Are you turning Rechabite?"

"There's something helluva funny going on," Cam insisted. "If it was me I could understand it — I've been bashing the tomato juice so long that if I took a glass of beer people would say I had gone berserk. But I'm just telling you I still hear you're caning the whisky. You'd better watch it."

"I have enough trouble watching Nick Gaylor," Tom said. "Get to hell out of here with your sermons."

He didn't hear from Gaylor at the end of a fortnight on the subject of the factory, but after three weeks Jack Fillimore telephoned to ask him to tread water, show a policy of masterly inactivity and maintain the status quo because negotiations were going on for the sale of the plant. Tom thanked him, and thought momentarily of going out to see Stiles, to let him know what was going on; but he decided against it. The sale might not come off, and if it didn't, there was no sense in getting the workers worried in the meantime.

Young Hugh Winton almost looked as if he might lose weight, he was driving himself so hard in his impersonation of the high-pressure head-office crackerjack. In fact, he was getting plumper than ever — probably through overeating to keep his strength up, Tom surmised.

"You're doing fine, Hugh," Tom told him. "Stop narking yourself into a decline or you'll burst out of your new suits."

"Ah, you've got to keep up the impetus, Tom. What I mean, Gaylor's have done all right by me, I've still got my job, so they deserve loyalty."

"They deserve a fair bargain. That's how Nick Gaylor describes it. Nobody deserves loyalty, Hugh, at least, companies don't deserve loyalty. Loyalty's for your friends if you've got any, or your wife and kids."

"Sure, but if the company treats you right, well, what I mean, you could call it a friend . . . in a way."

"Aye, right. Away you go, I've got to go out and be loyal for a couple of hours."

He was going out to call on David Thew, another old acquaintance who had grown up in business with him. Twenty years ago Thew had been assistant buyer in a big engineering company when Tom was a salesman. Now he was a director; and Tom was a director. Tom still sold and Thew still bought. They had a comfortable friendship that managed to subsist on a meeting once or twice a year, the kind of old-pal contact that would always irritate newcomers, like young Hugh, because it got in the way of newcomers. He was losing patience with Hugh's loyalty-oath syndrome, and he warned himself not to give in to those middle-aged irritations.

Thew was the same as always, he showed no aging in twenty years that Tom could see, but he looked rather hard at Tom.

"You're looking better," he said doubtfully.

"I haven't been ill."

"Well, you've, er, ah, you know, you looked a bit pale the last time I saw you."

"I'm fine. How is your health?"

"There's nothing wrong with *my* health." Thew was rather offended. "I keep myself fit. There's something wrong with two of the desks you sold me. The locks don't work. I've told your office about it."

"Let me see them."

They went to the accounts office and Tom failed to make anything of the malfunctioning locks. He was going to promise to send somebody to look at them, but Thew's attitude was frosty enough to annoy him, and he got down on his knees instead and after a struggle, removed the lock mechanisms entirely.

"I'll have them fixed or give you new ones," he said, a little breathlessly, and dropped them in his pocket.

"Aye, but when?"

"Tomorrow. No, the day after — I'm not going to promise you a date if I can't keep it. When did you get the desks?"

"It's hardly six months. They should last a lifetime."

"Aye," said Tom. "They will when they're fixed." They were walking slowly back to Thew's office, and Tom was sizing up the equipment en route.

"Three of your typewriters are ready for the scrap heap," he said. "Do you want me to fix you up?"

"Heavens above," said Thew, "you never stop trying to get money out of us."

"There's nothing in it for me," Tom said curtly, "it's more trouble than it's worth, but you need them, the girls can't do decent work on these machines." He looked round the rather shabby office. "You need a new desk, you're a big man. I would be ashamed to look at visitors across that old apple box."

"Well, that's funny, I was thinking something like that," Thew admitted. "I don't like the way you can read my mind. But nothing expensive, the board's gone very canny about expenditure."

"Damn the board, they eat off solid gold. I'll send you some prices that'll turn your hair white. You've got to act up to your exalted status."

"Yes, all right, Tom, I've always been able to trust your judgment. This whole room's a bit shabby, but I've never had the heart to complain about it. Is there anything else?"

"Aye, I'll buy you a drink before I go."

". . . I don't know that I feel like a drink. It's a bit early in the day," said Thew.

"For you? The heavens will fall. Okay, suit yourself, David, I can get back and do more business if I don't have to spend my money on you."

"Oh! Aye, well, all right, I've got time for a wee one. Just a wee one."

They went to a new bar and Thew asked for a double whisky without thinking.

"It's too hot for me," Tom said. "I'm having a beer." He looked hard at Thew, but the other man merely nodded, and they drank.

"Have another," said Tom.

"Aye, all right, I don't mind if I do. That'll be enough, though." He laughed nervously. "It's a terrible thing when it gets a grip of you."

Little bells rang in Tom's head. He twisted his face into solemn sympathy.

"Has it got a grip of you, David?" he murmured. "Surely not. You can hold it as well as you ever did."

"Me? Not at all!" Thew was easily touched on the raw, he always had been. "I enjoy a drink, I'll admit that."

"Who has it got a grip of, then?" Tom asked.

"It's only a general observation. I've seen some good chaps went down under it."

"So have I," Tom said, and stared hard at Thew. The other man lifted his glass and smiled.

"Cheers," he said. "You're looking fine, Tom. Here, don't charge too many thousands for that desk, will you? The company's got to make *some* profit over the year."

"No," Tom said slowly. "I won't."

Meg Macrae told him he was putting on beef, and he went out and weighed himself to prove her wrong. She was wrong.

"I don't care what the machine says," she said. "It must be that lassie you've got housekeeping. Is she giving you all your home comforts?"

"She feeds me, and switch off your filthy imagination, Meg."

"It beats me. I don't know how any lassie can trust herself living in the same house as you."

"It's strictly business, I'm too old for pleasure. Come and have dinner if you like, I think we're on scaloppine marsala tonight."

"Mercy me! And tell me, does your lady housekeeper sit down at table with you?"

"No, you snobbish old bitch, I fling her a bone in the kennel."

"I canny see it, I simply cannot see it. But you look well on it anyway."

It was not entirely strictly business, of course. It was impossible to have a woman living in the house and preserve the pristine atmosphere of formality. Acquaintance had to develop. Appleby was still quiet, and evidently quiet by nature, but it was a more informal quietness; guarded, but informal.

She worked as efficiently as she had promised, and the only dispute they had had so far was when he found that she had bought an expensive cookery book, the Larousse, with her own money, and he insisted that it should properly be classed as domestic equipment and purchased by the employer. She retorted that when she left, she would certainly take it with her, and refused to let him pay for it. No doubt she would leave, but he hoped not for some time. She made it possible to forget domestic problems completely, and Tommy clearly liked her.

She spent many evenings in her own room, reading or listening to the radio. It would have worried him to see her lock herself away in loneliness except that she didn't appear to regard it as loneliness, and as often as not would decline to spend the evening with him and Tommy because she said she had other things to do. When she did stay downstairs, she would look at television or sometimes discuss Tommy's homework with him, not very expertly but with an interest and patience he himself could never muster. It wasn't really like having a wife in the house, but it was as pleasant as having a sister or an aunt — more pleasant probably, from what he knew of sisters and aunts.

Curious about her hidden selves, as he would have been about anybody, he asked her one evening if she would like to play the piano, and got the astonishing information that she actually played the piano accordion. The idea was grotesque and he said so.

"My parents were professionals," she said. "They had a musical act."

"On the stage?" He was startled.

"Yes. I didn't like it." She didn't close a subject so much as let it trickle down a hole and vanish. But he was able to forget about laundries and window cleaners; his shirts constantly had buttons on them and his suits vanished regularly to the cleaners. And he was sure he was saving money.

"I'm making a profit on you," he said.

"I still think you pay me too much." She was washing dishes and he was hovering in the kitchen, unwilling to force his company on her. "Considering," she said, "that there's no end-product you can sell. It's pure expense."

"You've been listening to my patter."

"I would have to be deaf not to."

"But your last job must have been worth a lot more."

"I don't pay rent, I've got no fares to pay, I don't buy food. I'm better off financially. All the money I get I can spend on myself. I feel almost guilty about it."

"You're worth it," he said shortly, and made to leave. "As long as you're happy."

"Yes, I like it."

"Good." He left her.

A piano accordion, of all things. A violin, yes, even a cello. He felt like sniggering every time he thought about it. She would probably have been all right on the stage, with her long legs and a piano accordion. To his surprise, it was only a few weeks to Christmas, and he toyed with the notion of buying her one, but decided it was too expensive and would be too showy and opulent a gift, and that doubtless she didn't actually *like* piano accordions. It was a pity, because he thought he might quite like to learn a couple of tunes on the accordion, it looked so damned difficult. How did accordionists avoid getting their flesh mangled between all those pleats? Especially well-built women accordionists . . .

His daughter Joan telephoned to invite him and Tommy to spend Christmas Day, and it was this invitation that brought home to him how much he preferred not to leave his own house. He was going to accept, grudgingly, when he remembered the Problem of the Housekeeper, and he covered the phone and called for her.

"What are you doing for Christmas?" he asked.

She was wearing an apron over dark green tights. The outfit pleased him.

"Nothing," she said, and at once realized the implications. "I could go away for a few days."

"Do you want to?"

"No."

"Okay." He spoke into the telephone. "No, it's too difficult this year, Joan, we'd rather stay at home."

Without coming right out with it, Joan indicated that he was letting her down, and also that she was being kind to him and it would do him good to accept the invitation, and also, perhaps, that she didn't like the way things were working out, with odd unknown women from England worming their way into his house.

"My daughter thinks I'm hard," he told Gladys Appleby. "She's right."

"Yes, I'm sure she is." There was a derisive note in this, but she left the room without pursuing it. He noticed her back view, and he noticed that he was noticing it. It wasn't a bad back view. His domestic situation, he considered, was pretty well perfect. The Appleby woman — he insisted on calling her this when he thought about her, to maintain his lack of personal interest in her — the Appleby woman kept him comfortable and she had the kind of plain, ordinary looks that didn't obtrude and therefore didn't pall. It might even be admitted that she looked pretty good the more she was around. So he had his good food and a well-run establishment and a woman to look at, and the relationship was distant enough to have some of the qualities of interesting discovery without the troublesome need to develop any further.

This was how he explained it to himself, with the wry reservation that he could always be deceiving himself.

In the second week of December, she warned him one day to come home early because Tommy was going to a dance, and it was an occasion.

"He'll go to a million dances," Tom scoffed. "Don't start mothering him." Her face went grim, and he touched her arm in guilt and sorrow. "I didn't mean that," he said. "You do what you like with him, you're good for him. But a dance? Let's not exaggerate it."

"It doesn't matter," she said, and closed up. He looked at her back for a second and went to get the car out.

"This is not the game," he said aloud as he drove delicately towards Glasgow. There were patches of frost on the road. "Okay, have a wife, have tiffs. Not little emotional scenes with bloody servants. That is going to stop before it starts, boy. You don't pay wages for fits of temperament."

He was home early nevertheless, telling himself that he had nowhere else to go in any case. In the atmosphere of haggard excitement he felt half excluded. Tommy was having an enforced bath, and popping in and out of the bathroom in a towel to yell plaintive questions about underwear.

"I had a bath yesterday," he moaned. "Excessive cleanliness is a symptom of a disordered personality. Gladys! Did you hear that? Excessive cleanliness is a symptom of a disordered personality!"

"Shut up and scrub up!" she shouted from somewhere. There was no sign of food anywhere. He put the kettle on the cooker and started to cut sandwiches, and he tried to feel aggrieved, but he couldn't manage it. Gladys drifted past him carrying a clean white shirt on a hanger and said no more than Hello.

"Fine thing!" he shouted, but he spoiled this by laughing, and finally he abandoned the sandwiches and sat before the fire in the lounge with a whisky and water to let the commotion spend itself round him.

"She's put the creases too far round to the side, hasn't she, Dad?" Tommy appealed to him. Tom looked contemptuously at the boy's trousers and said, "It's the silly way you're standing."

Tommy looked thoughtfully down at his feet and said, "It's possible that I have eccentric ankle joints. My knees appear to occur at an obtuse angle to my femur."

"Have you eaten enough?" Gladys demanded, and the boy waved a world-weary hand.

"There are occasions on which nutrition recedes to a secondary position. Lay off, Gladys, it's time I was away."

"What the hell have you rubbed that leg against?" she said. It was the first time he had heard her use even a mild swearword. Tommy clapped hands to brow and groaned. She grabbed a clothes brush and knelt in front of him to rub away the white mark from the cloth.

"Don't make me utterly impeccable, my good woman," Tommy said, and patted her head. "Flesh and blood can stand only so much."

Gladys bowed her head, and Tom thought she was giggling, but in an instant of awful discomfort he saw that she was crying. Tommy's face flushed dark and his hand went on patting her head foolishly. He looked over at Tom and grimaced.

"Women," he choked. "I'll have to scram, honestly. Don't wait up for me." He backed out of the room stumbling and grinning horribly. Gladys Appleby was still sitting on her haunches, with her face averted. Tom reached out and touched her shoulder.

"You did fine," he said. "Have a drink."

She shook her head as if to fling away the tears or fling away his sympathy, but his hand stayed on her shoulder. She gave a shuddering sigh and turned and fell softly into his outstretched arm and lowered her face on to his knee. He let his hand rest on her hair and softly massaged it.

"You'll ruin my hair," she mumbled.

"Yes."

They stayed in the same position for perhaps three minutes, and then she slowly pulled herself to her feet and said, "I will have a drink, if you don't mind." She poured a glass and sipped it and put it down.

"Sorry to use you as a cushion," she said. "I don't know what I'm blubbering about."

"I didn't object," he said, amused. "I quite liked it."

"Really?"

"Yes, really."

She dropped naturally to her knees and laid her head on his chest. He held her with one arm.

"I'm hiding my face," she said. "I feel such a fool."

"Yes."

She made herself comfortable.

"I'm not making advances to you," she said. "I swear it. It's nothing like that."

"I know," he said. "It's comfort . . ."

"Yes, that's right. It's comfort."

He kissed the top of her head lightly.

"Thanks," she said. "I'll make some decent food for you now."

He let her go and they dined on thin-sliced underdone steaks and Burgundy.

"I've been meaning to ask you about buying wine," she said. "Yes, cheers. I keep all the newspaper cuttings about wine. It seems if you buy a lot of this year's Burgundy when it's cheap, it should be rather precious in five years."

"It's all right in theory," he said. "It would never last five years."

"But you have a cellar. You could lock it away. That's what I would do."

He grinned at her enthusiasm. "All right," he said. "Make up a list if it amuses you and we'll think about it."

"I have to talk about something," she complained. "I'm still extremely embarrassed."

"Don't be."

"I'll be terrified to brush past you now in case you imagine I'm trying to throw myself into your arms. I'm not, I swear it."

He smiled at her, in a mixture of sympathy and mean little triumph that she was finally discomfited.

"I swear it!" she insisted. A perverse devil was in him, and he looked at her closely.

"Why don't you come to bed with me?" he said. "Now."

Her breath stopped and she stared at him glassy-eyed. He laughed aloud.

"I was curious to see how you would react to that," he said, still laughing. "But that's the question lying at the bottom of it all. Now it's been said, it's lost its sting and we can both forget it."

She started breathing again.

"I don't think I would mind," she muttered into her plate.

"What?"

"I don't think I should mind," she said very loudly. "I don't *think* so. This is very difficult," she added wildly. "Perhaps I should go away. I've enjoyed it, honestly, I *like* housekeeping, it's so peaceful compared with working in an office, but the reason why I was sure it would be perfectly simple was that I didn't really like you in the first place. I imagined that that would make for a reasonable degree of simplicity. However, I've never lived with a man before — really lived, I mean, in the same house, seven days a week, making breakfast every morning and locking up every night. I've never been exposed to a prolonged regimen of propinquity, I suppose that is how Tommy would describe it."

"And has this worried you? I've never noticed a thing."

"No, I swear it hasn't, Mr. Fletcher. That's interesting, I've always thought of you as Mister Fletcher, you see. But it must have been there all the time, and now I've made that silly scene and you've said that, and I suppose everything's spoiled. I *was* enjoying it, honestly."

"You're not going away, don't be silly," he said. "You cook too well, and in any case, Tommy would die if you went away."

"Yes." She stared at the table. "I'm very fond of Tommy. I love him."

Tom laughed gloriously.

"Well that's a hell of a reason for going to bed with *me!*"

"There's no need to tease me," she chid him. "And in any case, I'm not." She paused and looked uncertain, almost afraid. "Am I?" she asked him shakily. Her expression wrung him curiously and he stared at her.

"I'll tell you something," he said. He pressed his hand on the table to still the tremor in his fingers. "I think you *are.*"

She put her fingertips to her cheeks and sat still. He stood up, confused and angry.

"I shouldn't do this," he said. "I'll be no good to you. In the plain ordinary physical sense. I've lost the knack. Do you understand that? I won't please you and I'll humiliate myself."

"I don't mind," she said, puzzled.

He looked down at her and wondered if she understood at all.

"You're a very kind woman, Miss Appleby," he said.

"Don't be silly," she said. She stood up and walked out of the room ahead of him.

Eighteen

IN THE middle of January he had a lunch date with Alice Wardell. She looked neat and luscious, as always, and she emanated warmth and titillation. Smiling and joking with her, he examined her clinically and admitted to himself that she was good.

"How is business?" she asked him.

"I don't know."

"Well, you know what they say, Tom. It's tough at the top."

"I'm three quarters of the way down from there," he said, "so I wouldn't know."

"Are you having a hard time," she asked, in quick curiosity.

"I don't know," he said. "Gaylor's are a tough shower and they've got me where they want me. Oh, I'm all right as long as I play the game, but sometimes I get a boyish notion to tell them to go to hell."

"Don't do it, Tom," she warned him. "You'd be making a big mistake. Oh, I know you're still as keen as ever, but let's face it, it's security that matters now."

"Is it?"

"Once you're past forty, Tom, need you ask?"

"No, I suppose not."

"You know very well in your own heart, Tom. There's

a time for taking chances and a time for sitting back. It's very *nice* to sit back, now admit it, isn't it?"

"Mm." He smiled at her and she lifted her glass to him and gave him a long bold look over the rim.

He consulted with Meg Macrae when he got back to the office.

"I've had a wee billet-doux from God," he said.

"It's nice to be remembered."

"It's the usual annual pep-talk sludge," he said, pushing at the many-paged letter distastefully. "And there's a wee paragraph tucked away in the middle, fixing my percentage of the profits for the next fiscal year."

"They'll have raised it, of course."

"No, but they've been generous in their way, they've only cut it by half."

"You've got too much money anyway."

"I wonder what I'll tell them," Tom said, and Meg snorted.

"If you dragged me in here to hold your hand and give you advice you're up a gum tree," she said.

"You think I should be a good boy and say thank you sir."

"I didn't say that, I didn't say eechy or ochy. You'll do what you decide yourself and you're not going to blame me for it."

"My God," said Tom. "Loyalty."

"Och! Loyalty my bottom! Let me away to get on with my work."

"And what'll you do if I chuck it?"

"I'll do as I think fit, Tom Fletcher, and whatever I do will be for me to decide when it happens, *if* it happens, so don't waste my time. Away and ask your housekeeper. And don't tell me you're not getting your nooky. There's a look about you."

"That look is night starvation, you dirty old besom. Get out, you're useless to man or beast."

"*That* depends on the nature of the beast," she said.

He did ask his housekeeper.

"You don't mind hearing about my business worries?" he asked her.

"No, I'm flattered. But how can I offer you an opinion? I don't know anything about it."

"Dammit," he said, "I either sit tight and work out the next few years being prepared for pasture, or I chuck it."

"Chuck it and what?"

"I don't know. I could retire. I've got money. I could sell this house. I have insurance policies coming up in a few years. I could grow roses."

"No. That's no good."

"Don't you think so?"

"No!"

"I could start something on my own."

"That sounds reasonable."

He got impatient with her.

"What do you mean, it sounds reasonable? You don't even know what it could be."

"I'm sorry, I told you I was ignorant."

"I could go bust if I started on my own."

"I don't think you would. And in any case, is it so awful to go . . . go bust?"

"It's hellish."

"All the same, you couldn't do *nothing*. I don't understand why you're getting so angry."

"Neither do I. I'm angry with you because I'm no good to you."

"I didn't complain."

"No, you're a very tolerant woman, Gladys. I'm sorry I'm such a hard man."

"Hard? Hard?" She laughed. "You have never been hard. You're always talking about how business is business, but you've spent weeks trying to find work for that old man in the office. The young one in the office — I can't remember his name, but *he*'s hard. He doesn't care about anybody but himself."

"Hugh? Hugh's all right. I trained him."

"You take more care of him than you do of your own son."

"*Now* you're overstepping your responsibilities as a housekeeper!"

"I don't care. You're not hard, you're only hard-working. If you were hard *you* would be in Nick Gaylor's place and he would be in yours."

"I don't care about money!" The woman was too thick-headed to comprehend him.

"It doesn't *matter!*" she said. "I'm not hard either — I'm the kind of person who always ends up taking care of things for other people. Francis was hard. Francis was the man I worked for. He often wept on my shoulder, it's shocking of me to tell anyone this, but he did, every time I told him the affair would have to finish, and it always went on, because he was so soft and vulnerable that he *had* to get his own way. Soft on the outside. I know this now because I've been thinking about it for weeks. People like that are really hard because they don't *care* about other people, they simply insist on their appetites being satisfied."

"So do I."

"I don't know what got into me," she said. "I expect most of what I've said is silly. But it's the way I see it. Only it doesn't help a great deal, does it?"

"Did he really weep on your shoulder?" Tom asked in astonishment.

"Yes, but I shouldn't have said that and please forget I did say it. It's not fair."

"He must have been a louse."

"Perhaps he was. It's awfully difficult to tell. I wasn't promiscuous, you know."

"I know. You would have had a better time if you had been."

"No!"

The doorbell had been ringing, and Tommy came into the kitchen.

"It's Joan," he said.

"Joan and Alan?" Tom asked.

"No, just Joan. I surmise she has experienced an emotional cataclysm and run home to Father."

"I can't take this," Tom said in a faraway voice. "I don't believe it, but I can't take it."

He went into the lounge and found Joan sitting upright on the sofa, wearing an overbright smile.

"Hello," he said warily.

"Now I know you're going to be shocked, Dad, because you have a soft spot for Alan, but I may as well tell you and get it over with. I've left him. Finished. Kaput! All over. I'm not having any more. Before you say anything, I may as well tell you my mind is made up. There's no use going on."

Tom sank gingerly into a chair. Tommy was leaning in the doorway, rapturously interested.

"Ask Miss Appleby to make some tea, will you, Tommy?" Tom asked, and the boy put on an imitation pout and withdrew.

"Oh? Is Miss Appleby still here? Is that what you call her? 'Miss'?"

"Where is Alan?" Tom asked, and Joan's mouth pursed grimly.

"I don't know, and I don't care!"

"Isn't he at home?"

"It's a matter of the utmost indifference to me."

Joan sat back, having delivered the bombshell. She was now waiting for Tom to make the next move, and as he gazed dreamily at her, he had the strongest inclination to do nothing whatever. He felt an impatient fury against the girl, with her tidy little body and her tidy little mind, solving her problems by handing them to him. Maliciously, he determined to leave the situation lying where Joan had dumped it and wait for her to do something. Moments stretched until the silence twanged, and he gazed thoughtfully at her and kept his mouth shut. It worked.

"Now we have to decide what to do next," she said.

"I don't understand, Joan," he said callously.

"Well what am I going to *do?*" she demanded. The prim purposeful tone was giving way to petulance.

"*I* don't know, Joan. What do you *want* to do?"

"I don't know," she complained. "That's why I came home."

Home. Home. Home.

"Do you want me to speak to Alan?" Tom asked.

"No, I don't care if I never see him again!"

"In that case you would have no problem, surely. But I'm sure you'll change your mind, Joan. Alan's a decent young fellow — it's very doubtful if you'll do any better."

"I won't discuss Alan."

Tommy came in with a tray. It was typical of Gladys that she would stay invisible when anybody else's business was being discussed.

"I suppose this is all the result of your dear old grandfather's rush of generosity," Tom said.

"That's got nothing to do with it! Well, I suppose that started it," Joan ended grudgingly.

"Have you got the money yet?"

"No, it takes a long time."

"Does it?" Tom was intrigued. "Does it really? It often takes a long time to *get* money, but I've never known any difficulty about giving it away. Now pay attention, Joan. Your grandfather, I know you quite like the old pig, is nevertheless an old pig, and he's the meanest old pig you're ever likely to meet. Giving money, to him, is like having toenails pulled out. If he's taking this long to get round to it, he's thinking better of it. How will you feel if it turns out you've had all this trouble with Alan for nothing?"

"Granddad *promised!* I'm not worried, I know the money's coming. Not that I care about the money itself anyway! It would have happened even without the money. I've just reached the end of my tether."

She scooped one, two, three spoonfuls of sugar into her tea and stirred it threateningly. Tom examined her and knew, rather sadly, that she would never willingly tell the whole truth about anything whatever. She avoided his eye.

"Where did you say Alan was?" he asked mildly.

"I have no idea and I have no interest."

"Dammit, where is he? I want to speak to him!"

"I don't *know!*"

Tom glared at her.

"*He*'s left *you!*"

"He wouldn't have the cheek," Joan cried in fury.

"He's left you, and that's why you've run home."

"Well the least I could expect was a bit of *sympathy!* I've never been so humiliated."

Why, he wondered, couldn't his daughter have been one of those guileless, candid, embarrassing children who spill everything? It had taken dreary minutes to establish one plain, unconcealable fact which Joan could have announced at once; but that was only the beginning. She had come to see him with some quite specific intention; there was some specific, precise thing she wanted from him, but being Joan, she was quite likely to sit out the whole evening without admitting what it was, and in the end, she would hope to get it forced upon her without having betrayed herself into asking for it. He was tempted to question her brutally, but this was an irrational, emotional impulse, because brutal questioning would merely produce more and more hysterical evasions. He sat and chatted with her and drank tea and wondered what he should do about Gaylor's and made mental calculations and planned a long talk with young Hugh Winton, and waited for Joan to sidle up to the point.

"It's time you redecorated this room," she said aimlessly.

"Yes," he said aimlessly. They sat.

"It'll be all right if I stay here tonight?" she said, and he said, "Of course. There's plenty of room."

"That's settled, then. And then I can get my mind settled."

Joan, he thought, had the kind of mind that would never settle; it would have to be swatted first.

"I'll get Miss Appleby to fix up the bedroom," he said, and she looked at him reproachfully.

"Really, Dad! At least I can find my way about in my own house!"

"Yes, of course."

If that was all she had wanted of him, it would have saved a lot of trouble to ask outright. And it wouldn't take her long to come to her senses and realize that old Shaw was fooling her with his promises of free fortunes. And Alan would come back too. Everything would be fine, or as fine as it could be between two people like Joan and Alan. He would explain it sketchily to Gladys Appleby.

It was extraordinarily difficult to explain it to Gladys, because it was impossible to get Gladys alone. As long as Joan was there, Gladys skillfully lurked out of sight and sent Tommy in with more food late in the evening. When he excused himself and went into the kitchen to see Gladys, she had vanished, and Joan was inquisitive about his disappearance.

"I wanted to see the housekeeper," he said vaguely, and infected by Joan's habit of tacking on a spurious excuse to everything, he added, "to arrange about food and things."

"Tsk tsk, you shouldn't have to bother with things like that when I'm sitting here! I'll see her."

"No, it's all right, it doesn't matter," he said. It was barely half past ten. He didn't usually go to bed till around midnight, but he searched his mind bleakly and could find no possibility of sustaining conversation with his own daughter for ninety minutes. He glued a fatherly smile over the glumness of his brain and looked for a book and announced that he had a hard day ahead and would have to get to bed.

"Just you do that, Dad, you do look a bit peaky," Joan said lovingly. "I'll turn in too — I'm in the wee bedroom downstairs. It feels *strange*," she giggled, "but I was very careful not to go near my old room with the housekeeper's things in it. You have to leave servants their own privacy, it's the only way to avoid unpleasantness."

"There isn't likely to be unpleasantness, she's a very quiet woman," he said impatiently.

"Of course! I could tell that right away. But it's just as well not to take any risks, you know what they say about two women in one house."

He was going to look at her suspiciously, but she was kissing him goodnight and he couldn't see her face. He was profoundly glad that she was only staying overnight.

When he came home on the following evening he realized again how much of a blind idiot he could be. It was Gladys' day off, she was away somewhere on her own, and instead of the casserole he had learned to expect, there was Joan; full of jollity and surprise.

"Well, I said to myself," she explained, "it's Appleby's day off, and Dad coming home to an empty house, and after all, I've got nothing to rush home for, have I? And I cooked you a proper meal."

The meal was perhaps the most crushing surprise. It was macaroni and cheese, and the table was loaded with buns and French cakes. Maybe that was why Alan had run away. *In petitioning for divorce, schoolteacher Alan Spurrier alleged that his wife, pretty brunette Joan Spurrier, had subjected him to repeated and barbarous carbohydrates* . . . Young Tommy wasn't at all put out. He liked sugary buns and French cakes even better than food. The most attractive thing about Gladys Appleby, Tom reflected, wasn't sex at all. It was her dedication to cooking.

"I'll take the food, and let the nooky go," he said.

"What?"

Joan was looking at him, uncomprehending. He had spoken aloud. It must definitely be the end of middle age and the beginning of senility. Soon he would be one of those mumbling old men who pass you in the street having long angry conversations with themselves.

"Nothing," he muttered, "I was thinking about something somebody said. Doesn't mean anything."

Again he went to bed early, in despair, but this time he lay awake and alert, and caught Gladys on her way to bed. He beckoned silently to her, and she came into his bedroom. Thank God, this woman didn't jump to any conclusions. She didn't protest that it was indiscreet, she merely waited.

"My daughter is obviously dug in for a little longer," he said. "Not for long, but for a few days."

"Yes?"

"You don't mind?"

"I don't understand. You're my employer — you don't have to ask me when you want to entertain your own children."

"No. Still, I wanted to warn you. Joan is . . . Frankly, she's a damned nuisance. Don't let her annoy you."

"All right." Gladys was honestly surprised. He let her out and never thought to touch her.

He still planned to have a talk with Hugh Winton, a carefully stage-managed talk, perferably over drink, but for the next few days Hugh was away and away and working like a Stakhanovite, and the opportunity never arose. Meg Macrae asked him once what he had decided to do about Gaylor, and he barked at her and she dropped the subject. It had taken more than a full working day to pursue the branch office of a desk manufacturer and dig out of them replacement desk locks for David Thew. This was the kind of job an office boy should have been doing, but his pride was involved in it. It was nevertheless an atrociously uneconomical way of spending time, and he grudged it and felt fairly sick of business.

At the weekend, he discovered Joan in a coverall, with her sleeves up, ready for a stern assault on household cleaning. The spectacle offended him, because since the beginning of the Gladys era he had never actually seen any housework being done at all. Cleaning and everything else appeared to happen in secret, during his absence, and the sound of a vacuum cleaner never disturbed his cloistered calm.

"The place is clean enough," he protested sourly, but Joan's mind was not to be lightly turned from duty.

"There's always a few special jobs that *have* to be done. You men would live in pigsties if there were no women in the world," she added archly.

"Gladys can do all that nonsense," he said. "That's what she's paid for."

"It's not the same thing," she said cryptically. He couldn't make any sense of this statement. "Oh, and incidentally, I've been thinking, Dad."

He saw it coming now. He had been blind and imbecile, but now he saw it coming.

"I can get rid of Gladys," he said smoothly, "because it's a waste of money when you can take care of the house for me."

"You've been thinking about it yourself!" Joan was tickled pink. "You're absolutely right."

"You're not on, Joan. Now please understand this before you think of any good reasons. You are not on."

"It's only commonsense." She was ignoring him. Joan was convinced that if you ignore anything hard enough it'll go away. "I know you don't want to come between me and Alan but that doesn't arise, I assure you." She started lifting ornaments and being busy and efficient. "Our marriage is completely on the rocks, and to tell you the truth, good riddance. And don't worry, I would *rather* be at home. I don't think I could stand living in that house again," she added dramatically. "Oh, Appleby! Talk about angels. We were just talking about you."

Gladys had incautiously come into the lounge. Tom watched her, and saw that she took in Joan's coverall, the bucket of water, the dusters, without a trace of surprise, resentment or anything except polite interest. She smiled pleasantly at Joan and said to Tom, "I thought about goulash tomorrow. Is that all right?"

"Urrgh," said Joan. Black anger started to grow in Tom's skull.

"Yes, goulash is fine," he said levelly.

"There's something else, Appleby, while you're here," said Joan. "We were discussing it this very minute."

"Joan, shut up."

"It's all right, Dad. It's like this, Appleby."

"Miss Appleby!" He was shouting. "Will you leave the room? Please? At once."

"Yes, of course."

She left the room. Please. At once. Joan turned to him, and he could see the little glints of light in her eyes, the tear signals.

"Put that damned bucket down," he said. "There isn't a speck of dirt anywhere in the room. Get your coat. I'm driving you back home now."

"I won't go! You can't! I've offered to stay and look after you," she said, explaining to an idiot dog.

"You are not on, Joan," he said again. "I don't know what I've got that everybody wants to look after me but get this into your head, I — am — not — going — to — be — looked after. I am not a refuge for runaway wives. You're a big girl now and you're going to live your own life. I am — As long as — hell! You're not getting your own way, Joan, do you understand that? You can babble or yell if you like, but you're leaving. You don't care, do you? I've just to turf my housekeeper into the street so that you can do your Pollyanna?"

"That kind can always get another job."

Blind with anger, he stamped into the downstairs bedroom and started to ram everything in sight into the lightweight air-traveler suitcase with Joan's monogram on it. Wails of agony and desolation followed him. He was a fool, he should never trust himself to speak, it only caused trouble; and he was a fool, he should be able to manipulate his own daughter without allowing hysterical crises to develop. He was a fool, but he was deeply relieved that he wasn't the kind of fool who was going to have Joan for his housekeeper.

"Christ," he said to the bedroom wall, "it must be an epidemic. I do nothing but fling women out of this house."

She wouldn't go in his car. He hated her, she wailed. She wanted a taxi. He telephoned for a taxi. She kept it waiting for fifteen minutes, and then tripped down the front path waving affectionately back at him while Tommy carried her suitcase. Not for Joan the shrieks on the lawn where neighbors could hear. Neighbors mattered to Joan.

"It's like prizing a limpet off, isn't it?" Tommy said chattily as the taxi drew away.

"You mind your tongue!" His anger spilled over on to the boy, who shrugged.

"It is, a bit," Tom admitted. "I didn't want you to hear that barney."

"I'm sorry for Alan," the boy said. "Alan's a very . . . he's a very decent type of man, isn't he? Incidentally, Joan's culinary performance is hardly up to Cordon Bleu standards, is it? When she dished up that macaroni the other night I thought for a dread moment that Mrs. Crow was back."

"You are too damned cheeky for your age," Tom gruffed.

"I can't help it if I'm far advanced into puberty," Tommy said, and Tom uttered a short hoot of helpless mirth.

Gladys wasn't in the house. Her tact was almost excessive. She came back late in the afternoon, and was told merely that Joan had gone. In a flush of guilt and relief, Tom proposed that they should all go over the hills to Drymen for dinner, and they dressed up and went. This could look like something significant, he warned himself — something about the old Scottish common-law process; if a woman appeared with you in public and was taken for your wife and you permitted her to be mistaken for your wife, the law held that mumble mumble mumble. He insisted on champagne with dinner although he had never liked champagne very much as a drink, and in spite of his stern orders, Gladys kept letting Tommy sip hers, and they all giggled. When they got back home, the boy shambled off to bed in inartistic imitation of a drunk, but possibly a little drunk in truth.

"Thank you for the evening," Gladys said. "I'll make some tea."

"I'll write to Gaylor on Monday," Tom said. "And tell him to ram his managing-directorship up his . . . his . . . up his jumper."

"Up his jacksy?"

"Miss Appleby," Tom protested. "That's not the kind of language I expect from my servants."

"I don't even know what it means. I heard it from you. I'm glad. I don't like Gaylor."

A quiet, passive woman, unexcitable, undemanding; a little pallid compared with other women he had known — he had never really known a long-quiet woman.

"So do I," he said. "Gaylor's a twit. I might just open up in opposition to him."

"Could you?"

"I feel tempestuous, that's the word. I'm a hard man, Miss Appleby, get that. Yes," he said in surprise. "I feel tempestuous. I do." He held out both hands and she took them, and he pulled her towards him.

"You don't have to be tempestuous for me," she said. "I don't even know if I would like you to be tempestest . . . tempestuous."

But she was wrong and he was right. The familiar fear of failure was still with him, but he crushed it down. She gasped, and in the gray blur of light in the bedroom he saw her eyes open and her mouth open in shock and surprise and felt her hands clamp rigid where they held him. A great shuddering sigh shook her, and at once she pulled his head down and was whispering fiercely into his ear, "I didn't believe it, I thought it was a scientific theory, I didn't believe it happened to people I was sure they made all the stories up I thought it was a confidence trick it's true it's true it's true what have you done to me oh oh oh I don't believe it." Tom, surfing on a giant ocean roller of release and relief, wondered at the same time what kind of creep her former boss had been, and real-

ized in alarm that she was all set to have his neck for breakfast.

"Gently, gently," he whispered. "That's the jugular vein."

"Oh! Oh I'm sorry, I'm sorry, I couldn't help it, oh dear!
You've ruined me, you've ruined me, I'll never be the same
again."

"You can always *try*," he said, and she had a fit of giggles
and had to bury her mouth in his neck again.

"Well," he said, "that's your birthday present."

"No, no," she giggled weakly. "It's too much, sir, I
couldn't accept it."

Nineteen

A MONTH passed, of bitter cold. The sight of snow had always pleased him, childishly, and he was the obsessional kind of driver who actually enjoyed the extra difficulty of motoring on ice. But there was no letup, and the fresh bright snow thawed briefly and froze again and lost its charm by outstaying its welcome. A weary depression came on him, and when he looked out of his office window at the white trees, he sometimes felt that hope was a fantasy and that the world was going to shrink away to dead ice and the human race pass from memory.

He felt the depression, but considered that he was getting by without letting it overwhelm him. As far as he knew, he was the kind of man who was known never to have moods. He had as many as other people, but he had always been suspicious of his own volatility, and kept it to himself. Depression or elation were too likely to be mere by-products of digestion, or of the weather, or of something chemical. They passed, and a man's job in the meantime was to accept them and remember that they were temporary. There had been plenty of times when he had considered the possibility of suicide, or at least considered the possibility that he could willingly die even if he wouldn't go the length of killing himself. But at the darkest times, he had always known, from simple experience, that the sun would shine again and that there was nothing to do but shut up and carry on.

In this at least he was sure he was adequately hard. He was nagged by Gladys Appleby's accusation that he was soft, because there was some kind of truth in it, but it wasn't the whole truth. He had always been hard enough to be gentle and to be patient and to wait his time and carve his way to what he wanted from life. And he could believe that he would go on making a life for himself.

Nevertheless, the depression persisted. It might, he thought, have nothing to do with the endless cold weather. It could be a post-orgastic depression, and he was familiar with that feeling after many tumbles with many women. So often, the next day or the next week brought the gloomy reflection that after all, it was an undignified and irrational pleasure. And then, of course, the following week would bring the reflection that such reflections were irrational.

Or perhaps it was Gladys herself who troubled him. What was she, after all? Only another woman. He still scarcely knew her; her past and her youth were blank mysteries, and her present existence was hardly exciting. Forcing himself to be fair, he recognized that he must be grateful to her. She was a good woman, and she was kind, and he could recognize a degree of unemphatic beauty in her body, without being exhilarated by it.

She had done him a service. For over a year, he had known himself incapable of enjoying the pleasure of women. Georgie's illness and her death had made sex seem obscene and unmanned him. It had taken a woman like Appleby, honest and reasonable and quite undemanding, to restore him. With her it had been possible to perform like a man because she expected nothing, she had no standards of comparison. But now that that was done, now that that was proved, what was the sense in it? He could find no excitement in being back in the old rough and tumble, in being the lusty ram of Meg Macrae's imagination. Well, perhaps just a trace of excitement, but at forty-seven where was the wonder? None of that was new any more.

That was especially true because, now that it had happened, there seemed to be nothing new or exciting in it for Gladys Appleby either. She had tasted the frenzy, but since then her quietness and withdrawal had been deeper if anything. She had reverted to demanding nothing, to expecting nothing. She was bland and efficient and helpful and more remote than ever. She annoyed him, in fact, and he wondered if it was this annoyance that was spilling over into the office and discoloring his enthusiasm for other things.

Meg Macrae caught him staring at the trees, with his coat on. The heating in the office had never been designed for genuine, cold cold; it was a symptom of the British dream, that Britain's climate is never very cold or very hot, the dream that Britons hold fast to through every heat wave and every blizzard.

"You'll no' make it any better looking at it," Meg said. "What's the coat for? Are you going somewhere?"

"No, I'm frozen. Old bones and crystallized marrow."

"Old rubbish. Whatever have you done about Gaylor? You're getting awful close and secret these days."

He wrapped his coat tighter.

"Oh, that. I resigned. I resigned a month ago, in fact."

"You're a rotten sod, Tom Fletcher! Was I not good enough to be told?"

"Ach, what difference does it make?" he asked her wearily. "You might as well wait till you meet your new boss before you start narking me. Whatever I do doesn't concern you."

Meg was genuinely hurt, but she only glared at him.

"A woman's got a right to be nosy, at least. Where are you going?"

He sat down at the desk and shook his head.

"Humph. Sounds stupid, that, doesn't it? Humph. I don't know Meg. I've got great plans, but to tell you the truth I'm tired and fed up, this damned cold is getting me down. I was thinking of opening up on my own."

"I should think so."

"Aye, I know, but the longer I think about it the less I know where to begin. This month's like a no man's land. I can't settle my mind to anything till I'm clean away."

"You're mad," she said. "Have you no' been spending the month getting yourself organized? My God, you must be getting senile right enough."

"I'm still working for English Brothers," he protested. "Hell, it would be too easy to start going round their customers poaching the business away. You can't do that. As long as they're paying me they're entitled to my attention. I can't think till I'm out and finished."

"Ach, away back to the Boy Scouts, for God's sake. 'Their' customers, did you say? They are *your* customers."

"Aye, well," he assented grudgingly. "I hope a few of them may trail after me, but I can't get myself organized yet."

"God, I never thought I would have to mother you at your age. If you're going to sit on your backside I'll have to start phoning everybody and telling them you'll be looking for their business. Not that you deserve any help."

"Don't be crazy, Meg," he said. "That's dishonest or I would have done it myself. Have you no scruples at all? You would even use English Brothers telephone to sabotage their business. And you still work here."

"Well that's gratitude! You mean you're not offering me a job?"

"A job? With me, Meg? I haven't got a business, you silly old fool."

"Ach, you make me sick. Come on, give yourself a shake and start doing something. You're not going to be a wee one-man traveler, you'll have to find yourself an office, and you'll need somebody to keep it going. Get excited, man! This is the best news I've had since the day the landlord dropped dead."

He responded feebly to her energy. It was what he needed, he knew. There was nothing difficult about starting a new business except finding the initial energy; but that was exactly what he couldn't find.

The mechanics of the business were simple to him, but he was in a kind of mental paralysis because he was still working for Gaylor; and some pride, or conscience, or guilt, compelled him to work for Gaylor to the bitter end, and inhibited him from putting any energy into his own affairs.

He needed a Georgie to give him a reason for getting ahead, and Gladys Appleby clearly was not a Georgie. She was nice, but she had no connection with him and she didn't really need anything from him and her pallid friendship would never drive him to anything.

Meg's brusque vitality was the next best thing, and he both welcomed it and resented it. He knew he needed to be pushed but his body didn't want to move.

She labored to get him unsettled, sat down opposite him and cross-examined him brutally to speak his plans so that she could write them on paper and make them real. He was a dogged, reluctant witness, though the sight of her pen jotting down notes evoked a faint flicker of his first enthusiasm.

"What about the Japanese mannie?" she demanded. "You said he was making you a free present of all kinds of stuff, but there's not a hair or hide of it to be seen. God, it's months ago!"

"Ah, I don't want to hold him to that. We parted in some ill-will, Meg — he's a volatile kind of guy."

"To hell with that, a promise is a promise. I'll write to him," she threatened.

"No, no. It's impossible to write that kind of letter. Forget about Kutsu."

"All right! Telephone him."

"He probably doesn't even remember me, for God's sake forget about him, Meg. That's a good start to a business, chucking away twenty quid on a phone call to nowhere."

"I've got the address in the file. I'll phone him now."

"Oh, women! It's three o'clock in the morning in Japan."

"It would serve him right. I'll put through a timed personal call for ten o'clock tonight, to your home number."

"And it goes on my telephone bill?"

"Well, now, it wouldn't be fair to make English Brothers pay for it, would it?" she said in sanctimonious tones. You'll be grateful before I'm done. Somebody's got to give you a prod."

He looked at her wearily while she deliberately booked the call. The enormity of telephoning Japan appealed to him in spite of his lethargy, and he knew the old bitch was doing it for his own good, but his appreciation of this was purely rational. He couldn't respond emotionally.

"Aye, all right," he said when she was finished. "Where's Hugh?"

"Uhuh, that's the question. He's hard to get a hold of these days," she said suspiciously. "He said he had to go and meet somebody."

"Aye, that's funny," Tom said. "I'm expecting somebody myself, from London. I wonder if it's the same man."

"Nothing would surprise me. Who are you expecting?"

"Your new boss."

"Not for long!" she said. "Honestly, Tom, you might have

let the cat out of the bag before now. I'm disappointed in you. I'm hurt, and that's the truth."

"It's the weather, Meg. Or something."

At four o'clock he was back at the window, in time to see Hugh Winton's M.G. drawing in to the curb, and Hugh and Jack Fillimore getting out of it. Seeing the two of them together saddened him. He took his coat off and tried to feel warm without it. Hugh knocked on his door and came in leading Fillimore.

"I met Jack at the airport," Hugh said evasively.

"What a climate!" Jack Fillimore said. "You look great, old man, it must be the Highland blood. You don't mind if Hugh stays, old boy, he'll be interested in this. Heigh ho. I was really sorry when N.G. told me about your decision, old man, I mean that. Frankly I envy you, I really do, I hope you've got some nice sunny spot looked out for yourself."

"Have a chair," said Tom.

"Get down to business and get it over, eh?" said Fillimore. "That's the system."

Hugh, ill at ease, sat down and tried to look poised and intelligent and keen without saying anything. Tom sat and kept his eyes on Fillimore, but his attention was on Hugh. This was a conference that Hugh would not enjoy until it was over, and his own careful disregard of Hugh would make the younger man even more uncomfortable than he was now. Fillimore prattled on, and Tom was able to follow him with a small part of his mind and think about other things at the same time. A gentle disgust was creeping through him, and it had the surprising effect of warming his blood and restoring his energy. For the first time since his resignation, he found himself planning ahead, and he was amazed at the number of things he had overlooked. He smiled suddenly at Fillimore and threw him off his stride.

"Sorry, did I say something?" Fillimore asked.

"No no, carry on, Jack," said Tom, still smiling. Fillimore returned the smile gratefully. He too had had some discomfort about the interview and it was good to find it going amiably.

"That, um, wraps it up," he said. "And of course, N.G. particularly sends his best wishes."

"It's good of him," Tom said dryly, and Fillimore alerted slightly at the harder tone.

"He has a high regard for you, Tom, I mean that. I know he's sorry you're retiring."

"Nick Gaylor has a high regard for Nick Gaylor," Tom said, impatient of Fillimore's flummery. "You can give him my love, but we don't need to vomit sweet sentiment over everybody. The reason why I'm out is that I'm too expensive for Nick Gaylor, and he aims to save money with somebody else." He still didn't look at young Hugh.

"I'm sorry you feel that way, old man," Jack Fillimore said earnestly. "I assure you N.G. is genuinely sorry to lose you."

"Don't be daft, I'm not complaining," said Tom. "Nick is a money man and he's good at it. I think he's making a big mistake this time, but that's his own business."

"Oh." Fillimore was deeply sorry that the conversation had taken this turn. "Well, old man, you don't have to worry about it now anyhow."

"No, I don't. And who's taking over for me? It's none of my business, of course, but I'm curious."

"Yes, naturally, old man. Well, you know how it is, I'm only one of the orbit team, I'll be organizing things for a few weeks, putting the N.G. trademark on things, and then Hugh is taking over, and I know you'll wish him the best. You taught him everything he knows, I suppose."

"Absolutely everything, and I'm grateful." It was the first time Hugh had spoken.

"Not absolutely," Tom said. Smiling. Hugh smiled too. "I'm glad you're getting a young fellow. It's a tough business, business. Most men are pretty well past it when they get to my age." He looked at Hugh in paternal affection and saw Hugh's mouth working nervously. "They often start hitting the bottle, in fact. We've all seen it happen. You've seen it yourself, Hugh."

"Eh? But not you, Tom!"

Tom stared straight into the young man's eyes, smiling, and admitted to himself what he had pigheadedly refused to admit for months. He couldn't find it in his heart to blame Hugh. He himself had preached that business was business and that there was no room for sentiment in it, and he ought to be glad to discover that Hugh had listened to every word and learned the lesson.

The business with David Thew should have been conclusive enough. Thew didn't mix with the business boozers in the city, and he could have heard about Tom's wild drinking only from somebody who made a point of telling him. And it was young Hugh who had sold Thew the desks with the lousy locks, only six months ago. Cam Jones, and Stiles, and Thew, had all somehow got the message that he, Tom Fletcher, was drinking himself to death, and Tom could now admit what he had suppressed all along, that young Hugh, his own protégé, must have helped to roll the story along. It wouldn't be quite deliberate malice, or quite conscious calculation, and the story wouldn't be entirely untrue. It was simply a question of that lifeboat, with only a few seats, and young Hugh's instinctive urge to grab one of the seats no matter who else had to be nudged into the water. Hugh had been a good pupil. He would survive.

"When are you taking over?" Tom asked.

"Any time." Hugh squirmed. "I'm not chasing you out, Tom, ha ha."

Tom sat back and laughed. He was happy and splendid and his muscles felt fine.

"Remember, Hugh," he said, "remember you were asking me what you would do if you found you were the boss and you sacked somebody and they wouldn't go away? It's not such a problem, is it?"

Hugh laughed, a nervous little giggle, and Jack Fillimore looked puzzled.

"An old private joke, Jack," Tom explained. "A bit of nonsense, it doesn't matter. Oh, by the way —" Tom smiled a quiet, sympathetic smile, "— where is your office going to be?"

"What do you mean, old boy?"

"You can't run the business without an office," Tom explained.

"I don't get the joke, old boy, honestly."

"It's not a joke, Jack. This is my office, you see — surely they must have told you. I own it. And I'm planning to use it."

The expressions on their faces were a joy.

"You can forbid me to use the telephone, of course, I hadn't thought of that. But then, you can't use it either, if you can't get in, can you? Then there's all the furniture and the files, but I don't mind storing them for you till you can find a place for them. Oh. This chair is my own. My wife bought me it to celebrate my directorship. Quite nice, isn't it? It swivels."

Jack Fillimore groped for reality.

"Now now, joke over, old man," he said. "I did hear that you owned the building, now that I think of it, but surely we have a lease. So don't give us a hard time, Tom."

"I don't know how much you know about Scottish property law," Tom said, and he knew he could say anything now without being contradicted. Slipping in the word "Scottish" pulled the feet from under Jack. It evoked an ancient mystery. "— but I assure you, you could go out to the street now and come back with a policeman, and all he could do would be to take a note of my complaint against you for trespass. How about that, old boy?"

"What are we going to do?" Hugh Winton asked Fillimore, in falsetto.

"We'll all have a cup of tea," Tom said paternally, "and then you can toddle off and forge ahead with the good old business."

They didn't wait for tea. He went to the door to shout for Meg Macrae, and she fell through as he opened it, with her hand still gripping the handle.

"Bloody eavesdropper," he said. She threw her arms round him and kissed him.

"When you've got your lust under control," he said, "you can phone the post office — at English Brothers' expense! The guilt will go with me to the grave! — and tell them we want a new telephone."

"As Thomas Fletcher, Limited?"

"Naturally. No. No, Meg. Fletcher and Macrae. How does that sound? Oh, we'll have to call Fraser and Sidmouth, we'll have to form a limited company. Just a minute, Cam Jones has a brother or a brother-in-law or something with a big yacht, hasn't he? He's always going away getting drowned at sea on weekends. Phone him, Meg, he can give us a line on boat equipment. Not that it matters urgently. Write all this down, you hysterical bitch. Just in case I get Comrade Kutsu, I'll want a look at some yachting magazines — is there a magazine for fishing boats or trawlers or something? We can't really stay in this office, you know, it's too big. We want two small rooms somewhere — we could take the attic floor here and let English Brothers keep the rest.

You know what I mean, we gave them a fright, we don't have to be lousy about it."

"That's enough," she said. "Be lousy. You canny make a living selling wirelesses to fishing boats yet. You'll be selling office stuff. You'll be competing with English Brothers."

"No, no. They'll be competing with us. Okay, they can stay in the gutter. Get me Mike Allardyce, Meg, I would like to start spreading the news a wee bit."

At five o'clock he took her to a pub in Sauchiehall Street and they had a ceremonial drink in a mood of suppressed hysteria and went back to the office. He left her at eight o'clock so that he could drive home slowly, because he suspected that he was in the mood to put his foot down and go through a wall on an icy curve. Nevertheless he was home in little over an hour.

"Tell me my dinner's ruined," he snarled, and smiled.

"Your dinner's ruined," Gladys said.

"Hell, I'm starving!" His amusement diminished.

"Good, there's a beautiful roast. You told me to tell you your dinner was ruined," she explained. "So I told you. You're the boss, after all."

"I don't know that I approve of you developing a sense of humor," he said. "That kid's infecting you. I think I preferred you when you were cold and hostile to the male sex and kept your place."

"What kid?"

"Tommy. You're beginning to make the same kind of moronic jokes as him. Tell him to stay off the telephone. I'm expecting a call to Japan at ten o'clock."

He sat down and prepared to eat.

"Just a telephone call to Japan. I see, sir."

He looked up at her and laughed.

"Yes, I'll tell you all about it. I'm in business."

"Will you go bust?"

"Maybe. It's quite probable. Why?"

"You won't be able to afford a housekeeper."

He looked at her thoughtfully. It was hopeless trying to find a way through to the inside of her. She pleased the eye when she was actually there, and suggested reserves of interest and strength, but it was possible that she was simply a firm introvert with an accidental quality of sensuality.

"Are you thinking of leaving, then?" he asked, and he knew he didn't want her to leave, but he wouldn't plead with her to stay. He could survive without her, or without anybody, rather than plead.

"I don't particularly want to leave," she said, "but I don't mind. I can stay or leave, whichever is practical."

"You're bloody cool, aren't you?" he asked, and she nodded. "Cold, even. I don't get, you, Gladys."

"There's nothing to get, I suppose."

"But you do like it here. You do, don't you? At least, you have so far?"

She gave one of her quarter-shrugs.

"Yes. If you really want to know, I've loved it here, it's the first time I've ever had a *place*. It's the best time I've ever had, and I'm grateful. I can't tell you how grateful I am because I'm not good at . . . talking, but I'm grateful for everything."

It was strange how she could speak words that would have been effusive from anybody else, in that level considered tone.

"For everything?" he asked, truly curious.

"Yes, of course. Especially for that, in fact. It made me realize something about myself. I never knew I was a . . . a sensualist?"

"Nobody would ever have suspected it," Tom said dryly. "You haven't been very impatient to repeat the experience."

"Oh. Oh? It's very difficult when one has . . . well, after all, no experience of living with a person. I don't know the — the procedure, or the etiquette, I suppose I mean." She was drawing circles on the table with a finger. "I didn't want to . . . to presume on our acquaintance," she ended with a nervous laugh. Tom looked at her in exasperation and wonderment.

"Who the hell am I supposed to be?" he demanded. "The King of Siam?"

"You know perfectly well I don't mean that," she said. "Even if we are two equals —"

"— which we are."

"Yes, all right, even if we are two equals, that's no reason why I should demand anything of you. Oh God, I hate people who demand things of people, I've had enough of them."

"Gladys, Gladys." He shook his head. He would have to recalculate this woman entirely, and retrospectively, but there was no time now. "Gladys, don't always be worrying about other people, you have your rights too. My wife always said people who are too unselfish only get other people confused because nobody knows what they really want."

"Three cheers for your wife," she mumbled.

"And you'll be staying."

"I don't know," she said.

"Gladys," he said. The idea was so ordinary and simple that it seemed like a great discovery. "We could get married. That would be easier for you, wouldn't it? My God, that must have sounded hellish. I'm sorry, but I'm not young any more. I can't make it sound very romantic, but it's reasonable, isn't it?"

She clenched both fists. "I'm not trying to drive you into that," she muttered.

"Oh, hell and damnation, woman, nobody drives me anywhere. It's not much of a deal for you — I'm getting on, and I can't tell you you're the only girl in the world. But I like you, and I'm too old to chase other women, I think."

The old calculation mechanism had been working automatically all the time, and the sudden decision continued to seem reasonable.

"Is it much of a deal for *you?*" she asked.

"Yes, clear profit — I would save your wages."

She smiled dutifully. Was it a foolish mistake? All he knew about her was that she was honest and quiet, as a servant, but marriage could change people. Momentarily, he hoped that she might refuse. Nevertheless, an offer was an offer.

"You can change your mind if you like," she said tightly. "But if you don't, yes, I accept, thank you."

"Good."

"But what if it changes me?" she asked him, and was pleasurably surprised to find that their thoughts had run parallel. "What if I became a harpie? I've been a spinster so long. I might turn into a termagant."

"I would beat you."

"You couldn't. Or I might start . . . I might suddenly demand to go to bed in the middle of the day, or at breakfast time. I've never had a husband . . . a *man* . . . in my own house . . . *there.*"

She laughed and turned away and waved her arm, nervously uncoordinated and trembling, and for an instant he saw her again on the evening when Tommy had left for his dance . . . submissive and afraid. It was strange how much cruelty there could be in the mixup of men and women. Had she been afraid of him, or of something in herself? He felt an odd tenderness that was also sharp and greedy.

"Never mind that," he said. "I want to keep you." He heard his own words, and their surprised tone. She put both hands to her face and drew a deep breath; and Tommy came in, carrying a geometry textbook.

"Are you busy?" he asked vaguely.

"Yes," Tom said. "Away and do your homework. Incidentally, Gladys and I are getting married."

"Both of you?" Tommy's mind came slowly back from geometry. "Oh. Are you not a bit old?"

"Yes, we are," Gladys said.

"Yes. Still, the expectation of life is constantly increasing," Tommy conceded. "I don't have to call you Mother, do I?"

"No."

"Well . . . Huh! That's a relief." Tommy blushed, now fully conscious. "I think you're well advised," he said. "It's more convenient, isn't it? If you didn't get married, Gladys might get a better job somewhere else and then we would have Mrs. Crow coming back for the kill. You're past the age of procreation, of course, I take it."

"I hope so," Tom said heavily. "I've had enough."

"Still," Tommy said judicially, "if you did have any children, by the time you died I would be old enough to act as father to them."

"My God!"

"That's the doorbell," said Tommy, and wandered out, thinking. "That kid frightens me," said Tom.

"He isn't a kid." Gladys snuffled.

"Don't cry, Gladys. I'm glad about this. I mean it."

"You don't know everything," she said.

"I don't care. We've got plenty of time."

"No, there's something I must tell you now."

Tommy reappeared and said, "It's Alan."

"Alan and Joan?" Tom asked quickly.

"No, Alan, alone and palely loitering, in the lounge. Do you want me to entertain him while you brace yourself?"

He withdrew without waiting for an answer, and Tom got up to follow, but Gladys grabbed his arm.

"Stop fretting, Gladys," he said. "Everything's fine. Japan'll be on the line at any minute and I don't know what to say to them and I want to get a hold of Cam Jones and Nick Gaylor is probably going to sue me and I've got to hold my son-in-law's hand, but we're getting married and everything's going to be fine and simple and we'll tackle everything one at a time. One thing is enough."

She wouldn't let his arm go.

"I've got to tell you," she insisted. "I'm pregnant."

"Don't be daft."

"I *am*."

"Why didn't you say so?"

"I *couldn't*."

"Oh, great!" he gasped. "Now I've got Nick Gaylor, and Alan, and Harry Hirohito, and bankruptcy, and a howling brat, at my age, prams and nappies and sleepless nights. I can't take, I just can't take it."

She looked crushed and humbled and said, "You can. You're hard."

He slumped against the doorway, and muttered, "A father! A father?"

His hand was on her shoulder, and he gripped the hair at the back of her neck, hard, and tears smarted in her eyes and she gritted her teeth and she smiled a brilliant painful smile. When he loosened his grip she fell against him and held fast, and a short burst of laughter was forced out of him.

She was speaking into his neck.

"Oh, dear. You lead a terrible life of trouble and worry, don't you?"

"I don't know," he said. He kissed her head. He was unaccountably delirious. "You never bought that Labrador," he said. "Get a Labrador. A family needs a dog."

"I wish I could stop blubbering," she said. "I love you."

"A fine time!" he said. "A fine time to start that kind of talk! Come on, woman, I've got work to do. And hand in hand they walked into the sunset, for God's sake."

"Your lapel's all wet," she said.

"Remind me to phone Cam Jones," he said. "And I'll have to get business cards engraved. I think I'll sell the Jag and buy a cheap station wagon. Come on, come on," he said. "There's a lot to do." She didn't look at all bad with her eyes full of tears. She looked fine, in fact. He took out his handkerchief.